DARK PASSIONS SUBDUE

Stephen Hollis is a young college student, living with his pious parents in the well-to-do Westmount suburb of Montreal. He is an attractive young man, intelligent, popular to a degree, but Stephen has a problem. His is also an insufferable, self-justifying snob who uses his intellect as a barrier against the world. Then he meets Fabien. Fabien is an impeccable bon vivant who lives in a large house with two young men, Duncan and Bill, where he entertains guests while dispensing his bon mots.

Stephen is immediately drawn to Fabien, but finds himself in a jealous triangle with Duncan, whom he sees as a rival for Fabien's affections. Duncan had been in the war, and now seems to be living off Fabien. He drinks a lot, takes a lot of showers, and is writing a novel. Stephen hates him.

Bill also fought in the war, and feels protective toward Duncan, watching Stephen's intrusion in their household with mounting resentment. In this enclosed world, where everything revolves around the scintillating Fabien, delusions will be shattered—and tragedy becomes inevitable.

Dark Passions Subdue

Douglas Sanderson

**INTRODUCTION BY
PAUL CHAROSH AND JONAS WESTOVER**

Stark House Press • Eureka California

DARK PASSIONS SUBDUE

Published by Stark House Press
1315 H Street
Eureka, CA 95501, USA
griffinskye3@sbcglobal.net
www.starkhousepress.com

ISBN: 978-1-951473-41-9

Book design by Mark Shepard, shepgraphics.com
Cover art by Stevan Kissel
Proofreading by Bill Kelly

First Stark House Press Edition: September 2021

Dark Passion Subdue: An Introduction

by Paul Charosh and Jonas Westover

Dark Passions Subdue is an outlier of a book. It resides within a realm chock full of novels that are published, commented upon, and soon left behind as new material takes their place. When the book was first published, in 1952, it met with mixed reviews. Never mind that it was the first novel written by Douglas Sanderson (aka Marin Brett and Malcolm Douglas), who surely had high hopes for a book that tackles a web of complicated topics and sensitive subject matter. Sanderson turned away from general fiction and found success penning crime novels. These twenty-plus hard-boiled detective stories were warmly received, so much so that he never looked back. But, unlike some of its forgotten brethren, *Dark Passions Subdue* deserves to be revisited. It may be unusual, but that is part of what makes the novel such a remarkable book.

The few websites and publications that comment on the novel place it squarely in the field of queer literature and there is no question that issues of sexuality permeate the book. The central character, Stephen Hollis, is a student struggling with self-actualization. One review says he is "a man who didn't belong," while another says he is "caught in an emotional maelstrom in which freedom and understanding get mixed with bitter jealousy and repulses as he discovers himself…in a homosexual triangle." Sanderson himself claimed that the novel was a "puritan ode to repressed sexuality." The (at the time illegal) homosexual urges explored in the book were a dangerous topic for a debut novel, but unlike the books that used similar characters in the post-war period, the author refused to pander to pure stereotype and sensationalism. Instead, the book deftly weaves together many threads between a web of characters, allowing for remarkable nuance. Even overt sex is frequently avoided. It is this devotion to fully-formed characterizations that pushes the novel beyond the pedestrian and demands that it be available for a new generation of readers to revisit.

The book is set in Montreal, Canada, and uses McGill University as a backdrop. This was an environment familiar to Sanderson, who, although he was English, emigrated to Canada and settled in that very city. Much of the book explores topics that were important to the Canadian white middle-class, and one can only speculate how much of this might be born from the author's experiences. Issues of class, family dynamics, religion, and personal identity are all given voice; Sanderson admitted that the book was "an analysis of Puritanism in Montreal's high society," and he pulls no punches in his scathing critique of the status quo.

It is with the varied characters that these issues are given flesh. The protagonist, Stephen Hollis, has grown up with a family he sees as stifling. His father is a religious zealot, while his sister demurs to church leaders, and his mother offers no opinions. The home, for Stephen, is not a place of security, but of false sentimentality and harsh scrutiny. He is pulled out of these oppressive walls when Bill Prescott, an army buddy, introduces Stephen to the mysterious, foreign Fabian and his roommate, the flirty Duncan. Both young men seethe physical sensuality; Fabian is from an unnamed country and is described as being impossibly handsome, with thick black hair and narrow hips, while Duncan has glittering eyes, red hair, and is often displaying his porcelain body in or out of a towel. Who has money and who does not is an important part of the narrative, but there is an underlying sense that everyone has more wealth than they really need. Fabian and Duncan's shared home becomes the site of most of the drama, allowing for a remarkable extended party scene and providing a place where the norms of middle-class life are shattered. The tension crackling between Stephen and these two new friends becomes palpable as Stephen tries—often crudely and unsuccessfully—to understand what their relationship is and what part he might play in their lives. The house itself becomes the closet, full of secrets and suggestion. Just what they do in their rooms when Stephen is gone becomes an obsession for the confused youth, and the enigmatic Fabian keeps him at bay enough that Stephen's drive leads inevitably to tragedy.

Most of the narrative revolves around these men, but two women are also featured, allowing alternative exploration of some of the book's main themes. Miriam is a wealthy woman who is unhappily married and is perpetually on the prowl for any young male escort. She views and presents herself as youthful in appearance, but is forty-four. She considers herself intellectual, cultured, and plays violin. She wants to establish a salon of which she is hostess, attended by similar people. Possibilities are limited: she is Jewish. Her religion, her age, and her ego make her stand out among the others, despite her desperate need to be included. Crystal is a college girl who also participated during the war, but in women's services. She is congenial, but while she is "attractive to men," she is "constitutionally, indefatigably, virtuous." These two become part of Fabian's household in strange, disjointed ways, but Sanderson paints all who visit as outsiders in one way or another.

The narrative leads to dramatic explosions between the characters, with many surprising outcomes, including tumultuous personal revelations. It is, in part, these disclosures that make *Dark Passions Subdue* such a fascinating book. Beyond the story itself, though, are Sanderson's sensitive depictions of a collection of outsiders. The strength of the book derives from the author's ability to create characters who are gregarious, voluble, smart, self-aware, but also sometimes ambivalent, experience self-deception, misread others, and can display both kindness and cruelty. The reader wonders what becomes of them after the book ends — in a sequel which does not exist and will never be written.

—January 2021

Paul Charosh is a retired member of the Brooklyn College faculty, and taught sociology and computer languages. During the 1970s, while traveling in Europe during summer holiday, he met Douglas Sanderson and his family in Alicante. They became friends, spending many hours together annually for a number of years, until he gave up traveling. The friendship deepened via much ongoing correspondence, until Douglas passed in 2002.

Dr. Jonas Westover is a music and theatre historian and is the author of *The Shuberts and their Passing Shows: The Untold Tale of Ziegfeld's Rivals* (Oxford University Press, 2016). He has taught at many colleges and universities throughout the United States.

Dark Passions Subdue

■ ■ ■ ■ ■ ■ ■

Douglas Sanderson

To René Fortier

Yield not to Temptation, for yielding is Sin;
Each Victory will help you some Other to win;
Fight manfully onward, Dark Passions subdue ...

HYMN

Part One

THE SHIRT

The last lecture of the day was finished. It was ten minutes past five o'clock, the second Friday of the first term of the new school year. All over the campus students were gathered in small packed groups that together constituted a large, bright, very animated, and sometimes very loud, crowd. The majority were Arts students—students of history, philosophy, languages, and literature. They erupted from the door of the Arts Building, down the steps, and onto the pathways, gathering on the grasses in a mass that tapered to extinction only at the top of the elm-lined avenue leading to the Roddick Gate and the city outside. They lingered.

Over to the left the engineers, whom everyone suspected had nothing to talk about, made quick clean movements in and out of their building. Either they were there or they were not. Only four of them loitered, leaning or sitting on the balustrade at the front of the building, not speaking to each other, gazing longingly at all those others with the animation and the talk. Misfits.

But Crystal was a medical student. She was having a party that evening. She ceased surveying the campus and brought her gaze to bear on that one of the six young men surrounding her who was making the joke. She had heard the joke before, but not for almost a year, and as she liked nearly any sort of joke provided it was not too dirty she was able to laugh with perfect sincerity. The youth looked gratified. And while the enjoyment still rippled through her fibers she studied his face, and the faces of the other five.

The two tall ones most affected her; their gangling, bony unjointedness made them so inescapably adolescent. And of the six, three had crew cuts. It suited the two with the round faces, but the boy with the pointed chin looked something like a lugubrious pixy. If she were nearer his own age she might be able to tell him so. But, she thought, I'm not.

She laughed at another clean joke, every word of which she had heard and enjoyed. The second jokester flashed a look of cheerful triumph at the first, then grinned happily at Crystal. "Gee, Crystal," he said. "You're all right."

"Hell," said another, "Crystal's one of the boys, ain't you, Cryst?"

She nodded. Had she not been gurgling with laughter she might have given vent to one of her rare sighs. One of the boys. Sure. But how about one of the girls? Here she was, giving a party, looking for eligible male guests, and finding only pals—juvenile pals at that.

The six nice lads all began to talk at once. She selected a single remark and said "Why sure," to it, wondered how she could possibly advise the pixy about his haircut, and went back to surveying the campus with a wider-ranging glance. At the entrance to the Arts Building Stephen Hollis was standing apparently lost in thought, his eyes narrowed in the rather lean face, his lips gently clenched. He looked, as always, neatly dressed, self-assured, and mature. She lifted a hand. He did not see it.

His headache had come on during the last lecture. He brushed a finger over his eyebrow. Good God! the man was ordinarily a fool, but today he had excelled himself. An examination into the causes of fascism, he called it. The birth in Bohemianism was permissible, as was the carry-over to the spirit of Christian crusading. But from there to the end! The quick skittering through missionary societies, imperialism, dictatorship—the mumbling of a continuous stream of disconnected thoughts like a patient on a couch—and then finally, "Thus, you see," and this, of all things, with a flourish, "we arrive inevitably at people like Hitler and Mussolini." Oh Jesus, the man was a complete idiot. And he had him again in the morning.

He was ticking off tomorrow's lectures in his mind when the hand beckoned again from near the memorial to James McGill. He picked his way through the crowd on the steps, acknowledging two greetings with a nod. Someone called his name; he pretended not to hear. He threaded his way across the strip to where Crystal was waiting with the six young men. He was smiling.

She greeted him with the usual lazy friendliness, her voice soft and promising. A nice compliment if he could make his ear slide up and down the side of his head in time to her melodious modulations. "Hello Stephen," she said, and the upper lids of her brandy-colored eyes drooped like those of a cat in sunlight.

"You look fine today, Crystal. How come you are on this part of the campus?"

Her gaze swiveled over him. "I get tired of med students. They get to think they're God after the first year. Something to do with dissection, I think. Horribly boring." She swept a slow grin around the circle of admirers. "It makes such a change to have a little intellectual conversation once in a while."

Automatically, with unresisting accord, the admirers all grinned back.

"Encouraging the freshmen, you mean?"

"And waiting for you." Her special smile would have ravished a marble statue. "I'm having a party tonight. I want you to come."

"Thanks. Nice of you. Who's going to be there?"

He listened with increasingly cold dubiety as she recited a list of names. "Are any of these going to be there?" he interrupted, acknowledging her companions for the first time. They were all at least four years younger than himself.

"One or two of them."

He turned his head slowly from one to the other, scrutinizing each face in turn. "Thanks again, Crystal," he said, "but no. I've had some before. See you later. 'By.'"

He walked off in the direction of the gates. Crystal watched his retreating figure, her face composed and smiling.

A youth broke the silence. He had ruddy cheeks and thick-soled shoes and was feeling defensive. "What's the matter with that guy?" he demanded hotly.

Crystal bent a melting gaze upon him. "Stephen is postgraduate," she explained, "and I'm afraid you can't come to the party tonight because you ask silly questions." She looked at the pixy who brightened visibly. "Would you like to come instead?"

He beamed widely, and she turned her head, biting her lip. It was despicably unfair, but one was going to have to be ruthless. She was suddenly prepared to sacrifice every one of them, one by painful one. And the hell with it! Tonight she would certainly tell the kid about his hair.

Dawdling by the gate, pretending to be immersed in a book, was Harrigan. He looked up and gave a start of false surprise at the sight of Stephen. He fell into step beside him and peered up earnestly, a little pitifully, from the brown eyes set close together in the small acned face. He said nervously: "Want to come over to the Union for a coffee, Stephen?"

This was the third time of asking. Next time, the fourth, Stephen would be morally obliged to accept. He shook his head. "Sorry, I have to get down and buy a shirt before the stores close."

They stood side by side, waiting for the gap in the traffic that would permit them to cross the road. Small buses, jammed with humanity, nudged ahead to the accompaniment of spasmodically hissing brakes. Cars, driven by hunched figures with pale, exhausted-looking faces, edged greedily into sudden unexpected gaps. A taxi halted momentarily at the curb, affording a glimpse of a hard-faced woman of about forty-five, eyes narrowed from the smoke of a cigarette poked in the corner of her painted mouth, looking fixedly, almost viciously, at the back of the driver's neck. A gust of cold wind, presaging winter, blew west along Sherbrooke Street, whirling the exhaust fumes in a noxious fog.

Stephen's headache increased.

"That was a pretty good lecture, wasn't it?" Harrigan said.

Stephen looked down at his companion and wished, beneath the surface irritation, that he could make some gesture of friendship. Surely something could be done about that appalling skin. Sulphur tablets? He said: "Well, it ran true to form."

Harrigan eagerly seized the assenting tone. "He's having a professor's tea next Monday. You going?"

"I don't think so."

"No, Tuesday. It's not until Tuesday." A note of appeal came creeping into Harrigan's voice. "All the other boys are going. Sid's going, and Tom and Holly and Jack. They're all going. All the boys."

"I don't doubt it. But I'm not."

Harrigan smiled uneasily. "Don't you like them? I mean, they all seem to like you, so you won't have to talk to the old boy, you can talk to the boys all the time."

"Yes, but I know already what they're going to talk about."

"Yes," Harrigan said, and he paused. "How do you mean?"

"I'm forecasting the absolute improbability of the desirable and the dead certainty of the unpalatable. Something like that. No, I'm not going."

"There might be some beer. Even though it is a tea they might serve beer."

"Under the circumstances there is no basic difference."

The traffic surged on unbrokenly.

Harrigan said: "It was a pretty good lecture, wasn't it?"

Stephen bit back a savage remark about the acne. He looked down into Harrigan's face, the face of all the boys who were going to the tea, and thought with impactual boredom of what extraordinary limits could sometimes be reached by sheer bloody ordinariness. He said, "I'll see you tomorrow, I suppose," and stepped out into the road where Harrigan had not the temerity to follow, ignoring the brakes and the honking horns and cutting a deliberate diagonal across the unending stream of traffic. Harrigan called something after him.

The bright autumn sky, dimming fast, still held enough color to render garish the neon signs switched on too early in the side streets; the shoeshop, the barber, the small café, and among the universal pinks a florist's grassy green. In the window the chrysanthemums ranged in hues from yellow through red to deepest bronze, and briefly he considered buying some for his mother. No, let Father do it. His mouth went wry. He walked on slowly toward St. Catherine Street, trying not to think of school, concentrating forcibly on the shirt he was about to buy. Not white, but something with a stripe, narrow but quite bold. And with a short tabbed collar that would permit a tie with a small knot. It must match the new suit he was going to start wearing next week to McGill, diffusing an air of simple elegance among the sartorial horrors of the campus. Loafer shoes, denims, sports jackets, sweaters: all the tomboys cavorting in comfortless ease. All still back there on the campus, making the five-o'clock charade last until six. All wanting him to go to the Union for coffee. And such coffee.

The doors of the huge store were being locked against tardy customers as he slipped in past a gaggle of chattering women and made his way to the second floor. Clerks grown drawn-faced by this hour were tidying the counters, drawing enormous white cloths over the piles of exposed merchandise, moving faster than at any time during the day. Stephen approached a display of shirts and stood tapping the counter gently with his fingernail.

"Yes, sir?"

The voice came from behind him, with no discernible trace of resentment. He did not turn round.

There was an element of interest in the situation. Assume that the man had a wife and child. Assume also that he was not a technician, for with a specialized trade he would not be in a store. A few weeks ago he might have been a student working through the vacation, but everyone was back at school now. The man, then, needed his job. Would he protest, even deviously, at the lateness of the hour? Stephen said: "I want to buy a shirt."

"Yes, sir. Did you have anything special in mind?"

The voice sounded completely subservient, a vague accent of some kind. The man came around to the other side of the counter and stood quietly, dutifully, while Stephen glanced along the row of merchandise.

"I have a blue suit," he said pleasantly, "with a faint red thread running through it. I'd like something to pick up the color."

"Yes, sir."

Stephen smiled at the counter. "The shirt to pick up the suit, not vice versa."

There was a silence during which from another floor someone's retreating footsteps echoed as in a cathedral.

"Do you have any suggestions?" He lifted his head to glance briefly at the man's own shirt and caught a glimpse of shiny red hair over a face that was much younger than the voice had intimated. He looked at the eyes. They were gazing into the middle distance, faraway, bored, utterly uninterested.

"Do you never look at your customers when you serve them?"

"I beg your pardon, sir, I was trying to visualize the suit." The voice was precisely as before, but the impression of subservience had been destroyed. "A red thread did you say?"

Stephen moved quickly along the display. "Show me this, this, and this!" His hand stabbed like the head of a striking snake. Foolish to have mentioned the suit. That remark about the red thread was completely asinine. He had an indefinite feeling of having been tricked. "I'm rather particular about shirts," he said, and was immediately more than ever idiotic. Without looking up again he considered the three presented to him and shook his head, making a vague gesture that included everything in view. "Show me some more."

A trim elderly man in a suit of youthful cut emerged hoveringly from the background. He drew nearer as the clerk returned with an armful of shirts. "Is everything all right, sir?" he asked with smooth deference, then turning to the clerk: "Will we be needing the cash tube?"

Stephen drew a small card from his pocket. "Thank you, I have a charge account here. Anything I order can be sent out to Westmount in the morning."

"Yes sir." The deference became more finely shaded at mention of the address.

"Are you the manager?" Stephen asked.

"Yes, sir, I am."

Stephen nodded slowly. "I think you are more likely to know what I need. Perhaps you will serve me." He turned to the clerk, his hand waving gently to and fro, like the tail of a goldfish, in a gesture of dismissal. "I'll not be needing you anymore. You can go now," he said, and he smiled.

The redheaded man smiled back absently, his eyes still dreamily out of focus. "Yes," he said, "good night," and was gone. He went light-footedly down the stairs, his head bobbing nearer and nearer to floor level, and then he disappeared.

"The suit I wish to match," Stephen said, turning back to the manager, "has a faint red thread."

While Crystal prepared for her party, Stephen was sitting in a dark-brown downstairs sitting room, his legs draped over one arm of the chair, and his back turned to the cabinet containing his father's large collection of Bibles. He was engrossed in Alfred North Whitehead's *Adventures of Ideas*.

On the heavy marble mantelpiece an ormolu clock struck seven. As the last chime shivered away, a door opened on the second floor, footsteps traversed the landing and the top stair creaked. Mr. Hollis began his slow descent, tunelessly mumbling a hymn.

The event did not impinge upon Stephen's consciousness, for familiarity had put it beyond his mental focus. Every evening his father did that precise thing, came downstairs from his anteprandial wash, trailed behind him a faint odor of carbolic soap, and varied from night to night only his choice of hymn.

> "'When they reach the land of strangers,
> And the prospect dark appears,
> Nothing seen but toils and dangers,
> Nothing felt but doubts and fears...'"

The voice passed the sitting room door, wafted slowly down the passage, and found extinction in the dining room.

Almost immediately the dinner gong clashed and Stephen heard his mother calling in her birdlike voice for himself, his brother, and his sister. He turned the leaf of his book. Another page and a half to end the chapter on "Appearance and Reality." He read on. An indistinguishable rumble of voices came from the dining room.

There was another, more furious rattle from the gong, and his mother's voice, calling this time only Stephen, was higher pitched and worried. With deliberation he marked his place, closed the book, and balanced it on the arm of the chair. A single uninterested look at himself in the hall mirror and he went down the passage and entered the dining room where the family sat waiting in uneasy silence. He took his place and saw his mother's pleading look before he bowed his head. They waited longer. Then Mr. Hollis spoke.

"Oh Lord our God and Father, punisher of the evil-doer, scourge of the wicked, Thou who hast in Thy goodness given this food unto us who are unworthy ..."

With lugubrious savor he rolled the words around his palate, as another might with Benedictine, tasting them with slow and morbid relish and allowing them, as if reluctantly, to fall from his tongue only when they had attained the requisite viscosity. Stephen knew from a life's experience how long the prayer would continue. He sat, as he had since he was twelve years old, a little impatient that the food should become cold, but deriving an undying pleasure from his suspicion that behind the rumbling pedantry his father was suffering a misery of self-damnation.

"And show us that Thy mercy is obtained only through repentance ..." On and on it went, intoned and monotonous, then abruptly Mr. Hollis said Amen and his head shot up and Stephen was fixed by the small, round eyes, always a little bloodshot under the scanty brows.

Again they waited; Esther, Stephen's sister, with her pathetically plain face downcast, brother Richard breathing a little more deeply and staring straight to the front. No one had yet started to eat. Mrs. Hollis began a frantic, twittering monologue concerning the difficulties she encountered in ordering the meat they saw before them. Stephen stopped her with an imperceptible shake of his head and a look that both thanked her and indicated the impossibility of diversion.

He knew well what he was waiting for. Unlike himself, Mr. Hollis had only a rudimentary education. Moreover, he had attended no wars. Indeed, his father's only valid claim was that he had worked hard—all his life, like a horse, as he was so fond of saying—and that by a combination of chance and cunning had reached the top of the hill to find the cart he pulled filled with an astonishing amount of money. Valid, yes, but insufficient to justify all that his father had been and wished to be. Stephen loathed his father. The game began.

Mr. Hollis picked up his knife and fork. "Why were you late for dinner?" With eyes still fixed on Stephen he took a mouthful of food and commenced eating.

"I was reading a book by a man named Whitehead, a university professor at Cambridge in England." He waited until his father swallowed the food and had taken a breath preparatory to answering. This was the latest and most delicate innovation. "It is said," he continued mildly, "that Whitehead will be remembered for bringing to the world the true spirit of Locke, and that he was also the greatest of the Cambridge Platonists. I'm not positive that he was, though. I feel that there were others as great. Not as lucid perhaps, but as great."

He paused and looked around the table. "Do any of you know what I am talking about?"

"Don't be so smart!" his brother said angrily.

"Keep out of this, Richard," Mr. Hollis snapped. "I'm quite capable of handling the situation."

"What situation?" Stephen asked.

"He's been coming home here with his rotten communist ideas ever since he got back from the war."

Stephen looked at his brother and wagged a finger. "The fear of the Lord is the beginning of knowledge," he said pleasantly, "but fools despise wisdom and instruction."

The words had their desired effect. Mr. Hollis leaned forward with glittering eyes. "Was that a quotation from the Book? Are you trying to be blasphemous?"

Now Stephen could eat in comfort. Relaxing, he commenced contentedly to chew. Unneeding of an answer, his father would talk religion for the rest of the meal, getting slowly more vehement and red in the face, calling down upon the world the vengeance of the God of the Canadian prairies where he had spent his boyhood before coming to Montreal, to a large bank account and a tattered conscience.

The prairie god: Jehovah, grim and relentless as his habitat, remorseless, unforgiving, watching with cold celestial eye the grievous faults of a Babylonian Canada and, especially, the sins of the young, heedless, and disobedient. Watching Stephen.

Occasionally, though not often, Mr. Hollis went to the New Testament and St. Paul. Stephen recited mentally: *Being filled with all unrighteousness, fornification, wickedness, covetousness, maliciousness. Backbiters, haters of God, despiteful, proud, boasters, inventors of evil things, disobedient to parents. Etcetera.* Mr. Hollis did not like St. John nearly so well.

Stephen had no strong feelings against the Apostle to the Gentiles, but a few weeks previously, extremely provoked, he had asked his father if he didn't think that St. Paul was sometimes just a little dirty-minded. The result of the question has been as appalling as unexpected. Mr. Hollis, who was shouting, stopped short as if poleaxed. His red face became colorless. His mouth opened and closed uselessly as little blobs of foam appeared at either corner. He seemed unable to move and suddenly unable to breath. When his wife ran to him he waved her aside with feeble little gestures, both feet scuffling on the floor, trying to find a purchase. Then he had lifted from the chair, painfully, supporting himself with two hands upon the table, seeming to tower, despite his small stature, above the cowering family who awaited the storm.

But no storm came. With his arms crossed tightly over his chest, his hands clutching his ribs as if in the bitterest cold, Mr. Hollis had staggered wordless from the room.

It had been Stephen's greatest triumph. None of the family dared speak to him for the rest of the evening. But he had reflected that henceforth he must confine himself to narrower limits. For he had seen his father as he really was, a frightened old man, more than seventy years old. The knowledge was common but the sight was rare and it made him uneasy. He felt indelicate, and slightly stupid.

Across the table his father was still talking, bringing forth the sound but timeworn formulations that Stephen enjoyed attacking. He did not underestimate his father's mental capacity on these religious issues.

Indeed, he admired the agility with which his father could parry the most deft and oblique thrusts. But, this was his satisfaction, Mr. Hollis used a cudgel as opposed to a rapier. He was clumsy and uncouth where his opponent was always graceful. And Stephen knew that at any time he could smoothly turn the discussion into paths where his father was too unlettered to follow. That was the culminant. He smiled genially round the table and decided not to argue tonight.

In a lull before coffee Mrs. Hollis said to Stephen: "Chester phoned today to see if you'd go to dinner on Saturday."

Chester Arden was minister at the Hollises' church, a large, muscular-jocular youth of forty, whose naïve and exuberant manner was perfectly complemented by a puddingy face. Stephen could tolerate his company only when it was well diluted. He said: "Who else is going to be there? Did he say?"

"Oh, he mentioned having met someone he knew when he was a padre in the air force," she answered vaguely. "He said something about a get-together for the boys. It might be nice," she added hopefully.

Stephen said: "It sounds lovely." He looked across to where his sister sat with lowered head. "But maybe Esther would like to go in my place."

She dropped her head even further. "Oh, you shut up," she said.

"What exactly do you mean, Stephen?" Mr. Hollis barked.

"Nothing, nothing at all." In the face of his father's inexhaustibility Stephen felt suddenly weary. "Excuse me," he said, standing up, "I must go and prepare for tomorrow's lectures."

"Wait until we have finished. I have something more to say to you."

"I'm sorry, but the lectures are important. You want me to get on in the world, don't you, Father?" He left the room. That last question was always effective.

In the darkened sitting room he looked from the window and watched the Millingtons from the opposite house back their car carefully from the garage and drive off down the hill. He wondered where they were going. The Millingtons seldom went out in the evening.

He pressed the main switch, flooding the room with light, and thought of the flowers in the shop window. He should have bought some—yellow ones for this dark-brown room. It was possible that he might have persuaded his mother into a conversation about them: he could have protracted it; they might even have laughed together at the idea of a man walking through the streets with flowers in his hand.

As he drew the curtains he pondered whether to go over the notes for tomorrow's lectures or read a little more Whitehead. One would be work, the other pleasure. It was a form of enjoyment, he felt, to meditate the decision.

And in about three hours it would be time for bed. He lowered himself into a chair. Christ Jesus, another day tomorrow just like this one!

▌▌

Miriam Sabel sat before her dressing table preparing her face for breakfast and the long morning that stretched afterward. A sunny morning, she noticed, looking at the window. She could wear the dark-tan pancake make-up that the snow in a few weeks would render impossibly mauve. Digging deep she applied it liberally, stroking her face gently upward and across. (She knew from a thousand sources that any other direction was injurious to the facial muscles, dragging them down and imparting to the countenance an eventual and unprepossessing sag.) Carefully she worked the paste into the corners of her eyes, drawing the center finger of either hand with graceful and delicate gestures over the upper lids. Now the throat, up to the chin, continuing in a sweeping line under the hair and behind the ears. Special attention needed here. She had seen too many women look disgusting on just this one small point.

She flung back her dark gold, beautifully brushed hair and folded her left ear forward to look at the scar. There was another, its mate, behind the right ear, souvenirs of the operation last year when she had had her face lifted. She smiled roguishly at herself in the mirror. Really, she had to laugh. Nobody had ever guessed, and of course she had told no one.

Don't even think about it. It makes you brood.

Wait, though. Sincerely now, Miriam, honestly, if you were somebody else looking at you how old would you say you were? Fiercely and, as she felt, impartially, she scrutinized her reflection. Thirty! Thirty-two! Perhaps—she steeled herself against her enemies—perhaps, but at the very outside, thirty-five! A woman of the world, blooming and ripe, not yet quite at her prime. Long cigarette holders and very much at home in the embassies of the world's capitals. Mysterious maturity. The older, understanding woman who is invariably a boy's first love.

She wiped her fingers on a tissue. But never forty-four!

The shiny magazines from which Miriam drew her religion told her that the sole purpose of this morning ritual was to draw indifferent husbands from behind their breakfast newspapers. On this point she was heretical. Her daily performance, she had long since concluded after serious self-examination, was for the World. And, in natural sequence, because she was a genuine lover of beauty, for herself.

As for husbands, Marvin, in point of fact, was away in Detroit on business. Shrugging her way into a light-green dress she hoped the trip would last even longer than he had anticipated. Marvin was apt to be a nuisance. He definitely did not understand her.

Miriam was now absorbed by the selection of suitable jewelry. A wide, diamond-set wedding band and the huge solitaire marquise diamond went on to the third finger of her left hand without a second thought, for she got a remote, rather sophisticated glow from the fact that she never tried to hide her married status. Still without serious perturbation she put the essential diamond-set watch on her left wrist and a massive but beautifully worked cocktail ring with a predominance of rubies on the little finger of her right hand. Then relaxing purposefully she contemplated the most difficult part of her morning toilet. What should she wear at her throat and on her breast?

Her fingers stirred thoughtfully through the drawer containing the substantial remainder of her jewelry. How difficult it was to find something that expressed at once her gay mood of freedom and the mellow dignity of this lovely season of the year. "That stippling, dappling melancholy encompassing my heart"; it was a line from "Autumn and You," one of the poems Neil had dedicated to her. She smiled gently, breathing deep. What a soul that boy had! How beautifully he expressed those things! Was he managing with the money, she wondered? When was he coming back from that cabin in the woods? His Muse *should* be refreshed by now. Just think of introducing him to Pierre and the two of them in one room, Pierre painting her portrait and Neil over in the corner composing a sonnet for her. They wouldn't, of course, speak to each other. They would exchange jealous looks, and she would soothe them by being equally nice to each of them. She sighed happily. Art was the only thing in life that mattered.

And now she had it. For her breast, negligently and at an angle, the cognac diamond brooch. Color for autumn, angle for her mood. Seized by inspiration she picked up the neckpiece of dull gold, exquisitely wrought and studded with diamonds, that had cost her thirty-five hundred dollars plus tax. Sometimes she was harassed by the thought that this piece did not look worth as much as she had paid for it, but at the time she had been quite unable to resist the blond young man at the jewelers'. Fleetingly she wondered what had become of Eric and made a mental note to check whether or not he had been fired. He had been a little rough, but he was thrilling.

Standing up she gazed with deep satisfaction into the mirror. The reflection looking back at her, she noted, was chic, well groomed, and wealthy. And, although not vulgarly so, young.

She was ready.

Head held high, to counteract the minute suggestion of chin sag she had seen recently, shoulders well back, bottom well in, with the utmost confidence and a slight but elegant movement of the hips, Miriam glided out of the room and down the stairs.

Partaking slowly of the grapefruit and toast prescribed by her latest diet, munching the food morsel by morsel with carefully closed lips, Miriam looked completely at her ease. But all her mental projections were going a scant ten feet away, to the electric clock on the mantelpiece. With the tenseness of a marathon starter she was watching the second hand as it crept around the face with agonizing slowness. Nine-thirty. Stores were opened now, covers removed from merchandise, delicate touches given to display cases. A twinge ran through her as she realized that this was Saturday and some of the stores would be closing at one o'clock. Nine-forty-five. Business left over from yesterday would have been checked and dispatched. The young men were combing their hair and straightening their ties, snatching a few minutes relaxation before the first onrush of customers. Nine-fifty-five. The young men by now were relaxed thoroughly.

Miriam stood up, taut as Diana's bow.

"I'm going out to make a few purchases," she said to the maid. She added, easily, "I shan't be home for lunch."

The sunlight poured through the windows, filling the room with great golden patches of dusty light, making the professor's bald head glint like a doorknob as he strode up and down in front of the class. Stephen looked up from a hastily taken note, pleased to see the old boy in such good form. In time with the rest of the students his head began turning from side to side as his eyes followed the moving figure.

A teacher was more than ordinary if he could interest these apathetic Canadian Liberals in the activities of seventeenth-century Levellers and Diggers. If Stephen was eventually to be a teacher, a fate that seemed inescapable, he would pattern himself on this model. The quick movements, the jerkily stabbing forefinger, the almost jabbering delivery containing at the unexpected moment a Rabelaisian joke. Above all, the lively warmth with which he spoke, imparting to the palest subject the air of hot gossip.

Examining this latest thought with customary dispassion, Stephen realized the impossibility of his ambition. He, Stephen, had no warmth in him. Moreover, he wanted none. His cool demeanor was an act of self-faith, a constant reiteration of individualism in a world where everyone radiated the same steamy heat. These students about him, the people he passed in the street, Chester Arden, with whom he was to dine that evening. No, thank you. No warmth for Stephen.

When he accepted the invitation over the phone the minister had literally bellowed bonhomie at him, exuding a boisterous eagerness that left Stephen limply regretting the meek way he had submitted to an unabated evening of this violent camaraderie.

"Just a few of the boys," Chester roared gaily, "and a very good old friend of mine named Bill Prescott. We can talk over some of the things we used to do in the war."

He even contrived to make it sound saucy, hinting of booze and women and mass copulations outside of officers' dances: Chester certainly knew how to pull in an audience, provided none of the audience had had previous experience. There was the remark he invariably made as he gripped the hand of a new acquaintance and looked earnestly into his eyes. "Never mind if I am a minister, I want you to call me Chet."

Chet! Stephen repressed a shudder. Tonight he would effect a reprisal by talking about Esther, the one topic that made Chester uncomfortable. With a grin he looked at his watch. Almost ten o'clock and the end of the lecture. An hour off before the next at eleven.

Hatless, wearing a short chinchilla coat, Miriam closed the front door and stood for an instant, motionless, in the molten light of the autumn sun. Unconsciously she was waiting, as she did each day, for the adjustment when the second Miriam beneath her skin would make herself felt for the imperceptible moment. The faint morning breeze caught her hair, and then the second Miriam jerked into a single movement, a taut crouching within that left her breathless without knowing why.

It had happened in a fraction of hesitance, then, quickly and unrecognised as it came, the movement was gone. She knew only an urgent desire to get away from these chaste and moneyed residential heights of the Montreal mountain, down into the warm, pulsing depths of the city where people looked at people with equal eye and women would admire her jewelry.

She got into the car and drove hastily away.

Miriam no longer dwelt upon the fact that she was Jewish, because in the past it had proved too worrying, too troublesome. All the miseries of her life, she had thought in the days when thought was still permissible, could be laid to the accident of her race. Except for the brief years in London and Paris, her life in retrospect appeared as a long and continuous road on which the avoiding of evasive glances and the ignoring of not-quite-heard whispers stuck up like ugly milestones. Miriam's resentment of her race had been more strong than that of the most rabid anti-Semite.

Europe had been different. In France everyone she knew had been too gay and occupied to bother with antecedents, and in England she had heard of Jews who were members of the peerage. She had had the opportunity of being introduced to one of these titled men—not a peer, only a baronet—at that lovely party in Chelsea, but strangely she had felt suddenly ill and had been obliged to leave the room. No one had said he was Jewish but she could see, and it occurred to her that this might be someone's idea of a joke. She had been unwell for almost a week.

But that was the only time in all those wonderful years. She realized later that she had allowed her happiness to dull certain memories, to lull her into a false sense of security that left her totally unprepared for her life in Montreal as Marvin's wife.

He was comfortably off when she married him. Not nearly so wealthy as now, for the war had more than tripled his money, but with enough to allow her easily to carry out her plan. She was going to be a great hostess, establishing permanently for herself in Montreal something of the life she had glimpsed abroad.

On thinking it over she was not quite sure now what that life had been, but she had definite visions of what she wanted in Montreal. *Art* was all that mattered. A room thronged with fascinating, chattering people. Men with beards, girls with blond hair and long legs, artists, models, poets, authors, musicians. My latest work. The most recent trend. Long fingers, hands stroking the air, shrugging shoulders, brilliant eyes.

And moving gracefully through them, like silver fish through a night sea, would be the people who made it all possible. The art lovers, the patrons, the ones with money. Decorous and sophisticated, murmuring apologetically of the latest acquisition to their collections, asking her discreet advice on the younger ones present.

"You have all these things at your fingertips, Miriam. Which is the up-and-coming, the really promising artist among them?"

And she, bridging the two worlds, a cocktail glass held lightly in her hand, directing. Subtle and cognizant. Suave. Of course, when I was in Paris. When I was in London. Cubism. Impressionism. Polytonality, whatever that was. Matisse? But no, not if you can get a Picasso. That lovely name with its long, broad second syllable!

The young poet shyly reading his latest work, dedicated to her, and, as the salon drew to a close, someone asking her to play her violin. Miriam had a clear picture of them, sitting in the same silence that had enrapt her audiences throughout the music halls of England and France, while she, accompanied at the piano by an adoring young student from the Conservatoire, played them her favourite tune. "Trees." With lovely words by Joyce Kilmer.

The dream never materialized. With inherent acumen she had realized that dilettantes, as important to the scheme as were artists, were infinitely more difficult to acquire and must therefore be acquired first. Knowing almost no one she cast her net by frequenting exhibitions and concerts, most of which bored her intensely and forced her to the realization that art, for her, was as nothing unless shared. At these gatherings she always picked out the most distinguished-looking people, tall, elderly men and hollow-cheeked women, and, in casual conversation during intermissions, dropped hints concerning her future plans. In every case the delicate invitations were firmly ignored.

Tightening her mesh somewhat, she began collecting names and addresses, dropping little notes indicating that she would be serving tea on certain afternoons. The notes remained unanswered.

Then one afternoon, as she sat in front of her silver tea service, hoping listlessly that someone would arrive, the maid brought in an envelope. Eagerly Miriam tore it open. The few lines enclosed were from a lady who omitted to sign her name. The content of the message was that her husband did not like her to mix with Jews so would Miriam please not send any more invitations.

Overlooking the vital fact that the ultra-conservative inhabitants of Montreal do not like to be solicited, Miriam had taken the note as a confirmation of all her suspicions. They had not come because she was Jewish. From that moment she had ceased to be a Jewess, outwardly or inwardly.

The first step had been to nag her husband into obtaining the house they now occupied in a "difficult" area on the heights of Montreal, an area coldly ignored by every self-respecting Jew in the city. In restaurants she asked with faint ostentation for ham sandwiches. The synagogue saw her not. Excepting her husband, she no longer spoke to any member of her own race; when she passed them in the street it was with a look of hostile defiance.

All her heritage was deliberately thrown aside because she had been unable to find a single Aryan dilettante. She saw no irony in the situation. In her search for the graceful and urbane patron, the gentle and decorous lover of the arts, how was she to know that she had picked the wrong city?

Stephen refused coffee on the grounds that he had to get weekend books from the Redpath Library. He beckoned Matt Lambert skipping nimbly by. "Do you know a guy called Bill Prescott?"

Matt pointed. "Over there on the grass, talking to the girl in the red hat." He whistled softly through his teeth.

Stephen saw a man of about his own age with a large, firm chin, a longish nose, and a head barbered in such a fashion that the remaining hair gave the impression of having been surprised in the act of springing from the scalp.

Matt said: "Why?"

"Nothing special. I have an invitation to dinner tonight and I was debating whether to plead a bilious attack."

"Are you sure you wouldn't like coffee?" Harrigan asked.

Without answering Stephen trailed off in the direction of the library.

She studied the array of ties and wondered which she should take as a gift for Pierre when she went for this afternoon's sitting. Choosing a tie for an artist who knew all about colors was fraught with all sorts of possible pitfalls. It might be wiser to buy him something else. At their last dinner together, at that wonderful little place down in the east end of the city, she had noticed that his cuffs were beginning to fray. Her head turned idly toward the shirt counter.

The young man with red hair was leaning against the wall, staring into space.

Her heart gave a violent wrench. From this windowless second story, artificially heated and impenetrable to the sun, with the Saturday crowds moving turgidly around her under the electric lights, she was transported to a woodland in soft April where the air was tinged with the fresh smell of primroses and filled with the sound of birds singing their delight at the awakening of this so beautiful spring. She was alone with him. The Miriam within sprang toward the sky uttering a frantic cry of yearning that echoed voicelessly across the gap made by all those other words, deeds, actions, thoughts, and desires. The gap that was now too wide to bridge or brook.

Someone brushed heavily against her and moved on without apology, but the moment was gone before that. Vibrant with old habit she bore down upon him. What imperfection would mar him? How about his teeth.

"Can you help me?" Oh God! wasn't he lovely. "I'm interested in buying a shirt. Something fairly bright and sporty."

The head with its helmet of burnished hair turned to her with remote gaze. Without a word he reached into a display case, drawing out several garments to be arranged precisely and automatically upon the counter. She didn't look at them. Her heart was pounding. She said:

"I wonder if you would help me choose? I know very little about shirts."

Perhaps it was the softness of her voice. The trance fell away from him and his expression became a mixture of shyness and something that looked to her very much like guilt. "Yes, madam, of course." The embarrassed smile revealed teeth of dazzling evenness. "I don't suppose I shall be much help. Did you have anything in mind? I mean, is he any special sort of man?"

I had thought so until now, dear, but he's not like you. He hasn't those soft, sad, violet-colored eyes or that curve to his underlip. What would you do if someone grasped you by the ears and sank their teeth into your mouth? Prettily she said: "Oh, but you have a cute accent. Say something else. Do you come from out West?"

He blushed deeply and lowered his gaze. "I picked up the accent at school in England," he explained, "but I'm really a Scotsman. That is, I spent my early childhood there."

"Lucky you," she said solemnly, "lucky, lucky you. I think Scotland is the most beautiful place in the world. The heather, the hills, all those beautiful sad songs." There had been the time when she sat up all night learning "Ye Banks and Braes" for her appearance the following evening at the Greenock Empire. And the moment she had put bow to violin the audience had chimed in, grimly singing verse after verse, evincing not the slightest interest in her hard-learned variations. "I think the heather is really beautiful," she said emphatically. "Whereabouts did you live?"

"Glasgow."

"Oh. Well, that's a lovely city. I know some people there named Gordon. Would you know them?"

"No."

"Oh."

There was a long, uncomfortable pause while they stared at each other.

"I know some people called Gordon up at Caithness," he said helpfully.

Wistfully she said: "I'm sorry, how could you possibly know them. I guess I'm not very intelligent, I'm always making a fool of myself." Taking her cue from him she lowered her head and added in a small voice: "I don't even know anything about shirts."

He gave a low, gurgling laugh. "To tell you the truth madam, neither do I. We should be able to perpetrate something really abominable together."

"Let's do," she said eagerly, and thought he looked like a naughty child about to get into mischief. Her captivation was complete.

"Do we like him?" he asked, eyes sparkling.

She wrinkled her nose in an exaggeration of thought. "Not very much," she answered at last, shaking her head. "He's nobody special."

"Then how about this?" He lifted a tan-colored shirt covered with pictures of hula girls, palm trees, and surf. Miriam knew instinctively that Pierre would like it.

"Much too refined," she said. "Try again."

Eyes wide and brow furrowed in mute question he held up the second garment, a multiplied hunting print complete with horses, riders, fox, and hounds, set on a background so violently puce that it hurt the eyes. Pierre would like neither the color nor the implied activity of the pictures. "This?" he asked, and chuckled again.

She took it from him, contriving to brush his hands lingeringly as she did so. How warm he was! "That's it exactly," she said, barely glancing at the shirt. Pierre wouldn't like it, but he'd wear it. She was paying him very well for the portrait.

"I'll have it packed for you."

He made out a bill and took the money. When he went down to the packaging counter she noticed with pleasure that the red head was turned indifferently away from the girl who did the wrapping. The girl was quite pretty.

"You've been very kind," she said when he returned. "Could I know your name so that I can ask for you when I come again?"

"McSurt. Duncan McSurt. I'm glad I was able to help you." He indicated the parcel, smiling faintly.

"Seriously, Duncan—I may call you Duncan?"

He nodded.

"Seriously, you don't know what it means to me. You see, usually I'm afraid to go into stores. People are so rude, and," her mouth gave a rueful little twist, "well, I guess I'm too timid. It restores my confidence when I meet someone like you." Putting out two fingers of her right hand she laid them lightly upon his wrist. "I'm very grateful," she added warmly.

"It's all right, madam." He seemed not at all embarrassed.

She pressed the fingers more firmly. "Thank you, Duncan. I hope I shall see you again sometime." Her smile was of the shyest.

"I hope so, madam," he said. "Good morning."

She walked away wondering what she would wear this evening. How about the black? Nice boy. His eyes would be following her now as she walked demurely toward the stairs.

But the young man was already back against the wall, staring idly off into space. Miriam did not look back.

Morning classes were over.

Crystal was walking slowly across the campus, lost in thought, trying to find a way out of this second major crisis of her life. Definitely, she told herself, a new method was needed, and that very soon. Which was too bad. The other method had worked so well, and for so long.

Early in life she had made two important discoveries: that she was attractive to men, and constitutionally, irrefragably virtuous. It had taken her many years to correlate the two facts to a state whereby she could live comfortably in North American society—a long, unhappy period during which she had made the same ghastly mistake over and over by saying "No!" at the very outset and with the utmost finality. For at least three and a half years after she reached the age of fifteen she had been coldly hostile to any male who made overtures to her; as a consequence she had arrived at nineteen without an apparent friend in the world, either male or female. She knew why. She was living in a small town. The males, chagrined at being so impersonally repulsed, had disparaged her to the females, the less solicited females, and they with delighted malice had done the rest.

She knew why, and sought a way out of the situation, desperately. The enforced solitude was weighing upon her gregarious nature, having a quite physical effect upon her. She was becoming wan and listless, almost unattractive; soon no one would want to make advances to her. Something had to be done, and immediately.

The first thing, obviously, was to get away from the place where the situation had arisen. She didn't much care for Wetaskiwin anyway. As Providence had decreed that there should be a war on at the time, a branch of the women's services received Crystal with open arms.

The combination of appearance and natural intelligence made it but a short step to a commission, and thus was Crystal able to devote the almost unlimited spare time of a female officer to pondering more deeply the resolution of her problem. Sitting behind the vase of seasonal flowers on her desk, interrupted only occasionally to sign an inconsequential paper, she had scanned the postpubescent years, considered her experiences, weighed the evidence, and made a decision.

Hostility and repulsions were definitely out: blunted weapons. "But when," she asked herself, "is a weapon not a weapon?" She answered: "When it is sheathed."

She metamorphosed. Almost overnight she became what fundamentally she had always been, a creature alluring and enticing, somewhat sophisticated, quintessentially feminine; quite consciously a sort of Albertan Marlene Dietrich. So naturally did the role fit her that she needed forcibly to prevent herself undulating when she walked. The males among her fellow officers loved it. Her inviolability was now as securely hidden as her defence of it.

Her new method, fancifully envisaged, eminently successful, was one of the most complex simplicity. She was going to be a female chum, a feminine pal. As men pierced each other's reserves, so would they be permitted to pierce hers. The difference was going to be one of speed.

Any man who now made advances to her was led with tantalizing slowness, dallying at each, through the six outer gates of the city. The inner, the seventh, the final gate? Bolted, barred, securely locked against all comers. "Nothing," she thought, with overtones of Hilton whom she liked, "nothing but the tinkling of far-off bells and dove-flutes vanishing fast upon the distant air." And there was always that ultimate reserve, gently put, of, "Tom, I'm sorry. I think you have misunderstood me."

The reserve was seldom necessary. The journey had been long and pleasant and, on thinking it over, Tom realized that her soft offerings had been all of friendship and nothing—well, only accidentally—of sex. He thought of the jokes and experiences they had shared, of the verbal intimacies they had exchanged, and he felt no resentment. She was not, after all, a teaser. She was that rarity among women, a real friend, thought Tom. And so did Dick and Harry. Crystal merely thought what satisfying fun it all was, and how successful. The only aspect of her earlier life that remained unaltered was her dislike of women.

With the war's end Crystal decided that the recent carnage would be nicely balanced if she became a doctor. She was subtle enough to suspect that her ambition had something to do with her attitude toward her own sex, and wise enough not to let the two facts interfere with each other. Enrolled in the medical school at McGill she discovered to her immense and humble surprise that she was an outstanding student. But she had brought her method with her.

And this was the commencement of her third year, she thought of which had sustained her through the blisteringly dreary summer vacation months in Alberta. She loved McGill. She looked about her, fondly; the sunlit campus; the old buildings; the gaudily turning leaves; the laughing groups of girls and young boys. Young boys. Kids. She saw Stephen Hollis going out through the gate. He turned and saw her.

By no means the least blistering experience of the summer vacation had been her encounter with no less than three unmarried female doctors. How many men, outside of patients, did unmarried female doctors ever get to meet? And how many of those men, including the patients, were not vaguely terrorized on sight? Oh, emphatically a new method was needed, was overdue. The essential thing was to plan ahead.

She turned out of the Roddick Gate and Stephen fell in beside her, walking in the direction of the house where she roomed. He was carrying a brief case containing his notes. He looked confident and well turned out.

"Hi," he said. "Good lecture?"

"Fascinating. Yours?"

"Nine to ten wasn't bad. Eleven to twelve was sheer idiocy."

"Too bad."

Sherbrooke Street had the airy, golden, well-swept look that it acquires suddenly every Saturday noon and retains until Monday morning. Crystal took several deep breaths from pure tingling joy of living. "Too bad," she repeated sympathetically.

"How did the party go last night?"

"Oh, wonderful!"

And the awful thing was that she was speaking the truth. It *had* been wonderful. From the moment of opening the door on her first ineligible guest she had enjoyed herself to the full. Despite anything she could do, she liked them. Come to that, she liked everybody, but most of all those, like the ones last night, who established the slightly boisterous officers-mess atmosphere that permitted her to be her natural self without necessitating that she pay for it later by fighting off gropers. The trouble was that, outside of an actual officers mess, those who qualified seemed never to be more than twenty years old. Twenty-one at the outside, and still wildly ineligible at that. She visualized an introduction, next year or the year after: "This is our new lady doctor. Her husband is still at school taking third-year Arts." No! A thousand times!

But the three unmarried female doctors were beginning to assume the outlines of cogent vision, standing on a blasted Alberta prairie—Act One, Scene One, *Macbeth*—beckoning to her.

A grin swam up, irrepressibly.

"What is it?" Stephen asked.

"I just thought of something beautifully silly."

Would it continue to amuse? Surely there was someone, somewhere, who was mature without being exacting. Or even eligible although juvenile.

Stephen said: "I sort of wish I had come last night."

"Oh, you're notoriously hard to get."

They came to the house. "Coming in?" she asked.

"What for?"

"I could make you some coffee."

He said: "I'm older than the freshmen."

"Don't be difficult, Stephen," she said. "We're friends, aren't we?"

"Not that, Crystal," he answered, shaking his head. "Not with me. But if you want to walk as far as Guy Street I'll buy you a Coke in the drugstore."

"Stephen, you're funny," she said.

He said: "Do you think so?"

III

She drove three times around the block before he came out of the store and began to walk wearily towards Sherbrooke Street. Drawing to the curb a little ahead of him, leaving the engine running, she leaned out of the side window and called softly as he passed. "Can I give you a lift, Duncan?"

He paused, bewildered, then came slowly over to the car. She opened the door. "I happened to catch sight of you as I passed by. Can I take you anywhere?"

"Thank you," he said, getting in beside her, and all at once the car was filled with a sense of intimacy almost unbearable to her.

"Where will it be?" she asked.

He said: "I live west from here."

"Oh, do you?" She was greatly interested. "So do I; up on the top of the hill. Do you have a house? Did your parents come out with you when you emigrated?"

"No, I'm alone. That is, I share a place with another fellow, but he's not related."

"I see. That must be nice."

One at a time, she thought. She didn't mind going with him to some buggy little room, but not if a friend was liable to turn up at any moment. A quick look from the corner of her eye reassured her that he was as presentable as she remembered.

"Were you going straight home without eating?"

"My friend usually cooks something for me in the evenings." After a pause he added, "My friend doesn't work."

She saw it all clearly. A room, disordered and not very clean, with a small window, two beds, and a single naked light-bulb hanging in the center. A chiffonier, the drawers not quite closed, crammed between the beds and covered with a litter of soiled underclothes, scuffed magazines, and unemptied ash trays. The room was particularly unpleasant at the moment because of the smell coming from the sausages and eggs being cooked on an electric ring in the corner by the unemployed friend, who had lank hair. She had a vague idea that all the unemployed had lank hair.

She said: "Will you think me very bold if I ask you something?"

He stared at her blankly.

"You were kind to me this morning, very kind, and I always say that kindness should be appreciated. I'd like to show my gratitude by taking you out to dinner. Would you come?"

The look on his face could only be consternation. Fearing what he was about to say, she resumed quickly and gaily. "Actually you'd be doing me a great favor. My husband has gone away for the week end and there is no one at home except the three maids. I get terribly lonely with no one to talk to and you were so kind to me this morning." Reaching into her handbag she pulled out a ten-dollar bill. "Look," she said, tucking it into his breast pocket, "if you take this you can pay the bill with it and no one will be embarrassed. And if you need any more I can slip it to you under the table."

He continued staring at her for so long that Miriam wondered if she had gone too far too quickly. These preliminaries, enjoyable as they were, were always the most difficult and trying part of the procedure. There were too many possible mistakes. This might be a case of that outraged masculine dignity she had heard so much about but never encountered. Or he might be balking at the mention of her husband. But instinctively she knew that this was a time when mentioning Marvin had been good tactics. Almost as good as saying that she was lonely. Experience had taught Miriam that in methods of approach her instinct was well-nigh infallible.

A surge of relief and pleasure ran through her as his face relaxed and she saw that she had won.

"You astonish me," he said.

She had not expected him to say that. He was not smiling, and his voice had a curiously humble ring. Perhaps the phrase was a Scottish term of approbation. In the same tone he said: "You must be very lonely."

With a resigned gesture, infinitely weary, she laid her hand on his knee. "Oh Duncan, I am, I am. Terribly." She turned her body toward him and gazed earnestly into his eyes. "And you are too, aren't you? Oh yes, I saw it in your face this morning when I first looked at you. I said to myself right then, 'those eyes are like a mirror of all my own loneliness and sadness.' And they are." She heaved a deep sigh. "That may have been what brought me back here tonight. That and Fate," she added hastily.

"Yes. I am lonely too." The statement was so ingenuously delivered that it left her wondering if he was younger than at first she had thought. She squeezed his knee encouragingly, trying to visualize him in a kilt. The thought made her a little dizzy.

"But there's nothing one can do about it, is there?" he continued, "because we are all in the same predicament. All of us rolling through life in little glass balls, trapped in a complete state of isolation. We can see each other; that's God's gift to us; and we can even communicate with each other after a fashion. But all our words are flung back at us by our own confined space, aren't they? And all our gestures are distorted by the curve on the two glass walls that lie between."

He chewed on his underlip. "The only real contact we ever have is when we stop rolling and two balls lie side by side, with each inhabitant realizing that the other is as lonely as he. Strange, isn't it, that the only respite from loneliness is the recognition of it?"

She was watching him with growing excitement, not understanding what he meant but immeasurably thrilled by his words and the way he delivered them. "Oh, I think it's all—it's all ..."

He looked at her anxiously while she sought for the word.

"It's just wonderful, wonderful!" she burst out. As she leaned close to him, her voice became intimately conversational. "Tell me something," she said. "Are you an intellectual?"

"I beg your pardon? Am I what?" He looked at her incredulously, then suddenly his head flung back and he burst into a great gale of uncontainable laughter that left Miriam disconcerted. "I'm sorry," he said between gasps, "I don't mean to be rude but you frightened me. I was completely at your mercy."

When the gusts had subsided to a sporadic giggle that refused to be suppressed he said: "Damn it, I don't want to laugh."

"I've been like that sometimes," Miriam said sympathetically, trying to re-establish the bond.

"I used to do it in church," he said. "Anything sacred moves me to mirth."

"You haven't answered my question yet."

"You're right," he said gravely. "And it merits a serious answer." He screwed up his eyes in concentration, and the tip of his tongue appeared at the corner of his mouth. "The matter really needs a great deal of thought, but if you will settle for a snap decision, just between friends mark you, then I'll say yes, I am an intellectual."

"I knew you were," she said.

He said: "Damn it, I'm going to giggle again."

When the bout had passed he said: "Good Lord, and I don't even know your name."

"If you come to dinner I'll tell you all about myself."

"You're very kind," he said.

Miriam let in the clutch.

"As this is a special occasion I thought we should have some wine," said Chester, clumsily pouring sauterne into each of the five glasses. Leaning his head back in the direction of the kitchen door, he roared to his housekeeper that she could bring in the soup now.

"And now," he resumed, lifting his glass and gazing round the table with misty eyes; "a toast."

The young man who was interested in mission work cleared his throat. "I never touch alcoholics, Chet," he said, mildly reproving; "it would be against my principles."

"Ah, principles," Stephen said. "Do you know my father?"

Chester said: "A very fine man, Stephen's father. A pillar of our church and a model to us all."

"He certainly would not approve of your plying me with liquor," Stephen remarked, clucking his tongue.

The mission-work young man nodded. "The thin end of the devil's wedge."

"You turn a pretty phrase."

The young man wearing a small flower in his buttonhole said seriously: "I expect some of the congregation would think that having wine in the house was a bit Romish, but personally I have nothing against wine so long as it's taken in moderation."

"One bottle between five is excessive," murmured Stephen.

Chester looked uneasily about him. "It was only for a special occasion," he said. "I never touch the stuff myself from one year to the other, but this is the first time Bill and I have met since the war. I thought it would be a good idea if we drank a toast to reunited friends." Simultaneously he raised his head and lowered his voice. "And to those friends, Bill's and mine, with whom we shall be reunited only in the hereafter."

"Hear, hear," Stephen said heartily, frowning at Mission-work.

"I apologize if I offended anyone," Chester continued, looking like a wounded St. Bernard, "but I felt it would be somehow mean if we drank water at a time like this."

"I know what you mean, Chet," Mission-work said in a conciliatory voice, "but really, water is good enough for me."

"Don't misunderstand me," Stephen said, "when I say that it certainly is."

Chester was looking appealingly at Bill Prescott, as if for some sort of bone. "Every man must follow the dictates of his own conscience," he said, raising his glass again, "but I sincerely hope that you will all join with Bill and me in a toast to our comrades of the good old days." With a reckless twist of his wrist he swigged off the wine in one gulp.

All drank except the young man interested in mission work, who was busy making mental notes for future reference.

Bill Prescott was looking at the minister's large, shiny face and thinking Hell he hasn't changed, he hasn't learned yet. Big, booming, genial Chester, still trying hard to do the right thing and putting his great flat feet into it every time. Wanting to make friends and making an enemy because he works too hard at it. He wondered if these other three had any special claim on Chester's affections. If so, how low he must feel he had fallen, how heartsick when he thought back to the days on the squadron when he had aspired to friendship only with proven heroes. These guys were probably all right, but Chester must notice the contraction when he compared types.

Dinner got under way. The young man who had refused wine began a lengthy disquisition on mission work among the Indians of Upper Quebec. They all suffered from the White Plague, he said, but their physical condition was as nothing compared to the state of their souls. The young man with the buttonhole knew exactly what he meant and punctuated the address with much sad shaking of the head, and Chester agreed that yes, there was a great work awaiting them up there. But there was a hint of impatience in his voice that made Bill realize with an empty feeling that the minister was determined to talk about the war.

Stephen, who had been saying nothing, said: "You are silent, Mr. Prescott. I understand you are taking engineering."

"Bill is from out West," Chester explained cheerily, then abruptly his voice plunged a whole octave, became lush and vibrant. A distant look, warm and moist, came into his eyes. "I guess I know what Bill is thinking of," he added.

"It is my belief," rattled on the young man, "that the Catholic priests could do a lot more on the reservations. They don't choose to, that's all."

"The old Stirlings?" Chester queried wistfully. "The old four-engine jobs?"

Chester, shut up. Please. You're a nice guy and you mean well, you always meant well. But I don't want to talk about it, not with you. Shut up before I get irritable.

"Say what you like," Chester mused on. "Stirlings were our best kites."

Yes, I remember now, you always called them kites. It was a point of honor with you to memorize every scrap of air force slang. Bang-on,

Wizard-prang, Good-show—especially Good-show. It made you feel like one of the boys, and that was the height of your ambition. But you never quite made it; the outsiders can never get in. And even the ground crews ran for cover when they saw you coming.

Chester said: "Are you remembering, Bill?"

Oh, sure. It's like a card trick. Pick a memory! There was the night I didn't go over the Ruhr because I was dead scared, and the M.O. let me get away with it instead of marking my records Lack of Moral Fibre the way they did with the British airmen. That was one of the nights you stayed up all night. I remember fine. And Don slumped down on the next bed at five o'clock in the morning, white-faced and beat and mad as hell. "Lovely trip!" he said. "Beautiful! Eight missing! And when we get back that goddamned padre is circling the perimeter on his bicycle like some son-of-a-bitch of a sea gull, fresh as a goddamned daisy. He approves of us. Told us what a good job we'd done. Onward Christian bloody soldiers." And then he rolled over on his back and said, "If that bastard is there tomorrow night I'm landing at another field. I'm sure as hell not coming back here."

He didn't come back the next night, but for another reason. I remember how red-eyed you were for about four days. You'd been especially fond of Don, and no one doubted your sincerity. People liked you. I like you. But move over. You were never one of the boys. Only the boys were that.

The mission man was saying, "And then again, most of them drink heavily. That makes them more prone to the disease."

Bill reached over and took the untouched glass of wine. "I guess you won't be needing this, will you." He began to sip, aware of Stephen's quick glance of approval. To Chester he said: "How do you like being settled down?"

"Fine. Never better. I've been very lucky. My congregation consists of some of the finest people I've ever met."

Stephen said dryly: "And they think that Chet is an absolute whiz."

"Name of God, she's got another new one," the barman said, looking unbelievingly at the waiter.

The waiter shrugged his thin shoulders. "Why not? There's plenty of 'em about."

At the other end of the narrow, dimly lit café Miriam and Duncan sat close together at a small corner table. In her heart was a gentle and steady heat that radiated its warm glow to every part of her body, bringing a consciousness of each pore and the root of every hair.

She was feeling good. She looked young, she knew, because she felt young; and no one needed to tell her how the indirect, amber-colored lighting made the luster dance in her hair every time she moved her head. She had been wise to decide on the black dress. Moods were important at a time like this, and the dress went well with the feeling she was getting from this boy who sat staring at her so somberly.

A tremor, almost mystical, ran through her. She had never had anyone brood over her before. It was new and different. It was somehow sad. Perhaps the loneliness he had mentioned. To indicate that she understood she looked deep into his eyes, noticing with pleasure the violet color and the fringe of long, dark-red lashes.

He looked young. No more than twenty-one or two. She refrained from asking his exact age, primarily because he might ask hers in return. That had happened once, catching her unawares. And experience had also taught her that young men in their twenties could be as touchy about age as women in their forties. Pierre, for instance. He never admitted to more than twenty-five, and she knew for a fact that he was twenty-nine. She had almost blurted it out at the sitting this afternoon when he started being so troublesome.

There was no need to think of Pierre when this beautiful, pale-skinned unknown was sitting opposite waiting to be discovered. How juicy he looked! She brought her eyes back into clear focus and was startled to see that his sadness was tinged now with a faint air of boredom. He might be thinking she was neglecting him. Leaning closer she managed by a concentrated effort to project a little extra soul into her eyes. There was no noticeable response.

"Would you like some oysters?" she questioned huskily.

He jumped.

"And a little wine?"

"Thank you."

They were served by the leering waiter.

Miriam, always very keen on table manners, was pleased to see that his behavior was good. He was not flashy with his wine glass as was Pierre, nor did he lift it as if it were a beer stein in the more jovial manner of Neil. And with the oysters, an unfailing test, he had a skill and silence that bespoke at least two previous encounters. Very satisfactory! All in all, she concluded, he had quite a—her mind shied from the word "class"—he had an air of quality that was pleasing in the extreme. It more than made up for his lack of conversation.

And anyway she preferred silent men—after the American boy at Gaspé last summer. He had a crew cut, nice features, and an unpublished book of poetry. Only after settling down to a sea-swept idyl had she discovered that his one vice exceeded all his virtues. He talked all the time. *All* the time. Supplying a running commentary in the present tense on every action and reaction. He explained that it was a new movement sweeping his part of the States.

Duncan finished his oysters and reached for the bottle. "You haven't touched your wine," he said.

Miriam smiled. "You're very silent. Is anything bothering you?"

"No. Nothing."

"What are you thinking about?"

He set his glass down carefully on the table. "It's hard to say. I'm never really sure, are you? It's like trying to catch soap bubbles." He laughed. "I'm full of spherical references tonight." This seemed an ideal opportunity for reopening the fascinating question of intellectualism, but she hesitated, sensing he was about to add something else. Smiling carefully, she waited while he finished his second glass of wine and poured another. He looked down at the full glass and when he spoke again it was in a curiously muffled voice. Even under the shock of his words Miriam had time to notice that his accent had become pronouncedly more Scottish. He said:

"Are you wanting me to make love to you later on?"

For an agonizing moment the curtain was drawn back and she saw the picture of an aging woman, raddled and painted, with two very unfunny scars behind her ears; a hag who went whoring around a big city procuring men twenty years younger than herself and paying them for services they would no longer give freely. The blood rushed to her face and pounded in her ears. She felt the sheen go from her hair.

"You dirty, rotten little swine," she said hoarsely. "How dare you speak to me like that." A detached corner of her mind wondered why she did not hit him in the face with the wine bottle.

There was a long silence and then he said, "I'm sorry," and raised his head slowly until he was looking full into her face. With an astonishment that almost mollified her she saw that his eyes were full of tears. "I'm sorry," he repeated, "I didn't mean it that way. It was rude of me." She watched wonderingly as a single drop brimmed over his lower lid and coursed slowly down his cheek. "I thought that the two of us, being as we are—" He stopped, lost for words.

"I don't understand," she said. As an afterthought she added, "You certainly are different."

Abruptly he wiped his cheek with his knuckles and broke into a grin that showed both lower and upper sets of teeth. "You mustn't mind me," he said. "I'm somewhat stupid. Outside of my stupidity I don't exist, I'm not really here."

She was angry still, but wondering now if this could all be part of a movement at present sweeping Scotland. She said: "That was an awful thing to say to anybody."

"I see that now," he said. "I apologize. My only excuse is that I am a stranger to the New World and unfamiliar with the customs."

And then a light, as of a tropic dawn, broke upon Miriam. Oh, what a fool! What a fool she had been for not bearing in mind all the time that he was a stranger here. He had come from across the ocean, from the places where she had spent those memorable years. He had offered her a glimpse of what had once been by asking her a direct, civilized question in the manner of that Old World she had wanted to bring to Montreal. And she had reacted like any of those provincial matrons she had seen during intermissions at the Plateau Hall concerts. She had failed herself.

Mentally she deleted every trace of the word "matron."

But he had shown by his question that he, as least, saw her as she really was. A mature and sophisticated woman, intellectual, artistic, very much in love with life. A woman whose generous impulses caused her to hurdle all social barriers, to bestow upon fortunate recipients friendship and charm and a liberal education in *savoir-vivre*. She was, of course, a type instantly recognizable to any young European.

Like a Scotch mist, thoughts of Glasgow and the Greenock Empire swirled damply through her mind. "Were you ever in Paris?" she asked.

"Yes," he said, "a few times."

She put her hand across the table and laid it lightly upon his sleeve. "Duncan," she said, "it is I who should apologize."

"You are very kind." Briefly he laid his hand upon hers and squeezed lightly. "I had no right to think that you would understand."

"But I do," she protested earnestly, tingling at his touch. "I understand perfectly."

"We are both in the same predicament, aren't we?" His smile this time showed no teeth at all.

Had he been American or Canadian she would have been startled at the apparent speed with which he moved, but her revelation was still upon her. Simply and bravely, she said: "Yes, we are, and I'll give you an honest answer. I want you to make love to me."

She failed to see the flicker that crossed his face, for she was lowering her eyelids and wishing, irrelevantly, for a cigarette in a long holder. When she looked at him again his eyes were blank.

"What shall we have for the next course?" she asked in a throaty purr. "I'll look at the menu and while I'm deciding I want you to think over all the things in your life that you're going to tell me about."

Dinner had been a dreary mixture of indifferent food and dull conversation. Only his scruples and thoughts of his father had prevented Stephen from thanking God that it was over. The present position was hardly better; there was no noticeable improvement in the quality of the conversation. But the sitting room had a comforting air of being nearer to the end of the evening. A sort of halfway house between the dining room and the front door.

He had attempted, during the meal, to halt Chester's flow of words by referring to Esther. "You must find my sister tiresome, constantly hanging around you. Isn't she a bit of a nuisance?" But Chester had only paused long enough to say earnestly, "Your sister is a very great help, both to me and the church," before resuming his swampily emotional reminiscences of the war. Stephen would have pressed the point, but he noticed that the young man interested in mission work was looking at them with quickening interest. Better, he decided, that Chester escape than the young man be gratified.

Looking covertly at these other three, he wondered if Chester was genuinely fond of them and whether they, in turn, were fond of him. There was no indication of feeling in the pietic features of the mission man; and the other one with the buttonhole, coughing now at the smoke from Chester's huge pipe, seemed incapable of any self-fabricated interest whatever. Both of them, thought Stephen, represented a type of Canadian male that he had avoided steadily since the time when his parents had been unable any longer to supervise the selection of his friends. They were a type that could be found in every church, on every campus, and, slightly older, in every large office building in Canada. A race of men with shiny, immobile faces covered with a distinguishable layer of flesh that, no matter what the age, showed wrinkles only at the corners of the eyes. During business hours they laughed a lot, slapped backs, boomed when they spoke. Once in a while they told faintly smutty jokes which they pointed up by nudging you in the ribs with their elbow. Their lives were a devoted emulation of the gusty American tycoon, the successful Unforgettable Character.

But their Scottish and English blood made them always conscious of what they were doing, forced them to realize they were only playing a part, made their most uproarious laughter merely a matter of eyes and mouths. And as they got older the smooth, undisturbed planes and curves of their cheeks made their eyes appear strange, as if they had wrinkled not from laughing but from peering. Stephen always felt in their presence that they wanted to spy on his innermost thoughts.

He looked across at Bill Prescott and felt more kindly disposed. The face, though not handsome, had character, emphasized by the pliable, gentle look that distinguishes the people of western Canada from those of the east. It was not a particularly intelligent face, Stephen thought, but neither did it have the aggressive stupidity current among the students who took part in the five-o'clock charade. And there had been that rather good business of silencing the wretched mission man by taking his wine glass. Stephen looked hastily away as Bill, aware of the scrutiny, gave an elaborate and conspiratorial wink.

There came now the moment that Stephen had been anticipating sadistically all evening. Conversation slid to a screeching halt. The young man interested in missions, having expended all his élan into the disquisition on Indians, was void of any other subject. The other young man, with nothing at which to cluck his tongue and murmur deprecatory monosyllables, lapsed into complete silence. Chester, like many Canadians, unable to talk without a background of the conversation of others, looked with uneasy hopefulness at each and then sank back miserably in his chair, dismay spreading over his face as he viewed a possible noiseless five minutes of social ruin.

In a surge of engendered good-fellowship Stephen, just as elaborately, returned Bill's wink.

The lull developed into a painful lag, broken only by the whistling and bubbling of Chester's pipe. Stephen smiled faintly at his knees. The others frantically sought objects in the room upon which to fix their attention. Chester, his face crimson, suffered abominably at the thought of his disgrace.

"Would anyone like some music?" he asked, leaping eagerly to his feet.

"Not unless," Stephen articulated, "you have some new records since last I was here."

Chester deflated back into his seat. The silence resumed.

This is Canada, Stephen thought dreamily, where a guest's duty to his host is nonexistent and the party giver who does not invite at least one naturally garrulous person is doomed to finish his evening under the stare of accusing eyes set in faces stiff with resentful boredom.

But also, this is Westmount, he thought, and fell into contemplation.

Westmount, the single Canadian manifestation of those hills, rising like gilded pimples on the face of the American continent, up which the Merchant and his Lady have ever fled to distinguish themselves from the Merchant and his Woman, financially obliged to remain in the town below. *Westmount*, the prosperous city within the encircling city of Montreal, where the clean, wide streets sweep sharply to the top of Mount Royal, and the prosperity of a resident can be judged by the altitude of his house. (Deep in the minds of many residents is the prompting that God—the president of many Westmount church clubs—

would dwell over the top of that small mountain were it not rendered uninhabitable by the proximity of a large electrically-illuminated cross, erected at the very peak by The Catholics. God is British, and therefore not Catholic. Catholics are French, and those are the people one sees down in the city, working as road menders or policemen or streetcar conductors, or as clerks in stores owned by The Jews.) *Westmount*, a city of wealth and plenty, a splendid isolation of the mind, a cult; a secret society of the soul whose members recognize each other psychically through gestures and nuances unrecognizable to nonmembers; an institution regarded with derisive awe throughout the length of Canada; a magic word, whose utterance can bring more deference to the purchase of a tie than another gets when buying a suit. A noble city, an immensely powerful, go-to-church-on-Sunday city, temperate, moderate, rigidly ethical and frigidly moral; adhering publicly to the high standards it has publicly set itself and decently confining its private life to cellars and upstairs rooms.

A city in which most of the inhabitants of Montreal would dearly love to live. A devout and religious city where the first dogma is Westmount.

In the face of languished conversation to what an infinitude of alternatives the residents and fellow members can at last resort! Who would begin, Stephen wondered?

"I have a funeral tomorrow afternoon," Chester said leaning forward, confidential but a little reluctant. "Matter of fact, it nearly took place in the morning." He paused, looked meaningful and decided to shoot the bolt. "In which case I would not have conducted the service."

Stephen pursed his lips and commenced to enjoy himself for the first time this evening. "Catholics?" he asked.

The mission man's eyes glinted as Chester nodded his head. A very difficult situation for a while. Mr. Fraser's sister." He paused again as he saw the uncomprehending looks. "Mr. *Nesbitt* Fraser's sister," he amplified. "The one who isn't married."

The heads nodded in unison, and the young man with the buttonhole murmured, "Poor Mr. Fraser."

"His sister lived with him for years, you know," Chester continued. "I remember she used to give me cookies when I was a kid."

"And now she's dead," someone said.

"Strange how things happen," Chester said ruminatively. "Everything seemed all right until the secret came out. It's out now, of course."

"She wasn't really his sister?" Stephen suggested.

"Terrible situation. It seems she was married. Thirty-four years ago last March she married a Catholic."

The mission man literally gasped with horror. "A sister of Mr. *Nesbitt*

Fraser?" he asked incredulously.

"I know how you feel," Chester said. He drew a shade closer. "I'm not breaking any confidences because everything has come out now, but it appears that the man drank or something. Well, you all know what a nice woman Miss Fraser was. She left him the moment she found out. Three days after the ceremony, I think it was."

"These mixed marriages are always a mistake," the young man with the buttonhole said with gloomy satisfaction.

"Yes, indeed!" The mission man nodded vigorous agreement. "What happened then?" he asked. "About the funeral?"

"Well," Chester said, "they hadn't heard from this husband for years, and then he turned up at Mr. Fraser's house yesterday and demanded that she be buried as a Catholic, if you ever heard of such a thing."

"Isn't that awful!"

"Quite a little skirmish for a while I believe, but Mr. Fraser won out in the end. A fine man, Mr. Fraser."

"The husband French?"

"Irish, I think."

"Hmmmm."

This was a sort of amusement that Stephen had been deriving for years. Happy to keep the subject going he said: "The Catholics do have a better cemetery, don't you think?"

Chester leapt. "I wouldn't say that exactly. Ours is pretty nice."

"Ours is lovely!" snorted the mission man. "Pity it's right next to the Catholic one." He turned to Bill. "We don't use the same entrance though."

"I'm glad," Bill said.

Stephen looked sharply at the unsmiling face and felt that he had an ally.

The young man with the buttonhole, looking considerably more vivacious, made his first gambit of the evening. "I was in ours the other day," he said, his voice lingering and dramatic. "And who do you think I saw walking there?"

"Who was it?" someone asked dutifully.

"Only a group of men from one of the Catholic seminaries."

"In our cemetery?" the mission man said, furiously indignant. "What were they doing in our cemetery?"

"Perhaps they mistook the gate," Bill suggested amateurishly.

"Arrogance!" Stephen said firmly. "Pretending to show their tolerance just because they're a majority in Quebec."

"They ought to be stopped." The mission man was thoroughly incensed. "And there's a few more things they ought to be stopped at, too," he added darkly.

With the exception of Bill, everyone started to speak at once. Unconsciously or otherwise, they had selected an alternative to the dreaded noiselessness, and conversation could now bowl merrily on, until the following morning if necessary. Indeed, until all the protagonists dropped dead with sheer fatigue.

Stephen was pleased to see how sincere they had all at once become. Sitting ducks, he thought.

The initial gaffe was forgotten, and Miriam was thinking that seldom had she spent a more delightful evening. True, Duncan had not proved communicative. Her most oblique questions had elicited nothing but scraps of information about his schooldays and a passing reference to the recent war. But he had listened with a more than gratifying attention while she sketched a version of her own life told so often before that she had almost come to believe it herself.

She skimmed lightly over her childhood in Ontario. "Just a small town, but quite charming. Daddy had a business there." She had learned to use the word "daddy" in England and considered it rather fashionable, but it conjured up for her no picture of the gentle little tailor whose one strictness had been to lock her in her room with a violin every other evening for two hours. He had died of a heart attack four months after she ran away from home, and when she learned of the fact ten years later she had already forgotten what he looked like.

"Daddy was lovely," she told Duncan warmly. "You'd have loved him. He used to say that nothing was too good for his little Miriam. Some more wine?" She leaned over, without waiting for an answer, and refilled his glass. "He sent me to all the best violin teachers in the country," she resumed. "Some of them were very great too, but Daddy never ever grumbled at the expense. He said it meant *that* much to him." She snapped her fingers to indicate how much and became reflective. "He stood behind me and encouraged me through all those years of grueling study that every true artist must endure, because, as he used to say to me, 'Miriam you are a true artist.'

"Then almost overnight I became a success. In New York, it was. An executive of a record company who was taking an interest in my work persuaded me to make a few recordings. I agreed because I knew by that time I had something to give the world. I've always had music in my blood."

Duncan was drinking again. "What pieces did you record?" he asked.

She knew that nothing dated one so irrevocably as a popular song. "Oh," she answered, airily waving a hand, "some concertos, a few sonatas, things like that. 'Blumenlied.' 'Humoresque!'"

"Dvořák?"

She said the first name that came into her head. She said it glibly and with an air of gentle correction. "Wagner."

"Oh."

"It sold thousands of copies, thousands. Made me a success almost overnight. That was how I came to be invited for my first European tour."

"You know Europe?" he asked.

"Like the palm of my hand. London. Paris. Oh, how I miss them all." She smiled dreamily, as at the memory of a thousand champagne waltzes.

He was staring at her in wide-eyed fascination. "Please go on," he urged.

Yes. She and her past life must appear dazzling and glamorous to this poor lovely boy after the drab room, the unemployed friend, the ugly nondescript crowds it was his duty each day to serve. "My biggest successes were in England and Scotland," she said. "You may have heard me there. I made quite a few appearances on the B.B.C."

"I expect I was still at school," Duncan said. "I didn't hear much music then."

A glance reassured her that the remark had been more innocent than it sounded. "Oh, I wasn't much more than a kid myself," she said, laughing lightly: and taking a deep breath she added, "Seventeen to be exact. Everyone was surprised at how young I was. Where did you say you were at school?"

"In Berkshire."

"That's a lovely place. I was there once myself." She was not quite sure of the truth of this last statement, but suddenly a thought occurred to her so authentically charming that two tears sprang to her eyes. She turned to Duncan that he might see them, but he was looking down at the tablecloth. She said: "To think we were in the same place at the same time and yet it took an ocean crossing of three thousand miles to bring us together. And some people say there is no such thing as Fate!"

Would the reference to Fate provoke him into saying something interesting and intellectual? Vaguely she felt that he had something different to offer, something to tell her that she could hold and ponder tomorrow when he was no longer there. She saw that he was becoming very drunk. His lower lip was thrust down revealing his lower teeth, his brows drawn over the blurring eyes as if in pain. He looked fierce and nearly wild, and yet she was conscious of an impression that in the past something, or someone, had tamed him completely. All through.

It reminded her of that time she had appeared at the Blackpool Tower. There was a professional Wild Man from Borneo on the same bill, a great frightening creature with thick arms and a mass of hair, whom she had never spoken to beyond a nod and a greeting. They were, after all, representing two totally different aspects of Art. They were, after all, on opposite ends of the bill. But he had disturbed her in a peculiarly pleasant way. She had met him in the long, rambling sequences of her dreams.

Until one night. She was waiting to go on stage, bejeweled, beautifully gowned, her specially sequined violin tucked under her right arm. Looking across the lighted stage to the wings on the other side she discerned the wild man standing with two stage hands. With little finger elegantly crooked, he was drinking tea from a dainty little china cup.

The sight haunted her for days. She dreamed of him no more. There was, she was thinking, somehow a connection between the wild man and Duncan.

He asked: "Do you still give concerts? I should like to hear you play."

The inevitable question was always difficult to answer because for years past she had not been offered a single engagement. She imagined the probable reason was that agents thought her too wealthy now to bother with the theater, but the few times she had put forward this explanation it had sounded like a weak admission of failure even to her own ears. She said: "That's all over now, I'm afraid." And having forgotten in this golden glow of afterdays that one of her reasons for marrying Marvin was to escape a succession of dirty theaters grown suddenly wearying to her, she added: "You see, my husband doesn't like me to appear in public."

Duncan nodded in tacit understanding. "What is he like, this husband who goes away on week ends?" he asked, reaching again for the bottle. "I beg your pardon. That sounded bloody rude."

"Oh, that's all right. I'm not sensitive about it. Marvin and I realized long ago that we didn't get on together. We've gone our separate ways for years. My husband drinks."

"So do I," Duncan said, smiling. "I'm nearly drunk."

She had no idea why she had said that, but now her infallible instinct, hitherto groping through the evening as in a dark passage, was impinged by a shaft of pure radiance. "It's different," she said. "Very different. Marvin is an alcoholic." And the words came tumbling forth in a sighing torrent, with a quiet passion and an immense natural skill.

"Duncan, Duncan, if you could only know what it has been like; the misery, the heartache, the unutterable loneliness of it. He was my sun, my whole world, all the melodies I had ever played made into one lovely melody that I sang constantly in my heart. I worshiped him, Duncan, I adored him. The day I married him I thought that no woman in the world could be happier than I. That I would spend the rest of my life in a state of continual bliss." She laughed bitterly. "Two months later I knew different.

"Oh, I did what I could. I begged him, implored him to stop drinking. I consulted doctors, I asked his relations to help me, I even got down on my knees and prayed to God. No use. He got steadily worse. He was drinking all day, every day. It was horrible. Sometimes he would disappear for weeks, gone on one of his bouts, and during all that time I daren't leave the house in case he came home and was in trouble. That was when I learned what loneliness was. I knew what you meant when you said those things tonight. I know what you were feeling.

"And then when he got home, dirty and unshaven and reeking of the stuff he had been drinking, he would come to my room. That was the worst part of it. Later on, you can imagine, I had to lock my door against him. I've kept it locked ever since. Wouldn't you think that life could hold no greater unhappiness for me? But no! The worst blow was still to come.

"It was one night at dinner. Marvin was sober for the first time in ages and I thought I'd talk to him, ask him again to try and give up drinking. I looked across the table at him and discovered that I was looking at a stranger. I didn't know the man who sat there. Marvin was gone from me. It was at that very moment that I realised I had stopped loving him." Her voice became piteously soft, anguished. "Oh Duncan, is there any greater loneliness than when you have loved and suddenly stop loving? I tried, I swear I did, but I suppose I just wasn't good enough. I guess I was too—too—"

Gently, attractively, Miriam broke down and wept.

Marvin Sabel, at that precise moment, was politely refusing a second whisky and soda offered by his Detroit host. Could he have heard Miriam's recital he would probably have wept also.

Duncan handed her a large, crumpled handkerchief and said: "Is that why you haven't been drinking all evening? I wondered."

Bill suggested a drink after they left the house, and Stephen, somewhat surprised at himself, accepted the invitation. Sitting now in the tavern, waiting for the first round, he began to wish that he had not come, feeling certain that the threatening conversation would be only slightly less uninteresting than that which had gone before.

The beer came, they muttered "Cheers" and drank half a glass, meanwhile watching each other with the faint but unembarrassed antagonism that a student shows when left alone with another student he doesn't know well. Stephen wondered whether the atmosphere would be enlivened if he made a few mildly hostile remarks.

"The pasty-faced one who talked about missions," Bill said. "How the hell can he have won the M.M. in the war?"

"It's dangerous to harbor preconceived ideas about heroes," Stephen replied. "As a soldier who spent the entire war in an office I once had the privilege of helping award a medal to a cook."

Bill laughed with such obvious delight that Stephen, who had not meant to be funny, felt more friendly towards him. He offered a cigarette. "What time does this place close?" Bill asked.

"About twelve-thirty."

Bill murmured approval, and Stephen was relieved to see that the conversational possibilities of licensing hours were not to be pursued. They sat in an easy silence, smoking and drinking their beer. The undertones of cockfighting ebbed away. After a while Bill said:

"Was Chester always like that?"

"Ever since I can remember. Jolly, merry, plenty of fresh air; Jesus as a baseball player and so on. His parishioners love it."

"He means well."

"He makes me puke," Stephen said mildly.

"He goes out with your sister, eh?" Bill asked.

"No, but it's not her fault. What gave you that idea?"

"Must have been something you said." Bill waved the waiter to bring more beer, and Stephen insisted on paying. Books and drinking were the only opportunities he had for spending money.

"I remember back in the war," Bill looked up at the ceiling, "when someone mentioned in the mess that it would be good to see a decent game of baseball again and Chester immediately got the idea we ought to form a squadron team. It would serve two purposes, he said—be a link with home and at the same time show the local inhabitants one of the better sides of Canadian life. Well, hell, none of us wanted to play baseball, except the guy who'd mentioned it, but Chester wouldn't take no for an answer. He used to sit in the mess every day with a pencil and paper and a miserable look on his face. Some of us had to give in, in the end." Bill grinned. "And by Jesus, you should have seen the team; scraggy as hell; and what made it worse was that no one ever turned up to watch us. That really hurt Chester's feelings. He used to talk about it every Sunday on his church parades. How did we expect to win the war if we didn't all pull together?"

"Sounds like our Chester."

"There were times when I could have kicked him."

"You'll probably feel like that when you hear his sermon tomorrow evening. Why did you promise to attend?"

"I sure wasn't going to get up for the morning one."

"I have to do one or the other," Stephen said. "*Noblesse oblige*. My father is a member of the hierarchy. You realize Chester'll probably want us to go up to the house again after the service."

"Not for me, I've got somewhere else to go. Hell, fancy coming three thousand miles across country and running into Chester. What a fate!"

"What made you come east in the first place?"

"I don't know: I've been like a blue-assed fly since the war ended. Fed up with Vancouver. Women. The usual reasons."

He is still talking, but Stephen no longer listens, being convinced that he knows where the conversation is leading and certain now that he was foolish to have come. He does not wish to discuss women and the usual reasons; they are too usual. And looking at his companion he is thinking wearily that Bill will have nothing fresh, nothing original to offer.

He turns over in his mind the possible alternatives. The war? Among recapitulations of shot and shell, flak and forced landings, there is always the consciousness that he spent the war behind a desk. This occasions no spiritual disquiet. After the First World War it was the vogue to suffer pangs of conscience because one had killed. Other times, other customs; it is now fashionable, the pendulum having swung, to be rent with remorse because you did not kill. All very enjoyable, but Stephen cannot enter into the spirit of the thing. He reacts only with an amused contempt. But he has found his lack of battle experience to be a conversational impediment. It makes him a mere recipient of monologues. Stephen's god is Participation. No. Not the war.

We can perhaps talk of our studies at McGill. But this, at best, is only mock participation. I shall quote my professors and lecturers and, in turn, I'll be met by other quotations. If I venture a conclusion of my own that can possibly be countered by something a professor has said, then my conclusion will be immediately void and nonsensical. I am academically unqualified. I cannot meet my masters as equals and I refuse to join my fellow students in the mass worship of professorial oracles. At my age that would be the most disgusting form of self-castration.

So what else? The movies? Magazines? Hockey? Historical novels? I am sitting in this cheerless, marble-floored tavern where it is against the provincial law for women to enter and Bill is still talking and I am unbelievably, stupendously bored.

His mind wanders back to England, where he was stationed during the war. London; the theaters and concert halls he lost when he returned to the land of the enduring amateur; the soft envelopment of antiquity and the jazzed-up, brittle excitement that came with the air raids. The soft, blue-gray texture of London air on an autumn evening, the unexpected squares filled with green trees and amethyst shadows, the walk at night from Charing Cross down to the Embankment where everything was misty and muffled, and a coolness rose up from the moving river. He thought of the pubs down in the East End, not spittle-covered taverns like this one, where he would sit alone in a corner and watch the women. Some of them were fat and middle-aged; they had snub noses and red shiny faces, and sometimes they wore flat black hats with a long pin stuck in at the back. All of them were noisy. They pushed each other and shook when they laughed and sang songs like "Down at the Old Bull and Bush." And when they moved they tightened their thick, firm thighs in such a way that it set up a pleasant tingling in the back of one's stomach. It would soon be winter in Montreal.

"What did you say?" Stephen asked.

"I said what sort of office was it where you spent the war?"

Of course he had been foolish to come tonight. This was as unsuccessful as the last time he tried. But he had realized more than ever of late that he couldn't go on living like this. One day his father would die and then the great, rolling mesa of ennui would be completely unbroken. He stood up, buttoning his coat.

"I've had enough beer for tonight. Think I'll be running along. See you."

"Yeah, sure thing. See you tomorrow," Bill said. A thought struck him. As the figure retreated he called out, laughing: "See you in church."

When Duncan, with slurring voice, suggested that she drop him off outside the City Hall, Miriam laughed girlishly at the unfailing coquettishness of young men and pressed a little harder on the accelerator. The tires hummed over the paving, the streetcars passed with little bursts of noise that she found exhilarating. She knew that she was a good driver.

"You must have one more drink," she said. "I have something very nice at home."

He moved and she thought he was coming nearer to her, but he was only adjusting his position on the shiny leather upholstery so that he could lean his head on the back of the seat. She changed gear as they came to an incline and went soaring up Cote St. Antoine. Even sitting apart like this she could feel the warmth coming off his body.

The car crunched quietly on the gravel and into the garage. "Don't slam the door too hard," she whispered as he got out. She noticed how loud his breathing sounded up here among the still residences.

At the door, with her key in the lock, she hesitated. "Better take off your shoes," she said. "We might wake the maids." He was peering at her in the dim light, his body swaying slightly. She wondered if three bottles of wine had been too much for him.

"No," he answered finally, and began to laugh as he had done earlier in the evening. "I have a large hole in the heel of my sock and your advantage is too great already."

She turned the key and beckoned him in, making small, quieting sounds. His giggle snapped off as the door closed gently behind them. The breathing came even louder here in the hall, and he made faint sounds, like tiny moans, as the exhalations caught at his vocal chords. Miriam was reminded of the irritating noises that kept her awake when she shared a room with her husband. "Hush," she said again, and took his hand, leading him in the direction of the stairway. Forty-four years old? God, how ridiculous! A woman was as young as she felt.

She pulled him close and whispered in his ear.

"That's the dining room through there. I had it specially done, all from my own ideas. Cost me a fortune. I wish I could turn the lights on and show it to you."

"Why can you not?" Duncan asked loudly.

"Duncan, sshh! Be sensible!" No one had asked that question before. She realized that there was nothing on earth to prevent her turning them on except that she preferred it like this. The darkness lent an air of greater excitement, almost of conspiracy. The word "rendezvous" crossed her mind as they ascended the stairs. Then the word "tryst." Her flesh gave a tiny ripple of ecstatic anticipation.

"In here," she said, throbbing with excitement, and they entered the music room. From around the walls the busts of numerous long-dead composers seemed to glow through the darkness in dull disapproval. As Duncan sank onto the couch Miriam crossed to the farthest corner and turned on a dim, pink-shaded lamp, throwing into faint discernment the piano, the violin stand, and the stave-patterned wallpaper that had been so difficult to procure. From the glass-covered liquor cabinet she drew out a bottle and one glass.

"I save this for special occasions," she said, very low. "What better time than now?"

"None for me." His voice sounded choked, causing her to suck the air in sharply through her teeth. "Please no more. I've had enough."

"But this is special. Very special. You'll notice it the moment you taste." She three-parts filled the tumbler and carried it across to the small table beside him. "I don't know what has happened to the proper glasses," she said. "I'll have to speak to the maids in the morning."

He was lying with his head back, unmoving as in the car, looking up at her with pupils dilated by the half-light. His legs were stretched apart in front of him, hands limply at his sides, his hair in tangled disarray over his brow. Miriam, thinking she had never seen anything more beautiful, felt an impulse to lean over and kiss softly his parted lips.

She was standing quite still, and then all at once there came upon her that peculiar emotion she had experienced in the morning when first she caught sight of him; a great yawning, yearning, tender feeling, mingled with a mounting something that was strangely like pity, frightening in its intensity. It was as if, like a drowning man, she suddenly sensed her whole life; all the lies, the mistakes, the disappointments, all the wrong choices she had made. And now vaguely she perceived that this was another moment of choice.

In the darkness she smiled and blinked her eyes, and chose wrongly.

She said: "Take your jacket off. You won't feel the benefit of it when you go out."

"I—I think I'm all right, thank you," he replied, not stirring.

"Then wait just a second." She was still smiling. "I'm going to make myself more comfortable."

In her room across the landing she turned on the lights around the dressing table and stared hard at herself in the mirror. The sight shocked her, but pleasantly. She looked superlatively well. The bright eyes danced as they looked back at her, the skin was smooth and firm. She put her hands on either side of her head and lifted her hair, holding it high a moment then letting it fall in a cascade of gleaming locks.

She stood in the middle of the room and undressed slowly, allowing each smooth article to slip gradually from her fingers into a neat heap on the floor. Afterwards, she would cram them into a drawer. A man had once told her that nothing nauseated him so much as the sight of a woman's apparel strewn about a room.

She went back and looked into the mirror. Well, nobody could say she didn't have a good figure. She pinched herself two or three times and stood sideways to view the flatness of her stomach. Good! And the way she lifted here! Just coming to the full bloom of mature ripeness.

Crossing her arms over her breasts she hugged herself, stroking her shoulders, reveling in the satiny feel of the skin under her fingers. She wondered if possibly she were immortal, and laughed delightedly at her own foolishness. The fingers stole from her shoulders to her face. Back again to her shoulders. Standing perfectly still she found the line on her neck where the texture of the skin changed and became coarse.

"He's just a pathetic kid and I ought to send him home," she thought. "He's suffering about something. I know about suffering. I ought to be trying to comfort him."

She turned abruptly back to the dressing table, picked up a puff and dusted herself from shoulder to toe with talcum powder, so liberally that when she had finished she was standing in a fine cloud. With a spray she applied perfume—ears, throat, armpits—then she robed herself in a single garment of shimmering white silk that swept the floor. She had bought it as a nightgown, knowing full well that no one could possibly sleep in it; but she had been attracted by the extreme length of the shoulder straps, by the way they fastened with a little snap in the center of each bare shoulder. She shook her body and the material crackled over her in the dry air.

A few last arranging strokes of the brush in her hair; a last look at her reflection. She turned out the lights and went back into the other room, surrounded by an aura of perfume.

At first she thought Duncan was asleep. He was stretched full length on the couch, his feet extending over the end, the fingertips of one hand dangling to the floor. He stirred as she advanced. "No, don't move," she whispered, "I want to talk to you." She sat beside him, balancing herself on the edge of the couch, taking his hand. "You look so comfortable."

"I wasn't asleep," he said. "I was watching you from under my eyelids as you came in."

For no reason she gave a low, throaty laugh, releasing his hand so that it fell limply upon her thigh. "Move over Duncan, or I shall slip." Putting one hand on either side of his head she leaned over him, close enough to feel the hot, wine-laden breath that panted from his mouth.

"Still comfortable?" she asked huskily, and, helpless, swooped to press her mouth on his.

She was not quite sure what happened then. There was a brief whir of arms and legs and heads and suddenly she was sitting upright on the couch with Duncan beside her. His arm was outstretched, his finger pointing to one of the busts against the opposite wall.

"Is that Beethoven?" he asked in a high voice.

What was it? What the devil was the matter with him? A possible answer came and her annoyance was swept away, supplanted by a thought so titillating she could scarcely find her voice. Grasping his arms she drew him round until she was looking into his eyes. "Duncan," she said, "I want to know. Why are you afraid of me? Is it—is it because this hasn't happened before?"

He looked back as if trying to say something, then with a sound suspiciously like a sob he lowered his head onto her breast, his body shaking, his arms groping around her till his hands met in the center of her back.

"I wish I could tell you," he whispered. "I want to tell someone."

"Oh, you darling," she said, running her fingers through his hair. "I understand, I understand. Imagine that!" Over his shoulder she saw the glass of wine, still untouched. "You haven't had your nice wine. Didn't you want it?" He shook his head, seeming to nuzzle deeper into her. "And you didn't take off your jacket. Here, let me help you."

With fingers that trembled slightly she picked at the buttons until his jacket came open. "I like you very much," she murmured, and wrapped her arms around him, drawing him close, feeling through the thin shirt his ribs pressing into the soft flesh of her underarm. "Duncan," she said softly, "Duncan."

The sweet damp smell of him seeped up through her nostrils. The ridges of muscle on either side of his spine quivered under her fingers. In an uncontrollable access her grip became a vise that tightened until she felt his back bend. "Duncan." The words rattled from her throat. "Duncan, kiss me, hit me, do something to me." Freeing one of her hands she grabbed his hair, dragging his face to within an inch of her own. "Duncan!"

"No no no no no no NO!" It burst from him like machine gun fire and with a fierce wrench he tore himself away from her, standing up so rapidly that he almost upset the couch.

"I can't," he said, his breath coming in sobs; "I'm sorry, but I can't." His hands were over his face, muffling his voice so that she could barely understand what he was saying.

"Duncan—"

"No, it's no use. I tried, honestly. When you came into the room I told myself I could do it because I was a man. I even told myself," he added, with a short, high burst of laughter, "that I must do it because I was a gentleman. What an archaic notion." He was silent for a moment, turning his back upon her, and she could see that he was buttoning his jacket and straightening his tie. "But it simply wasn't possible," he said finally. "I couldn't make it." As he walked out of the room she heard him repeating quietly to himself: "It simply wasn't possible. It simply wasn't possible."

He was gone. She stayed where she was until she heard the front door close behind him, then she stood up, wondering what she had done and what she should do now. The scars behind her ears were smarting and the smell of the perfume on her was getting to her stomach, making her feel sick. She wondered if it would help her if she screamed, but decided against it because it might wake the maids.

A drink. Sinking back on the couch she picked up the untouched glass of wine and drained it off.

Ah, yes. There it was. She had half expected this when he walked out of the room. She knew there was something missing, that some final little touch was needed. Call it the cherry on top of the sundae. How could anyone live to be forty-four and still be such a fool?

Lying on the table, where Duncan had tucked it carefully under the wine glass, was the ten-dollar bill. He had had no intention all the time. Not from the moment she picked him up. The dirty rotten little bastard of a store clerk!

She said once more, "Duncan," and with the wine glass in one hand and the ten-dollar bill screwed tightly in the other she began most miserably to weep. She knew that she looked hideous as she did so.

I would be wiser, Stephen thought, to go in by the back door and sneak quietly up to bed by way of the back stairs. He was conscious of the smell of drink upon him, and a light in the window of the downstairs sitting room indicated that Mr. Hollis had not yet retired. But he rebelled at the thought of allowing his father even so small a moral victory. He inserted his key in the lock and noisily opened the front door.

"Is that you, Stephen?" Mr. Hollis looked up from his copy of *The Sermons and Letters of the Rev. Dr. Andrew Harkness* and peered out into the darkened hall. "Where have you been until this hour?"

"Up at Chester's place. I was there for dinner."

"Oh. I hope you were able to derive some good from it. A fine man, Chester." He was looking at his son's motionless figure with quickening suspicion. "Why are you standing out there in the hall? What have you been doing that you are afraid for me to see?"

"Father, it's too late to quarrel, and I'm not in the mood. But please realize that it's many years since I was afraid of you in any way at all." Stephen continued on to the foot of the stairs and turned to see his father staring angrily after him from the chair in the lighted sitting room. "Believe me, Father," he said, quite loudly, "when I do do anything that is at all likely to enrage you or shame you I shall make a point of seeing that you are the first to know about it. Good night."

Up in his room he reflected upon his defeat, wondering why, at the last moment, he was unable to say that he had been drinking. Undressing slowly, carefully putting the wooden trees into his shoes, he reflected that it had always been thus, this ability to confront his father with the greatest sins of the spirit while yet being afraid to reveal even the smallest sins of the flesh.

And pondering on these latter sins he thought how pitifully few were those he had committed. He turned on his bedside lamp, picked up *Adventures of Ideas*, and commenced to read.

Shivering with cold, Duncan let himself into the house and began crossing the darkened hall toward the stairs.

Halfway across he shouted: "Hello, I'm back. Are you home?"

Up on the landing a shaft of light appeared from an opening door and a figure, smoking a cigarette and wearing a bronze-colored Charvet dressing gown, emerged, advanced, and leaned nonchalantly over the bannister. The voice was as pleasantly languid as the pose.

"Greetings, you infamous cow. You won't mind if I mention that I cooked a perfectly delicious Lobster Newburg and opened a bottle of Chablis?"

Duncan laughed. "I beg your pardon."

"Granted, of course."

"I was out with a woman. She wanted to know if I was intellectual."

"You are, my dear. Far too. Did you convince her?"

"I don't know. I went home with her and she offered me some wine." He sat down on the bottom stair. "I suppose there is no way of helping anyone. That poor lonely woman. Christ, it was ghastly." He burst into tears.

The figure did not move. The voice softened. "Come upstairs and have a shower and tell me about it, my pet. And let that great heart bleed for the world if it must, but please, please don't weep on the staircase. It simply isn't done. Come now."

IV

The evening sermon was one of Chester's favorites.

"All of us adrift in our little boats, frail vessels on the broad, turbulent river of life, must choose whether we are going against the current or," a dramatic gesture of the arm, "or the other way. It is a great temptation to let the waters take us where they will, but let us remember that God has given us oars to enable us to pull *against* the current. Pull we must, and in that pulling, which we do of our own, divinely-given free will, what joy is to be experienced when we feel our spiritual muscles bulge, strengthen, and grow firm." He gazed down on the smooth, contented faces of the congregation. "Life is a struggle," he said, "but who, in the face of divine revelation, can say that the struggle naught availeth. So I say to you, leap to the oars, and we will all pull together for that beautiful shore. We will find in the end that it has been well worth our while."

"Too profound for me," Stephen muttered. Bill whispered that he recognized the sermon as one he had heard during the war, when it had been thinly disguised with bicycles, head winds, and high hills to give it more local color. Stephen liked that.

They dodged out of a side door when the service ended to avoid Chester, who stood in the main entrance, wringing the hand of each member of the departing congregation and accepting congratulations with modest concurrence.

"He'll be hurt," Stephen said when they were standing outside on the shiny sidewalk. A shower had fallen while they were in church.

"Sure he will, but this sort of thing could go on forever."

"So what now?"

Bill looked dubiously at his companion, thinking of the previous evening. "Come on," he said, "we'll go and visit a guy I know. He'll give us a drink."

Stephen was thinking of the lengthy disquisition on Chester's sermon that his father would be giving at home. Once was enough for any man. "All right," he said. "Come on."

Later, walking up the driveway of a large, three-storied house ablaze with lights, he was assailed by doubts, felt wary. "What's he like, this friend of yours?"

"Just a young guy. Some sort of foreigner, but he speaks good English." Bill paused, about to bestow the highest Canadian accolade. "In fact," he said, "Fabien's a damn good head."

Stephen groaned inwardly. "I hope we don't have to meet his parents."

"They're away somewhere."

Bill rang the bell. They waited.

"My precious Bill Prescott! Come in and transmute all the baser metals for me." The deep voice was peculiarly devoid of accent, and so musical that Stephen thought it must be affected.

"Hi, kid," Bill said cheerfully. "I brought someone with me; his name's Steve."

"Stephen," Stephen corrected stiffly.

"Ah, I shall make an especial point of remembering. Do come in. The hospitality is humble but heartfelt."

Stephen stared, startled.

He was handsome. Tall—as tall as Stephen; thick, fair hair, cut short; large, unrevealing eyes in a face completely patrician until one noticed the shortness of the nose. His perfect composure of expression made impossible an accurate guess of his age, but in the cheeks there was a roundness that indicated a recent adolescence. Twenty-one, Stephen thought, or possibly twenty-two; and with those shoulders, the narrow hips, the long, immaculately clad legs, a faint hint of the average tailor's impossible advertisement. A football player? Stephen wondered. Fabien led them into the house and there was an indolence, a poise that would have been immediately shattered had its owner made a single appearance in a football game. Stephen felt strangely gauche as he took the extended hand. "How do you do," he murmured.

They had entered a large hall, paneled walls, beamed ceilings, and wrought-iron chandeliers. On opposite walls sliding doors led to other rooms. A great, black-carpeted staircase curved gracefully to the upper regions. It was impressive. Whoever lived in this house had money. "Quite a hall," Stephen said.

"Shocking, isn't it?" Fabien remarked gloomily. "But my dear, the worst is yet to come." He led them through one of the sliding doors into a long, highly polished sitting room. "There!" he said, "mock Adams furniture and the most spurious Grinling Gibbons chimney that anyone has ever seen. Accept my humblest apologies and have a seat."

Stephen relaxed onto a settee. There seemed no necessity for anyone to say anything. He watched with interest as Fabien moved gracefully about the room, gathering magazines into a tidy pile on the window seat, adjusting the drapes, straightening ash trays, picking up a glass that had obviously and quite recently contained beer. It took but a few seconds.

"Now," he said, going back to the door. "Now I'll get you both a drink." His smile embraced them. "If you can contrive to smash any of this hideous furniture whilst I am gone I'll get you two drinks." He went, and Stephen thought how suddenly empty the room had become.

"Good head, eh?" Bill said.

"Yes," Stephen replied. It was inadequate, he knew, but he could think of no other comment.

"Damned good head," Bill said, and leaned back contentedly in the easy chair that was at variance with the rest of the furniture in the room. "I met him at McGill."

"Did you?" He was about to question Bill further on the extent of the acquaintanceship when Fabien returned bearing a tray set with four glasses and a silver cradle in which reposed a bottle of wine.

"My father, God bless him," Fabien said, lifting the bottle respectfully from its cradle, "has recently sent me six bottles of Trockenbeeren Auslese, and you shall be the first to try it." He removed the metal cap and wiped the neck gently, almost reverently, with a napkin. "My father is a religious man," he continued, reaching for the corkscrew, "and I strongly suspect that he invoked the assistance of St. Anthony in finding this lovely, lovely stuff. There is no other possible explanation." He sighed with relief as the cork came out with a clean little pop.

Carefully wiping the lip of the bottle he filled three of the glasses with a cool, clear liquid. They each took one.

Fabien turned to Stephen with an anxious look. "Tell me if the temperature is right."

Stephen sipped. "Exactly," he said, hoping desperately that it was and wondering why all at once he felt nervous.

Fabien took a mouthful, thoughtfully. "Perhaps a shade colder?" he suggested, raising his eyebrows.

"No, this is fine." Why did it sound so utterly the wrong thing to say?

"You could serve it to me boiling," Bill said, "and I wouldn't know the difference."

"Dear Billy, you bring the smell of the soil right into the house. Loads of beer in the second icebox when you've finished that."

They were grinning at each other, friendly and intimate, like members of the same family sharing a private humor. Feeling isolated, cut off, Stephen sought around for some remark he could make. Fabien seemed to be watching him with an air of amused patience, for all the world, Stephen thought, like a large, marmalade cat about to purr.

Stephen said: "Are you at McGill?" and immediately flushed with annoyance at himself because the question had sounded strained and juvenile.

"I thought so at first," Fabien answered politely, "but I changed my mind after the first week. My dear, I've been the victim of far too many schools already. So provincializing, all this formal education, don't you think? I am going to give myself over completely to Life during the next year in an attempt at counteraction. My father always says that Life does so broaden the mind."

"I see." Stephen felt he could not afford the error of further questioning. Lifting his wine glass he added, "This is excellent," and was unaccountably relieved at having said something he meant.

"Thank you." Fabien made his way elegantly to a phonograph that stood in the corner beside a grand piano. "I don't know if you care for music?" he added, turning the phrase into the politest of enquiries.

"Play that thing on the piano that you played last time," Bill said, with such eagerness that Stephen felt instantly on more familiar territory. He was certain that Bill knew nothing of music; this was simply a means of showing off his friend. Without searching for reasons he found himself hoping that Fabien would prove an indifferent performer. Uncertain, he was relieved when Fabien demurred.

"Charming of you to remember, Bill, but we must not ask our guest to suffer too much. I think probably a little Mahler would be more in keeping with the prevailing mood." He searched through the cabinet and selected some records, which he adjusted on the machine. "So drearily restful," he continued, coming over and taking a seat beside Stephen. "Are you familiar with *The Song of the Earth?*"

A trick, a gimmick, Stephen thought, for with the question the atmosphere in the room seemed to change, to become thicker, almost soporific. "I'm afraid not," he answered.

"It's lunatic, of course, according to modern viewpoints," Fabien said, looking suddenly very young. "But it's very beautiful. I hope you like it."

Stephen listened to the sounds coming from the phonograph in the corner, deep bass sounds, soft and long-held, like the dying sighs of a large golden gong. Or like, he corrected himself, the slow heaving of a volcanic mass of black treacle. Came the muffled rhythm of horns; a solitary oboe rose and fell, languished, and was lost in a sad upsurging of muted strings. Then the horns again, descending, halting the strings. The sighs longer now, and deeper. A last wail from the oboe and the whole orchestra sweeping in, majestically, slowly downward, expiring.

A flute rose like a skylark at night, soared once to the heavens, took fright and swooped down to the warmth of the dying murmurs. The low plucking of a harp and then silence, broken only by the thin, dark-brown note of a cello.

A woman's voice poured forth in a soft, silvery column, rising and swelling until the room was filled with the ineffable poignancy of her song. She sang alone until the flute, encouraged, rose again above her to chirp a paradoxical counterpoint of sublimated melancholy. The song continued.

"Later on," said Fabien, "it becomes quite unbearable."

"What is she singing?"

"The song of the earth. *Das ewige Lied*. Farewell and distance and death. Death and resignation. You will find it all on the inside covers of the record album." He smiled lightly and leaned across, touching Stephen momentarily on the sleeve. "Forgive me," he said, "I have no wish to spoil anything."

"You haven't." Stephen found he was smiling back as earlier he had seen Bill do. "It will always be there." Good Lord, what was he saying, and how was he saying it?

"Yes, I suppose so. A little more wine and then we'll have another wallow." He refilled Stephen's glass.

"None for me," Bill said. "I'll get some beer later on. And shut up will you, so we can hear the next record?"

"I have only known Bill since last night," Stephen remarked acidly.

Speaking from over by the phonograph Fabien said to Stephen: "Now that we are such good friends it is only fair to warn you that you are not going to approve of this song when you discover the literal meaning of the words. Your face, very charming, shows traces of a quite devastating Calvinism, and your manner, I think you will proudly agree, is emphatically twentieth century. *Das Lied von der Erde*, unfortunately, is nineteenth century and wildly pantheistic. Anthropocentric philosophy at its ultimate. Poor old Goethe's prize bull, all begarlanded with passion flowers. Not your cup of tea at all, my dear, do you think? And then when I share with you my suspicion that the whole business was really written for a boy alto you will realize at once that it's quite beyond the bounds. Too naughtily Teutonic."

The words were purring out from behind a disarming smile. "If you earnestly desire a remedy I suggest that you bring yourself up to par by drinking lots of beer, in the Germanic fashion. It does wonders along that line. I know, my dear, that I am being quite shockingly honest, but there is something about your face that simply forces one."

"Are you always so articulate?" Stephen asked.

"I beg your pardon. Was there some point at which you wished to interrupt?"

"For God's sake," said Bill, "play the christly records." He seemed to be having a wonderful time.

Fabien restarted the phonograph and closed the lid. Placing his elbows upon it, he rested his face in his hands and, with a deep sigh, closed his eyes. The music, weirder now and oriental, fell upon Stephen's ears in wide ribbons of plushy sound. He leaned back and vainly attempted to recapture his former mood.

"I thought it was Mahler," a voice said. "Are we burying someone?"

A man stood with one shoulder leaning against the sliding doors, damp hair falling over his eyes, his shining face split by a broad, very amiable, and slightly tipsy grin. Wet prints from his bare feet tracked back across the hall to the foot of the stairs. In his hand was a white towel with which he dabbed idly at the glistening beads of water on his naked body.

"You're not going to play it right to the bitter end, are you?" he asked.

"No, pet," Fabien answered, without opening his eyes. "We're merely conducting a small experiment. The stranger in our midst is Stephen. Go over and say how do you do."

But Stephen, with crimson face averted, was fumbling in his pocket for a cigarette, his mind already whirling off into an untraceable pattern of concentricity that spun and changed, went deeper and became smaller, until, at the point in time where his burden was changed, all that remained was the last tiny, tremorous circle, the core that had no place in connected memory and registered unnoticed only in the sweating palms of his hands.

He was almost twelve years old. His mother told him not to go far because breakfast would soon be ready, but he sneaked out of the gate at the front of the bungalow, knowing his father would be unable to see him from the room where he dressed, and went right down to the lake shore.

The straggling remnants of a morning mist hung over the dark-green, wooded hills of the opposite shore. Insects buzzed around his head, birds sang noisily in the trees behind him. In front was the great expanse of water, glittering in the early morning sunlight, cool and inviting.

But Stephen did not go swimming. It was forbidden, because of currents. Besides, his father said, he should be satisfied that they had the means to come out here to the lake shore, away from the heat of Montreal, for four months every year. How would he like to be one of the boys who had to spend the summer sweltering in the St. Henri district of the city? Did he ever think of the inconvenience his father suffered, having to rise an hour earlier to catch the train that carried him to the intolerable temperatures in which he must work so that the family could stay at the lake shore? Fortunate boys should thank God most humbly for having been born into such a family.

Stephen failed to see what all this had to do with swimming but was wise enough to hold his tongue.

A small boat with leaning white sails glided across the water, noiseless and beautiful, certain of its course. Crossing his fingers in his trousers pockets, Stephen wished earnestly for a boat on his birthday next Sunday. Anything would do, even a canoe. Perhaps from an uncle he had never heard of, smitten with remorse over his hitherto neglected nephew.

Impossible. Between himself and this unknown uncle stood the high wall of his father and God over which nothing so frivolous as a boat could ever pass. He watched while the white sails disappeared around the bend of the shore then strooched dejectedly back to the house.

The day, ordinary enough in its beginning, was to end for Stephen in a welter of excitement and breathless curiosity that kept him awake for almost all the night. For this was the day that Stephen first heard the word.

Breakfast was over. Mr. Hollis was in the hall, making final preparations to leave for the city, when Stephen became aware that his parents were whispering together. Standing behind the half-opened door he strained his ears until his head rang, but he was at first able to make out only the word "doctor." His mother said it urgently, several times, to be answered by a burring rumble from his father. And then his mother said that other word. His father answered sharply, loudly, "Be quiet, woman, be quiet," but it was too late. Stephen had heard. Hernia! He had not the faintest idea of what it meant, but the word filled him with a strange rapture. It smacked of old sins. He could hardly wait for his father to get out of the house.

The day was spent with three dictionaries, a medical book, and the Encyclopedia Britannica, over which he pored with widening eyes and an increasing sense of fascinated horror that received its final macabre fillip during a half hour of intense conversation with Jimmy Ryan, who lived down the road and with whom Stephen was forbidden to play. Jimmy was poorer, older, more blasé, and infinitely wiser. He could most impressively describe a hernia, give its almost certain location, and speculate with a great deal of gusto and incredible salacity on its probable cause.

Stephen had almost fainted.

In the days that followed, the hernia became an obsession that filled all Stephen's waking thoughts and, sleeping gave him unending dreams of thrusting protrusions, long as human arms and rock-hard. He watched his father surreptitiously, fiercely, seeking an indication, wondering how, with this dread thing upon him, Mr. Hollis could still pretend to be the stern, implacable tyrant he had been previously. Slowly the suspicion grew that all his father's former conduct might have been a pose, a deception with which he covered up the approach of this secret and shameful disease. His father, he began to think, was perhaps not quite all he pretended to be.

On the somnolent Sunday of his twelfth birthday there were no presents. This was the Lord's Day and Mr. Hollis was going to permit no pagan celebrations in his house. He would take Stephen into Montreal the following Saturday and permit him to select a suit of clothes. Meanwhile, the day would be spent in church-going and prayer. Mr. Hollis went to take his morning bath.

In the clear, early morning heat of the garden there was no sound. The trees hung motionless in the windless air, and no footsteps passed on the road outside. The majority of the inhabitants of this pretty Canadian summer village were rolling over for their second sleep, ridding themselves of the effects of last night's dance at the hotel, or the midnight swimming-picnic of beer and sandwiches on the flat black mirror of the lake.

Stephen knew what he must do. With his heart beating in his throat he went to the shed at the bottom of the garden and took a small ladder. Creeping back, he placed the ladder stealthily, silently, against the wall beside the bathroom window, frosted except for the narrow strip across the top which could be opened. At present it was shut tight.

Painfully slow, his nose almost touching the rough-cast wall of the bungalow, he ascended rung by rung until he had reached a suitable height, then keeping his right foot on the ladder he swung the other out and round, placed it delicately on the narrow sill of the window, and moved his body gently to center. He tilted his chin and peeped.

He froze. He was looking straight down into the small, upturned eyes of Mr. Hollis. They stared at each other, expressionless, rigidly unmoving, transfixed by sin. An eternity passed.

With a slow and awful deliberation Mr. Hollis reached for a towel and wrapped it about him. It was over. Stephen descended from the ladder and entered the house, going directly to the bedroom that he shared with his brother Richard. A hush had fallen over the entire world.

The hours dragged on. The bedroom door remained closed. No one came near Stephen, he had no food, no one called him. Sitting on his bed he heard the family leave for morning church, return, and have lunch. His brother and sister departed for afternoon Sunday school. The day lengthened. The sun went to the other side of the house, and the shadows grew deeper. He heard the clink of cutlery at the evening meal. The family departed for evening service. The house was silent.

At nine o'clock the door opened and closed. Mr. Hollis stood in the dim room, a large piece of kindling in his hand. He advanced upon his son, his face set stonily in an expression of stern, vengeful wrath. With an overwhelming, a ludicrous sense of anticlimax, it occurred to Stephen that his father, in the words of Jimmy Ryan, looked pretty damn silly.

"You will lean over the bed." Mechanically, Stephen complied with the familiar command.

"You have committed a heinous sin that will make you forever evil in the eyes of God." Mr. Hollis's voice was low and strangled, as if he were choking. "Your vile and filthy act has caused me a day of great misery, of torment. I have spent the hours in anguished prayer, but I can find no ease. I can find in my heart no forgiveness for you. You have committed against me the sin of the son of Noah." His voice dropped to a horrified whisper as he forced himself to say the next words. "You have uncovered your father's nakedness."

The kindling came whistling down. "Unnatural, unspeakable son!" With these words Mr. Hollis seemed to lose control. "Instrument of Satan!" A cry that was almost a snarl broke from his throat, rising in volume and pitch until it became a continuous, bubbling scream. Blows rained down with such unremitting force that Stephen's limp body became numb, refusing to register pain.

He did not cry out.

Then suddenly the door burst open, and Stephen thought it might be his mother. She had never interfered before, but this time she might have been impelled by the special quality of the occasion. He was disappointed. It was his elder brother Richard who stood there, eyes glittering and face livid with excitement. Stephen guessed he had been listening behind the door.

"Father, I want to tell you." Richard's voice was a shrill gabble. "Stephen plays with himself in bed, too."

The blood spurted from Richard's nose as the piece of kindling caught him full in the face. He fled, bellowing like a bull.

But the interruption, or perhaps the open door, seemed to have drained all emotion from Mr. Hollis. Quivering with the attempt to regain his self-control he turned to Stephen, his voice once again little more than a whisper.

"I hope you have realized the depth of your iniquity," he said. "And I advise you to spend the rest of the night on your knees, praying to God that He does not visit upon you the punishment of Ham and turn you black."

He spun on his heel and left the room, closing the door behind him.

Stephen lay in the darkness, turning over in his mind the events of the day and wondering why he felt so little pain from the blows. It had certainly been quite a birthday, he thought.

And all at once he began to laugh, for he had pictured to himself his father's face when at breakfast the next morning he, Stephen, would walk into the room with fuzzy hair and a skin that was jet-black from head to toe. The laughter welled up in him until he shook. Would he get a melon for breakfast? By the time Richard came to bed, still blubbering over his swollen nose, Stephen was quietly shrieking in uncontrollable mirth.

And when the next morning arrived and he, pink as a flamingo, exchanged a single glance with his father over the breakfast table, they both realized instantly that one regime had ended.

"Hello, kid," Bill said, cheery and pleased. "How's it going?"

"Fine. Better than fine; I'm a little drunk." The man entered the room, trailing the end of the towel on the floor.

"What, then, should I play?" Fabien asked.

"Oh, anything. Something jazzy. How about Ravel?"

Stephen noticed, for the first time, that the supple body was clad in a brief article of underwear. But the relief engendered was only momentary, for the man advanced upon him and thrust the towel into his hands.

"Will you dry me, please?" he said, and sitting a scant four inches away on the settee he presented an expanse of gleaming wet back to Stephen's unwilling gaze. "There's a place just about here that I can't reach," he added, putting a hand behind him and indicating the position.

Scarlet-faced and semi-hypnotized, Stephen began to rub. The man moved his back contentedly and grunted.

From the phonograph came the first strains of Ravel's *La Valse*, heaving nascently in staggered three-quarter time, waiting for the violins, lifting, and finally lilting. The bare feet took up the beat, one tap with the left, two with the right, carrying the rhythm from the toes to the heels, up the leg, past the knee to the thighs. The fingers tapped the tempo on the cushions of the settee, the head beat time from side to side. To Stephen's infinite discomposure the back began to sway under his hands. The orchestra gathered itself together at last, and the waltz, fully born now, suddenly zipped into the room with unexpected sound and gaiety.

With a cry like that of a drunken cowboy the man leapt into the air, came down on his toes, paused, rose again to an *entrechat*, and began dancing, hair in his eyes, a shining grin of pure enjoyment on his face.

Moving with the litheness and unabashed carnality of an animal, his body filled with an exuberant energy that must be spent, he sprang on and off the furniture, uttering hilarious cries, pirouetted, stood poised on his toes, made prodigious leaps, gave a rhythmic performance that would have been remarkable if only for its acrobatic agility. Yet there was with it all a peculiar hint of formality, a strange gracefulness that gave to the dance a patterned air, as of some primitive rite, fierce and intensely masculine.

Watching the muscles move fluidly under the pale, smooth skin, Stephen felt ill at ease, and wished the man would go away and put some clothes on his boy's body. This was the worst display of exhibitionism he had ever seen.

He studied the flushed face and changed his mind. There was something in the expression that indicated the man was dancing only for himself.

Fabien moved away from the phonograph. "I haven't seen you all day."

The man halted, feet apart, his hands sliding down his body until they rested on his thighs. "I was working up on the third floor," he said. "Did you get anything done? I didn't hear you."

"My cherished lamb, I have been working all day like a veritable slave. I used the piano in the basement in order not to disturb you."

Each was looking into the face of the other, neither smiling. Stephen thought he sensed something flowing between them. Fabien said gravely: "It's very nice to see you again."

"It certainly is." A gentle smile, sickening to Stephen, spread over the man's face. "It certainly is," he repeated.

Lifting a bare foot he studied the sole, marked now with the grime he had picked up from the floor. A look of disgust writhed across his face. "I'm all dirty and sweaty," he said, walking to the door. "I'll just go and have another shower."

From halfway up the stairs he called out: "Hey, Bill! Bring us up a couple of beers. I have something I want you to read." Bill rose to his feet, smiled at Stephen, did a high jump in silent imitation of what had gone before, and left the room.

Stephen was feeling intensely annoyed.

Turning to Fabien, who was pouring himself another drink, he said: "I've met him somewhere before. He works in a store, doesn't he?"

"Who, Duncan? Yes, he does."

The annoyance welled up into an antagonism that made Stephen's words sound sharp and deprecatory. "I thought so. I bought a shirt from him the other day."

"How nice. Are you wearing it tonight?"

The murmured enquiry left him no foothold, and he saw that he was being childish. Yes, if the topic had been pursued the conclusion, not five minutes away, would have been disparagement of such an employment. He admired Fabien's lightning anticipation and the deft way he had made further pursuance impossible.

Stephen said: "I'm not really a snob, but one slips easily into these habitual methods of attack. He is a menial; I am not. I chose the weapon nearest at hand."

"My dear, I am only an unenlightened foreigner but isn't your attitude rather at variance with the customs of the country?"

"I don't think so. You must remember that we are British. Equality lasted only so long as the country was full of have-nots. Once the balance was disrupted by some acquiring more than others the whole doctrine was thrown out as being incompatible with human nature. The aristocracy of the successful was established. Your friend does not belong to it because he works in a store. I belong to it because my father is a success and I do not work in a store. Your friend, moreover, does not wear the coronet of formal education. I do. Any North American can tell you that formal education is a wonderful thing, an end in itself."

"How do you know that Duncan has none?"

"You are certainly an unenlightened foreigner. The answer is that he would not be working in a store if he had it. *It*. The air over here is full of *Its* and they all merge. You have a great deal to learn."

"I shall be very grateful for any instruction you can give me," Fabien said. "But the tone of your voice does not indicate which side you are on."

"Why are you so protective toward him?" Stephen asked.

"Ah, then even you are not sure which side." Fabien extracted a cigarette from a monogrammed gold cigarette case. "We are being terribly pedantic, but isn't it intriguing? Why are you attacking him?"

Stephen, trying to be fair, could find no discernible reason. "I don't know," he replied. "Perhaps a natural antipathy. He's a horrible little narcissist."

"And is your body awfully saggy under that beautifully cut blue suit?" Fabien asked, smiling. "I must say it doesn't look it."

"I'll admit it's not like his, not so smooth, not so many muscles, but that would hardly be a reason. If I allowed myself physical jealousy life would be unendurable. I have too many shortcomings. How did you meet him?" He paused and added, "Of course, it's none of my business."

Fabien laughed aloud. "Come Stephen, don't be disingenuous. We both know it's your business and I don't mind telling you at all. It was the way, I suppose, that thousands of others must have met him, but I am so much wiser than the average. He merely looked up from behind the counter with that drenching, Dionysian gaze, and I immediately asked him if he would go for a drink. It was as simple as that."

"And naturally he accepted immediately."

"My, but you're snide. Yes, naturally, but only, I think, because he is seeking something. The invitation must have looked like an opportunity to widen the search. I was pleased but not at all flattered, but then I am an altruist."

"What is he seeking?"

"I'm not sure. Perhaps just the drink."

"May I make a guess?"

"Not yet, my dear, not until you are a kindred spirit. You will be in time, you know, but until then—" Fabien spread his hands in mock despair.

"We had a lovely time," he continued. "The drink became several drinks, we had dinner at Drury's, and then he told me that he was living at the Y.M.C.A. Well, my dear, *nobody* lives at the Y.M.C.A., so it was the easiest thing in the world to tempt him into coming here to live with me. And now the lovely time goes on unabated. His company is as enjoyable as I knew it would be."

"Does he usually walk around undressed?" Stephen asked.

"Mostly, yes. He spends most of his time taking showers and I assume he feels it not worth while dressing in between."

Fabien walked over to the piano, and Stephen realized that the topic was closed. He would reopen it again, he thought, at leisure. For the present he was content to lean back and filter the previous conversation, meticulously examining each sentence and intonation for possible loopholes through which he could later thrust one of the prepolished and lethal phrases that he used in annihilating his acquaintances and his father. It would need to be something different to those he usually forged, he thought, looking over to where Fabien sat with his hands resting lightly on the piano keyboard. Here was an unknown quantity, new and different, with God knows what reserves at his back, a man with references. The idea gave extra zest to Stephen's search.

He hoped that Bill and Duncan would stay wherever they were, wondering what it was that Fabien had in common with these other two that made them all friends. Fabien was obviously well traveled, wealthy, and, with a tiny hesitation he added, cultured. He was not sure about the red-haired one, there was the dance to be considered, but he expected that Duncan would turn out to be just as ordinary as Bill. People invariably did.

And suddenly all his boredom crystallized in a single, aching conception. Stretching out behind him was an endless line of ordinary people saying ordinary things, a procession of prosaic events that reached its drab length right back to the cradle that stood in the attic of the gray house in Westmount. What, at any time, had there ever been?

His earliest memories were of his father, always old, monotonously declaiming passages from the Scriptures while the wife sat quietly by, hands folded in her lap, mouth pursed, showing that she lived separately only when the mild, oddly opaque eyes flickered behind her spectacles. A sounding board for her husband, a piece of pliable rubber from which his judgments could ricochet even when he was no longer present, Mrs. Hollis went ploddingly through life, performing her duties with just a hint of abnegation, supervising the ever-changing servants, keeping the children in check, seldom unkind, and, by the same token, seldom affectionate.

No one had ever declared as much, but affection, in the Hollis household, was considered both indecent and unnecessary. When he became older Stephen often wondered how his parents had come to marry. More puzzling, how had they come to have three children? This indicated something happening. Even now he felt sick at the thought of his father participating.

Stephen was the youngest of the three but this had caused nobody to spoil him; on the contrary, his father seemed under an obligation to select Stephen for special disciplinary measures that the others escaped, an inclination greatly assisted by the taletelling of Richard, for whom Stephen had felt a contemptuous dislike ever since he could remember. At present learning the family business, growing fat and bald, nearly thirty but looking older, Richard still approached his father with the same oblique sycophancy he had used in his childhood and still received as little response. Mr. Hollis had always treated his eldest son with a cold disdain that no amount of deference could overcome. As for Stephen, he had long ceased to regard his brother as a worthy opponent.

Esther, five years older than Richard, had never been an opponent. Fulfilling in maturity the distressing plainness she had shown as a child, she was ignored by the whole family except for an occasional mockery from Richard or, from her father, a brief and approving remark on her devotion to the local church. Esther left the house only when she attended a meeting of one of the church's numerous societies or had found an excuse for helping the unwilling Chester, for whom Stephen suspected she had a fixation. The remaining hours of each creeping week she devoted to helping her mother, who had little to do, or staring vacantly from the window of the upstairs sitting room. And yet she was not of a placid disposition, Stephen thought. Rather was she compressed, as if her spirit, her vitality had been screwed into a tiny hard ball that was pushed deep inside herself. She gave him the impression, not so much of being deadened, as of being in wait. There was something secretive about her that grated on him. He disliked her more than any other member of the family because there was nothing about her upon which he could realize himself, no way in which he could illustrate the vital difference between them.

Looking back he saw his life as a long struggle for self-identity, a flight to escape his family and all like them, their friends, their neighbours, the people with blandly smiling faces that he saw at church every week, the inhabitants of a territory that lay, seemingly forever, in the gloom of a religious shadow that had survived, intact, the crossing from Scotland two centuries before. He had thought that the war would provide an escape, and indeed for a time it had, but when he returned, with heightened perceptions and an increased capacity for comparison and criticism, conditions seemed even worse. For now he discovered that he must withstand not only his family but the entire society in which he lived. If he must fight his family for having a false and fabricated set of values, then he must fight society for having no values at all.

Over the world was hanging a pall of uniformity through which moved figures indistinguishable from each other. Under strong lights everyone ate the same foods, sang the same songs, mouthed identical words in a uniform manner and with an identical lack of meaning behind them. Stephen suspected that they also experienced identical emotions, and certain it was that his feeling for them was unvarying. He despised them. At first he listened carefully to what they said, watching how they moved, how they reacted, wondering what was the motivation for this mass behavior and what was its goal. He found the answer.

They were all, each and every one of them, trying with desperate earnestness to be cute. Winsomely, lovably, smooth and peachy, gee is it ever, cute! Patterning themselves with minute care on the glittering idols of movies, magazines, and radios, contriving to people the entire visible world with a horde of male and female ingénues, all talking and looking and acting alike. The girls made demure glances no matter how tired their eyes, and their lips were always parted slightly in the magazine-cover travesty of allurement. The boys writhed their shoulders and shuffled their feet and said Gee, implying inarticulation with wry and rugged grins. They were all boys and girls now, there were no men and women left; everyone lived in an eager, kittenish state of suspended adolescence. He noticed how sometimes the patterns would become momentarily confused, when briefly the boys became girls and the girls became boys. It was the only amusement he could derive from the whole display.

For it was a display. They were playing to an audience, offering for approbation their most piddling utterances, their smallest gestures; making their words a shade too exaggerated, their movements a trifle larger than life, outside of the cinema, would seem to demand. Everyone was in on the trick. He could see an entire group of people, all working the same routine one upon the other, achieving a pattern that was gay and animated in the superficial details and drearily symmetrical when viewed as a unit. He loathed this eurythmic simulation and set out to learn how to throw it out of gear. It was too easy. There needed only one member who refused to be receptive, one nonplayer in the game, and a party could be made to collapse in fifteen minutes, leaving the actors without cues, openmouthed, shuffling, and lost. At such moments he would say with unfailing politeness, "Oh, sorry; haven't you seen that movie?" It gave him a pure pleasure to think that by raising the age limit a scant six months he had defeated a whole army of script writers who admitted they wrote for no one over fourteen. Stephen was not popular.

But the wreckage he created soon reassembled itself, was waiting afresh for him everywhere he turned, and he realized that he must either lose his identity by himself becoming fourteen years old or forgo society almost completely. He chose the second course. Tonight, watching these other three, he wondered if perhaps he had been unwise.

Then— No, he thought. It was neither so simple nor so obvious. There was a difference here, something that was far removed from the haw-haw arm punching of the campus and the beery camaraderie of taverns. An ease, a polish he had not encountered before; a competitive touch that made conversation a duel instead of a bludgeoning fight for individual existence.

A flicker of self-derision appeared in his thoughts and was swiftly quenched. He said:

"I've just made a decision."

Fabien's hands were moving idly over the keyboard, picking at random a few soft chords. "My dear, do be careful," he said. "A decision in a young man these days seems invariably to lead to a Trappist monastery. You will be forced to write scores of best sellers and then the reading public will canonize you. And only think of what happened to the original St. Stephen, poor thing. Stones, my dear. Big ones."

He commenced playing a thin, brilliant melody that was a distillation of three single-note melodies in counterpoint, criss-crossing from a tinkling treble through a juxtaposition of sad, oddly moving bass notes.

"Pretty," Stephen commented.

"Delightful boy," Fabien said, pleased. "I've been working on it all day. You will notice that the idea is pinched from a Bach invention."

"Three voice?" Stephen asked, glad of this opportunity of showing his musical cognizance.

"Four," Fabien corrected him. "I should be singing. It is a setting for a poem by Blake and the voice is an integral part." In a rich and effortless baritone he broke into the fourth counter-melody.

> "'Little Fly,
> Thy summer's play
> My thoughtless hand
> Has brushed away.
> Am I not
> A fly like thee ...?'"

"*Merde!*" he said, striking the piano discordantly. "I've fallen splosh into the trap of old Blake's easy rhythm. But I must not complain. That is the problem of composition I set myself. I have two for the year, you know; one rhythmic, the other interpretive. My second attempt is going to be a setting for part of the trial scene in *Alice in Wonderland*." He quoted with relish, "'And gave me a good character but said I could not swim.'"

"The Blake," Stephen asked, "is for Duncan?"

Fabien removed his hands from the keyboard and flexed his fingers. "I am nineteen years old and an only child," he said, conversationally.

"You, I think, are a genuine vintage bitch."

"And the Alice?" Stephen said gleefully.

Fabien closed the piano and crossed the room, standing over Stephen and looking down. "About your decision," he remarked softly. "Would you care to get drunk?"

Stephen nodded, grinning maliciously.

"Good, I have some champagne in the cellar."

They looked fixedly at each other and Stephen guessed what was coming next. "Will you call the other two," Fabien said, "while I get it?"

They went to the sliding doors together. Still grinning, Stephen called out. "Hey, Bill! Duncan! Bill! Duncan!"

There was a heavy scampering on the landing and they appeared at the top of the stairs, wrestling furiously.

"You silly bastard," Bill was saying breathlessly, his face flushed and laughing. "You'll have me down the stairs in a minute."

Duncan was wearing gray slacks and a vivid green sweat shirt that made his hair redder than ever. He's older than I suspected, Stephen thought. Much older. Older than I am. Probably his hair is beginning to thin, and his teeth are going bad.

"Champagne," he called nonchalantly. "Gentlemen."

It was raining again when he left at one o'clock and the air was full of the sharp, raw smells of autumn, of smoke and decay and the bark of trees. Car headlights reflected brokenly in the wet roads, and patches of fallen leaves, red and gold, shuffed under his feet as he walked.

The light was on. Entering the room, he stood motionless, looking coldly at his father as the head was raised slowly from the book.

"Don't lie. I can see by your face that you have been drinking."

He continued to stand there, wordless and staring, for almost a minute.

"Well, answer me. You've been drinking."

"Drinking, Father? Drinking?" The conversational quietness of the words surprised even himself. "Make no mistake about it, Father, I'm drunk. I'm rotten drunk."

Without waiting for further comment he left the room.

And upstairs, rummaging through the back of the cupboard for his childhood copy of *Alice in Wonderland*, he laughed to himself at how easy it had been.

PART TWO

THE HAIR SHIRT

Fat flakes of snow sifted down lazily from the blue morning sky and settled gently on the thick carpet that already overlay the city. From overhead the sun shone bright yellow through the thin veil, making the streets glitter and sparkle as if strewn with the purest white granulated sugar. The snow, under the heels of the passers-by, made tiny squeaks of protest that echoed loudly in the cold quietness of the brittle air. The cries of the children who snowballed each other at the end of the street sounded isolated, as though they played in a gigantic canyon.

Stephen surveyed the scene with pleasure from his bedroom window. The others would probably be willing to go again to the mountains this week end to ski. He smiled at the thought.

The ride in the car, the drink in the hotel at Ste. Agathe, a tingling skin, a meal eaten with appetite; noise, laughter, the colored clothes showing vivid against the glaring whiteness of the snow. The figure of Fabien, poised and graceful, soaring down the slope with the brown skin of his face drawing nearer and nearer until at last it was there among them, taut and shining. Glowing.

With broadening smile, Stephen turned to the mirror to knot his tie.

The bedroom door opened behind him and Richard came in. Stephen turned his head slightly and watched the reflection as his brother sat down on the edge of the bed.

"It's snowing," Richard said.

"Yes." Stephen lay in wait.

This was to be another of the blunderingly amateur investigations that his family had been conducting, singly and together, for the past ten weeks. Each had become suddenly like a flypaper, hanging in a wind of curiosity, swinging wildly with each breeze in an attempt to catch the single elusive fly. Each one, that is, except his father, who had not spoken to Stephen since the night he returned from Fabien's house and now stiffly ignored his presence, hurrying from any room in which inadvertently they happened to find themselves alone.

Yet his father also was consumed with curiosity, sticky as the others but more subtle; a flytrap—yes—but a web rather than a paper. However, he was just as inadequate as the others, for the successful spider must weave in a dark corner and somehow there were no dark corners now. None whatever.

Richard feigned a yawn, swung his feet up, and lay full length on the bed. "Gee, I'm tired." He stretched his arms above his head in a huge extension of the yawn that set his body quivering. "Guess you're pretty tired too, eh?"

"You're probably working too much. You shouldn't let Father drive you so hard."

"Father's all right." Richard sounded nervous.

"A fine man, Mr. Hollis, everyone agrees." Stephen kept his face bland. "Aren't you working today?"

"Father says I don't have to work Saturdays anymore. Don't you have a lecture?"

"Not until eleven."

"Guess you're pretty glad about that." Richard's tone was warm, amicably interrogative. He waited encouragingly, his face falling a little when no response was forthcoming. "I mean," he added, "you got in late last night."

"Two-thirty, to be exact." Stephen was combing his hair.

"Gee, two-thirty!" Richard exclaimed with genuine admiration. He hesitated, dropping his voice to a whisper. "Is it a babe?"

Stephen put his tongue on his teeth and made the clicking noise currently indicative of aroused lust and anticipated satisfaction.

"Gee!" Richard sat up abruptly, eyes bright and mouth slightly open. "Who is she? Someone I know? Someone from McGill?"

"Gentlemen don't talk," Stephen said primly.

"Aw, come on, you can tell me," Richard pleaded. "I know, I bet she's someone from down at the church." His face brightened as Stephen laid down the comb and leaned confidentially toward him.

"Is my parting straight?"

"To hell with your parting. What about this babe?" Again the whisper: "Is she hot?"

"Would I be seeing her every night if she wasn't?" Stephen skidded his gaze around the room in an appallingly lascivious leer.

Richard nodded eager encouragement, the tip of his tongue flickering momentarily over his upper lip. "Go on."

"She's only sixteen. You wouldn't think she knew anything to look at her, but oh!" Once more he made the clicking noise with his tongue, and Richard's mouth twisted in imitative sympathy. "Most of them haven't got sense enough to put a pillow under them, but not this one. What a hot tamale!"

"Jesus!" Richard said. "What does she look like?"

"About this high, small, soft, dark hair, big eyes." His twinging fingers laced a descriptive pattern through the air. "Her top is a little big for her age and she'll probably start sagging in a few years, although I'm not complaining at the moment. Nice handful; snub-nosed, firm."

"And she's really hot?"

"Five times a week—at least."

They had not liked each other since they were children, but, looking at his brother, Stephen saw in the eyes an expression of almost idolatrous admiration. The past could be passed now and this moment made the beginning of a lifetime's affection and intimacy. They could be friends.

His stomach turned at the prospect of how horribly far a joke could be carried. Physically impelled he turned away.

"Get off my bed before you have your orgasm. Who sent you up here, Mother or Father? Go back and say it didn't work."

"What's the matter with you?" Richard demanded, springing to his feet, scowling. "What are you talking about?"

Stephen had turned back to the mirror, tilting his head to look at the parting and placidly combing his hair again. "The assumption then is that you dropped in for a brotherly chat and some astral masturbation. A charming custom; I believe it's carried out in all the best families. Only we have left the inception a little too late. Moreover we are not one of the best families."

Richard's face flushed in anger. He was almost shouting. "You needn't think Father doesn't know what you're up to."

Very well, Richard, you pig, you shall have the last twist of the knife. "Don't lose your hair, Richard," Stephen said jovially: "I was only kidding. You don't understand me."

"Well, what's the idea? What were you getting so darned nasty about?"

"I was kidding. You misunderstood me. As a matter of fact, this girl friend has a girl friend."

It was Stephen who now flung himself full length on the bed, flat on his back with legs in the air at a right angle from his body and arms straight out like the crosspiece of a crucifix. Under his brother's interested gaze he lowered his legs, parting them slowly, until at last he lay spread-eagled on the counterpane.

With a long, sensual grunt he bumped himself three times.

"They share the same apartment. The other girl has asked me if I can bring a friend."

"Who are you thinking of?" Richard asked warily.

"Who are you thinking of?"

"You mean tonight?" The tongue was flickering. "Yeah, we could get a bottle from the liquor commission and have a few drinks and maybe dance a bit. Do they have a phonograph?"

Stephen nodded. "There's only one bedroom. We'd have to take it in turns."

"You could go first."

"That's magnanimous. But what if Father finds out?"

"He won't. I won't tell him."

"Oh, but I may."

Richard looked at him uncertainly. "Are you getting funny again?"

Stephen gave a deep, smiling sigh and rolled off the bed. "Just a couple of whoremongers, aren't we?" he remarked. "I don't know what Father will say when he discovers you've been tempting me with liquor and whoring parties. No, Richard, you're a big boy and you'll have to do your own procuring. Better still, if you really want to scratch your dirty little itch, go down to the Gaiety Theatre where it's safe and legal.

"I haven't had breakfast yet and I've suddenly got an appetite," he exclaimed brightly as he walked to the door followed by Richard's uncomprehending eyes. "But remember, dear brother, no more spying on me or I might think it my duty to inform Father of your naughty tendencies." Enunciating each word clearly, he added, "You know, you really are a bloody disgusting pig, aren't you?"

From the bedroom behind him he heard the sound of reprisal that had been familiar since childhood. Richard was destroying a book, ripping the pages into small pieces that would afterwards be scattered over the floor. Not *Alice in Wonderland*, he hoped. It had afforded him great pleasure during the past few weeks. Quietly he recited to himself:

> "'Tis the voice of the lobster; I heard him declare,
> You have baked me too brown, I must sugar my hair.'"

In the study on the second floor his father coughed. Abruptly sobered, feeling indefinably soiled, Stephen went down the second heavily carpeted flight and entered the dining room, sitting at the table where a place was set for one. Over the mantelpiece the clock was ticking heavily and it occurred to Stephen that this house had too many clocks and insufficient ash trays. He inserted two slices of bread in the toaster and plugged in the table percolator. He was not in the least hungry.

"Would you like something cooked?" Mrs. Hollis came up quietly behind him.

"No, thank you." As her dress rustled away a feeling of horrible desperation forced him to speak. "Will you have a cup of coffee with me, Mother?"

Without turning round he sensed her surprise by the suddenness with which she halted. "Why, yes, I think I could use another cup of coffee. I was up very early this morning. I have such a lot to do on Saturdays as you know and it's quite difficult with everyone at home. Do you have a lecture this morning, Stephen?" Her dress rustled round his shoulder as she took a seat across the corner of the table from him.

"Yes." They looked away from each other with an expression that was the Hollis equivalent of looking at each other. Embarrassment settled upon them with a silence so flat and padded that Stephen felt disproportionate relief when the percolator suddenly began bubbling.

"This coffee must have been almost boiling."

"Your father had a late breakfast." She was putting the cream and sugar in the cups with quick, nervous gestures. "He was a little upset when he heard you were still upstairs."

No! Please! It was like a merry-go-round. No matter how much you paid or with what care you selected the wooden animal, invariably the music played the same tune and you were whirled in the inescapable circle until sickness descended upon you. Upstairs, downstairs, and in my lady's chamber. There must be a method whereby the spinning and the hurdy-gurdy tune were halted. How could he find it?

A sadness enveloped him. What could he do when they so beggared him mentally? He had tried desperately of late, but it was impossible to follow in his mind the numerous levels of sin and society, God and gospel, morals and magistrality on which they conducted their enquiry into himself and perhaps into living itself. How was it possible for them to dig and dredge and muck-out and then stand proud-eyed and chidingly arrogant before him, still claiming temperateness of soul and a soul still temperate and untarnished?

The remedy was simple when at night he walked through the silent streets and rehearsed the conversations he would hold with them. Then the brake was applied—then—when he said warm, human things that penetrated the intellect while embracing the heart. The Galileo-Schopenhauer-Kant pastiche he had devised must surely shatter their cosmic conception of pride and anger, so that the entire family were left dancing together as mere motes on the one ray of light.

He would not, of course, apply the mixture as a paste with the trade name visible on the label, for that would frighten his mother and outrage his father: but presented as a manifestation of the might of Jehovah—that was it, the Might—surely it would persuade them that they, with him, were fellow infinitesimals.

How beautiful the conversations were when planned to the accompaniment of solitary, snow-muffled footsteps! He would be clever because his father had invested in his education. He would be kind because his own former tendency had, of late weeks, become a positive yearning to be kind. He would start the discussion gently and not until it was well under way would he say to his father:

"Father, you must realize that I am two separate entities: I am what you think I am and what I think I am—and never the twain shall meet." His father would like that because he was fond of Kipling. "In the same manner, whilst I look at you, you are two entities. But if there were five or ten people in the room then you would be five or ten entities, all varying in desirability according to the desire in the eye of the beholder. The different individuals might envy you, admire you, deplore you, respect you—in short, might subject you to a barrage of all the emotions whether real or imagined. And not only might, but would. Some of them, Father"—and this was the part that almost brought tears to Stephen's eyes in rehearsal—"some of them, Father, would love you. It must be so. Even if we need to leave the room and go to a great hall filled with people, there would have to be one who loved you. And because of that love, an actual not hypothetical love, it is impossible for me to hate you as I do and for you to despise me.

"I know my reasoning is somewhat elementary...."

And, God! so bloody illogical! He looked across the table to where his mother sat fidgety and uncomfortable at this situation where two members of the family were together for none other than social reasons. Shards of fractured intimacy lay between them, and suddenly Stephen seemed to hear his father's voice intoning one of the favourite evening hymns.

> "'Jesus loves me, this I know,
> For the Bible tells me so....
> Yes, Jesus loves me,
> Yes, Jesus loves me.... '"

The love of Stephen, of this small, indifferent woman who sat at the table, of the rest of the world, was rendered unnecessary, superfluous, by the hymn. The One who loved was sufficient.

And Stephen thought: Poor Jesus! Everything of yours they touch is turned into another Calvary.

To his mother he said: "I hope I'm not keeping you from anything."

"Well, no." She shifted her position and looked a little more sideways. The room immediately became charged with an inquisitorial air.

"How's Father?" Stephen asked, using diversionary tactics. "Esther says he wasn't well the other night."

"It was one of his little attacks. The doctor says he needs a change, so he's going up to visit your Aunt Lou in Ontario. For the week end."

"Now?"

"He's getting ready."

Perhaps his father was about to die and, like an elephant, was going into the hinterland, never again to be seen by human eye. Stephen got a quick mental picture of a huge, time-haunted cemetery to which old presbyteric pachyderms lumbered off to spend their last moments among the bleaching bones of their own kind. He smiled and his mother apprehended it.

"I hope you'll not be in late tonight. I get worried when your father is not at home."

"Talking of late, I shall be late for my lecture."

"Didn't you say it wasn't until eleven?"

"I have to go to the library first."

"Oh."

He put on his coat and overshoes and went out into the morning sunlight, walking with a springy tread down the sloping street. The air was crisp, invigorating; the sun strong. He was not at all sure what the time would be when he got in tonight.

A snowball hit him in the back of the neck, scattering in a shower round his ears and dropping small spots of cold down his back. He turned quickly, and another, softer snowball burst in his face.

"Got you, Stephen! Got you double!" The voice was high-pitched and gleeful.

Stephen wiped his face with a gloved hand and saw the small son of a neighbour, an importer of chinaware, stooping to the lawn to gather more snow, his eyes shining with an urchin light that might have disquieted his parents had they seen it.

"Little brat!" Swooping his hand to the ground, Stephen snatched and hurled a loosely packed handful of snow at the pink, smiling face. The ball disintegrated, scattering ineffectually over the ground that lay between.

"Missed me." The child, all at once determined, raised his hand to throw again, and became paralyzed with delighted terror as Stephen hurled himself across the intervening space.

"Right, Phillip, you asked for it." He seized the laughing boy by the collar and the seat of his pants and thrust him face downward into the snow, surprised at the vigor that suddenly coursed through the squirming body under his hands, feeling his fingertips tingle with the muffled shrieks of joy that vibrated the column of the small neck. Stephen was laughing, too, and with the realization came an impulse to stretch himself full length on the snow. He slackened his grip a little, giving the boy a chance to turn and grasp him by the leg. Off-balance, he sprawled upon the lawn.

"Got you!" The boy leapt agilely upon Stephen and thrust snow down the front of his collar. For a moment they floundered, then Stephen flung his arms around the small heaving chest and the two rolled over the sloping lawn in a kicking tangle, each trying to halt the progress and push the face of the other into the deep snow.

"Just a minute," Stephen panted. "Just a minute." The boy rolled over and they separated, sitting side by side with their knees up and palms flat on the ground, grinning at each other, triumphant and surprised.

The child turned his head a little. "Where is your father going?" he asked, pointing to where Mr. Hollis surveyed them from beside a waiting taxi.

"To Ontario. And I'm going to a lecture." Stephen rose to his feet, brushing the snow from his clothes, seeing from the corner of his eye that his father had entered the cab. "So long. See you later."

"You're a lousy shot," the boy called after him in a clear, treble voice. The cab drove by with Mr. Hollis in the back seat looking rigidly ahead.

He walks in anger like a blight. To hell with him! Stephen waved a farewell to where the boy still sat upon the lawn.

No—to hell with him was too strong. Away with him was sufficient. Away with him and his everlasting vague thundercloud, his perpetual overhanging threat that never materialized. The Damoclean sword would never, *could* never, fall. It was not suspended by a hair but by a length of high-grade tungsten steel wire. Its very permanency was its undoing.

Stephen bent down to brush off the snow that still adhered to the cuffs of his trousers. Then he stood up and almost cried aloud, for all at once the entire world jolted into a beautifully composed picture in which everything vibrated with color. Taking a deep breath, he looked over his shoulder and saw that the small boy was entering the house. The small boy's hair shone in the sunlight.

Stephen set off down the road toward Sherbrooke Street, walking near the inner edge of the pavement where no one else had trod. He left behind him a trail of deep, almost symmetrical footsteps.

He let himself into the house with a key presented to him some weeks before and found Fabien, clad in a plain cerise dressing gown and already beautifully groomed, smoking a cigarette in front of the remains of a breakfast of eggs and mushrooms.

"Ah, John Knox. Some Turkish coffee?"

Stephen took the proffered cup, sipped, and grimaced at the slightly brackish taste. "Duncan gone to work, or taking a shower?" For the past few weeks he had been trying to make a standing joke of Duncan's innumerable ablutions. No one was taking it up.

"He is upstairs, pounding a typewriter. Drunk as an eft."

"He was that when I left last night."

"Oh but no, the serious drinking didn't begin until after you had gone. Bill got positively confessional. Did you know that after he graduates he's going back to Vancouver to be a *fisherman?*"

Stephen shook his head and grinned, amused not so much that Bill was to be a fisherman as that Fabien, however remotely, should be connected with anyone of that intention.

"I say, did you mind that?"

"What?"

"About the serious drinking not beginning until after you left."

"No. Should I? Why?"

"That wound complex of yours. You are sometimes so determined a wounding shall take place that if no one else is handy you madly stab yourself. I've always considered it such a terribly obvious form of autoeroticism."

"All in the past," Stephen said, not thinking. And then the certainty of it descended upon him and he wanted to repeat the words over and over, to etch the passionless conviction of their message upon his mind. Instead, he said: "I feel like the Nietzschean ultimate this morning," and was immediately apprehensive lest it be turned into the wrong sort of joke.

"May the dear Lord preserve us from a race of *Obermenschen* who are Calvinistic, Anglo-Saxon, *and* North American." Fabien crossed himself with a delicate wave of the hand, too elegantly for devoutness. Stephen almost sighed aloud with relief.

"It's a beautiful morning," he said.

Fabien glanced out of the window at a snow-clad tree. "So different to everything at home."

"You haven't told me about that."

"No." Fabien blew a perfect smoke ring. "Everything is different. I'm different. I adore being a foreigner in a foreign land, speaking a foreign language, doing things foreignly. A delightful game. And such an assistance to me when I am obliged to pick out the fools."

"How's that?" Stephen asked. "Most people are fools."

"Only to themselves, my dear. Not in my customary orbit at all. I was thinking of the more exalted fools who cannot see beyond the foreignness to the imperishable, utterly lovable me."

"You force me to say this silly thing," Stephen said, "but I don't think of you as a foreigner."

"That is not in any way nice when I've just finished telling you how hard I work at it." Fabien dropped his cigarette into the coffee cup and stood up. "Do you have a lecture this morning?"

"Eleven o'clock."

"I too have a duty. After years of patient search I have received through this morning's mail a copy of that favorite ballad of Samuel Pepys, 'Gaze Not on Swans.' Did you ever, in your quieter moments, ponder the reason, for that adjuration? So did I. I go now to uncover their secret, nasty long-necked hissing things."

He wilted from the room, humming, his voice trailing back presently in an afterthought invitation for Stephen to return to lunch when the lecture was over.

In the shining white kitchen, loneliness assailed Stephen like a doubt, bringing a faint resentment at Fabien for departing before a conversation had been developed. Finishing his coffee in a quick gulp he wandered aimlessly through the pantry, the paneled dining room. Emerging into the hall he heard the clacking of the typewriter.

He was unable to stay away. From halfway up the black-carpeted stairs he could hear Duncan's voice coming from one of the bedrooms, mumbling in a sporadic undertone.

He was sitting on an unmade bed, pillows propped behind him, picking with two fingers at the portable typewriter balanced uncertainly upon his knees. He was wearing a suit of blue-striped pajamas. He looked thick, but cheerful.

"Glad to see you. Hello. You supply an excellent excuse for me to stop work." He put aside the typewriter and scratched at his red hair. "Do you know what? I've been sitting here for hours, digging for something of myself to put down on paper and coming up with nothing that doesn't already belong to someone else."

"What are you writing? Something important?"

"I'm rather like a larcenous squirrel," Duncan continued with a dazzling grin. "Got a drink?"

"I can get you one."

"Damn! God damn!" Duncan stood up, kicking viciously at the screwed up sheets of paper that littered the floor around his bed. "Do you like 'God damn'? You know, we don't use it where I'm from. I think we should." Seizing Stephen by one arm he began to propel him from the room. "I'm a vampire. I never realized how much of the blood of others flowed through me until I severed a vein. Don't you consider that a tragedy?"

"Where are you taking me?" In all the times Stephen had visited the house Duncan had barely spoken to him, had not especially been encouraged to do so. In this onslaught of unsolicited intimacy Stephen wanted time in which to adopt a mental attitude.

"It's not a tragedy," Duncan said fiercely, halting suddenly and swinging Stephen round until they stared into each other's eyes. "It's tragic when a man stands in fearful contemplation of the sea, but if the fool goes and drowns himself he's just another dead body." Incontinently he burst into laughter. "Do you like that? I do. I cherish its pretended originality."

They traversed the landing nearly at a canter and burst into another bedroom where Bill lay sleeping on an almost unruffled pillow. Two glasses and assorted bottles were at the bedside, and a faint, sweet smell of alcohol hung in the air, mingling oddly with the other odors of fluff and distilled dreams.

"Hey, Bill!" Duncan shouted. "Wake up, Bill, we have company." The figure in the bed grunted and rolled onto its face, thrusting into the air a hummock of backside.

"It must have been quite a night," Stephen said. "He looks drunk, too."

"Do I detect a note of reproach in your voice? I have a reason for being drunk. I'm looking for a new art form."

"Don't you have to be at the store today?" Stephen asked.

Duncan filled the two soiled glasses with rye whisky and sat on the edge of the bed. "It's a question of perspective, I think," he said. "We've all been tricked into seeing the world through the dutiful eyes of others. Seeing things in their proper perspective, my teachers used to say. But I don't see things clearly that way, do you? The only time I can clearly encompass anything is in the morning when I'm waking up and my solitary, disperspective eye is making the selection by its untrammeled self."

He thrust one of the glasses into Stephen's hand. "Now if I can carry that clarity through to the waking stage I won't have to steal from anyone, will I? And the nearest thing to being nearly awake is being nearly drunk, isn't it? Let's drink to it." Draining his glass, he lifted his free hand in the air. "Disperspectiveness," he yelled, and on the third syllable brought the hand down with a terrific whack upon Bill's extended backside, an action that Stephen had himself been contemplating for some seconds.

Bill uttered a long groan and rolled onto his back, peering about the room with bleary eyes until finally he fixed Stephen with an owlish stare.

"You should have stayed longer last night," he said limply. "Junior here would have enlightened you on his theory of the continuum of existence."

"I think he's working up to it now."

"Oh, God!" Bill groaned again and struggled to a sitting position, refusing with a shudder Stephen's offer of the extra glass of whisky.

"He doesn't have any trousers on, either," Duncan crowed, patting Bill's bare chest. "Before he went to bed he was demonstrating some of the dances of the West Coast Indians."

Stephen wondered why it was that the wilder manifestations of this household usually occurred when he was not present. Was it accident or design? "It must have been very edifying," he said, and noticed immediately that Bill's gaze had perceptibly hardened. "Don't worry, Bill, I shan't tell anybody."

Bill shrugged. "Do you have a lecture this morning?"

"At eleven, do you?"

"Supposedly. I'm not going."

"You won't need to if you're going to be a fisherman." Stephen meant the words to sound light. They cut the atmosphere like hail.

"Who told you that?"

"Fabien. Wasn't I supposed to know?"

"It doesn't matter." Bill grinned genially, obviously friendly, as if trying to withdraw the harshness of his previous question.

"We all sang 'Caller Herring' when he told us last night," Duncan said, reaching for the bottle and pouring another drink. "It was before the Indian dances."

"We were discussing future professions," Bill said. "Fabien is going to be a Jesuit priest."

"The lushest of the puritanisms. It should suit him."

"He's going to do missionary work in Darkest Paris," Duncan added, and both he and Bill laughed—like members of the same club, Stephen thought bitterly.

"And what are you going to be?" he asked of Duncan. "Don't you have to be at the store today?"

"I'm not going anymore."

"Not at all?"

"No, not at all."

Bill was looking fixedly at Stephen, appeal or defiance in his eyes, it was difficult to tell which. Stephen smiled faintly. "I'm glad to hear that," he said. "It must have been a deadly place to work."

"It wasn't so bad. Except for the middle-aged women with glasses who used to come in and peer at us, all clenched eyebrows and pursed mouths. I always felt they were blaming me for the fallen erections that lay behind them, and is isn't my fault."

"They blame everyone," Bill said. "You can't blame them, they're probably the wives of businessmen. Primary victims of the American way of life."

"Anyway," Stephen said, "it's good that Duncan doesn't have to be subjected to that anymore, isn't it?"

And he waited while the ensuing silence, of which only he and Bill were conscious, began to palpitate around them.

Duncan spoke first, mumbling indistinctly into the glass from which he was drinking. "Coleridge was wrong when he maintained that writers should have a job and write only in their spare time. I know because I've tried."

Bill said: "Fabien has persuaded him to give up work and spend all his time writing."

"That's my bonnie wee Fabien." Duncan stretched himself on the bed and closed his eyes, moving his head closer until the cheek lay against Bill's bare arm. With his toes he eased the slippers from his feet, dropping them over the side of the bed to the floor. "Bonnie wee Fabien," he murmured again, and began to snore.

"It'll be nice for the three of you, living here together," Stephen said.

"I just stayed the night. I haven't been invited to live here."

"Oh." Much can be done with an inflection. Stephen indicated Duncan with a nod of the head. "I'd like to see the stuff he writes."

"Why don't you ask him?"

"I don't have time now. Have to get to the lecture. Sure you're not going?"

"Not with this head."

"See you later, then. At lunch, probably. So long." He went out, not caring to look back.

Down in the hall he met Fabien, who had changed to a suit of herringbone tweed that made him look English.

"Duncan has passed out. I guess he's celebrating his release from work. Nice, that."

"Very."

"You must have a great deal of faith in his ability."

"I have never seen a thing he has written. The Scots are a very close race."

"And thrifty."

"Mainly in jokes," Fabien said. "But they are, I believe, a very vengeful race. Their history is absolutely crammed with the reciprocal gesture."

"Interesting," Stephen said. "I don't take Scotch history."

"Scottish," Fabien corrected gently. "Scottish. Aren't you going to be late for your lecture?"

"Yes. I'd better cut. I'll see you at lunch."

The door slammed. Fabien stood motionless a moment, a thoughtful expression on his face, then he smiled and turned and ran nimbly up the stairs. In the bedroom Bill was easing himself from under Duncan's flung arm. He got down on his hands and knees, extracted some underwear from beneath the bed, straightened up and closed his eyes, groaning faintly.

"By hell, I had a good time last night."

"You poor lamb, I know how it can be. Caused by beer, cured by beer and tomato juice."

Bill gave an exaggerated shudder. Duncan snored and rolled over onto his face. Bill reached out and drew the covers over the pajama-clad body, then stood with the waistband of his shorts stretched for entry.

"That's the one who can really cork it down," he said. "Christ! Gallons! He's a funny guy, ain't he?"

"That at least."

"I'm not knocking him. He's one of the boys. He reminds me of a lot of other guys I've known."

"One of the boys. Enviable condition. Am I?"

"You? You're nothing but a bloody foreigner."

Fabien smiled. "My dear!"

"See? You just proved it. My dear. Foreign as hell."

"Stephen doesn't think so."

"Him," Bill snorted. "That one. He was just in here."

Fabien said: "Will you *please* put on those underpants. If you only knew what a horrible unesthetic appearance you present, standing there like that."

Stephen did not comprehend the lecture, simple though it was. After the first few minutes he ceased to listen. The anger was boiling through him with a vitality that by comparison made the lesson seem dead words upon dead air, a tale told by a corpse to corpses. He was seething.

The fury had seized him as he entered the Roddick Gate, growing swiftly as he crossed the campus, filling him with such surprise that he was unable at first to discover the cause of it. The immediate reason suggesting itself was that Fabien had been, well, *cavalier* with him this morning, in both the kitchen and the hall, treating him with an indifference, brushing him aside. But no, that was ridiculous, for Fabien was in a sense unvarying in his behavior, and why should this morning above others be so affecting?

Then it was the scene in the bedroom. On looking back, he was sure now that the behavior of Bill and Duncan and their conversation with himself had left him with a peculiar feeling of physical sickness; not in the stomach, but rather in the head and chest. Only his interest—and, strangely, he had been intensely interested—had prevented him from noticing the sickness before he left the house.

Again, why? Why sick? Not the naked flesh, for he had grown used to that long since. Indeed, he had once walked into a bathroom when Duncan was emerging from a shower, finding himself intensely pleased at the lack of shock in what he saw. And not the contact of naked flesh, Duncan's face against Bill's bare arm with the rest of Bill stretched stripped beneath the bedclothes. For Stephen had been noticing of late how often people did touch each other in the normal course of everyday living, touching not to hold but for enjoyment purely. Stephen liked to see people do it now that he had noticed.

And finally he decided that the nausea was caused by Duncan not going to work. It was true that Fabien was rich and unstinted by his parents, but that, surely, was an insufficient reason for allowing Duncan to live like a parasite. Perhaps, really, that wasn't the reason, though; perhaps there was another. But that gave no cause for Fabien to use Duncan as a threat. Vengeful, he had said. What did that mean? It meant something; everything did. Stephen had not moved from under one sword merely to take his place beneath another.

That took care of the feeling of sickness. But the fury had succeeded the sickness and was not, he felt perfectly sure, at all contingent upon it. What then? He examined himself closely, fully conscious of the limitations of self-honesty and determined to extend them to the farthest possible boundaries.

It was toward the end of the lecture that he discovered he was enjoying the anger, and at once it was as if in his mind a door had opened through which he could pass at will. He crossed the threshold, timorously then bravely, completely engrossed, and at once he saw clearly the imprinted picture of which he had carried the negative for an hour or more.

The composition had changed, differed from the held memory. Although he still held the body of the child under his hands, the world had already become the clarified integration he was not to see until minutes later. And even as he felt the energy surging through his fingers to his arms, the child with his shining hair was disappearing into the house.

But these were details, vague background.

Through the center of his mind, large and startling in its multi-dimensions, ran the taxicab, quickly, smoothly, pausing only long enough for the crouched figure in the back to waver, become dim and unrecognizable, before moving silently ahead to vanish around the corner. Forever. Of course, forever. Father had gone to Ontario. And beyond. There was no return for him now, whatever disguise he affected. He remained only as a nebulous memory, a thin echo of a dry cough in the study on the second floor.

All in the past, Stephen had said to Fabien. All in the past, and now he was angry because the occasion was slipping past, was about to vanish in the inconsequent stream awaiting all occasions uncelebrated and unheld. A medal must be struck, a monument erected: something which at a later date could be shown as commemorating the moment of cleavage between the old and the fully new.

What, though? Could Fabien have told him? He felt relief that he had refrained from asking the question. Fabien would have erected a monument completely of his own design, making of Stephen a dead hero, a soldier perished in some obscure war; removing him from the tomb to the grave beneath a tomb. No, Stephen would instead raise something of his own, a towering edifice full of doors and painted windows, an erection that indicated unmistakably by its design the identity of its architect. In my father's house, Stephen thought, there is but one mansion, and through it I shall roam at my pleasure.

Or he could have taken the drink proffered by Duncan in the bedroom. But the glass was dirty, and Duncan was already drunk.

Every oath and obscenity he ever heard or imagined fell from his brain to his throat and was spat in a silent stream at the back of the vanished taxicab. Then the cab was gone, the child was gone, and the entire world fell clicking into place like the magnetized pieces of some tossed jigsaw puzzle. He smiled, and looked up to find the lecture was over.

The erection.

Out on the campus Matt Lambert fell in beside him and began talking. The snow had ceased, the world scintillated in the sun, and Sherbrooke Street glowed more than ever with its Saturday spick-and-span. The snow crunched under their slowly sauntering feet, emphasizing Lambert's unusual gait. He gave the impression always that he walked through olive oil up to his ankles.

"Did you ever get to meet your friend? Bill Whatsisname?"

As if seeing Matt Lambert for the first time, Stephen remarked with pleasure that the mobile, inquisitive face was good-looking, ripe, receptive. There came an urge to confide the entire morning's happenings to these amiable features. It was diverted by the rackety passage of three men and two girls, going in the same direction, talking and laughing, leaning forward into the sunlight.

"Yes," Stephen answered. "He's all right." One of the girls had disengaged from the group and was waiting at the Roddick Gates. Stephen added: "See you later, Matt. Got a heavy date," and increased his pace. Actions today must be accomplished positively and alone. He knew that already the foundation of his monument was being laid.

There was no denying Crystal's attractiveness, and, weaned as she was in Alberta, this bright day of crisp snow became her best. Even without his present, pressing necessity he suspected that he would have pursued exactly the same course of action. He said:

"You look fine today, Crystal. I'm taking you to lunch."

She rippled her own brand of bonhomie at him. "Swept off my feet like the feeblest of Sabines. Somewhere expensive?"

"The best place in town." He lifted his hand to a passing taxi, and the promptitude with which it stopped lifted them both into another world. Seated in the back he took her hand, stroking it gently from the pointed fingers down deep into the plump palm, laughing suddenly when she continued to gaze dreamily out of the side window. "Crystal, this is Stephen," he said, moving nearer and pressing his arm gently into her side. "Pay attention."

Her gaze turned full upon him without losing a fraction of its dreaminess. "I know. I'm trying to figure out what's up."

"Lunch. Aren't you hungry?"

Her eyes brightened. "Ravenous!"

"Then?"

She lifted the hand that held hers and pressed it to her cheek.

But when they arrived at the house her languor departed abruptly. "God!" she whispered, looking around the hall and up the black-carpeted stairs. "Do you think your mother is going to like me? Should I try to be demure? She may believe me when she finds I'm from Alberta."

The house was completely silent. "In here," Stephen said, ushering her into the sitting room. "I'll get you a glass of Dubonnet."

"Oh, ravishing!"

"There doesn't seem to be anyone at home," he said, clearing his throat. "Can you cook?"

She looked at him blankly for a second, then a hoot of mirth came from her throat. "Trapped again. Stephen, you bloody beast." Arm in arm they wandered out to the kitchen, gurgling at each other in a completion of the light mood that had seized them when they entered the cab.

She sat in the chair where Fabien had been that morning, sipping her wine, radiant with the amusement that filled her. And now that the time had arrived he began to feel apprehensive. Previously there had been only the snatched kiss at the dance or church social, the momentary, frightened groping on the dark shore of a lakeside in summer. There had been, too, although it didn't count, the girl in the pub in Manchester, England, with whom he had gone home because the last train had left for camp and he had nowhere else to go.

It was raining, Manchester rain, and through the wet streets she talked of her passion for dog-racing in a high, one-level Lancashire voice, holding his hand and swinging their arms while she prattled on. When he enquired about the wedding ring he could feel on her finger she had said harshly that her husband was a prisoner of the Japanese. But immediately she went back to the dog-racing and it seemed that her harshness had been merely a gesture to popular wartime feeling. He had felt empty and homeless.

At her house, after a great deal more drink, they went to bed. He had disgraced himself, he knew, for no matter how fiercely he tried to do what he did, it became apparent that he had no wish to do it. She had not laughed or complained, but in a while, drunk though they both were, her ennui had become undisguisable. And from the moment she awoke in the morning she had resumed her monologue on racing, giving him a kipper for breakfast and hurrying him on his way with almost indecent haste. The dogs, she said, were running today and she had to be off. He couldn't remember her name. Perhaps he never knew it. She was extremely pretty.

"No more for me," Crystal said as he made to refill her glass. "This stuff is making me hungrier."

"Me too." He moved round the table toward her and, sensing what was coming she stood up, her back to the wall, smiling. "You've guessed, haven't you," he said, "that I brought you here to seduce you."

"Oh, sir." Crystal giggled. "Tuesdays and Thursdays are my days."

"I'm in earnest." Stephen spoke with as much hoarse passion as he could muster.

"My reference to the Sabines was supposed to be a joke." Becoming serious, she said: "Stephen, you astonish me."

"What a Victorian remark."

"I don't mean it like that. I mean, I had theories about you. You're exploding them."

"What sort of theories?" He moved closer, pressing her to the wall with his body, becoming excited as she struggled a little to avoid his oncoming mouth. The kiss landed just below her ear; he slid his mouth down her cheek and managed finally to imprison her lips, forcing them closer by pressing with his hands at the back of her head. Her struggling ceased. She kissed him back, returning evenly the pressure so that for an instant they rocked off balance.

Her head drew back, eyes wide and pleased, and a shaft of sunlight through the kitchen window fell on the side of her face, illuminating the faint, fair down on her rounded cheek. "You're like a big, golden honeybee," he murmured, brushing a light kiss across her eyebrow.

"Not me, I'm the water-buffalo type." She was chuckling again and he said: "You're not taking this business seriously enough." His hands were stroking over her body in long, smooth gestures. The trepidation had left him, now; a hard core of excitement was rising. Easing her to the wall again he dropped his head and thrust his mouth into the open neck of her dress, opening his lips and sustaining the kiss until he was feeling her collarbone against his front teeth. He felt Crystal relax, go limp, her chin resting on his bent shoulder.

"Hello," she said, in a cool, rather amused voice.

"Hello," Fabien answered. "May I play, too. It looks like a lovely game."

He was leaning nonchalantly against the door, eyebrows raised and lower lip outthrust in a burlesque of bashfulness. "Terribly sorry," he mumbled to Stephen, hanging his head. "But the young lady saw me and I couldn't run away lest she thought I was spying. Do forgive me."

"How long were you two looking at each other?" Stephen asked suspiciously.

"You must be Stephen's brother." Crystal ignored the question and offered a gracious hand to Fabien. "We didn't hear you come in."

"My dear, I was having a preprandial siesta." He straightened up, becoming completely himself, shaking hands, and giving a slight bow in which there was no trace of mockery. And Stephen, now that at last he and Fabien were meeting on grounds of complete equality, although it was through the handshake of another, thought that he had never seen, or even conceived, anyone more charming. A wave of sweet relaxation went through him, and the shaft of sunshine on the back of his neck was like a warm, approving hand.

"This is Fabien, a friend of mine," he said. "No relation, but try to like him."

"Why, of course! Didn't he save me from a fate-worse-than?"

"In the nick-of," Fabien said. "I shall pay the mortgage for you. Have you had lunch?"

"I was invited. But what about Mum?" She turned to Stephen.

"Didn't you say I should meet Mum?"

"No, I don't live here. This is Fabien's house."

They were standing in a group, all candidly smiling, like children; as if in the air between hovered some obscure joke, the point of which had not yet been reached but was certain to prove hilariously funny.

"Do you like to cook, my dear?" Fabien asked. "With garlic?"

"Mmmm." She uttered a deep sigh, falling into a posture of complete surrender. "Garlic," she murmured. "I am yours."

Fabien began to move with the deft accuracy that characterized all his physical actions. From the icebox he brought lobster, sole, haddock, and a small unidentifiable fish, all of which he dumped on the table in front of Stephen. "Roll up your sleeves and cut everything into slices," he commanded. "We are going to make a bouillabaisse." The mere name was enough to make Stephen attack the task with gusto. He fell to marveling that three such exciting people should be together in one room.

Crystal was set to heating olive oil in a saucepan while Fabien himself chopped and sliced a variety of vegetables—onions, leeks, tomatoes, carrots, parsley—putting on rubber gloves and averting his head painfully when he crushed two cloves of garlic. The onions and carrots were cooked in the hot olive oil until they turned the exact shade of light brown. The remainder of the vegetables followed after.

"The fish now?" Stephen asked.

Fabien shuddered, as would a pure priest confronted with blasphemy. "We have barely begun," he said. "Have you finished the fish? Would you be a lamb and set the table? You know where the cutlery is."

"For how many?" Stephen asked.

"Please, for four."

Crystal was looking from one to the other with interest, her expression asking an explanation. "Watch the saucepan," Fabien told her gently, "whilst I get the shrimps and the clams and the wine and the herbs. And the spices. Then you can brush the bread with garlic and make the toast."

"Lovely," she murmured.

Stephen lingered, fascinated by the ritual of the saffron, happier than he could remember having been before. And as he laid the first knife in the dining room he found he was singing a cheerful, slightly bawdy song that they used to sing in the army. His volume increased noticeably as the first heavenly aroma came wafting from the kitchen. He was taking great pains with the table.

And now, somehow, the monument was already erected. The fork in the road lay behind, and it no longer mattered whether or not he made love successfully to Crystal. How nice she was, sweet, what fun! She had more than served her purpose. Fabien, though, he was almost certain, had not been terribly impressed by her. There was no need to bring her here anymore. But, out of gratitude, Stephen decided in the future to be more friendly with her, to encourage her, even to seek her company. She would be one of the host of friends with which this new road was to be lined. And at the end of the road—

Out in the kitchen they were laughing. Stephen hurried in to share the joke.

The steaming bouillabaisse, a beautiful color, was carried in ceremony by Crystal and placed at the head of the table; Stephen, still humming, bringing up in the rear with plates of golden, aromatic toast. Fabien went into the hall and stood at the foot of the stairs.

"Lunch is ready," he boomed, in a voice so stentorian that Stephen looked up in surprise. "Excuse me." Fabien addressed the room at large. "Shall we commence?"

The slow pattering of feet came across the hall, and Duncan appeared in the doorway. He was clad only in sandals and a brief nether-garment. His hair, as usual, was damp; he looked handsome, clean, drunk. He paused at the sight of Crystal, crossing his hands in front of him.

"I beg your pardon. I didn't know."

"Crystal," Fabien said, "this is Duncan."

"A bohemian," Stephen added.

She was eyeing Duncan appreciatively, smiling, and under her gaze he began slowly to smile in return. "I'm not startled, I'm a medical student," she said. "But there's nothing like you in the dissecting room, so won't you come in before the meal gets cold?"

He advanced a few paces, made a deep bow, crossed the room lightly to where she sat, and planted a soft, respectful kiss upon her cheek. "Is it fish?" he asked.

"Bouillabaisse," Stephen corrected him, savoring the word as he would the dish.

"Hello, Stephen."

They commenced eating.

The food was ambrosial. Between sighs and sudden exclamations of delight the conversation slowly picked up and, under Fabien's direction, began to sparkle. The presence of the woman had changed the tenor of the household. Or perhaps, thought Stephen, it is simply I who have changed. Fabien, while polite as ever, had dropped the trace of mockery usually present in his address. Duncan, with head drooping over his naked body like a shy satyr, was maintaining a steady stream of inconsequential talk that was flattering to all present by its inclusion of them. Both gave their full attention to Crystal, begging with quick glances her approbation on every word they uttered.

And Crystal, opening like a passion flower under the sun of their consent, indulged in flirtatious skirmishes with each man in turn, assuming by their tacit invitation the aura of hostess, speeding the conversation, even when not speaking, by her contrapuntal femininity. Male voices became deeper, more resonant; points were stated with greater emphasis. It occurred to Stephen that Duncan was infinitely more naked than he had appeared when first entering the room.

They were discussing, among other things, music and medicine, helping each other over the barren places where knowledge failed. Stephen noted with approval that when Crystal and Fabien had discerned separately that each was a possible authority, they neatly exchanged subjects, prolonging the conversation and giving wider scope for humor. Crystal, strongly advocating the wider therapeutic use of music, freely admitted that her favourite tune was "Red River Valley." Fabien championed the cause of medicine on the strength of a former treatment, he claimed, of hormone injections. Duncan, dancing from side to side of the conversation, urged on the principal protagonists, looking to Stephen to join him in laughter.

Out of sheer delight, Stephen laughed. At times he wondered if perhaps he laughed immoderately, being fully aware that the conversation was not so amusing as his laughter would appear to make it. Yet how pleasant it was to sit here, participating in enjoyment and adding to it by encouragement. How wonderfully refreshing to be with people who listened to one's lightest words with appreciation and interest, who respected one because of—because of the sheathed weapons which, in the enjoyment, need not be unsheathed.

Hail to friendship—the sheathed weapon. Himself, like every living person, had an armory of stored viciousness compounded of every resentment and humiliation he had suffered; a cutting array that could be used, as they had been acquired, in the cause of inflicting suffering. He could, of course, if he wished, do something now; call Duncan a drunkard and worse, Crystal a tease and worse, Fabien a—Fabien, something. But why? Where was the need when they did nothing to him? This was friendship, society, civilization; the eternal human compromise, the state of sweet armed peace.

He perceived now how it could be at home if each member of the family would decide to become an entity instead of an adjunct to the group. In his mind's eye he saw sunlight flooding into his home, heard them at meals laughing warmly at each other's foibles, imagined himself sitting at that table as he sat at this.

He looked over to where Fabien was inclining his cropped golden head in confidence toward Crystal. "I shall be like Fabien," Stephen thought, and he said:

"How about coming to my place for dinner tonight? I think I could arrange it with Mother."

"At last," Crystal cried, "the mother!"

"Well, no." They were all friends, and Stephen did not feel in the least embarrassed. "Not you, Crystal. I'd have to break it to my mother more gently if I were going to bring a girl. But Fabien can come."

"Thank you," Fabien said. "Is Duncan included?"

"Well, yes, I suppose."

But the bouillabaisse was finished and now, for some reason, no one could get the conversation racing again. It became desultory, hesitant; it sputtered and died. Stephen felt an urge to leave the house with the memory intact. Also, he needed time to prepare his mother.

Before he departed with Crystal he was able to whisper to Fabien a plea that Duncan be sobered up before the evening. "My mother is temperance." Fabien nodded and cocked his head on one side at a curious angle.

Outside on the sunny, snowy street, Crystal said, "You certainly have some exciting friends," then she, too, nodded, and Stephen and she both went their different ways.

Downstairs in the hall the clock struck ten. Stephen rolled over on the bed, pressing his aching head between his hands, trying desperately to remember some small detail by which he could pretend that the past evening had not been a hopeless failure. The effort was too much. He allowed himself to sink unchecked into depths of the angry misery that had assailed him when first he opened the door that evening.

He had been excited. The dinner, he knew, was not to be an interesting one, for his mother had refused to serve what she called "silly, fancy dishes." But the atmosphere in the house compensated, was novelly fresh, revivified by the prospect of these approaching visitors. Already there was a difference.

Mrs. Hollis had shown unexpected interest in the visitors' identity and plied Stephen with questions as to their schooling, social standing, and plans for the future. In answer he had concentrated mainly on Fabien, minimizing the foreign birth in favor of the size of the house, the good manners, the wealth, and the ability at the piano. Duncan had been barely mentioned, partly through indifference, but mainly because Stephen suddenly realized that he knew nothing about Duncan except that he drank and had recently worked in a store. Neither of these facts would have appealed to Mrs. Hollis.

She took great trouble with the table, more in fact than the forthcoming meal of beef, potatoes, and mashed turnips would seem to justify. She spent almost an hour nervously straightening the cutlery and picking at the huge bowl of flowers that threatened to hide the diners from each other's view. Stephen was more than once tempted to make a suggestion to help the meal go more smoothly, but there was a look about her that kept him silent, a look rarely seen. With the few damp vestiges that comprised all her husband had left her, Mrs. Hollis was happy.

Stephen said gratefully: "Thanks for all the trouble, Mother."

"Oh, it's nothing. Of course, if Father and Richard were going to be here I probably couldn't manage it, but there's just Esther so there'll be only five of us." She looked thoughtful. "If it turns out well you can perhaps bring some more of your friends here in the future." Both of them knew it was impossible, but Stephen was happy to think that just for tonight Father was in Ontario for her, too.

If it turns out well! When the bell rang Stephen opened the door to find Duncan silhouetted against the snow. He was alone and weaving. He clutched in his hand a note from Fabien.

A thousand pardons! Had last minute call to attend absolutely essential dinner at consulate. Terrible bore! Hope you managed to arrange things with your mother. Tender my apologies. Will make it up to you by throwing huge party next week. Duncan perfectly sober. Enjoy yourselves. Love.

The handwriting was exquisite.

Stephen's anger was so intense that it was he who made the first *faux pas*, consciously, after which there seemed no time at which the evening could be salvaged. Mrs. Hollis had bustled forward with an outstretched hand, and he saw by her glance that she was not unimpressed by Duncan's appearance.

"You must be Fabien," she murmured with a little smile, "and this is my daughter, Esther." The almost unruffled way in which they were encompassing the arrival of only one guest infuriated Stephen, who saw only that he had been made to look foolish.

"This is Duncan," he said. He felt barely able to speak.

"Oh." The smile faded a little. "I don't know a great deal about you, Mr. Duncan. Are you one of Stephen's classmates?"

"Duncan," Stephen said, "works downtown in a store." Feeling his intention not fully accomplished, he added, "He sells underwear." He had thought the remark would abate the savagery that gripped him, but, on the contrary, he felt the vise tighten until his lips trembled.

They were moving into the dining room and, under the wavering light of the candles on the table, Duncan looked very drunk indeed. It was patently obvious that all the preparations—the room, the table, the illuminations, and probably the meal—were going to leave him totally unimpressed. He said: "I used to sell underwear, but I got fed up with it. I quit."

Mrs. Hollis had stiffened perceptibly. Her husband was in Ontario, the fort was unmanned and the enemy approaching. "Stephen goes to McGill," she said. "He's doing very well."

"I know," Duncan rejoined, aiming a light punch at Stephen's arm and grinning amiably. "But it's awful darn hard to tell sometimes from his conversation."

The silence that ensued was agonizing. It settled and congealed, lasting more than halfway through the meal to the infinite discomposure of everyone but Duncan, who, after a few attempts at conversation, lapsed into a genial silence and smiled around the table at anyone who caught his eye. Stephen could see that his mother was affronted by this casual acceptance of her hospitality by such a person. The absence of what she considered to be nice conversation and the all too obvious difference between Duncan and the people she usually met were engendering in her an almost visible sense of outrage. Perhaps later on she would be rude, for in her quiet manner, away from and in reaction to her husband, Mrs. Hollis prided herself that she always spoke her mind, particularly to inferiors. And it had been painfully apparent from the moment of introduction that she regarded Duncan as being most emphatically inferior.

For Stephen's part, he did not care if his mother decided to destroy their guest entirely. From the ashes of the evening there rose like a phoenix the indisputable knowledge that his early aversion to this man was solidifying into a deep hatred. He had been tricked into having Duncan here tonight. What did the Scotsman possess that commanded him as a guest? Nothing! Not his shower baths, his drunkenness, his unemployment, nor yet his wish to write. Not his perpetual, stupid, wet nakedness and not—most certainly not his willingness to hang like a leech on Fabien. One shuddered at the amorality of it. Fabien must be told. Duncan must be gotten rid of.

Oddly, it was the usually uncommunicative Esther who broke the painful silence. She had been watching him throughout the meal with quick, secretive glances and now she asked him how it felt to be an immigrant. He turned upon her his brightest smile and said it was excellent.

"Duncan is having it easy," Stephen said. "He's attempting to write a book and living in luxury. It's one of the benefits of making useful friends."

His mother had caught the implication, for she looked at him sharply. He was pleased that they could now link their mutual disapproval.

"It must be wonderful to write a book," Esther said softly. "Is it about the French Canadian problem? Will you tell us about it?"

The smile had vanished from Duncan's face and when he turned to Esther there was a look in his eyes of almost spaniel gratitude. "I'd rather not," he said. "I'm not sure yet that it's going to be worth anything." She nodded understandingly. "Are you interested in writing?" he asked.

"Esther is interested in the work of the church," Mrs. Hollis said sharply.

"And the ministers of the church." Stephen saw and was indifferent to his mother's angry glance.

"Is your friend a minister?" Esther and Duncan were looking at each other with the soft, unseeing stare that people wear when daydreaming and Stephen was shocked at the resemblance in their two faces, a similarity of expression that momentarily made them look like brother and sister. Good God! Could it be that, after all this time, Esther was feeling the first stirrings of sex?

"I beg your pardon," Duncan said. "I see I've made a gaffe. I guess we had better talk about books."

It was possible that he might have discoursed learnedly. At the beginning he appeared to be working up a discussion on the position of literature in modern society, or something akin, and Stephen was interested despite himself. But Duncan was directing most of his remarks to Esther, soliciting her opinion on the significance of authors of the caliber of Gide and Mann. Stephen saw it was quite hopeless. When for the fifth or sixth time she murmured "I don't know," the conversation swiftly degenerated into the swapping of titles.

"Have you read *The Robe?*"

"Yes, wasn't it lovely!"

On and on it went, boring Stephen as much as it seemed to irritate his mother, who read very little. Esther was enjoying herself, but surely Duncan was making fun of her. Or had he really read *The Robe* and added another crime to his calendar?

"You didn't eat much, Mr. Duncan," Mrs. Hollis said stiffly when the meal was over.

"I was not very hungry, thank you. I know what I would like, though. I'd like a drink."

There could be no mistake. The tone of voice could not possibly be implying a glass of water or a cup of tea. In the second deathly hush, Mrs. Hollis's words fell like pebbles on a kettledrum.

"If you are referring to alcoholic drinks, Mr. Duncan, I should tell you that we belong to the Temperance Union. There has never been a drop of alcohol under this roof, and there never will be so long as I am here." She was blazing at him.

"Oh, but that isn't a temperate attitude, Mrs. Hollis. It sounds most immoderate." Under the politeness Duncan was plainly very much annoyed.

"I'm sorry we don't see eye to eye on the subject." Mrs. Hollis's expression was entirely opaque, her voice curiously strained. "But really, Mr. Duncan, you must permit me to run my own household. If I listened to everyone's advice on the subject I don't know where I'd be. Why, before I knew what was happening I should probably be walking into the stores downtown and getting advice from the people behind the counter."

"I'm sorry," Duncan said. "I had no right to say anything." Ten minutes later he had made his excuses and departed. On the doorstep he apologized to Stephen. "Sorry, but I really have got a terrific drouth. See you soon." He jumped nimbly off the steps and was gone.

In the house Mrs. Hollis, her normal, timorous self again, looked at Stephen with half-frightened eyes. "I thought he was drunk when he first got here," she said faintly.

"His surname is McSurt, not Duncan."

She said: "I hope you'll not be seeing much of him. How can this Fabien person be so friendly with him when he's like that?" And then, fearfully: "I don't think we'd better mention to Father that he was here."

"It would have been different if Fabien had come," Stephen said.

He went slowly upstairs to his room and lay on the bed, suffering, unable to read, tortured by the thought of what Fabien would think when he heard Duncan's version of the evening's proceedings. Eventually he fell into an uneasy, sweating sleep, and everything changed.

He sat up, wide-awake and frightened, and saw that he had been sleeping on a cot in a narrow prison cell that was windowless and illuminated only by a single bulb set without fittings in the center of the ceiling. The cell was empty, he was quite alone, but from somewhere, somewhere not far distant, he heard the sound that had awakened him. A woman was laughing, a sustained, beautiful song of pure mirth that rose and fell through the entire scale like an aria from some unthinkable opera.

For a long time he listened enchanted, and then the horror fell upon him. The sound was going on too long. Why did she not stop now? He was frightened. What was she laughing at?

She was drawing nearer now, louder, and his head began to ring. Even when he had his fingers in his ears he could still hear her. He buried his face in the straw pillow, seeking silence in darkness, and a deep voice said: "You'll have to come along, Hollis. You're making a disturbance." The two warders who had appeared at the door grasped him brutally by the shoulders and dragged him out.

Marching down the long, narrow corridor, their footfalls made no sound. At first he tried to struggle, but after a while the laughter grew fainter and ceased, so that he didn't care much where he was being taken. His guards marched rigidly, lock step, grim-faced and unspeaking, never once relaxing their grip.

When, at the end of the corridor, the sunlight burst upon them, he saw they had arrived at Westmount railway station. They are going to put me on a train, he thought, and instantly came the knowledge that he could escape. With scarcely a twitch he flung the restraining arms from his shoulders and, straight as an arrow, rose up, up into the air—high—until the station below looked like a tiny hut. "Free, free," he shouted, and began to laugh.

"Oh no you don't."

The guards were at either side of him, hovering in mid-air, smiling secretively at each other from under their heavy mustaches. Slowly they moved in on him, enfolding him in their arms, beginning to caress him. To his unspeakable horror he saw that one of them was going to kiss him.

With a scream he hurled them off and plummeted to earth, hurtling himself across the station yard and into the entrance of the soundless tunnel. It had grown longer now, and he was running forever. He could scarcely breathe. The lights were getting dimmer. He ran although he knew they no longer pursued him.

Broken-winded and in terror he reached at last the door of his cell and flung it open, sobbing with relief. The woman was waiting for him.

He knew at once that she was the one who had laughed, and she laughed now, softly, raising her shapely arms until they stood out straight from her shoulders, the palms of the hands turned downwards, the fingers bent in a curve.

"My dearest friend," she said. "You knew where I was."

She was advancing upon him, laughing still, her mouth opening wider, until he saw, shuddering, that all her teeth were black and rotting.

"Hello," he said, while her laughter grew louder, wilder.

"Hello." And he began to laugh, too. What a pathetic deception! He saw the joke now and it was funny. It was in the eyes, somewhere about the forehead. The ears could not be disguised. Watching closely he saw tiny pieces of skin and flesh beginning to peel and flake from the face. He was convinced.

He said to the woman: "Hello, Fabien."

With an awful scream the figure leapt at him.

He was awake, staring at the ceiling of his bedroom, the muscles of his face still set in the smile. The small clock on his bureau said ten-thirty, and he wondered if he should go and see Fabien and explain how the evening and Duncan and Mrs. Hollis didn't really matter.

"But I mustn't lose my temper again," he whispered to himself.

In the shelves by his bedside stood the books of Huxley, Waugh, Ronald Firbank, Cyril Connolly, Christopher Isherwood, and the rest of the *quarantaine dorée*. He selected one at random and began to read.

II

Telephone calls were always a source of excitement to Miriam, and they had been scarce in the past few weeks. She leapt at the instrument the moment it started to ring, calling to the maid that it was all right, she would take it.

"Yes," she said, "this is Mrs. Sabel speaking."

The thumb in her mind riffled rapidly through the index of audial memory, trying without success to place the voice of the questioner. Such a soft voice it was, smooth and young. She sank into the chair beside the telephone table and unconsciously lowered her lids until her eyes were half obscured.

Yes, it was a cold day, but nice and bright. Miriam waited in pleasant anticipation.

"I've called to ask if you would like to attend a party on Saturday evening. Please forgive the unseemly method of invitation."

The intoxicating graciousness of the voice made the word "unseemly" seem a witticism, and Miriam laughed throatily, gay and beguiling.

"A party? I love parties. Are you going to make it very tempting? Wait till I light a cigarette and we'll talk it over."

She was positive he was a stranger, yet already her being was responding like a crystal bowl being rung by a rare and liquid tenor. She struck a match and inhaled deeply. So much could be destroyed by an impetuous lack of caution. She picked up the phone again.

"I don't know about Saturday. I'm usually entertaining at home."

"Oh, Mrs. Sabel! I'm desolate. We need you desperately. There will be a positive plethora of handsome men and almost no lovely women. Please say you'll come."

"What sort of party will it be?" she asked archly. "Tempt me some more."

The voice at the other end appreciated her challenge with a deep, lingeringly masculine laugh that embraced them both and left her feeling utterly feminine. Without releasing the phone she screwed her cigarette into the holder that lay on the table, inhaled again, and blew out the smoke in a thin blue stream.

"It will be quite ordinary, I'm afraid, as far as food and drink are concerned. Our only claim to distinction is that Ivan Simpson has promised to come."

The cogs of Miriam's memory clicked like a ratchet screwdriver and she heard Neil, his usually truculent voice dimmed with awe and admiration, telling her of the glories of Ivan Simpson. One of those mystical poetic phrases of his dropped intact into her mind, and she realized that even boredom can be turned to profit.

"You mean the Dylan Thomas of Canada?" she asked.

"That's right. Do you know him?"

"I've heard of him. And, of course, I've read him." A tiny pulse of excitement was beating in her throat. She felt a little breathless.

"'If with turgidity my soul should cease,'" quoted the voice, "'and wrackéd eyes grow wrackier yet ...'"

"Lovely," breathed Miriam. "One of my favorites."

"There may be others for you. Ivan has promised to read us excerpts from his latest unpublished work, 'Shabby Candles.'"

Then God be praised, for here she was at the end of that long, unwinding road. She stood now on the verge of the clearing wherein was fixed the magic circle. In the face of seemingly irrefutable evidence to the contrary, she had remained convinced that even in Montreal were real people who lived real lives. Her faith was about to be rewarded. In a muted voice she asked:

"Is it going to be an artistic party?"

The phone went dead at the other end and for a panic-stricken moment she thought he had hung up. But he was back immediately. He must have been covering the mouthpiece in order to cough.

"An artistic party? In a way, I suppose, yes. Most of the guests will be young and untutored, but I can promise a mitigation of those who know what they're doing. You will love it, I'm sure, and we will love having you. Promise that you'll come."

A tiny doubt flickered in the back of her mind and was instantly extinguished. Nothing could dampen those high spirits engendered by the warm effusion of this voice and the promise it held. Love, life, and laughter were beckoning. Strange music played on soft flutes irresolute, and gentle winds a-blowing through the aeolian harps of Youth. Her laugh was like a tinkling of bells.

"Why, of course I can come. I've just remembered my husband will be away this week end. It's usually his friends that I entertain on Saturdays."

"Bravo!" the voice cried. "You've transformed my whole morning."

Miriam hesitated, poised, and plunged.

"Shall I bring my violin with me. I play the violin, you know."

"Oh, please do. I've looked forward to hearing you play ever since Duncan mentioned it."

"Who? Since who mentioned it?"

"Duncan. Duncan McSurt."

"Oh! Do you know him?"

"Very well, indeed. He lives at my place."

"Yes. Then you must be the friend he spoke of," Miriam said in a dead voice. "I hope you've managed to get a job."

"I beg your pardon?"

"Duncan told me you were unemployed. I hope you've found something by now." It was terribly difficult to keep the depression out of her voice.

"Well, no, I haven't, but how extremely nice of you to think of it."

And yet he didn't sound at all as if dandruff fell from his lank hair to spread in a shower over the shoulders of his shiny blue suit. Maybe he worked in radio and was between contracts. Maybe he was an unemployed journalist, or something to do with advertising. Miriam brightened a little.

"Something will turn up soon," she said, projecting encouragement to both the young man and herself.

"Yes." The voice was wistful. "Although Ivan Simpson claims that he hasn't worked regularly for more than ten years. He's very poor."

It was a bombshell. For there, she saw immediately, lay her long-sought explanation. She had imagined while listening to Neil that Canada's leading poet was rich as well as respected, whereas in reality he was poor. Poor! Of course he was! They were all poor.

How fatally she had erred in the past by thinking that Art could be discovered over teacups, or through the intermissions of the Plateau Hall concerts. Art had never been, could never be—what was that word?—bourgeois. No, not Real Art. Countless incidents related by innumerable young men came crowding into her mind. There was Van-something, the painter who had been forced to cut off his ear to pay a woman for her favors when he had no money. There was that French boy-poet, so poverty-stricken that he was able to pick off his lice and throw them at passing priests, and who had not written a line of poetry after he ruined himself by getting a regular job at eighteen. And there was the greatest French poet of them all—what was his name—who spent his entire life in debt. And the musician, Bar-something, who died completely broke; Thousands of them, the true artists, spending their lives in want and starvation and denial, so as not to be distracted by worldly things from the pursuit of the only thing that really mattered.

In a flash Miriam perceived how her own great ability might have been dulled by commercialism and the presence of too much comfort. Had Duncan seen that? Surrounded by the luxuries of her home, had he, in reality, wept at the sight of an artist being smothered? Unusual, yes, but he was a very unusual boy. And now he was extending the helping hand, the second chance.

"Did Duncan ask you to invite me?" she enquired tenderly.

"Not exactly."

"Oh."

"It is a surprise party for him," the voice explained. "We want to invite everyone he's fond of. There are not many, of course, because he's so extremely sensitive—"

"Oh, he is," Miriam interrupted, happily corroborating her own conjecture. "He is indeed. One of the most sensitive persons I ever met, and such a lovely disposition."

"It will be a delicious surprise for him when you walk in."

"Then I shall come," Miriam said determinedly. "Oh, and by the way, what's your name?"

"Fabien."

"Hello, Fabien. You must call me Miriam."

"Thank you, Miriam."

She hesitated. "Fabien, is there anything I can bring to help out? I'd like to very much if I may."

"How extremely kind of you. You *are* a darling. I think we shall manage without putting you to any such bother. The formal invitation will arrive by tomorrow's post."

This was a delightful and unexpected touch. Miriam sought a rejoinder in kind.

"I suppose I should wear evening dress," she said.

"Miriam, my dear, there are absolutely no restrictions. Come entirely as you wish, and be assured of a warm, grateful welcome."

"Till Saturday, then," Miriam lilted.

"Till Saturday, then. Good-by. And thank you again."

"Good-by."

"Good-by."

She held the humming phone, enwrapped in a cloud of pink thought. It was here, *la vie de bohème*, the beckoning Left Bank; and she was more than prepared to meet its challenge. Like a cool and radiant queen about to receive her rightful crown she would go forth, gliding, over the cobblestones of the Latin Quarter's checkered streets. It was of no consequence that the first promenade led only to a small, stuffy room where dwelt the redheaded boy of dubious weeping and his unemployed friend with the hair. The twin wands of Art and Culture would transform and transfigure, would lend luster where before seemed only drabness.

And this first step was certain to lead to others. A plethora of handsome men? That meant a great many. Undeniably, there would be some that she was bound to interest and excite—Ivan Simpson perhaps; young boys, students, looking at her as she stood up and applied the first stroke to her violin, admiring her, respecting her, tinged slightly by desire. They would recognize a true spirit. And it was inevitable that after a while they insist she come also to their parties. Perhaps there would come a time when they held parties solely in her honor. Miriam smiled happily, surrounded by a thousand visions. She gave a deep sigh.

"Did you say something, madam?" The maid entered the hall.

Miriam hung up the phone and rose to pat the girl warmly on the arm. "You manage everything beautifully, Shirley. I must think of something nice to do for you."

The girl looked at her mistress affectionately. She had worked in the house for a year now, and never known better employment. "But you're always doing nice things for us, madam."

"You deserve it. You all treat me so well," Miriam said, and wafted airily up the stairs, followed by the maid's approving smile.

But there was a practical side to this, she told herself, sitting on her bed. She knew through hearsay and reading that there was a carelessness attached to the behavior of bohemians, a certain amorality that precluded several very desirable methods of procedure. She could not, for example, much as she would love it, appear at the party wearing all her most expensive jewelry. Artists were not subject to the rules that governed conventional humanity, and there was an anarchistic possibility that she might be robbed—by a starving painter needing funds to complete a major opus, by a fierce tigress of a girl who was devoting her life to the care of some fragile and dying poet. Apart even from that, it was more than likely her opulence would be taken as a personal affront, making them despise her, turning this precious first step into a false one.

Much the same thing applied to what she wore. At the read-about bohemian parties someone was usually sick, or violent hands were laid upon the womenfolk by a young man, or several young men, who had been carried away by transcendental desires. She objected to the sickness, if not to the hands, but what if either should happen whilst she was wearing one of her best dresses? And, too, the question of the smallness of the room. Sitting huddled on a bed or floor was part of the legitimate bohemian fun, but not if a two-hundred-dollar dress was losing its lines and being ruined. A two-hundred-dollar dress, moreover, that had already aroused the jealous antipathy of every female in the room, including the poet's tigress.

Wanting very much to do the right thing, Miriam opened the door of a wardrobe cupboard and ran eye and hand along the row of garments, ruminating, selecting at last an afternoon gown of soft gray. She crossed to the mirror and held it against herself. The color ebbed, became ashy, impossibly inappropriate and unfestal. She bit her lower lip thoughtfully.

And then the brilliant, the exciting idea occurred to her. Within minutes she had gone tingling to the attic and returned carrying on her arm a dress barely thought of in years. Her mind was a confused and wholly delightful mass of emotions, things remembered and things to come. She smiled excitedly at her reflection as she passed the mirror, pleased with the sparkle in her eyes so unexpected at this hour of the morning.

The sparkle became a scrutiny. Every sequin on the dress was in place, each fold retained its creamy whiteness. She pulled it over her head and adjusted the familiar low neck, waves of nostalgia coursing through her as she thought of those long-departed nights when a hushed audience had sat in the darkness beyond the glaring bar of footlights, watching this very dress vary its scintillating way through the entire spectrum while the lights blended from one hue to another to accommodate the mood of her sobbing violin. Those were the nights! That was the glory! She drew in half a sigh and discovered a difficulty in properly filling her lungs. Anxiously she went to the mirror.

The dress seemed to have shrunk. She turned her back and looked over her shoulder, viewing with dismay the taut, glossy area of her posterior. Tentatively she walked up and down the room, keeping her knees well together, toning down the insouciant sway of her hips.

It would do! Definitely! Her corset, though not slovenly, was a trifle loose this morning, and a somewhat tighter lashing would probably turn the trick. Failing that, a swift trip to the dressmaker with the matching bolero that still lay in the attic trunk, and a piece could be let in at the side. It could be fixed.

But not right away, not now! For now her heart was lifting and lilting like a tune by Ivor Novello. Humming a few bars from "Glamorous Night," she picked up the gray afternoon dress and walked with careful gaiety out onto the landing. "Shirley!" she called over the bannister. "Shirley!"

The maid appeared in the well of the stairs, face upturned. "Madam?"

"For you, Shirley. Something nice." She opened her hand and let the dress go fluttering down. She smiled and gave a little wave and went on into the music room, barely hearing the girl's excited cries, her exclamations that this would exactly match the shoes Madam had given her last week, but happier still that she had been able to make someone else happy.

She flung open a window and under the eyes of the departed masters took up her violin. Her loving hands stroked its shining surfaces. Each tuning was a caress.

Seconds passed and then the trembling air of the quiet street was filled with globules of melody. Miriam was practicing her favorite tune. "Trees."

"Well, that takes care of the food," Fabien said, laying down the phone. "The man at the store sounded delighted, but slightly incredulous."

"We Canadians are plain livers," Stephen said. "The jars of caviar have probably been there since colonial days. We're a Dominion now."

"Are we? Delightful." Fabien was sitting sideways in the chair, his legs draped over the arm. He had on the boots and trousers he had worn while skiing that morning on Mount Royal, and his shirt was open at the neck, showing a brown throat.

"Unless they ask for tequila, or something equally outrageous, there should be no trouble about drinks with what we have in the cellar."

"If I know my Canadians," said Stephen, intimately condescending, "they'll probably ask for home-brewed rotgut wines. Most of them are out of their depth beyond a sauterne."

"You mucky little snob," Fabien remarked mildly, his expression taking the sting from the words. "Stop trying to delude me after that performance with the Trockenbeeren Auslese. I remember it vividly."

"I didn't fool you?" Stephen asked.

"At the risk of sounding a snob myself: No."

"Am I fooling you now?"

"Are you trying to?"

"Maybe. Am I?"

Fabien began slowly to unlace his ski boots, keeping his legs perfectly still and twisting his body. "Canada isn't a wine-drinking country. I had great hopes of the French element when I arrived, but all they have offered me are noisome concoctions of dandelions and parsnips." His boots dropped to the carpet with a thud. "Vomitous," he said, "with all sorts of weird bacteria floating around the glass."

"That's exactly what the guests will want when they arrive." Certainly there was to be a party, but apart from that Stephen knew nothing. His impatience for details engendered in him an irritation difficult to suppress. He looked at Fabien from the corners of his eyes, then hastily away again as he saw that he was being coolly observed.

"Or have you invited only the *haut monde?*"

"Who would they be?"

"Your people from consulates, and so on."

"Are they?"

"All right, you win. Who the hell have you invited?"

"As an inquisitive swine, Stephen, you should learn to ask outright questions."

It was the first time he had known Fabien to speak sharply to him. A peculiar feeling of void appeared suddenly behind Stephen's solar plexus and spread to his breast in a mounting sensation akin to panic. Perplexed and frightened he sought its cause and meaning, only to discover that his customary sense of self-analysis had fled. His mind began fluttering like a frightened bird. His mouth went dry. Panic fed upon panic, and he feared lest this bewildering rawness within him should begin to bleed and somehow cause Fabien to depart the room, leaving behind a loose end that could never again be incorporated into the main skein. With a detached part of his brain Stephen became aware that another part was frantically seeking something placatory to say.

"I didn't mean to be offensive."

"You weren't at all. I should be used to you by now."

Fabien smiled as he spoke, but now he was staring abstractedly at his stockinged feet, head turned sideways to show the too-short nose and the smooth, brown planes of his cheeks. The hair, usually so neat, had tumbled onto his forehead as he untied his boots. It clustered in unexpected curls at the temples.

I must be ill, Stephen thought, for the panic in his breast had turned to a tormenting ache. In his stomach was a sick emptiness that he knew no amount of vomiting would ease. He moistened his lips.

"I should be used to you by now," and then turned indifferently away. Why had Fabien done that? Why was it?

Beyond a shadow of doubt, this was Duncan's doing. He had stayed out of the way since last Saturday, and, in the meantime, Fabien had said nothing to indicate he knew what had happened at the Hollis house. But there must have been a great deal of discussion between them, that was certain. In all probability they talked about it immediately after Duncan returned from the dinner; sat around, laughing and getting drunk, deriding Stephen for his family and saying, "after the bouillabaisse comes the beef and mashed turnips."

Not that Fabien could be blamed. From his point of view a description of that ghastly dinner must have been funny beyond words. Stephen himself, in the position of observer, would have sharpened a quiverful of epigrams to mark the occasion. But for Duncan, a participant, there was no excuse.

Unless he had a definite reason.

Stephen had a clear vision of Duncan sitting across the room from Fabien, glass in hand, eyes fogged, mouth hanging slightly open; looking very young, despite whatever his age was, and blowing dart after dart to poison that other friendship which threatened the one between himself and Fabien. He may even have called in Bill to aid the murder; open, amiable, stupid Bill, whom Duncan, whether drunk or sober, manipulated cleverly under a guise of roistering mutual fellowship. With a little prompting, Bill must have said things of which he barely knew the meaning, statements to which his stupidity lent an apparent sincerity. And while Fabien listened, Duncan must have sat back and smiled quietly to himself.

Duncan rarely smiled to the public view, now that one came to think about it. There was about him an inborn secrecy that approximated furtiveness, pointed up by the fact that he never mentioned his early life as did most people, even Stephen himself. It was not like the understandable and aristocratic reticence of Fabien, but rather a soft-footedness of mind that bespoke a preoccupation with matters both selfish and underhanded. And his only-too-obvious present preoccupation was to alienate Fabien from Stephen. It was even conceivable that his behavior the previous Saturday evening had been merely another dexterous move to further his cause.

Stephen lit a cigarette. Could any cause be more despicable than Duncan's filthy parasitism? It was not to be wondered that he went to extremes to keep Fabien from the confidence of others less stupid than Bill, when a clear eye and a dropped word would expose this transparent deceit of writing a book. Strange, wasn't it, that not even Fabien had seen the book. On such terms the writing could be strung out endlessly, while the supposed writer lived in comfort and ease at the expense of another. At the expense of my friendship with Fabien, Stephen thought.

Immediately he was profoundly shocked. In the self-sufficiency that had been forced upon him since childhood Stephen had seldom thought of friendship in clear terms. Now, all at once, the conception of it sat in his mind, tangible as a dove in an olive tree, and he knew he was reaching toward it with a desperate earnestness. An ineffable longing for self-abnegation came over him. He looked across to where Fabien sat gazing abstractedly at his own feet.

It was as if the room suddenly widened into an awful expanse, filling the air with a gushing sound that rang in Stephen's ears. Fabien was a distant speck on an opposite shore. Between them lay a great salt sea whose waves lapped within Stephen's breast in unendurable surges. Wild with loneliness, he lifted his hands and allowed them to drop again to his lap.

"You're the only friend I have," he said.

Fabien lifted his head with a charming smile, his eyes coming back into focus. "You overwhelm me. Thank you."

"It's damn nice of you to give me a party simply because I asked you to dinner. No one has treated me like that before."

"What? Oh!" Fabien straightened himself and lit a cigarette. "Now you've made me feel utterly heartless."

"You mean about the guests? I didn't mind."

"You're incredible." Fabien laughed softly. "Really quite incredible. As a matter of fact I need your help. I know very few local people and Duncan, I think, knows fewer. Would you like to invite some of your acquaintances to make up a decent party?"

"Sure." Stephen cast around gratefully in his mind seeking a list of desirables, but all he could conjure for the moment was the acne-blotched image of Harrigan. "What about Crystal?" he asked.

"I've invited her." Fabien grinned, apprehending the look of enquiry that Stephen could not hide. "I phoned this morning. The official invitations go by post tonight. It's rather short notice, I'm afraid."

"This is only Wednesday," Stephen said. "In Canada you can decide to have a party at six-thirty on Saturday evening and still have the house full by nine. Who else is coming?"

"Ivan Simpson—"

"Hell, where did you meet him?"

"At a consulate dinner. He was discussing some Canadian cultural mission to one of the lesser Latin-American countries. Poetry. Nobody understood a word."

"I'm not surprised. Any other country and he would be laughed out of existence. Here, he gets a complete issue of the *Northern Review*."

"It takes some talent to make bricks in a country with so little straw," Fabien protested.

"He don't make 'em, he drops 'em." Stephen was happily confident of his grounds on the strength of a review written in the *New York Times Book Review*. "I've seen better poetry on lavatory walls. Funnier, anyway."

"At least he makes a change from your usual poets with their fresh air and everlasting thews," Fabien said. And Stephen was delighted that at last they were having a conversation in which both were nominally interested. He strove to keep it going.

"Simpson would love that. His one desire is to appear a breath from the graveyard. Unfortunately, most of his poems sound like a compound of the *Railway Guide*, the *Ontario Farmers' Weekly*, and Eaton's mail-order catalogue. And," he added as an afterthought, "a handful of pamphlets from the Ministry of Mines and Resources."

"You know him?" Fabien asked with interest.

"Vaguely. He gave a couple of lectures one time—"

"Who did?" asked a voice. Duncan came into the room and went across to sit on the arm of Fabien's chair. He was wearing a white turtle-necked sweater and a pair of green slacks. His eyes sparkled a deep pansy color. He was redolent of sobriety.

"Who gave lectures?" he asked, nodding to Stephen. "How's your mother?"

"Very well," Stephen answered stiffly, stemming his anger at the obviousness of the tactics. "We were talking about Ivan Simpson."

The focus of Fabien's attention had shifted entirely to Duncan. "I called your lady friend. She has consented to come."

"Did you have a long talk with her?"

"Not terribly, but she sounded exactly as you described her. Souls, art, and coquettishness."

"Who's this?" Stephen asked.

"Someone Duncan knows," Fabien answered, not shifting his gaze. He reached up and put an arm round Duncan's neck, pulling him down so that they both sat asprawl in the one chair. "You miserable Scotsman, don't be so lugubrious. There'll be someone here for her."

"Perhaps I shouldn't have invited her," Duncan said uncertainly.

"You didn't, I did. I told her it was a surprise party for you. The idea appealed to her immensely."

"A surprise party for Duncan?" Stephen asked. "Saturday's party?"

But Fabien was speaking again. "Don't forget to look agreeably astonished when she walks in. You're not supposed to know she's coming."

Duncan was beginning to smile. "My expression will be that of a nun who has accidentally wandered into a gentlemen's lavatory. By the way, did she—?"

They looked gravely at each other, and Fabien nodded. "She did."

"Ah."

"She made a special point of asking if she could."

"Then I guess we can look forward to a few selections."

"Oh, God," Fabien said with a groan, and they both exploded into a fit of helpless laughter, clinging to each other and shaking until the tears ran down their faces.

"She plays the violin, Stephen," Fabien gasped in explanation. Stephen attempted to smile in understanding sympathy.

But the tormenting sickness was more than he could bear, and the smile congealed before it reached his lips. This easy, intimate merriment should have been his. He knew he must get away before he said something for which he would be sorry. He rose to his feet and murmured something about a lecture, but to intrude upon such mirth was an impossibility. Duncan, sobbing with hilarity, paid no attention. Fabien merely waved a hand in perfunctory farewell.

"I'll see about inviting those other people." Stephen left the room, while the laughter continued behind him in a series of anguished chokes.

It was cold outside. The weather was gray and the snow had the grimy look that comes with a partial thaw. Stephen walked as far as Sherbrooke Street and boarded the little bus that would carry him to the Roddick Gate, sitting in his seat with his overcoat wrapped tightly around him and his ankles pressed together. His analytical ability had reasserted itself by the time he reached the campus.

But there was no ease for him in realizing that for the first time in his life he was consumed with jealousy. The ache in his breast was threatening to burst his heart. He stood quite still and wondered what he should do, and the tears came into his eyes. He felt an urge to stamp his feet. Instead he stood and quietly cursed to himself.

Then he looked up and smiled at the overcast sky.

It was possible that Duncan had unconsciously tipped his hand this morning, with the green slacks, the loose-jointed comportment. It could be that the decisive counteraction lay somewhere in that direction. There was someone else who moved almost exactly like him.

Fabien could not possibly face that.

Matt Lambert was wending his preoccupied way toward the Redpath Library.

Stephen placed his fingers in his mouth and gave a piercing whistle, a trick acquired through assiduous practice in his army days.

Matt turned and waved and came undulating across the campus with knees together and ankles delicately awash. "Hello," he said. "What a thoroughly coarse greeting."

They sauntered down past the Three Bares, a group of statuary that had represented three nude youths before a moral hammer transformed them, by rude operation, into hermaphrodites. At this time of the morning, with no one around, the statues looked more than ever lonely and wistful. And they looked cold.

"What are you doing Saturday night?"

Matt pressed interlocked hands on his chest and opened wide his eyes. "A proposition, Stephen?" he asked, assuming a high, simpering voice. "I shall do what I usually do on Saturday nights. And all the week end, for that matter."

Stephen forced himself to grin. "Want to come to a party?"

Matt laid a mock-earnest hand on his arm. "Stevie, you're one of my sincerest friends. But not my type."

"There'll be others there besides me," Stephen said. "Want to come?"

"Oh, *that* sort of party! But *what* sort of that sort of party?"

"Conversation, poetry, music, smoked salmon, Saumur Rosé."

"Good God! Do you know about Saumur Rosé?"

"That's ordinaire. Do you know about Trockenbeeren Auslese?"

"No," breathed Matt, elongating the vowel and looking admiringly at Stephen. "I'd love to come to your party."

"Good."

"Oh, but what about Bobbie? We seldom go out at the weekend and never without each other."

"I was hoping you'd bring him, too."

Matt stopped walking and leaned close. "You're not up to anything, are you Hollis? You understand that I want neither good nor bad done to me?"

Stephen rid himself of the hand with an angry shake. "Go to hell, Lambert. I'm inviting you to a party. If you don't want to come, say so."

"That's what I like," Matt cried approvingly, "the hearty masculine rejoinder. It's simply that you have a faint air of mission about you. I'll be delighted to come to your party."

"And Bobbie?"

"Don't worry, he'll come if I do. Dress or tux?"

"Neither."

"Good, we have neither. But how delicious to think we might have worn them."

"You'll be more than amply compensated," Stephen said. "There'll be poets and musicians and writers with red hair. It'll be better than Christmas."

"It sounds marvelous. Where, and at what time?"

"The invitation will be at your frat house first thing in the morning."

"Invitation? Whoops! Lovelier and lovelier. Wild horses couldn't keep me away."

He showed tendencies to linger, but Stephen was anxious to get away now that his purpose was accomplished. There were certain inferences to be drawn from being seen in the company of Matt Lambert. Stephen watched the elegant figure retrace its steps to the Redpath Library.

"There's one on every campus," remarked a meek voice at his elbow. Harrigan had evidently found a new pill. His face, though still pimply, was noticeably clearer.

"There's more than one on this campus," Stephen said, staring ahead. "Considerably more." He turned and took a direct look at Harrigan. "Hey," he said, as if noticing for the first time. "Your acne is almost gone. What have you been doing with it?"

Harrigan blushed deep crimson with pleasure. "Nothing. It just went away."

In an onset of warm fellowship, Stephen put an arm around the thin shoulders. "What say we go over to the Union for a coffee?"

Harrigan looked at him unbelievingly.

He'll be speechless with gratitude, Stephen thought, when I invite him to the party. And I intend to. He reflected upon the joy that was attainable through making others happy, and once again he wished, though only fleetingly, that it was possible to give parties in his own home.

Harrigan toddled along beside him. It was warm and cozy inside the Union; one of those rare days when the coffee is good.

III

A perfectly beautiful young man opened the door. He bowed, kissed her hand and ushered her into a large paneled hall, murmuring in her ear the most exquisite formalities of welcome.

She was sunk.

Smart, poised young people swirled about her, chattering over cocktail glasses at each other with a fantastic sophistication. From another room a tinkling piano was playing a thin, gay tune whose strains were punctuated by bursts of polished laughter. Beyond sliding doors at her left, a gay group picked like delicate starlings at a buffet that entirely covered a long dining table. A solid mahogany dining table, she noticed.

Miriam clutched her third-best fur coat tightly around her and wished miserably that the floor would open and swallow her up. She should have taken warning from that invitation. Instead of something interesting and a little tatty—a tiny, hand-painted figure in orange and green bidding her from limp and thumb-printed paper to come out and play—the opened envelope had disclosed an unexpected card, thick and creamy and heavily embossed with expensive lettering. What a fool to explain to herself that they had friends in the printing trade! More foolish yet—why had she not heeded the foreboding as she turned her car into the driveway? Since when were rooming houses so ablaze with light, even in Westmount where allegedly they did not exist?

"Good evening," she said in a feeble, unhappy whisper.

Two girls passed by on their way to the buffet, clad in simple gowns that Miriam could high-price at a glance. They called something in a foreign tongue to the beautiful young man, and Miriam felt their eyes skim over her from head to foot in languid enquiry. Underneath the third-best coat every sequin of her dress burned into her flesh like a red-hot iron.

"Fellow countrywomen of mine," explained the young man. "May I take your coat?"

"Well, I—I—"

"Forgive me, I did not introduce myself." He bent over her hand again, and she could see the thick blond hair curling crisply over his head. "I'm Fabien."

"Yes," she murmured weakly. "Yes, I spoke to you on the phone, didn't I?"

A burst of laughter near at hand made her look around fearfully, and for the first time she saw the thick, black stair-carpet. "What a nice place you have here," she said abjectly. "Very nice."

How was it that Duncan had wept at the comparative poverty of her own miserable villa? He had been laughing at her all the time. Tonight's party was to be his humiliating revenge upon her for that ten-dollar bill.

"You're as charming as Duncan said you were." Fabien squeezed her hand lightly without offering to release it. "And lo, here he comes."

She had seen him already, immaculately clad in tails, threading his way through the crowd toward her with his eyes wide in surprise. She felt a wild impulse to turn and run, but then he was standing before her, saying nothing, smiling a quiet, warm smile of welcome.

"Let me introduce your guest of honor," Fabien said to Duncan. "Secured with great difficulty and worth every bit of it."

"Hello Miriam." He extended a hand only to drop it on seeing that her free hand was carrying a violin. "What a beautiful surprise. And how nice of you to remember that I wanted to hear you play." The voice and the words were soft, the expression tender. Everything indicated that he was meaning what he said. Miriam felt a little less ill at ease.

But oh! the weight of that costume jewelry as a woman walks past wearing a glittering pair of pendant diamond earrings. They were smaller than either of the pairs that nestled in the jewelry box back in Miriam's bedroom. Costume jewelry and a sequin-studded dress! God!

if someone should mistake her for a professional entertainer hired for the evening! There was no denying that the dress, theatrically undated though it might be, was infinitely too tight. She should never have settled for merely girding up her corset. With great difficulty she drew a deep, shuddering breath.

"May I take this?" Duncan asked. "I'll put it on the piano." She released the violin as if suddenly it had become red-hot.

"I hope you'll allow me the pleasure of playing your accompaniments later on," Fabien said.

"Unhand that woman. I wish to introduce my guest of honor to the other guests."

"Go play that violin," retorted Fabien. "I who did the work shall receive the just reward."

They both began laughing, and Miriam was frightened again. She was at their mercy. Her panicky eyes skittered from one to the other with an imploring look.

And then she almost cried with relief, for she saw the mutual invitation on their faces. Behind the mirth was a sort of humility, a kindness, a plea that she be kind in return. She who had known unkind enemies sensed at once that these were friends. And suddenly there were the three of them, companions, standing in the hall and sharing an intimate pleasantry unknown to the other guests. And to hell with the other guests, anyway, so long as the hosts liked her.

And it was done. The wave carried her through. Duncan had the third-best fur coat draped over his arm, and she was standing with her cream-colored sequin dress making a vivid patch among the sartorial quietness of her surroundings.

With one hypersensitive glance she encompassed their matching expressions. The last hurdle. Something caught in her throat. Sweet, sweet, lovely young boys. In a deluge of unselfish emotion she offered up a prayer for the endurance of this household and the continuation of their friendship.

Fabien took her elbow and steered her gently, shimmering, toward a large wall mirror. "*Regarde,*" he said.

There was no need. She ignored her own reflection, her eyes riveted to his mirrored gaze. Her answer was there, as it had been when she removed her coat. What cause to scrutinize herself.

Fabien and Duncan, her hosts, persons of impeccable taste, had told her unequivocally what she wanted to know, what she had felt all the time and was foolish ever to have doubted. Their eyes had spoken, telling her she was a poised, exciting woman of sophisticated and mature beauty. Fabien had not looked at the foreign girls as he was looking now at her.

He said: "My dear, you're stunning."

Yes, the dress had been an inspiration, compared with which the others were drab. Without releasing his gaze she fumbled in her handbag and withdrew a long amber holder and a cigarette. "A light please," she commanded, smiling a little mysteriously as she put the holder between her gleaming teeth. "Then you may introduce me to the guests."

"A good idea." Fabien flicked the flame from a golden lighter. "While they can still recognize each other."

She took his arm gracefully, suavely, and moved with him toward the sitting room, proud in her appearance and happy in her pride. The heads that lifted, the eyes that followed, she met them with a happy smile. She moved with undulant precision, languorous eyed.

The first two young men inside the door received her with a flattering eagerness that made her miss their names in the murmured introductions. They stared at her unashamedly from head to foot.

"By Jesus!" one of them said. "In the flesh! A Rubens!"

Reubens. The Miriam inside stiffened horribly. Not that! Not now, tonight, on the threshold.

"Foo!" said the other immediately. "If ever I saw one, a Botticelli."

Pierre's boring monologues. Canvases. Painters. She removed the cigarette holder and gave a long, smoke-filled, ineffably gratified smile. "How utterly sweet of you to say so. Are you artists?"

"They are," Fabien broke in. "We shall move along before they ask you to pose for them." Everyone laughed. For Miriam it was an elixir.

Realization. Art. Bliss of purest ray serene. Others were looking toward her now, awaiting her coming, legions of beautiful and interesting young men who wanted to meet her, who eventually would seek her. She tightened her grip on the arm that led her and looked up into Fabien's eyes. But none more beautiful than he, none more interesting. He smiled down at her and she felt the waves of mutual understanding vibrate between them. No, none better than Fabien. He was her type, her class.

This was exactly her sort of household.

"Who's the old bag with the junk jewelry?" Stephen asked without needing an answer. "She looks like the result of a mating between Kundry and the Dragon of Wantley."

"Her name is Miriam Sabel," Duncan answered coldly.

"A Jewess?"

"I didn't check."

"There's no way is there, except with the men? Is she the one you were laughing about, who plays the violin?" He saw Duncan's nervous start and laughed tolerantly, loathing himself for his tactics yet unable to do otherwise. "Don't worry, I shan't tell her. I'd hate to spoil the friendship between her and Fabien."

The thrust did not go home. Duncan said indifferently, "Have all your friends arrived yet? I've lost count."

"Two more to come. They've probably left it late in order to make an entrance. I think you'll like them."

"I hope so. I shall try." To watch the emotions flit across Duncan's face was like fanning open a hand of cards. In a flash he had gone from the aces to the twos. His voice was earnest with the sincerity that comes of timorousness. Stephen saw that Duncan was making a special attempt to be nice to him.

"Crystal arrived yet?"

"No," Duncan said. "She told Fabien yesterday that she might be a little late."

"Did he see her?"

"I think so. I'm not sure. Perhaps she phoned."

"I see." Stephen looked around for a drink. "Duncan, why are you always so cautious with me?"

Duncan hesitated. "I don't know. I think you don't like me. I feel that you're always trying to get something on me."

"What a ridiculous notion!" The heartiness of Stephen's laugh surprised himself. "Let's go to the kitchen and get a drink. I want to hear all about that book you're writing."

Duncan shied like a nervous horse under the arm that was put around his shoulders. "I don't like to be touched," he explained apologetically, and drew away. Stephen could have struck him, the more so because suddenly he felt like his brother Richard.

"What about a drink?" he asked.

"Bill's mixing them. They're not very good. Fabien is going to fix a batch of specials every so often."

"You haven't had anything yet, have you?"

"No, I want to be sober tonight."

"Stay right there," Stephen said reassuringly. "I'll fix something really special and bring it to you. After all the party is in your honor, and we have to do something to celebrate that evening dress you're wearing. Don't go away, now."

He made his way to the kitchen, nodding and smiling at everyone he passed, overt admiration for the women and quizzical understanding for the men. It didn't matter for the present that he knew only half of them.

Harrigan was standing at the buffet, cramming ripe olives into his mouth and dropping the stones into a nearby ash tray. "Have something to eat," he urged, looking happily into Stephen's face. "Some party, huh?"

"It's barely begun. Away to hell and enjoy yourself." Stephen pushed the swing door and entered the kitchen where Bill, with flushed face and glazing eye, gaily rattled a cocktail shaker to the encouraging cries of some of the more impatient guests.

"There is positively no one after Bach. All the rest ..."

"Ach, come on. Crepuscularity doesn't suit you at all. If you'll just listen to the sustained C Major after the murder in Wozzeck you'll know what ..."

"I feel more than a little rocky."

"Je me pris à songer près de ce corps vendu ..."

"And now he feels obliged to go through another Blue Period ..."

"Who, *who* is mixing these drinks? He deserves the *Croix de guerre*."

"Qu'on lui ferme la porte au nez, it reviendra par les fenêtres."

Miriam took the plunge. "In a tossup," she said, "I'll take Picasso every time." The second syllable rang magnificently through her brain, and she flung back her head and laughed for no other reason than that she was deliriously happy.

This—was *It*.

From all around her the conversation came clinking like a familiar but forgotten melody played on Chinese wind-bells. A flush of arrival tingled to the very soles of her feet, and it was only her dress that prevented her from breaking into a jubilant bacchante jig. No one would mind it. No one would mind anything she did. They liked her; admired her. She had been embraced into their confidence. As Fabien introduced her to group after group they saluted her warmly, continuing with their vibrant talk and inviting her by look and demeanor to join their conversations. They paid her the supreme compliment of solicitation. And why? Because they *knew*.

Eyes flickered over her from head to toe and back, admiringly, to her face. They knew, and they wanted. They perceived the true Miriam. For the first time in her life she experienced the rapture of being desired by the desirable.

What variety was in this house, what a supreme audience! Here, with no footlights intervening, the stalls, the pit, the gallery, and dress circle were welded into one. No longer was there a need to localize the performance, to pitch the selected tune to that part of the house where it was most suited. For here, through choice, there was a unity of feeling, a oneness like that which pervaded a ballet audience no matter where they sat. Yes, here, in a word, Art was hovering, and who would dare say which person would be its epitome when the evening had drawn to an end.

The babble of talk was swelling. No one appeared to be drinking much, but everyone had got much drunker in the past ten minutes. Hands were flashing, foreign voices could be heard, the groups became less of groups and more a single party as people standing back to back turned and harangued each other cheerfully, encouraged by yet more who called from the other sides of the room. Only a few remained above and beyond and they were those who drank most: a group of cropped young men drinking in a corner—could it be beer?—and discussing esoteric things in low voices; a girl with an Eton crop, leaning trancelike against the piano and rattling her teeth with a stubby, black cigarette holder; a pimply-faced youth sitting on the end of the sofa, watching with excited eagerness everything that went on.

Miriam winced slightly and turned away. Without the pimples he would resemble a great many young men she had known intimately. She hastily generalized her attention again and allowed the conversation to lap gratefully about her.

"Even Hemingway cried at Velásquez ..."

"But only Alyosha Karamazov was honest ..."

"Toute réaction est vraie ..."

"Do you seriously suggest that Art's potency is dependent upon the continuation of human suffering? Cojones ..."

"It is a peculiarity of cardinals that they are invariable ..."

"Except for the one and the hundred ..."

"Eventually they will be forced to admit that Sibelius' *Tapiola* has blown up the cozy Catholic Hell and substituted something really horrific ..."

"But Kierkegaard is so sexless when you come down to it ..."

"Who did you say was mixing these drinks?"

Each captured phrase plucked a string of memory and in the continuation she heard at last a melody where before had been but a few faltering bars. The young men had been useful after all. Instead of the makeshifts she in her darkest hours suspected, she saw them now as stages in her cultural evolution, necessary steppingstones in the stream she had needed to cross to reach this other bank. In her restored pride, she felt a deep gratitude. Bless them all. Though they had but one word to spread, may they forever spread the Word.

Secure upon her bank, the Left Bank, with the message being spelt out all around her, she turned adoringly to Fabien.

"I love your friends. They have so much artistic—verve!"

The soft eyes kindled. "My dear, I don't know them all. Many of them belong to Duncan."

"He looks awfully nice in his evening dress, doesn't he?"

"Perhaps a mite out of place."

Miriam examined the remark for traces of bitchery. There were none. "He's entitled to be the only one," she protested warmly. "It's his party."

Fabien nodded approval. "An agreeable point of view. And now, my angel, do you mind if we forgo the rest of the introductions. I begin to feel like the wife of an American ambassador." His tone indicated that they were already friends of long standing. Miriam's heart glowed.

Together they stood by the piano, reaching behind the unmoving Eton-crop girl for a glass of champagne. The violin, unsheathed from its case, lay within easy reach, but Miriam knew that the moment had not yet arrived. Sipping at the drink she pondered whether she dare pursue the line of enquiry which would allow her to repay in understanding what she had received so amply in friendship. Her self-question received an affirmative answer. Indeed yes, for to withhold from friends was to make a denial of their friendship. She turned, poised, judicious, and interested.

"Are you Duncan's patron?"

"I beg your pardon?"

Fabien's head jerked up from his glass, displaying a face of completely unreadable expression. Miriam staggered and sank under a veritable hammer-blow of fear.

What had she done? Had she been Canadian—bourgeois—Jewish? Had she ruined everything? Is that what his eyes meant? She faltered.

"I mean—I was at the store the other day, where the shirts are. They told me Duncan had left. They said he said he wasn't going to work anymore. He was going to write a book. I wondered if—"

"A perfectly natural question," Fabien said amiably. "I'm glad you asked it. Have some more champagne."

Tears of gratitude stood in her eyes as she accepted the fresh glass. She had almost betrayed her own cause, and he had saved her. Of course he understood! She should never have doubted, even for a moment. This was a different world, new as the untasted drink in her hand. It would be criminal to judge him on past standards, to regard him as another of the young men she had taken for nocturnal rides. She cast the unpleasant memories from her, limp with shame. There were to be no more doubts. This household, these enchanting people were to be accepted by her as freely and honestly as they themselves had accepted her.

She said softly, "Would you lean closer a minute?"

Chastely she kissed Fabien on his soft, brown cheek.

"Miriam, my dear, I believe you're crying. Is there anything I can do?"

"No, no, no." She laid down her glass and faced him directly, gripping his arms fervently in her two hands. "Oh Fabien," she breathed, "there is nothing you need to do. Nothing at all. I'm having a lovely, lovely time."

Bill knew they were telling lies when they insisted his drinks were good. He understood perfectly. This was a night for lying. Let them lose themselves in these ridiculous conversations, shelve their problems, pretend that what was did not really exist.

He filled several glasses with rye whisky, rescued one from the swooping hands, and leaned with his back against the wall.

At a party the people with problems always congregated in the kitchen. They came through that swing door under a thousand fabricated pretenses, to hide from the other, untroubled guests whose eyes might seek them out and lay them bare. They came for sanctuary, and once here, safe from scrutiny, they established a sanctified aristocracy of the troubled. The sensitivity that made them flee could be put now to the general benefit. They pretended for each other even more strongly than for themselves. Bless them.

Only occasionally did they move, to get a drink or allow passage for a transient drink-getter from the outside. The remainder of the time they looked earnestly at each other's faces, laughing, encouraging, admiring. Above all, believing.

Bill studied the faces, relating expressions to the problems they were hiding. It's a hobby of sorts, he thought. Some he was forced to conjecture, others he knew personally, for they belonged to people he had invited at Fabien's request to swell the throng.

Mick was telling Phil Anglo-French jokes. One might wonder why Phil was so careful always to retain the same glass. If one didn't know, one would never guess the lousy luck he had had four weeks ago with the tart on St. Lawrence Main. And Mick, of course, could tell his Anglo-French jokes without a qualm. He had recently married a French Canadian in Notre Dame Cathedral. It necessitated breaking with his violently anti-French family and, naturally, he had to give up his theological studies at McGill, but hear the gusto with which he described his new job in the advertising agency. His wife, who was pretty, was proud of him. She stayed out of the kitchen, and that proved she also understood him.

Was Daphne, the girl with the martini, really expecting a baby? Did it matter when every student in the kitchen was certain to pass the May exams? Listen to them! Their professors, in not so many words, had assured them of it.

The girl with the fair hair was not badly cross-eyed, but her brown eyes made it conspicuous. She was gazing at the ceiling and talking brilliantly. Her companion had his hand on the nape of her neck. He was a stranger.

And in the war, Bill thought, all those men were killed. The halt of spirit, the lame of heart, the troubled of mind, the problem children. Few who survived were afflicted, for they had gone back immediately to swell the suety ranks where Chester Arden was major general and the absent were absent because they had paid what the general referred to as the supreme sacrifice.

Chester Arden was a liar. They had died because of their problems. The world and its circumstances persuaded them to regard their problems as sins against uniformity, and they had permitted an avenging force to take their lives as expiation. Bill had seen the telltale looks they wore on the night before it happened.

They had known, and in their secret hearts they thought it only right.

Goodness how sad, when they could have stayed somewhere in a kitchen and pretended their difficulties out of existence. Or was it the statesmen who should have stayed in kitchens? Did a politician, for that matter, regard his crippled tongue as a problem?

"Everyone have a drink," Bill shouted. They clustered about him, interjecting requests without releasing their conversations. He was pleased at the dexterity with which he wielded the bottles and glasses. Nothing was too good for these people.

Stephen was standing beside him. "Where's the peach brandy?" he asked. "I want to make another 'kiss the trolley wires.'"

"You're going to get drunk." Bill indicated with a pointing finger. "That's the third of those things you've had." He came closer and peered intently into Stephen's face. "No, you haven't had anything at all," he accused.

Stephen remained silent, deftly adding a dash of Cointreau.

"Who's it for?"

"Where's the rum?" Stephen asked, scanning the array of bottles.

"Who's it for?"

"Are you keeping count?"

"It's for Duncan. It's for Duncan, isn't it?"

"Now don't do anything dramatic," Stephen adjured, "like knocking the glass out of my hand. I'm simply helping him have a good time."

Bill was regarding him fixedly. "What a bastard you are, Hollis. What a dirty rotten bastard. Why don't you leave him alone?"

"This," said Stephen, "is something special for a friend."

"Yes, I know." Bill's voice all at once became gentle. "Stay in the kitchen, Steve," he said. "You'll enjoy it here."

Stephen looked around him and pulled a face. "Everyone's too drunk. I'll send Duncan."

"Leave him alone." Stephen's wrist was seized in a fierce grip, and he knew that Bill was trying to hurt him. "You stick your nose into anything, don't you, Hollis. Is it something you learned in the war behind that desk?"

"That's enough." Stephen disengaged his wrist. He felt no animosity toward Bill and they had spoken in low, dispassionate voices, but heads were turning their way and he wanted to get out. "Forget it, Bill," he said.

"Forget it? Just don't you forget that a lot of men were killed in that war."

"You mean that Duncan was?"

"I don't know what I mean," Bill said hoarsely. "For Christ's sake, muck off."

When Stephen had picked up the drink and departed, Bill turned and smilingly addressed the kitchen at large. "A damn good head, that," he said. "We fight all the time. Anyone want more drink?"

Some did, some didn't. All of them smiled back.

The girl with the Eton crop snapped out of her trance, looked briefly hopeful, and drifted away to a new position, a disappointed look on her face.

"Sorry I'm late," Crystal said. "That damned hospital."

Fabien was still shaking her hand. "All your friends arrived safely, I think."

"Thanks for letting me ask them."

Miriam saw an imminent danger of being entirely cut out of the conversation. "Crystal," she said. "What a pretty name."

"It was in remembrance of one of my parents' wedding presents," Crystal told her. "A chandelier."

They exchanged a sweet smile.

"Excuse me a moment." Fabien made his way to a figure dramatically posed in the sitting room doorway, and they were left alone.

Ivan Simpson, after much deliberation, had decided to arrive in his tattered old naval raincoat and with shoelaces of string. His long hair hung over his eyes, and the bare hand that clasped the manuscript was blue with cold. Gratified at the attention he was drawing, but nevertheless in dire need of a drink, he held forth his other hand and made known his needs.

"That's Ivan Simpson," Miriam explained with a trace of smugness. "Author of 'The Golden Ringpiece.'"

"I know," Crystal said. "I read it yesterday. Didn't understand a word."

"Don't you think, though, that he's a lot like Dylan Thomas?"

"I've never read Dylan Thomas. I only looked at Simpson because I knew he'd be here tonight."

"'The snow dilates my heart with crystalline contusion,'" Miriam suggested with happy relish. "'And lacteous bottles, swollen, die at dawn.'"

The hard-learned lines were brushed away with a gesture. "I understood that least of all," Crystal said.

There was a pause during which the two women regarded each other curiously.

A faint mist of cigarette smoke hung over the entire lower story of the house. One could see it curling around the high-hung lights in the hall.

"Have you seen Duncan?" Fabien asked. The question was devoid of guile.

"The last I saw of him," Stephen answered, "he was wandering around in a blank-eyed condition with a particularly venomous drink clutched in his hand."

"Was he all right?"

"Oh, sure. Showing his teeth."

"I must find him. Ivan Simpson begins soon, and no one should miss that."

"You're going to have trouble getting Bill out of the kitchen. He's stinking."

"Dear Bill," Fabien said, smiling fondly. "Are you having a good time, Stephen?"

"Fine. Never met so many interesting people. Who's the woman with the earrings and the dress?"

"Miriam Sabel. Extremely nice, and utterly defenceless."

"Is she? She plays the violin, doesn't she?"

They laughed together, and Stephen glimpsed the time when they would have references and counter-references, a private language to afford them endless pleasure.

"Do me a favor," Fabien begged.

"Anything, gladly."

"Spread the word that she's a satirist. It will help her get away with murder."

"Why all the trouble?"

"Oh—she's defenceless, and nice. Foolish, but nice."

Stephen nodded a reassurance.

"Then I'll resume my search for the wandering boy."

He moved away, to Stephen's great relief, for from the corner of his eye he had seen someone open the front door and admit Matt and Bobbie. He did not intend that Fabien should see them till later, and before that time the two arrivals must be apprised of the most interesting people to meet.

"Hello," he said, going toward them.

Under the cover of general chatter Crystal studied Miriam covertly, marveling that the first competition she had ever received should be from a woman almost twice her age. The average Canadian woman, convinced that the requisite organ is a sufficiency of itself, does not compete for her men with quite the fierceness of her foreign sisters. This general fact, combined with Crystal's unique man-to-man technique, had until now always left her a clear field, and she herself had scorned competition on the grounds that the fish in the sea were more silvery by half than those that came out of it. But no such elegant fish had ever before swum so near her shores. She was determined to land him should it mean open combat with every other female in the city and a public spreading of her nets.

Damn, she thought irritably. I think I'm in love.

Talking pointedly of nothing, her busy brain was drawing on past experiences in order to visualize the situations in which she might find herself with Fabien. Nothing seemed adequate. Here was no groping Albertan adolescent, neither could she imagine him stumbling around kitchens as had poor Stephen (and how weird he had been). Fabien would spot the old man-to-man business in a flash. Tonight she must bring out as much as was devised of her new method, establish that Fabien was the man and she, unquestionably, the woman.

In a momentary flight of panic she wondered if it could be done. The anachronism of being virtuous made competition infinitely more difficult. What sacrifices were demanded in the sacred name of things learned at a mother's knee!

She searched Miriam's face again, wondering afresh that this overdone creature could attract anyone like Fabien, or anyone else for that matter. There must be a gimmick to it, a device, some peculiarly subtle trick of feminine allurement. Well, whatever she can do, Crystal told herself, I can. She settled down to watch.

"Fabien is very young, isn't he," Miriam said softly.

"I wouldn't say so. At least, he doesn't seem so young as the kids I meet on the campus." She thought: So that's how I'm trying to square it with myself. Interesting.

"Have you known the boys long?" Miriam asked politely.

"Oh, ages."

"I suppose you know about Duncan, then. Fabien was telling me just this evening. Isn't it strange. I never dreamt."

"Duncan?" Crystal said. "So far my studies have only touched on abnormal psychology."

Miriam nodded. She had no idea what the remark meant and thought Crystal a bitch for making it. But all was fair in love and war, and even though Crystal had turned out to be a form of the anticipated tigress, Miriam rather liked her. There was a directness about her that let you know where you stood. And she was probably only one of Fabien's many lovers.

Miriam diverted the channel. "It's wonderful to see two boys get on like Duncan and Fabien. Rather like old literature."

"Or the Bible," Crystal said. "Only there are three of them, didn't you know? That's the third member over there."

Stephen had intercepted her glance and was coming over. Matt and Bobbie, safely ensconced in a corner, were sipping their first drinks and looking forward eagerly to the interesting persons they were going to meet. The girl with the Eton crop was edging around the wall toward them, her stocky cigarette holder clenched tightly in her teeth. They looked at her, and Bobbie whispered something to Matt. They began to giggle.

"What lovely hair you have," Crystal said to Miriam. "How do you keep it like that?"

Miriam was thinking how handsome and determined-looking this new one was. Everybody smiled at everyone else.

"Angel child, what are you doing?" Fabien shouted above the hiss of the water. "God, no, not a *cold* shower!"

"I felt grubby." Duncan emerged from behind the curtain and began drying himself on a rough towel. "How goes it with Miriam?"

"She really is a pet, poor darling. There will be someone for her before the night ends."

"I hope someone permanent. Did you say she's a satirist?"

"They're expecting her to break into impersonations at any moment."

Duncan said: "It was good of you to let her come."

"My dear, will you stop making it sound like a bright deed in a dark world. It was a very little thing for you to ask, and I'm perfectly willing to indulge your lame-dog complex to any limit short of assisting lame dogs. I loathe dogs. Now cats—"

"Crystal here yet?"

"Looking perfectly beautiful and just a mite predatory. Not so Ivan Simpson, who also has arrived looking like the incarnation of modern poetry. You'd better hurry or he'll not be reading tonight. I judge from the speed with which he is getting drunk that he has not eaten for a week. I wonder if he'll let me feed him."

"Fabien, I love you," Duncan said. "Tonight I love everyone—but you especially." He regarded his naked image in the full-length mirror on the door, leaning back and running his hands down his smooth sides.

"See how clean I am. I shall write tonight if I stay as clean as this and can remember. I shall write a great deal."

They had simply carried her off.

"Look!" someone whispered. "Ninon de Lenclos."

Miriam stood in the center of a large group, bathing in a warm stream of scintillant epigram and mystic reference. The dear young men, the sweet young men! Of what consequence if the other girl enjoyed a temporary victory tonight with Fabien? Miriam was now a part of this enchanted household, and that, tonight, was all that mattered. And if she failed with Fabien, failed completely, there were the other two key-holders, Duncan and—whatsisname—Stephen. Stephen, who at this moment was watching her interestedly from the fringe of the crowd.

Between them lay gloriously the others: the two artists, the doctor, the famous poet, who looked at her so curiously, the student-one who kept saying "*Weldschmertz*," the slim, dark foreign boy who looked like Valentino; myriad young men with smiles and glossy hair, with eyes turned towards her, awaiting her words, applauding her wit.

They laughed uproariously at most everything she said, sometimes unaccountably. On this enchanted evening she did not pause to question. There was magic in the air.

Miriam's color mounted. Her eyes glowed, beacons of joy.

The two foreign young ladies were conversing in their own laconic native tongue. "The Duncan has changed his clothes," remarked one. "Ravishing, isn't he! Clean. Fresh. That red hair gives me quite a frisson."

"Obviously just taken a bath," commented the other, who worked in a consulate.

Her friend lifted enquiring eyebrows. "Perhaps more approachable than the unapproachable Fabien?" she ventured. "Oh, but the countless times I've tried with him."

"Too late," said the second young lady. "Those *Ones* in the corner are beckoning to him. The Duncan is going over." She gave a shrug, characteristic of her nation. "This is becoming like the capital city at home. There are hordes of them there. And now I come to Canada because I am assured the men have hairy chests, and they are here also. Sad for me."

The friend looked anxious. "Is Fabien from the capital?"

"Not from what I have heard," the second young lady said with quiet relish. "No, the estates of his parents are in the southern provinces. When they drive to Mass on Sunday, the peasants wave their babies at the passing carriage. And there is the trouble. We are peasants, you and I. That is all. Nothing more."

"I would happily wave a baby for him."

"He doesn't see you. Tonight he sees no one except the Canadian peasant who pursues him everywhere with her eyes."

"Oh, and perhaps the old woman in *that* dress."

"It is possible he wishes to make bizarre love to her in order to feel the scars behind her ears."

They exchanged a tiny smile.

"In my province," said the first young lady, "they say that the cheese most aromatic baits the trap most big."

They smiled again and looked across at Crystal, then they both shrugged characteristically. In a little while they edged simultaneously to where the cropped young men were still drinking beer in the corner.

"Who are the two gentlemen with all the *joie de vivre?*" Fabien asked.

"Friends of yours, aren't they Stephen?" Crystal said, eying him curiously.

Under her glance he became halting and apologetic. "I'm sorry. I had no idea they would behave like that, or I wouldn't have asked them."

"Oh, come," Fabien said with a tolerant smile. "It takes all kinds to make a world."

"Caught you," Stephen cried. "And history repeats itself."

"Because a bird in the hand's worth two in the bush," Crystal said.

"And birds of a feather flock together," Stephen ended.

The improvised maneuver was successful. Fabien's eyes flicked over to where Duncan's head bobbed animatedly between Matt Lambert and his friend. At that moment Bobbie emitted a screech of mirth and made a limp-wristed gesture under Duncan's nose. Duncan laughed, and the three heads drew closer.

"They're only acquaintances of mine," Stephen said. "I didn't know. They make me almost approve of Edward II's murder."

"Don't be vile," Fabien muttered.

"They're not so singular from a medical point of view," Crystal said. "Dr. Kinsey claims that two out of every five American men either have been or are."

"What?" asked Stephen.

"Fags."

"Fruits?"

"Flits, fairies, *tapettes*, *galbarnati*, men out of Utrecht, and those who walk with the fishermen," Fabien said impatiently. "Choose your geographical location."

"I suppose the two out of five is universal," Stephen surmised. "Africa, Europe, England, Scotland—"

"Lord," Crystal said. "Look at them wave those imaginary fans. They'll go straight up through the roof in a minute."

"I hope they don't take Duncan with them."

"Can't we drop the subject?" Fabien snapped. "I find it unpleasant."

"I'll tell them to leave."

"No!" The word cracked out like a pistol shot, causing several nearby people to turn their heads.

"Just tell them not to be so voluptuously queer," Crystal suggested.

"I'm sorry, I'm sorry," Stephen said. "The last thing I wish is to have this house contaminated. Believe me."

"I told you it didn't matter." Fabien's lips were a thin line and his eyes blazed briefly. "If you'll excuse me I'll get Ivan Simpson to read his poems before he keels over." With a little nod he moved to the other side of the room.

"You've upset him," Crystal said. "What's the game, and why?"

"He's just a child. He needs protection against his own generous nature."

A switch was tripped in Crystal's brain, and she bit back the remark that had formed on her tongue. Her eyes flickered about the room, and when they came back to Stephen they sparkled with an artfulness he failed to notice.

"I think you're right," she agreed. "There are plenty here tonight to protect him from."

Like a shepherd with a sheep, she led his assenting glance to Miriam.

"A bas les tantes" growled the thick-set French Canadian with bristly hair.

His supple friend contradicted him. "Vive le sport!"

The thick-set gentleman sighed deeply. "Aaah," he said, "que faites-tu de to jeunesse. Que faites-tu...."

The girl with the Eton crop was explaining her philosophy of life to the two foreign young ladies. Her voice was deep, vibrant, and desperate, for she couldn't tell whether they were interested or not.

But, she thought, if they shrug like that just once more I'll crack their thick, stupid heads together.

Everyone looked up from his or her drink.

Ivan Simpson walked uncertainly to the center of the floor, clutching his manuscript tightly in one hand and waving the other to clear away the surrounding crowd. They moved back dutifully to the walls, nursing their drinks and seeking seats, the unlucky ones squatting on the floor and crossing their trousered legs or tastefully arranging the flare of their skirts. Miriam was standing by the piano between the two painters, who were now discussing Edward Burra. Mentally she practiced rolling the double "r." Booorrrah! Eminently satisfactory!

"I'm sure you all understand perfectly how it is," the poet said, waving them all to silence. "If I see you clearly it will only discompose me. Poetry is essentially a solitary thing."

The company gave a general murmur of assent.

"I know exactly what he means," Miriam whispered reverently. "He wants to be alone with his Muse."

She was rewarded by stifled gasps of mirth from the two painters.

"*If* you don't mind, please." The quiet politeness of Ivan Simpson's request was belied by the icy glance he flung in the direction of the piano. The painters fell into a strangled silence, and everyone else looked hopefully in Miriam's direction.

How they loved her!

A straight-backed chair had been placed in the center of the room, and behind it Fabien erected a small standard lamp whose feeble glimmer was all but indiscernible under the blaze from the chandeliers. Gingerly, the poet sat down and opened his manuscript, a look on his face like one who had been awakened suddenly from a deep sleep. He thumbed through the manuscript, found his place, and nodded in the direction of the light switch. The room was plunged into darkness, relieved only by the gleam that shone over the poet's shoulder, illuminating his profile and making him look like the high-nosed head on a William III penny. He cleared his throat. Silence reigned.

Miriam shivered in near-ecstasy. This was going to be Art. Living Art. Delivered with authority by an Authority. Straight from the horse's mouth.

Ivan Simpson cleared his throat a second time. There was a dramatic pause of seven seconds.

"I don't want to hear any poets, do any of you?" Bill asked the kitchen.

"No," they chorused raggedly, and resumed their conversations, secretly marveling on the mystery that anything so brief as Life could glow so brightly.

"We're crude," Bill chortled, addressing no one in particular. "All of us, horrible damn crude."

He poured himself another drink. Only those that suffered the common sorrows hallowed by universal tradition could derive comfort from poetry. For these with the solitary sadness, the personal, incommunicable problem, there was no ease except in the touch of a hand.

Tears came to his eyes.

The voice rolled on like a deep and dark blue ocean—rolled: aided considerably in its waviness by the quantities of liquor consumed by its owner earlier in the evening. In the room remained not a shadow of man's ravage but his own. Ivan Simpson was pouring out his soul to its auditors.

He sank into the depths with bubbling groans; rose again to thunderstrike the walls of rock-built cities, bidding his nation quake. And, forcedly inarticulate, the representatives of his nation listened in a silence that was broken only by heavy breathing or the sound of a clinking glass.

They had been noisily receptive at first, applauding each item with spontaneity and cheer. Especially had they liked his "Ode to the Provincial Institute of Technology and Art, Calgary, Alberta," which began "... O! Seat of Learning nestled in the Plains...."

But now a pin could have been heard to drop, the end of each piece was greeted with the same hush that received its reading. For Ivan Simpson had ceased to pander to their lower, commercial senses. The last seven poems had been the real stuff, the true expression of his Absolute Self. And they were rapidly becoming absolutely truer and realer.

Miriam's eyes were riveted to the patch of light at the center of the floor, the oasis where she, the parched traveler, had at last arrived to take long, quenching sups at the deep, clear pools of Art. The enharmonic cadences had in turn lashed her, exalted her, shriven her; had boomed her sonorous funeral knell and wafted her into heaven with a soft plinking of harps. By the middle of the first stanza her heart had taken flight on fluttering wings, to wheel its mad way around the orbit of the lamp in a frenzy of lepidopterous intoxication.

She and the voice and these other dim guests were one, a solid rock of art against which the gates of Philistinism would never prevail. Definitely and most emphatically this was it: the Super-It for which she had waited patiently all of her life.

The beautiful sound mellifluated on, pouring from the painfully shaping lips and sweeping with velvet brushes the corners where the audience sat huddled. Through the fraught gloom Miriam could see their heads, their darkly gleaming eyeballs, turned in her direction. She felt a smile play all unbidden upon her features, a warmth enfold her from head to foot. And then she felt bewilderment, incompletion. *But why were they looking in her direction?* What part had she to play in this unsurpassable moment, to play now, to play?

The answer came. She knew. They had sent and she received. It was simple, natural, obvious. A wedding of the Arts. They would be as one again. More so.

Already her hand was sliding along the top of the piano, finger after encroaching finger.

Ivan Simpson read on:

> "... Striking from mine eyes the labial palimpsest
> Jocasta-bred, gestate translucent in vice;
> Seeing now 'gainst gurgitant blue on craggéd red hearts growing,
> White, gray-white, the edelweiss."

The luscious strains of a Musical Romance by Rubinstein pulsated into the room in quivering vibrati of unendurable sweetness, as if someone had filled a gigantic money-box with syrup and was allowing it to escape through the narrow slot in a continuous, wavering stream. A mass of startled eyes swung to the piano, peering toward the spot where Miriam, with body swaying and eyes closed in rapturous submission, was scraping succulently at the violin clenched firmly between her chin and collarbone.

In complete oblivion she wrought the sinuous melody, sending it writhing forth to wind a glistening, serpentine way between the phrases, the words, between the very syllables of Ivan Simpson's soul-soaked verse. The wedding was on.

But soul did not call to soul. With an expression of complete incredulity on his face, the poet slowly raised his head. His eyes widened, his words faltered in a drying throat. It was then that Miriam was inspired to improvise a short passage of pizzicato. Ivan Simpson rose weakly to his feet, mute, beaten.

"Very well," he said. The words that followed were lost in a great roar of laughing applause. Miriam opened her astonished eyes just as someone switched on the main lights.

"Very well." Ivan Simpson called through the din in an extremely huffy voice. "If you want the floor, by all means take it!"

"I couldn't help it," Miriam began. She was about to continue with an explanation of the technicalities of being carried away. But the crowd was gathering around her, laughing, applauding, congratulating. Her attention was drawn from the one to the many.

Had she done anything wrong? The moment of bewilderment passed as she surveyed her public, whose faces showed nothing but admiration and approval. Why, then, did the poet survey her so, his chin tucked into his shoulder, such bitter glances?

Ah, yes! Realization flowed over her like the contents of a gently breaking egg. There was art, and Art. Many months ago one of her young men had told her that music was the greatest art because it incorporated the time-factor. Whatever that meant, it was certainly being proved true. In trying to be merely supplementary to the poet she had, by acclaim, proved herself supreme. And Vox Populi, Vox Dei. Another young man had not only told her that but translated it.

The voice of the people had spoken and she was the elect of God. With a final commiserating glance at Ivan Simpson, for whom, in her generosity, she was truly sorry, she turned and graciously faced her public.

"Would you care for me to play something?"

In the ensuing roar of assent, Fabien slipped behind her and sat at the piano. She leaned and whispered in his ear.

"'Trees.'"

"You should have seen it!" The guy with peculiar eyebrows was recounting the incident to the kitchen, barely able to speak for his laughter. "She stopped him dead in his tracks."

"She's a friend of Duncan's, I think," said Bill proudly. "He's got lots of interesting friends."

"Yeah?" The laughter abated and the eyebrows twitched into place to accommodate a bland look. "Yeah, I agree. He sure has! Very interesting!"

"What d'you mean?" Bill asked. "Eh? What d'you mean?"

"Nothing at all." The guy with the eyebrows walked out, chuckling to himself.

The engineer was shaking with uncontainable laughter. "Oh, hell," he choked. "Just listen to the way she plays that. The funniest woman I ever saw."

"Yes," Stephen said.

"Intelligently funny, too," the engineer amplified. "Have you talked to her yet?"

"No," Stephen answered, and moved away. He did not want his observations interrupted.

All over the room they craned admiringly in Miriam's direction, stifling their delighted mirth as much as possible lest they miss one of the preciously satirical phrases that dropped so fruitily from her sawing bow. Two people only failed to give her their undivided attention. Ivan Simpson sat in a corner with averted head and whispered tart disparagements to which no one paid heed. Stephen was edging nearer the piano, watching the face of the pianist.

Watching Miriam.

Fabien played a tinkling arpeggio and smiled over his shoulder. Miriam leaned a little closer, returning the smile with the curiously constipated grimace reserved by restaurant violinists for their more spendthrift clientele.

The curious ache appeared again in Stephen's breast and numbed him with a constricting sickness. He saw now the full import of Crystal's warning. Fabien needed protection, would always need it. Throughout his life he would attract people of this sort, soiled people like Miriam and Duncan who came in the hope of regaining their purity by contact with his immaculate person, and who never considered the contamination with which they, in turn, might infect the unsullied mind and the white body.

He shuddered at the thought of contact between Fabien and this aging woman in her ridiculous tight dress, the rough to the smooth, the porous to the satin, the old and sagging to the young and firm. He glanced behind, to where Duncan was settled between Matt and Bobbie, and felt his justification. The foreseeable future must be diverted as it had been in the recent past. He threaded through the crowd and leaned against the piano, nodding to Fabien.

But Fabien was not looking, and when his head moved it was as a signal to Miriam.

The song was ending. The slender hands mounted the keyboard in a procession of lightly played chords, then swooped to the bass in a flurrying cascade that swelled, diminished, and almost died. The violin stayed above. It was the ultimate note. Wearing an expression of extreme pain, Miriam coaxed from the violin one single, sweet, and long-drawn sound that was an octave higher than any musical convention could possibly demand. It laved, it bathed, it quivered with the tenuousness of a streak of treacle.

"'For only Goood can maaake a Treeeeee.'"

The hand that held the bow dropped to Miriam's side in a weary gesture of utter completion. She awaited her applause, eyes closed, resigned, replete.

It came in a tumult of clapping and laughter that exceeded her wildest anticipations. They crowded around her, calling her name, drawing near to touch her, begging for encores. She opened her eyes and inclined her body in a series of bows, wearing upon her face that smile of wistful humility which is the hallmark of all great artists. The laughter grew. The clapping mounted to greater volume with each bow. They were demanding more and more and more.

What did she have well-enough rehearsed for an immediate encore?

Her hands tightened. Someone was trying to take the violin from her.

"Leave them wanting," a voice whispered in her ear. "It will do them good."

"I'll Walk Beside You" and "Smiling Through" were very poor seconds to anything of the magnitude of "Trees." "Scotch Fantasia" and "A Medley of Haunting Irish Airs" were right out of the artistic question. She released the instrument and turned in time to see Stephen put it on the piano.

"Come for a drink. You've earned it," he said, taking her arm and drawing her gently away.

Unresisting, she allowed herself to be led into the hall. Her feet were no longer touching the ground, her heart was singing. The diminishing applause at her back soughed like the waves of a golden sea in which she could bathe at will. Life! Art! Her whole skin was a serrulation of goose-bumps. This house, these people, this lovely young man who was part of it all—

"I haven't yet had a chance to speak to you properly," he said. "I was beginning to get jealous of Fabien."

"Were you, Stephen?"

The delicate nuance contained within her question filled her with a peculiar joy that had no parallel in previous experience. And suddenly her head reeled, for she had glimpsed a complete picture of what the world would be like if everyone conducted themselves with sophistication and delicate formality, said nothing to each other except that which charmed. The conception was sustained. She envisaged a world that was like this house, serene and joyous, purged of all ugliness. For one blinding moment Miriam felt radiantly, ineffably pure.

"People have been keeping us apart," she said, and sank onto the lowest of the black-carpeted stairs, basking in the approbation of this handsome key-holder who had carried her off under the noses of everyone present.

Towering over her like this he looked very tall. He was nodding gravely. "You play beautifully," he said.

"Do I?" Her smile was modest.

"We were lucky that you came."

"I was lucky to be invited." A wave of transcendental gratitude swept through her, bringing tears of happiness to her eyes. "You really are three lovely fellows. I think it's wonderful the way you get on."

"Oh, yes," he said, "yes, it is."

"You're all so good and kind and you know lots of interesting people—"

"None more so than you."

She acknowledged it with a smile. "And you have a marvelous place here."

He grasped her forearms, drawing her to her feet so that she faced him, almost touching. "I'd like to show it to you. All of it."

Shivering a little, she took his arm and they went together up the wide staircase. Several pairs of amused eyes followed their progress. Miriam was oblivious. Stephen saw and ignored. In the sitting room Fabien was playing his song.

> "'Little Fly,
> Thy summer's play
> My thoughtless hand
> Has brushed away...'"

Stephen had not known previously that the composition was completed, but now he smiled.

"Isn't it odd about Duncan," Miriam said as she finished admiring the library. "Fabien was telling me about it."

"What's odd?"

"Him belonging to a rich family and working at that store just for experience for a book and everything. I think it's thrilling, don't you? Sort of courageous, and real?"

"Oh, that," Stephen said. "Yes, it is." He drew a book from one of the shelves and leafed through it, angry that the lie had glorified Duncan yet strangely pleased that Fabien should have thought the invention necessary. It indicated a cognizance of a lack in Duncan that needed to be hidden by grandiose excuses. Was Fabien lying to himself to cover Duncan's conduct this evening?

"When I first met him," Miriam continued, "I never dreamt he was anything out of the ordinary."

"He doesn't look it, does he?"

"Well, no," she said. "He doesn't, really."

"And I'm afraid he isn't." Stephen replaced the book and came over to her. "I'm afraid someone's been pulling your leg."

"You mean that—that Fabien lied to me?"

He shook his head. "Duncan lied to Fabien. Duncan is inclined to take advantage of people."

The ramparts of her newly constructed world were beginning to crumble. She said faintly, "Don't you like Duncan?"

He smiled ruefully. "Do you?"

Without knowing it, thought Miriam, this nice fellow with his grave eyes is saying that Duncan laughed at me on that awful night. Oh God! The ramparts collapsed completely and she was toppled into a briny sea of disillusionment. Like a drowning woman she saw the events of that evening with Duncan pass before her eyes in humiliating succession. Possibly he had related them to anyone who would listen. She flushed scarlet with shame under Stephen's scrutinizing gaze.

"Never mind," he said kindly. "It was an improper question. How would you like to see the bedrooms?"

She nodded mutely, snatching gratefully at the extended arm as though it were a straw. They went out along the landing.

"In here," Stephen said. "It's decorated in green and gold, and there's a black and green bathroom. Fabien sleeps here." He opened the door and shut it again abruptly in his own face. "Perhaps we should look at the bedrooms on the third floor," he suggested. "They won't have penetrated that far yet."

The top back bedroom was a maid's room.

"Did you know that couple downstairs?" Miriam asked.

Stephen sat down on the bed. "No, but I read somewhere that male seals raise themselves on their elbows in exactly the same manner."

Miriam giggled. "They were funny. He stared right at the door and she turned right away from it. All in one movement."

"The difference in the sexes," Stephen explained.

Despite the recent setbacks, Miriam's spirits were lightening. He is being very kind to me, she thought, and pondered what she could do in return. She moved closer.

"About Duncan," she began.

"Yes?" He raised his eyes to her.

"Don't mind too much. I know how you feel, it's affecting me the same way. I've been very disappointed in Duncan, too." She paused thoughtfully. "He's strange."

"He's queer!" Stephen said savagely.

"Don't lose your temper about him, he's not worth it." Miriam sat down on the bed beside him, feeling the springs vibrate beneath her. "After all, he's only one of your trio. There is another member."

"Yes," Stephen said.

"There is Fabien," she reminded him. "And Fabien's worth fifty of Duncan."

"Yes," he repeated.

"Isn't he lovely?"

"Yes."

"Who," she continued, "could even think of looking at Duncan when Fabien was in the same room? He's a wonderful fellow, isn't he, handsome and well-mannered and charming. I think I almost fell in love with him at first sight."

They were sitting very close together, their thighs touching, and when Stephen turned his head he was whispering in her ear. "He seems very fond of you."

"I think so, too," she mused. "He has a way of holding my arm and saying things. And the way he looks at me—oh, you know, lots of things. But he does it all in a nice way, of course."

"I saw him," Stephen said. "And you never looked at anyone else."

She heard the note of reproach in his voice and drew back her head for a better view. There was a look of happy perplexity on her face. "Why, Stephen—" she began.

She saw what was coming at her and lay back upon the pillow, eyes closed and mouth slightly open. The hands and then the weight descended full upon her, and she began suddenly to struggle, beating at his back with her fists and saying his name over and over.

Her protests were stifled under his mouth and she lay still, letting his hands run over her.

The springs creaked in protest. An ominous whirring sound at the side of her dress proclaimed that a seam had split.

"I'll mix you a drink," Bill suggested, casting a wavering eye along the depleted contents of the bottles. "Something really special."

"Something strong," Fabien said. He looked thoughtfully at the other occupants of the kitchen. "There'll be a great many brandy eggnogs drunk tomorrow morning."

"They're most of them corked," Bill confided in a whisper. "They're having a great time."

"And you? I haven't seen you all evening."

"Oh, me too. Handing out drinks to everyone makes me feel like Jesus."

"I'm glad," Fabien said. He took the glass from Bill's hand and began drinking in quick little sips. "Good," he said approvingly.

"Is everyone else having a good time?" Bill asked.

Fabien nodded.

"Is Duncan?"

"Yes, I think so. He's extremely drunk, but he looks happy enough."

"What's he doing?" Bill asked fondly.

"I believe he's taking another shower. He and two other fellows."

Bill laughed. "Let's hope it doesn't start a fashion. We'll have the morality squad in."

"Yes." Fabien continued drinking. "Bill, you make the most awful drinks."

"I know, but nobody sees the difference." Bill interrupted himself to replenish the glasses of three petitioning guests, pouring quickly so that the glasses overflowed. Conversation in the kitchen was now little more than an exchange of whispers. Voices were muted to a nocturnal pitch that invited and confided, comprehended and forgave. Behind the array of reddening eyes was a collective look of deep, sad happiness. Bill's glance went right around the room and back to Fabien.

"All right, tell me what's wrong?"

"Nothing," Fabien said.

"Did someone wet on the carpet or are you running out of drinks? What about Duncan?"

"I told you, he's taking a shower."

"That's right, with two other guys. What two other guys?"

"I don't know," Fabien answered. "I never saw them before this evening."

"Who are they?"

"I don't know. Friends of Stephen's I believe."

Bill put down his glass with a bang. "That's fine," he said harshly. "That's just dandy. Stephen's a damn good head, even if he is a no-good bastard, only none of us ever knows what the hell he's up to. And he's usually up to it with Duncan. I'm going up to fetch him. I don't like Stephen's friends."

"You're a little tight, Bill. There's nothing wrong. Duncan knows what he's doing."

"You're a treacherous bloody liar if you say that. You know the poor little bastard never has a clue. I'm going to fetch him down to the kitchen."

"Well, I'll get back to the other guests." Fabien finished his drink and licked his upper lip with the tip of his tongue. "That's good, Bill. That's very good. I don't know what I'd do without you."

"That's okay," Bill said, smiling. He gave Fabien a light punch on the arm, crossed the kitchen, and disappeared up the back stairs. Within him was a sense of outraged justice.

"Have you seen Stephen?" Harrigan asked the girl with the Eton crop.

Her expression indicated that she was regarding some lower form of insect life. "I don't know any Stephen," she replied, haughty with disgust.

Harrigan went back to the buffet and hurriedly began eating the last of the ripe olives. The nearby ash tray was overflowing with stones.

Miriam sat up, straightened her hair, and took the lighted cigarette that Stephen offered. They sat side by side and smoked in silence, blowing out puffs of smoke that hung billowing in the still air of the small room. There seemed to be nothing to say.

She was pleased that he had proved amateur, for it quelled her suspicion that he was one of those who snatched at any and every passing morsel, going from victory to easy victory and gaining experience. His almost pitiful lack of it had been a compliment to her, indicating that she was the one for whom he had waited so long, the one for whom he had reserved himself. She touched his arm, but he did not look at her.

And after what has happened, she told herself, I belong here. This house and I are indissoluble. I shall come and go as I please.

Stephen would give her a key. At first she would not come often, perhaps twice or thrice a week on her way to or from the downtown shopping area, to ask their advice on what she should buy or to show her purchases, to bring them little gifts. But later, after each in turn had beseeched her, she would become more of a permanent fixture in the household, visiting whenever it was possible and maybe staying for the week end when Marvin was out of town. There would be nothing immoral in those week ends. The house had more than enough bedrooms.

She imagined those Saturday nights, those early Sunday mornings. The party, for which she had shared expenses, was over. Everyone had gone home. Everyone had had a marvelous time. She was sitting alone before the dressing table in her appointed bedroom, musing on the night's happenings, toying mentally with this personality and that, remembering the advice she had given. Footsteps outside.

There would be a tap on the door. She would call and the three boys would troop in, Stephen, Fabien, and Duncan—

The thought of Duncan gave her pause and she pondered her way through to an answer. There was obviously an understanding about Duncan, something tolerant and kindly. She would be invited to enter upon it. A second, related thought struck her. She said, very quietly, "Are you going to tell the others about this?"

Stephen got to his feet with a hint of impatience. "Let's get back to the party," he said. "People will be wondering where we are." He moved to the door.

She was not sure exactly when the pangs began, or if they had any specific cause, but as they stole softly down the flight of stairs to the second floor she became aware that her happiness was not as great as she had imagined. This should have been an ecstatic culmination. The young man was beside her, the crowd below awaited her presence, an endless vista of joyous days and nights stretched as far as the mental eye could see. And yet at the moment she felt no happier than—than after a bout of snatched sensuality with one of the unworthy young men in her car.

She made the involuntary comparison and was at once filled with horror. Something was wrong, dreadfully wrong.

They were walking along the second-floor landing to the flight of black-carpeted stairs that led down into the hall. Searching for something to allay her fears, she looked up at him. "Stephen," she asked, "do you love me?" In her own ears the question sounded ridiculous, but suddenly it became imperative that she receive an honest answer.

"Stephen," she said again. "Do you love me?"

"Get back!" The hissed command, coupled with a rough push at her shoulder, made her cringe. "Get back," he repeated. "The whole damn bunch is gathered in the hall."

She managed to find her voice. "Stephen," she began, and then the courage left her completely. "What are they doing?" she asked.

"Look!"

They peered round the bannister and surveyed the scene below. Duncan was standing in the center of an assembly of guests, barefooted and clad in an undershirt and a pair of trousers. In his hand he grasped a telephone into which he was talking in ringing tones, to the obvious and intense enjoyment of his audience. Stephen recognized the declamation as a quatrain from the *Rubáiyát of Omar Khayyám*.

"I'm sure you're right, sir. Yes, sir." Duncan had forsaken poetry for more mundane speech, but his voice still rang theatrically. He covered the mouthpiece with his hand and addressed the listeners, his wide eyes guilefully innocent like those of a night owl.

"He says the flames of Hell will consume us. He says that we're all whores and whoremongers. Isn't that terrible!"

The announcement was greeted with a shout of laughter that lasted until Duncan silenced the crowd with frantic shakings of his head. Everyone leaned forward eagerly for more.

"Oh, sir!" Duncan exclaimed in shocked tones, removing his hand from the mouthpiece. "Oh, sir, not Babylon. Babylon had only one whore."

"Come on," Stephen said to Miriam. "We'll go down by the back stairs."

"What was happening down there?" Miriam asked, trying to make her voice normal. The evening was ebbing from her. She must try and hold it fast a little longer. If Stephen would only say he loved her. But he was already disappearing down the landing toward the back of the house. She hurried after him, not wishing to lose her way and wander into another bedroom.

Later on it might be different. When he had seen his two friends, when the Trinity had been reunited, he might turn to her as he had upstairs, with softness and sweet, passionate words. Then she would know again that she belonged to this night, that her rightful place was here in this house. For she did belong here, she *did*, and he must assure her before the conviction had completely evaporated. He must stem the growing panic that made her feel like a derelict on a tideless sea.

She stumbled behind him, down the narrow stairway to the lighted door, teetering on her high heels, breathless from the dress she wore. The torn seam gaped at her left side. A feeling of profound depression engulfed her. Oh God, she thought, I feel like hell. Her head was aching. She emerged into the kitchen.

"Would you like a drink?" asked the drunk young man holding the bottle.

She nodded. Stephen was filling a glass for himself. He looked pale. The only other occupants of the kitchen were a couple in the corner by the refrigerator who whispered inaudibly.

"This is Bill," Stephen said.

The young man gave her the drink, making no word or gesture of greeting, looking at her from cold, drunken eyes. He reminded her of a great many intoxicated young men that she had known before and was now trying desperately to forget. She hated him, instantly, with a miserable, fearful hate. He looked at Stephen and she saw the supercilious expression change to one of disgust.

"Welcome to the kitchen," the young man said to her with a broad, unamiable smile. "Bring us your troubles and we'll solve 'em for you."

Miriam lowered her eyes to the glass and said nothing.

"What?" Bill demanded. "Am I to infer from this silence that you have no troubles? I would have put you down as a woman with a load of trouble, wouldn't you Stevie boy? Wouldn't you put her down as a woman with a load of trouble?"

"Don't be so damned silly," Stephen snapped, pouring himself another drink. "What's going on out there in the hall?"

"I haven't the foggiest idea. What is?"

"Duncan is making some sort of public phone call—"

"Aha, Duncan," Bill interrupted. He lifted an accusing finger. "You got him drunk tonight."

"Since when did he need assistance?" Stephen demanded acidly.

Bill wagged his head, slowly, patiently. "I can't understand why you don't like Duncan. He has the softest heart of anyone I know. He means everybody well. Do you know Duncan?" he asked, looking at Miriam.

She nodded.

"Then you know what I mean. He's kind, isn't he? Why, only just a minute ago he was in here telling me about all the people he feels sorry for, asking what he could do to help them. He was drunk, of course."

"Of course," Stephen said.

"Yes." Bill was taking his time, drawling out each word with drunken precision. "Your sister, for example, the one who's in love with Chester Arden. Dear old Chester, what a lovely man."

"What about my sister?" Stephen had a horrible premonition of what was coming next. He felt sick. "What about her?"

"Did you know that Duncan likes her? He likes her very much."

"I'm not interested."

"Well, he does. He says he feels sorry for her because she lives in a gloomy house where nobody ever laughs and the furniture comes up and bites you when you're not looking. Do you live there?"

"What are you trying to say?" Stephen stared back into the half-closed eyes and saw the light of saturnine satisfaction that Bill no longer attempted to disguise, an expression of amusement, maliciously triumphant and completely sober.

"Well," the drunken voice droned on, "as I say, we were talking about your sister, and Duncan wondered what we could do to bring a little happiness into her life. It was a difficult question. Duncan was so drunk he couldn't think of anything, but I had a good idea. What do you think it was?"

"What?" Stephen asked in a flat voice.

"I suggested that he phone her up and invite her to the party. Wasn't that a good idea, to ask your sister to come down to the party? What's her name again?" Bill screwed up his face, snapping his fingers in the air in a parody of forgetfulness. "I can't remember her name."

"Esther," Stephen said. "I don't think Duncan has managed to contact her. Did you count on that?"

"I hope we didn't do wrong." Bill stood up straight, rolling his shoulders to loosen the muscles. "Don't get angry and hit me, Steve, or we'll probably smash up the kitchen."

They were staring at each other, unmoving, like fighting cocks that have been placed in a pit but are still held by their masters' hands. Miriam's heart was thudding with a violence that echoed in her temples and threatened to split her head. Her fear had intensified unbearably, the more so because she had no idea what they were talking about. Something awful was going to happen.

"Stephen," she whispered frantically.

He was already striding from the room. The door swung noiselessly behind him, and she was left alone with the horrible young man who reminded her so much of the others she wanted to forget.

"And another stinker bit the dust," the horrible young man murmured. "By the clappers, I've learned a lot from that guy."

He removed the glass from her hand and refilled it, tilting an almost empty bottle so that the last few drops fell with an audible plopping. "You have a peculiar choice of friends," he told her dryly. "It amounts to what Fabien would call an indiscretion. Here, have another drink."

She took the proffered glass and drank deeply, conscious of the sneering contempt with which the horrible young man was regarding her.

Her misery went sliding down to its nadir.

"Drink," Duncan explained patiently to the telephone, "provokes nose-painting, sleep, and urine. Lechery, sir, it provokes and unprovokes. It provokes the desire, but it takes away the performance...."

Nobody was bothering any longer to keep silent. They crowded about him, laughing loudly, leaning close to the mouthpiece to shout witticisms and insults. One man had mounted a chair to denounce the company in a roaring, mock-rhetorical impersonation of a Hell-fire preacher. A girl who had announced that she was Jezebel began singing "'I'm a red-hot woman from the red-light end of town'" in a lusty contralto. A group of assorted males and females were gathered together, booing steadily. A quartet of engineers harmonized on their own version of "Jesus Wants Me for a Sunbeam."

Stephen edged into position beside Fabien. "What's going on?" he shouted above the din.

"I think we're all a little hysterical," Fabien answered. He may have been laughing against his will, but laughing he was indisputably, and

Stephen's heart withered as though the bared and shining teeth threatened its existence. "I'm not sure how it happened," Fabien said, "but Duncan has contacted an excruciatingly funny old gentleman who insists upon fulminating against us. I should not permit it, but it is quite hilarious."

The man on the chair was calling upon them to repent, and the noise swelled as everyone began clamorously confessing to impossible sins. Duncan turned on them. "Shut up!" he roared in a voice that must have split the eardrums of the man at the other end. "The gentleman refuses to speak to us anymore. We are all inhabitants of either Sodom or Gomorrah. Which one did you say it was?" he enquired politely of the mouthpiece.

"He's talking to my father," Stephen said.

"Oh, no! No!" Fabien's face froze into a mask and he made a quick, involuntary movement in the direction of the phone, his right hand raising automatically in a futile gesture of restraint. The action carried him only to the tips of his toes, the arm fell to his side, and he turned his wide eyes back upon Stephen. "Oh, Lord," he said, "Oh, Lord," and lowered his head until his chin was resting upon his chest. "Oh, Lord," he said once more, and collapsed into a paroxysm of helpless laughter that shook his entire body and brought the tears of mirth coursing in twin streams down his smooth, brown cheeks.

"No, you may not speak to your son," Duncan said, as if addressing a wayward child. "And for the last time I insist that I had no fell designs upon your daughter." He turned from the telephone. "I believe the gentleman is going now."

There were scattered cries of shame and a few boos, and over in a corner an engineer began to sing "Good night Sweetheart." It was a song they all knew and they snatched it up eagerly, determined to wring the last drop of amusement from this incident with which the party had been unexpectedly blessed.

"'Good night Sweetheart, all my dreams are for you.'"

The sight that Stephen carried with him as he fled the house was of Duncan holding the telephone at arm's length and executing a series of vigorous steps that seemed to stimulate the flaccid rhythms of the melody that rang like a dirge from every throat about him.

Outside it was snowing. The singing could be heard clearly in the street.

I am going to be punished, Miriam thought, for every wrong thing I have ever done. And this horrible person with his reminiscent face is going to be the instrument of my judgment.

Her glass was nearly empty. Without a word, he reached over and refilled it from a newly opened bottle.

The liquid trickled down her throat and exploded into heat like an opening fist, making her stomach contract with nausea. She shuddered. A lifelong rule was being broken by this drinking in the company of a young male, but she was unable to stop. Alcohol was the only means whereby she might deaden the impact of his disdainful stare. It would be fatal to run away, for she knew now that his eyes were going to follow her wherever she went. There would be no release until she saw his expression change. And, until then, she must drink.

"Why do you look at me like that?" she demanded in a whisper.

"I'm admiring the way you drink." He continued to stare.

Her mind was writhing in an agony of incomprehension. What had happened to the glory of this lovely evening? What evil chemistry had so rapidly tarnished the gold of its promise? The ingredients, the accoutrements were here still: the light, the talk, the sophistication, the youth. Her triumph was unsullied, the golden moment of exaltation remained intact. Yet the enchantment of this household had flown, the magic gone. She was empty and forsaken, alone and afraid, with nowhere to go, no one to talk to, nowhere to look except into the pitiless stare of this drunken boy who dispensed drinks.

She looked at him now and wondered hopefully if it were possible to establish a bridge between them at whose middle they could meet without regarding each other too closely.

"What are you thinking?" she asked. The question, which she had meant to be harsh and peremptory, sounded revoltingly coy. She bit her lip and waited. But it was so long before he spoke that she despaired of a reply and turned back to her drink. His return question caught her right off balance.

"Do you know many men like Stephen?"

"Yes." The answer came automatically and immediately a million angels fell down from heaven on broken wings, shrieking a chorus of dreadful affirmatives that rocketed around the recesses of her memory until it seemed that her brain must burst. Yes yes yes yes yes, she knew them, scores of them: hands behind doors, legs under tables, bodies in cars and darkened rooms, fingers groping, feeling, picking, she knew them all in every furtive place contrived by man. And Eyes.

She opened her mouth a tiny fraction and the other Miriam gave an awful, noiseless scream of agony.

The door burst open and the guests irrupted into the kitchen, chattering in high, laughing voices and calling for drinks.

Miriam tilted her glass right back and drank a deep, shuddering draught.

"Some people!" said Matt Lambert, still smarting under the rough treatment. "Always sticking their noses in things."

The supple young French Canadian was sitting on the arm of the sofa. "Un disapointement," he exclaimed wistfully, "est toujours suivit de près par un autre. Ma vie a été marquée d'une infinité de peines."

"I'm not very good at French," Matt said, "but when you speak I understand every word. I think it must be something about the way you talk."

"I speak English also."

"Yes," sighed Matt. "I wish I could speak French as well as you speak English. I consider it the duty of all of us to speak the two languages, don't you? I mean, Canada is a bilingual country."

"We are all Canadians," agreed the supple one. "You should find someone to practice with."

Bobbie and the thick-set French Canadian watched the scene from the same side of the room, but with varying expressions.

Bill had moved away from her temporarily, the better to serve drinks to the clamorous influx of guests, but Miriam remained where she stood, knowing he would return at the first opportunity. She saw how his face had become mobile. He was talking and laughing now, exchanging jocosities with whoever would listen. He reminded her of no one. But his expression had not changed for her sake. Until he turned away, his face had been cold and hard, and the transfixing eyes still penetrated her defences to rake across those memories that hitherto had been seen only one at a time. The expression, she knew, would return with his presence.

Perhaps, she thought, it is because he has seen that I am a Jewess.

She seized the excuse avidly, kneading it like putty until it achieved strange shapes, patting and smearing it in a perfectly conscious attempt to fortify her vulnerability. It's because I am a Jewess, she repeated, and thus was the race against which she had defended herself called in by her as a means of self-defence. She had turned her back upon her people, and now, in a moment of supreme irony, she was trying to use them in an effort to turn her back upon herself.

But the race was triumphant. The jesuitical scrupulosity of the Jewish mind would permit her only emotional deceptions. The quality of mind which gave the world its greatest chess players forced her to checkmate herself.

All at once she perceived that in the face of what was happening it meant nothing to anyone, least of all herself, whether she was a Jewess or not. Momentarily she was stunned. What had she been doing all these years? What was the point of the impersonation? How could she have hoped to come to glorious rest when she was neither Jew nor Gentile, but a hybrid bird perched on the barbed wire of prejudice that lay between the two? Through the confusing fumes that filled her mind she discerned vaguely that it was she who had been truly anti-Semitic, not the bigoted fools from whom she had tried tortuously to escape. She had been running away from her own persecution.

I've been stupid, she thought, in genuine astonishment.

Then habit asserted itself and she tried to obscure the greater stupidity with the lesser. Mentally she bared her breast and, with superficial honesty, she stood at the wailing wall to lament her sins and suffer self-inflicted castigation. She had sinned, sinned grievously. She would cleanse herself with the self-torment that had come now of her realization. From her deception had grown the dark flowers that were discernible to the supernatural gaze of the young man who served drinks. She would pluck them out by the roots, and when he returned he would find her whole and natural, her true, unaffected self. The look would go from his eyes and he would smile as did other young men, the other young men of whom he reminded her.

Like dried clay, the lie crumbled to pieces in her hands. The whips of chastisement snapped like brittle twigs. For she was feeling no torment. In her mind was only a clear, cold realization that she had been a fool to waste time in pretending and a resolve not to do it again. There was no suffering at that level. With one sweep, her intelligence brushed away the pretense that sprang from the pretense.

But now the real suffering could begin.

He would come back soon with that look unchanged, turning to her the face she knew too well. Different in mold, but always the same in stamp, it was the face that had looked sideways at her from every place where, during the past few years, she had gone to seek her pleasure. It was the face of the young men who even now were marching across her mind in sickening procession, smiling and nodding, wanting her with their mouths, holding out their hands for gifts.

They had not been deceived, nor had they tried to deceive. They knew of the one who went before; they were aware that one was to come after. Each one had known he was a unit in a column, but they didn't mind, they were honest. They had held her in their arms, loved her in their fashion, and was it deception when they held out their hands for their due reward? No, it was she who suffered deception, for she had deceived herself. She had pretended to find fresh rapture in each new arrival. They, for their part, had merely marched to the saluting base, saluted, hitched their trousers, and passed on, leaving her alone on the platform to scan the place from whence they came, looking for the newest arrival who would come with desire in his face, looking for the latest deception. But how much deeper did the deception go? Was there yet another behind it?

Bill appeared beside her with an abruptness that made him seem but a continuation of her thoughts. The cold stare transfixed her, turning her to stone, and suddenly all the faces that circled her mind came rushing out in a nebulous fog and settled into his features. *He* was the newest arrival. He was the first and the last and all those between. He was the original pattern, the archetype from which they all had sprung. She gazed at him in horror.

For his look was one of complete revulsion, and in the token expression was the incontrovertible truth that all of those he resembled had regarded her in the same manner. While she disported herself in attempted beguilement they must have been watching her with this identical cold loathing behind their eyes, wondering, even as she moved in to touch them, whether her behavior had been the same with all of those who preceded them. For she had overlooked the essence of their masculinity, and they had hated her for it. They had been aware of their predecessors as Bill had been aware that she came downstairs with Stephen, and in his reaction she could gauge what their reactions must have been.

Then what did they think of me, she asked herself. What were they thinking of me all the time?

She held out her glass for refilling and as Bill turned his back all the ghostly young men gathered round her again, pressing close. She had not known before how many they were nor how near, but suddenly she realized that they had followed her always. They had come with her to this house tonight, silently, all of them, biding their time until, with former experience, they might assist in her present pleasure. The talk, the art, the music had been an illusion, a resting period during which the shadowy young men formulated their plan. And as she ascended the stairs they glided into place, until in the bedroom they assumed the positions for which they had trained so arduously.

How they must have laughed about her dress! And when she arose from the bed their numbers were greater by one. Stephen had become a wafting, bodiless memory with all the others, and she descended to meet the ultimate, the one who looked like all of them, the one whose face was speeding her along the avenue of misery that lay ahead. She looked full into his face for the last time.

There was not the slightest simulation of desire in his eyes. She knew that under no circumstances would she ever be able to beg or borrow or buy it from him. Then what of the others? She had paid them. But how had she paid them, and at what cost to herself? Why was he still looking at her like that?

"Thank you," she said, taking back the glass. From the depth of her unhappy desolation she hated him.

"Hello, I've been looking for you to play us something," Fabien said. "Enjoying yourself?" He moved into her vision and stood beside Bill, smiling a charming, ready smile and looking poised and clean.

"I don't think I'm very good company for the lady," Bill muttered without shifting his gaze.

Fabien was looking from one to the other with pleasure spreading over his face. "I'm glad you two have met. I was wondering how I could bring you together."

"Stephen introduced us," Bill explained.

"Good." Fabien clinked his glass against Miriam's with an insouciant gesture that almost broke her heart. "If you come as often as I hope you will, you'll be seeing a lot of Bill. We're more or less of a trio here, and it simplifies matters if you like us all."

"A trio?" Miriam whispered.

"Bill, Duncan, and myself. We spend so much time together that it wouldn't at all surprise me if soon we began to look like each other."

"God forbid," Bill said.

"Yes, yes. Excuse me." In a moment of searing recognition Miriam had seen the resemblance between them. "Excuse me," she said. "I really must go and powder my nose."

"I hope you were kind to her. She's awfully nice in her way."

Bill shrugged helplessly. "I did my best, but she just stood and stared and I couldn't think of anything to say. I guess she was embarrassed because I saw her come downstairs with that bum Stephen. They'd been knobbing, I think."

"Stephen?" Fabien raised his eyebrows. "Stephen? Well, good! I'm glad she found somebody. That was the idea in inviting her in the first place."

"Yeah?" said Bill. "Well, that's all right, then. But I didn't think she was as witty as everyone said she was. Did you?"

She had put on her third-best fur coat and was crossing the hall to the front door, when Duncan called to her.

"Miriam. Going so soon?"

"It's so late," she said. "I have to."

He studied her with drunken intentness, leaning forward until she could smell the liquor on his breath. "You don't look well," he said. "I'm sorry you have to go. Did you have a good time?"

The room had begun to tilt a little and the sickness at her stomach put her in fear of fainting. "I have to go," she said.

"You're forgetting something." He skipped away into the sitting room and returned in a few seconds carrying the neat black case. "Your violin," he said, thrusting it into her hand. Despite his obvious drunkenness, or perhaps because of it, his face was relaxed into an expression of serene innocence. He looked about sixteen.

"Are you coming again soon?" he asked.

Over his shoulder Miriam saw that they were being watched by the girl who had told her Stephen was the third member of the trio. The girl caught her eye and waved a hand in mocking farewell, moving away with triumph written large in every predatory line of her body.

"You are coming again soon, aren't you?" Duncan insisted.

All the unhappiness within her was drawn together in a tight nub of livid agony that threatened to destroy her mind if she did not find an immediate outlet. "No," she answered hoarsely, "I'm not," and drawing back her hand she fetched him a stinging slap right across his smiling mouth.

He looked at her in vacant astonishment, his face gone suddenly white and screwing up like that of a perplexed child. His body had become rigid, and she did not see the movement of his arm until it was too late. His open hand caught her flat on the side of the jaw, rocking her on her heels and almost bringing her to the floor.

"I'm sorry, but I believe I've wanted to do that since the first time I met you," he said quietly, and walked away across the hall followed by the interested and faintly approving eyes of the few guests who had witnessed the scene.

No one came to open the front door for her, and, as she let herself out into the cold, she began to cry in a succession of deep, wrenching sobs. She stumbled to her car through a rising wind that whipped the snow, and the tears froze upon her cheeks in icy channels. She found herself wishing that Marvin was going to be home, but Marvin was away on one of his business trips and would not return until Monday afternoon at the earliest. With whom could she talk, and what, anymore, was there to talk of.

Crying openly, she let in the clutch of her car.

"Why are you hiding in the kitchen?" Crystal asked. "The party's just beginning."

"They usually wait till one o'clock," Bill said, slapping her on the shoulder with hearty affection. She smiled upon him kindly, but there were other fish to fry.

"I can see where I'll have to stay and help you clean up," she said to Fabien. "They're going to leave chaos behind."

"It's, sweet of you," he answered, linking one of her arms to his, "but I have two cleaners coming in the morning."

"I'll stay anyway, just to see that everything's all right. Let's go into the hall and have fun."

"Me too," exclaimed Bill, linking her other arm. "I haven't left this bloody kitchen all night."

"Well, come on then."

They forsook the shiny white room, loosing their holds to get through the door and linking arms again in the dining room. Out in the hall a mass of couples were dipping and swaying to the music of a samba that someone had put on the phonograph, the men shaking their hips and wriggling their shoulders, and the girls whirling away, linked only by the barest touch of fingertips, and making their skirts flare up like the petals of flowers. Everyone was in motion.

"I don't see Duncan dancing."

"He's corked," Bill observed. "Some of Stephen's work."

"What a pity," Crystal said, "that your violinist friend has left. She could have played him a lively little jig."

"Has she gone?"

"A few minutes ago; I watched her. In fact I've been watching her most of the evening. Fascinating, isn't she?"

"Weird," corrected Bill. "All she does is stand and stare. I wonder why she left in such a hurry."

"Stephen has gone too," Fabien said.

"Ah! Aha-ha!" Bill gave a knowing wink. "So that's it. There's something between those two, and I think it's a pair of trousers."

"Spare my innocent ears," Crystal pleaded.

"It's snowing like the devil outside," Bill continued. "Pretty cold if Stephen and thingummy decide to have it in the open."

"Shall we dance?" enquired Fabien, and he and Crystal clasped each other in a polite embrace, moving away in a series of rhythmic jerks and letting the dancers close around them.

Bliss for Miriam and Stephen. Bliss for everybody, Bill thought, and bliss for me. He said: "Who are you?"

"I am told," Ivan Simpson said with massive dignity, "that there is food in this house. Cold duck!"

"That there is," Bill replied, taking his arm. "That there is."

The two foreign young ladies, who danced sublimely, passed each other in the middle of the floor and peeped around the burly arms of their respective partners, exchanging a slow smile of secret satisfaction.

"You haven't told me your name yet," Harrigan said, and the girl with the Eton crop winced as he stamped once more on her right foot.

"Quand je vois le monde heureux," sighed the supple one, "je suis heureux aussi."

"Oh, me too," cried Matt Lambert. "Moi aussi."

IV

Westmount Park was bitterly cold. A light wind blew the snow into flurrying patches of pattern, geometric areas of dancing particles that retained their borders until they were disintegrated by a whim of the wind and carried off into the dark night air under the trees. Stephen stood hunched in the doorway of the red-brick public lavatory, head down and hands thrust deep into his trousers pockets, thinking of the overcoat he had left behind and wishing miserably that he had not left so hurriedly. Epaulettes of snow melted slowly on his shoulders and penetrated to the skin beneath. A fine white matting overlay his breast, and his hair was caked in a kindly semblance of age. He shivered deeply and drew one hand from his pocket to test his nose for frostbite. If only he could light a cigarette.

But it had to come eventually. He stepped out of the doorway and turned in the direction of home, leaning against the fall of snow so that it drifted over the back of his bent head and touched with small, wet fingers on his neck. A respondent, strangely hopeful reaction tugged from somewhere in the depths of his mind, as if something like this had happened before and led to a joyful ending. He groped feebly for the reminiscence, seeking to nurture the unexpected fiber of faint warmth, but even so slight a concentration of thought brought a return of the evening's happenings, and he shivered with an intensified chill.

I am afraid, he thought. And that which had passed was partially supplanted by what was to come.

He was going home from a party. To other guests the phrase must surely conjure a different scene from that which he knew was awaiting him. He visualized how they would let themselves into warm, quiet houses, stepping softly to sideboards where loving parents had laid out sandwiches and a nightcap. He imagined conversations: "Goodness, how it snows! Stephen will be cold and wet when he gets home from that party. We'll leave out the decanter and he can warm himself with a drink before he goes to bed."

The mere conception was like a vision of some impossible heaven, yet the poorest of the others might expect it when they returned to their families. Not the drink, necessarily, nor even the sandwiches, but some spiritual sustenance more filling than food and drink, the envelopment of loved ones dreaming, to satisfy the hunger always aroused by noisy places and send them contented to bed.

The deep snow was mounting his insteps, soaking through the eyelets of his shoes and numbing his feet.

Nonsense, he thought. Rubbish! I am working myself into a welter of spurious self-pity. Most of the others live in overcrowded frat houses, or dubious and drab lodgings forced upon them by the needs of student economy. No one is interested in their return except an occasional landlady, lying awake in her room on the ground floor, anticipating the disturbance which will cause her to speak strongly tomorrow to her boarder. The returning guest must mount the creaking stair cautiously, and when he entered the room where his books were must close the door with a minimum of noise. There would be no drinks or food, and, when he had carefully placed each shoe on the floor, the guest would go to sleep in the certainty that no one knew, or cared, where he had been.

God, he thought, how incalculably blessed must such a life be, where there are none to wait with intolerable question, and sin lies dead for want of the query that brings its resurrection. What sweet peace must lie in those paths where no one watched and wound, and guilt was found only in the farthest reaches of heretical conscience. Wasn't it Oscar Wilde who said that a truth ceases to be a truth when more than one person believes in it? How rancorously true was the reverse side of the coin which read that a sin is not a sin *until* more than one person believes in it.

And there is nobody like a religious person, Stephen told himself bitterly, for teaching one about one's sins. "Sin," said St. Paul, "is not imputed when there is no law. Moreover, the law entered, that the offence might abound."

His father was sitting at home, convinced of the sin's existence, waiting to bring it to active life by forcing conviction upon the supposedly guilty sinner. All my life I have sinned, Stephen thought. All my life Father has arranged that I be a great sinner by forcing me to be an unwilling parent to my own sins. He has torn them from me, as Macduff was torn from his mother, and what a singular pleasure he has derived from the operation. He has been not only my father but the father of every sin I ever committed. And because I realize the double sense of parenthood with which he awaits me, the taint of my guilt is already rising strong. Soon it will be so powerful as to eclipse my fear of him, and then I shall be completely at his mercy. Again at his mercy, for Stephen saw now that his experience of the previous week had been a partial illusion. Mr. Hollis had indeed gone away for the week end only; the sight of his huddled body disappearing in the cab had meant merely an extirpation of the physical fear of his presence, and into the vacancy had rushed an expansion of the moral fear. In the street with the snow flurrying round him, Stephen saw clearly for the first time how great was the moral terror in which his father held him.

It's the party, he told himself, that has made me susceptible; the party and the phone call and what I did with that awful woman. And it was moral fear that drove me from the house, for Father can foster my sins even through another person, even through so unlikely a channel as Duncan.

But why had his father been unable to resurrect the sins that lay dormant in the other guests? Why had they been able to laugh and treat the matter as a joke? Was not sin universal?

For as long as he could remember Stephen's every action had been colored or dulled, quickened or stopped, by the omnipresent consciousness of his father's sin-detecting eye. How would Father look at me if he saw me doing this? What will he say when he finds out? Dare I do it in the face of salvation? And as he grew older—dare I *not* do it for the sake of my own salvation? The eye remained unwinking before him and must be appeased or spat into. No action was taken, no state of mind assumed, without the watching eye as its motivation. I honestly believe, Stephen reflected, that I brush my teeth in a way he would, or would not, wish.

Yet all those others had laughed—at an excruciatingly funny old man who insisted upon fulminating. I allowed him to drag me from that house, the only place in which I can remember being happy, while the others simply laughed. I allowed him morally to pull me forth as surely as if he held me by the collar, and I did it merely to afford him an opportunity of minting further sins for me. I must be insane! I have taken no step since the cradle that he has not guided by his devious means, and he will continue to guide me until he dies unless I do something to prevent him. What am I to do? How long will he live? Who is he, besides being my father?

The others had laughed and Fabien laughed with them. He had seen no necessity for exercising restraint. The situation had been funny, honestly funny, and Fabien refused to be falsely directed even by the presence of a close friend.

Stephen drew his hands from his pockets and walked a little more briskly. The snowfall was lessening now, the street lamps blanched glittering paths along the white pavements. He began to swing his arms.

He let himself in by the front door, making no more or less sound than was absolutely essential, moving across the hall with each footfall making its scrupulously correct amount of squelchy sound. This was not laughing at a funny old man, and neither was it *not* laughing at him. This was behavior without a trace of direction.

The expected voice came to him through the gloom. "I've been waiting for you. Come in here immediately."

"Coming, Father." Pleased with the genuine equanimity of his voice, Stephen changed direction and entered the faintly lighted sitting room.

On the threshold he almost faltered. Had it been another man, or conceivably another occasion, he might have cried out at the figure that confronted him, but now the exclamation could only flicker and die at birth. By the light of a solitary standard lamp Mr. Hollis was sitting bolt upright in a chair, his pale round eyes burning like tiny pits of molten glass in a face so putty white that the scant eyebrows lent to it the appearance of an improperly finished wax mask. A faint tracery of dried spittle outlined the shape of his pale lips, and his mouth was curiously drawn down, disclosing only the lower teeth. He was sucking at the air like a man suffering slow asphyxia. He trembled from head to foot.

If it were a dog, Stephen thought, I could do something, but he has rendered me incapable of helping him as a man. He would strike me away if I went to his assistance. He doesn't want me. He wants only another session with sin.

But what a disappointment he's in for. Rather like a schoolboy who has read medical books for furtive pleasure and now finds himself in the dispassionate atmosphere of the delivery room in a maternity hospital.

"Sit down."

Stephen carried a chair across the room and seated himself a few feet from his father. A part of his mind had detached itself to watch the scene. He tried to imagine that he sat in a theater, watching the stage with critical eye. An interesting scene, faintly comic. Fabien would have laughed at this, too.

"Where have you been?" The question was little more than a whisper. Mr. Hollis was clenching the arms of his chair until the patches of brown on the backs of his hands stood out with a fungoid indecency. "Where have you been?"

"To a party." Stephen would have liked to say that it was an enjoyable party, but that would have broken the compact he made with himself as he strode through the falling snow. There was to be no provoking and no unprovoking. The cyclops eye was extinguished.

"I asked where you've been."

"Just to a friend's house."

"To the house of a harlot!"

"No, Father, to a friend's house."

"Don't lie to me, you—" The words dried in his mouth. When he spoke again his voice had slid up a little in pitch, the trembling had increased. "A cesspool," he said. "An iniquitous den of Satan. Don't deny it! I heard their drunken shouts with my own ears, the filthy carnal songs they were singing. What were they doing? I want to know what they were doing."

"Nothing wrong, Father," Stephen said mildly, and for an unguarded moment he wished it had been as wildly exciting as his father made it sound.

"Do you think I'm a fool?" Not even his wrath could hide the glint of triumph in Mr. Hollis's blazing eyes. "Perhaps you don't know that they phoned this house and invited your own sister to join them."

"I knew about that. It was a mistake."

"You knew about it?" His father drew a long, shuddering breath. "You knew and you did nothing when they spat upon the Word, when they mocked the name of the Lord? You did nothing to prevent the insults they heaped on me?"

"There were too many of them. There was nothing I could do."

"You lie!" The accusation rushed from a strangling throat. "You didn't want to do anything. You were too busy wallowing in the slime you've been heading for since you were a child. Lost to every decency, even the word given in the fifth commandment by the Lord God Almighty Himself."

"You should have hung up," Stephen said quietly. "There was no need to listen."

"What did you say?" An incredulous silence hung between them, and Stephen heard the clock ticking in the hall. "Are you trying to defend the behavior of that filthy, dissolute scum—"

"It's strange, Father," Stephen interrupted, "but they weren't like that until you spoke to them. I thought them charming and well behaved."

"Harlots!" It was a dry sob. "Whoremongers! They insulted me."

"You insulted them, Father," Stephen replied. "Moreover, you insulted me, far more deeply than anything you have ever received. I doubt that I can show my face among those people again. I'm ashamed of you."

His father's lunging weight hit him with a force that tumbled the chair backward and toppled them both in a heap on the floor. An incoherent torrent of vilification was pouring from Mr. Hollis's mouth, his legs and arms thrashed in a frenzy. Stephen lay motionless until the thin fingers began clawing at his eyes, then as gently as possible he thrust aside the old man's frail body and rose to his feet. "I don't wish to hurt you, Father," he said. "Please don't do that again."

Mr. Hollis lifted himself up, slowly and shakily, his gaze fixed immovably on his son's face. In the intensity of his expression there was something obscene, and Stephen would have liked to turn away. But he knew that he was lost if he failed this final challenge. He said: "Please sit down, Father. You'll have a bad attack."

Mr. Hollis tottered towards the chair with feeble steps, and Stephen could have laughed aloud at this sight of the man who had always kept him in fear. He stooped and picked up his own fallen chair, and as he straightened himself a shaft of unendurable hatred shot through him, vanishing as swiftly as it had come. He was calm again.

Under the light Mr. Hollis looked like a vague caricature of Ivan Simpson.

"That was an unpleasant scene," Stephen said, "to be indulged in by two grown men. It happened because you constantly overlook the fact that I am a grown man. Don't you see that I'm entitled to go to any sort of party I want, to drink if I wish—"

Mr. Hollis gathered up his withered lips and spat. The ball of spittle fell harmlessly between them. "Whoremonger!" he said.

"No, Father, I think that's a slight misunderstanding of terms on your part. A whoremonger is one who procures whores, what in common parlance we call a pimp. That's not what you mean, is it? You mean something quite different. Well, in that respect you're perfectly right. I'm exactly what you think I am. Tonight I went upstairs to a back bedroom with a woman old enough to be my mother. She was all painted and powdered and her body was flabby. You know what happened, of course, Father. I had *it*. I rolled on the bed with this fat hag and had *It*. Sins of the flesh, Father, lustful desires, hot moist bodies."

Suddenly he shouted "IT!" A feeling of ferocious contempt consumed him and he emphasized the word with a graphic gesture. "I enjoyed every minute of it, Father. I loved it. I shall do it again whenever I have the chance. Good night."

He went from the room without looking back, expecting the shouts to follow him but hearing only the sucked-in breathing become deeper, more rapid, the panting of a sick dog.

My feet are wet, he thought, as he continued up the stairs. I shall sleep well tonight.

On the first-floor landing a white nightgowned figure fluttered out of sight.

"Wake up," the voice pleaded again. "Wake up. He's having a bad attack."

The light above his head was switched on, and he saw his mother bending over him clad in a dressing gown, her pinched face drained of all color. From over by the door his brother Richard gaped into the room with goggling eyes.

"What's going on?" He sprang out of bed and reached for a robe. One glance sufficed to tell him that this constituted something far beyond the normal exigencies of the family. The air was charged with a nervous excitement foreign to the house, and his mother and brother, despite the fear on their faces, had about them an aura of anticipation, almost of eagerness. He tied the robe around him, casting off the vestiges of sleep. The scene with his father came back with infinite clarity.

"Is it Father?"

"What are we going to do?" Mrs. Hollis was wringing her hands. "He's terribly ill."

"You'd better get out of the house right away," Richard said in an awestruck voice. "He says you've got to go. Now!"

"Does he?" From downstairs came a faint cry, like that of a trapped animal. Stephen pushed his brother aside and went out onto the landing. "I'll go and see him."

He ignored the frantically whispered persuasions of his mother. He was descending the stairs when the cry sounded again, bringing him to an involuntary halt. I am not afraid, he told himself. But how damned unpleasant this was going to be.

"Stay away from him," Mrs. Hollis whispered. She was beginning to cry. "Stay away, you'll only make him worse."

He shook off her restraining hand and continued his descent, fearful that if he listened longer the temptation would prove too great and he would run away. Poor Father! Everyone was deserting him. Maybe Stephen could help him now that he was really ill, could establish even at this late hour some form of filial relationship that would work to their mutual benefit. He walked firmly along the landing and started down the second flight of stairs, then he looked up, conscious that his mother and Richard were no longer following. They were huddled together on the landing, peering over the bannisters, following his progress with fearful eyes.

His bare feet made no sound. He walked across the hall and looked through the sitting room door.

Mr. Hollis was in the chair where his son had last seen him, but there was a singular difference in his pose. His head was down, his body bent almost double. He was crouching over his knees, upon which lay an open book that apparently he was attempting to read aloud. Stephen recognized the book as one of the many Bibles, but whether or not it was truly being read he was unable to tell. In the stream of mumbling gibberish that issued from his father's mouth the individual words were indistinguishable.

He took in the details of the room at a glance during that first apprehensive moment—the open bookcases, the Bibles littering the floor, the way the bald crown of his father's unmoving head shone in the light of the lamp. But by the second moment he was aware of only one thing. He was staring at his father's legs, feeling a wild desire to break into a kind of laughter hitherto unknown to him. For Mr. Hollis had removed his trousers. His legs emerged from under his shirt, pale as the stems of clay pipes, forming a knobbly right angle at his knees and descending thin and brittle-seeming directly to his shoes.

Stephen had not realized before that his father had such enormous feet. The desire to laugh was almost irrepressible. All at once he went limp with pity.

"Father," he said. The quietly spoken word was lost as Mr. Hollis flung back his head, stared at the ceiling, and made the strange sound again. It sounded no louder than from upstairs.

"Father," Stephen repeated, remaining at the door. "Father!" The head came down slowly, cautiously. The mouth was still open, the eyes looking from the corners of their sockets with incalculable cunning. Then the ridiculous thin white legs shifted their position, and Mr. Hollis looked fully at his son with the mildest expression Stephen could remember ever having seen upon his father's face.

This poor old man *is* my father, he thought. He said: "You're ill, Father. I'm going to send for a doctor."

"You're wrong, Stephen." The tone was regretfully corrective. "There's nothing the matter with me, my boy."

"You're not well," Stephen persisted gently. "I'll phone Dr. Raddon."

The cunning look returned to Mr. Hollis's face. He turned his head away and appeared to be pondering the matter. Stephen relaxed and stepped forward into the room, and immediately the Bible fell to the floor with a loud thwack. His father leapt from the chair and rushed at him like a scuttling white spider, a thin whistle coming from between the pale lips. Stephen fled across the hall and up the stairs, disemboweled by fear.

He had not been followed. He stood catching his breath. Damn him, he thought, shivering with anger. God damn and blast and curse the filthy old devil. It was now or never. Swiftly he crossed the dark landing and entered his father's study to make the phone call that would irrefutably enforce his undirected and dispassionate victory.

"What are you going to do?" Mrs. Hollis stepped out from behind the study door and came to the center of the room. All the muscular power seemed to have departed from her face, leaving it drained and expressionless. Her opaque eyes were without depth, two areas of enamel painted on the inside of her spectacles. "What did he say to you?" she asked.

"Nothing at all. I'm going to call Dr. Raddon. Where are Richard and Esther?"

"I don't know." His mother came very close. For a moment he thought she was going to put her arms around him, shattering the taboo of affection, but she arrested her movement and stared into his face.

She said in a firm, clear voice: "Don't let your father die in the house. I couldn't bear that." A lifetime of indescribable misery swam briefly into the two patches of paint behind her spectacles. Her colorless face gathered in a tiny frown. "Don't let him die in the house."

"No," Stephen said, staring back at her with a feeling of awe. "No, of course not." He wanted to kiss her, but she wouldn't have liked it. He picked up the telephone and dialed a number.

"What are you doing?" The peculiarly breathless voice sounded loudly in his ear.

"Dr. Raddon, please." The words came of their own volition. He knew as he opened his mouth that it was all quite useless. The breathing increased in intensity. There was a deep gulping of air.

"The Lord God Jehovah shall purge them with fire...."

He lowered the telephone and put his hand over the mouthpiece, but the declamation still floated up to him faintly from downstairs. "I can't get an outside call," he explained. "Father is on the hall extension. Can you keep him away from this phone if I get him up here?"

His mother looked helplessly about the room. "Perhaps I can. I'll try." Stephen nodded and lifted the telephone.

"Praise ye the Lord," he said. "He delighteth not in the strength of a horse. He taketh not pleasure in the legs of a man."

There was a long silence, and from the noise that followed Stephen deduced that his father had flung the phone to the floor. "Keep him away from that," he said, carefully replacing the telephone. "He'll be up here in a minute."

Mrs. Hollis was crying. "He—he's awful," she said. "Don't let him get you."

"That's fine." Stephen paused indeterminately, then slipped across the dark landing and hid in the bathroom.

"And now the axe is laid unto the root of the tree. He will burn up the chaff with unquenchable fire." Mr. Hollis's voice ascended waveringly from the well of the hall and dispersed in the pressing silence that lay over the house. Stephen tried to visualize what would happen if his father should enter the bathroom. His heart began to beat in his throat. My victory is being taken from me, he thought, my position is ignominious. He put out his hand and squeezed the bathroom doorknob.

"'Jesus loves me, this I know.'" Mr. Hollis had started to sing. His quavering voice drew nearer, his feet performing a shuffling obligato on the stairs. Stephen released his grip on the handle. He couldn't go out there. The old man was too ridiculous in his shirt and his shoes, with those spindly legs, those huge feet. He couldn't look at his father in that condition, it would be indecent. He broke into a sweat. He felt foolish and afraid, undecided now whether he should even call the doctor.

"'Yes, Jesus loves me, the Bible tells me so.'" Mr. Hollis was on the landing, and Stephen heard distinctly the sobbing breath with which the song ended. A thick, gluey silence fell again upon the house, and he wondered if the ears of everyone else had suddenly begun ringing. His eardrums seemed to have dilated. He could hear nothing but a high, singing whine. I shall be sick in a moment, he thought, and was vaguely relieved to be in a bathroom.

"Get out of my house!" The shouted command was near and loud and Stephen thought it must be meant for him alone. "Get out of my house, all of you! Leave me alone!" Mr. Hollis's footsteps receded along the landing. He began to sing again. His voice became suddenly muffled as the door of the study was closed. Stephen emerged from the bathroom and descended to the hall, his bare feet whispering to him as he ran. He picked the phone from the floor and dialed with a trembling forefinger.

"May I speak to Dr. Raddon?"

"Yes, what it is?" demanded a sleepy, testy voice. "This is Raddon speaking."

"Stephen Hollis," Stephen said, trying to remain calm and indifferent. "I'm afraid my father is ill. Would you come over as soon as you can?"

"Oh, yes," the doctor replied, and his voice had changed to a polite, almost feline purr. "A heart attack, I presume. I have given him some medicine, and if you keep him quiet—"

"You don't understand," Stephen interrupted. "He's taken off his trousers."

"He's done what?" And yet there was a tone to the question that indicated this was not an entirely unexpected development. "Oh well, in that case—"

There was a click as the upstairs phone was lifted from its cradle. "A generation of vipers," Mr. Hollis said. "Bring forth therefore fruits meet for repentance. I want to speak to my office. They're trying to ruin me. They shall be destroyed. Every tree which bringeth not forth good fruit is hewn down and cast into the fire."

His breath was coming faster. "Get out of my house! All of you, out of my house!" The voice rose until the words tumbled one into another in a high-pitched stream of incomprehensible sound. Stephen realized that the doctor also was speaking. He strained his ears. "Would you say that again, please."

"I'll be over right away. In the meantime I suggest you get the police."

"Thank you," Stephen said, and his father's voice ceased. In the gulf of silence that followed he heard the doctor say, "Oh Christ, what a bloody nuisance," and then there was a click. He replaced his own telephone and walked into the sitting room, picking his way over the scattered Bibles and dropping into the chair where his father had been sitting a thousand years before. To hell with him, he thought, I can't go on any longer. Let him come down and I'll smash his face in.

But calling the police was out of the question. It had happened many times since he was a boy, the spicy whisper sibilated into the shrinking ear. "The police took Mr. Soandso away last night. The police came and fetched Mr. Suchandsuch this morning." No more was needed, except the succeeding exchanged look. Everyone knew it was one of the duties of the Westmount police to remove lunatics, to take them away to the Verdun Protestant Mental Hospital, whence few of them returned. These happenings were seldom discussed openly, but everyone whispered, even the children. Stephen could hear them now, furtively moving their lips in every corner of the room. "Mr. Hollis, early this morning. They say he was dangerous. Poor Mrs. Hollis."

The hissing minutes passed and nothing occurred. His ears began unbearably to ring again. If anything happens to Mother, he told himself, she will cry out, so I needn't worry about that. Then what *am* I worrying about? The silence was crushing him, making it impossible to sit still. He rose from his chair and began gathering the Bibles, carrying them in twos and threes across the room and restacking them neatly in the cabinet. Perhaps I ought to read them all, he thought savagely, and then I shall be a wonderful man like that wonderful Mr. Hollis. He picked up the last copy, the one that had fallen from his father's knees, and opened it at random. Then he looked for a specific passage.

And the battle went sore against Saul, and the archers hit him; and he was sore wounded of the archers. Then said Saul unto his armour bearer, Draw thy sword and thrust me through therewith, lest these uncircumcised come and thrust me through, and abuse me. But his armour-bearer would not; for he was sore afraid: therefore Saul took a sword, and fell upon it.

He read it through several times, the last time reading it aloud to himself, quietly. A peace descended upon the house, a tangible, velvety softness of infinite tranquillity. He sank back in the chair and closed his eyes.

He heard the doctor's car drive up. Someone answered the front door, and the doctor's hard footsteps went clattering up the stairs and along the landing above. Stephen counted slowly up to two hundred and fifty and got to his feet. There was a rustle behind him and Esther came into the room, clad in a white nightgown.

"Father's dead," she said, "he's dead," and sank down onto the settee, regarding her brother with a blank gaze.

"Is he? Oh." He could think of nothing else to say. He turned his back on her and crossed to the window. The doctor's car stood outside, its gray bodywork growing slowly silver in the light of the false dawn that crept over the roofs of the opposite houses. Stephen flung the window open and the air rushed in, icy cold and fresh. He took a deep breath, and all at once he felt the power in him that had been suppressed since childhood come bursting through its dams, filling him, inflating him, engulfing him. He shivered, as with an ague.

That's the doctor's car out there, he said under his breath, and this is myself. His eyes bulged with astonishment, he folded his arms slowly and dug into his biceps with the tips of his fingers. This was himself! It was an incredible fact.

"Stephen." Esther had not moved. She sat on the settee, hands folded in her lap. The blank look had vanished from her eyes, and they were large and luminous in the half-light. Stephen thought his sister was about to cry.

"Stephen," she asked, "is it true?"

"What?" he said.

She moistened her lips. "Did someone really phone up last night and ask me to a party?"

He looked at her for a long moment, resisting an impulse to touch her hair. "Sure, Esther," he answered softly, nodding his head. "Several people wanted you to come. It was a very good party, you'd have enjoyed it."

She rose to her feet, standing very erect, and the tiny smile which played around her lips transfigured her whole face. "I only wondered," she said, and with a little nod went gliding from the room, a queenly female figure dressed all in white.

Richard was coming down the stairs, crying loudly in a series of shuddering childish sobs. Stephen heard a low murmur of voices and the weeping ceased, and he guessed that Esther was offering words of comfort to their brother. He felt surprised until he realized again that his father was dead, then he wondered if the taboos had died also, all of them. Only the broad light of day would tell. He resumed his close study of the doctor's car.

The silver light over the roofs grew stronger. The shadows were disappearing. The snow changed to a faint hue of pale lavender.

Miriam turned from the window and went back to the mirror for a last good look at her reflection. Her face was heavily lined, sagging from lack of sleep, her eyes red and swollen from weeping. The tears had left grimy channels on the smeared remnants of last night's make-up.

I look horrible, she thought, as if I'd spent the whole night on the streets. She turned away, her throat becoming dry, and she wondered if the uncontrollable weeping was about to begin again. If she could sleep, but there was no point in trying to sleep at this hour. She went downstairs, treading gently lest she wake the maids, and put a percolator of coffee on the stove.

It was the first time in many months she had looked closely at her kitchen, and now its brightly colored neatness seemed to act as a soothing agent upon her nerves. With nothing else to do, she opened a few cupboards, admiring the display of food, wondering if she might find something to tempt her nonexistent appetite. The aroma of coffee began to permeate the room.

She thought: I need it black, good and black, and for some reason the idea made her laugh. This really was rather like the movies, the sort of thing that Greer Garson or Joan Crawford or any of the more mature actresses did when about to emerge triumphant from an exceedingly dramatic emotional trial. And then the camera showed them smiling reflectively, ruefully, bravely.

Miriam's mouth quirked greerishly, her eyes became crawford. In a sparkling kitchen, in the morning—black coffee. After the storm, the sweet reasoned calm.

She walked out into the hall and picked up the telephone. "I want long-distance to Chicago," she said. "The Mirimar Hotel." The fact that she had to redial did not at all interfere with the cresting flow of her mood. "The Mirimar Hotel," she repeated and waited patiently, smoothing back the soft hair from her forehead.

"Mr. Marvin Sabel, please," she said, and almost immediately he was talking to her, his voice all grumpy and growly like a lovable bear.

"Guess who this is."

"Miriam!" And now she could imagine him sitting up suddenly in bed, his eyes gone all wide, his hair tousled and curly. "Is anything the matter?" he asked in a worried voice.

"Nothing at all, Marvin dear. But I got up early and it's a lovely morning and I was making myself some coffee and I suddenly realized that I missed you very, very much. It's lovely just to hear your voice. How are you, Marvin?"

There was a stunned pause at the other end, then his kind, gentle tones came over the wire, brimming with happiness. "This is really very sweet of you, honey. How are you this morning? It's raining like hell down here."

"I'm fine," Miriam answered, and the fact that it wasn't raining in Montreal made her laugh aloud. "Oh Marvin, isn't it marvelous," she cried, "how we can speak to each other over all these hundreds of miles of wire just as if we were in the next room."

She discovered that she was weeping again.

The cab disappeared around the gateway. The sun rose higher.

"That," said Fabien, "was the last person capable of leaving. The party, I think, is over."

Crystal smiled, and wondered that he could remain so fresh. They walked across the hall hand in hand. "A wonderful party," she said. "The best I was ever at. A success. They'll be talking about it for months."

"But not immediately." Fabien indicated the sleeping figures, reclining on chairs and settees. "I wonder what happened to Bill and Duncan."

"In the cellar."

"Bless their sweet drunken hearts," Fabien said merrily. "And now, my darling, what about you?"

"Me? Coffee. In the kitchen. For two. I'll make it. And after that I must get some sleep."

"It is possible," Fabien said dubiously, "that all the bedrooms are occupied." He paused. "But never mind. We'll find something for you, won't we, my darling? We'll find something."

They pushed open the kitchen door. Ivan Simpson was still eating.

PART THREE

THE SACKCLOTH

The singular springtime of the city of Montreal was upon them. Its advent had been a slow, almost unnoticeable procedure, a melting creep remarked by so few of those who filled the busy streets that when, indisputably, it had arrived they looked at each other in the stone canyon of St. Catherine Street and exclaimed, "Why, hello. Spring's here!" while dodging through the chaotic traffic on their way to work or to the ever gaping stores.

The procedure was unvarying throughout the years, which perhaps explained the absence of that slowly growing excitement in the hearts and faces of the populace that characterizes the coming of spring in other, more gentle climes. In France or England, for example, and in many parts of the United States, when March comes around there is a subtle quickening discernible in the demeanor of the inhabitants, a way of looking from side to side and slightly dilating the nostrils, of giving cursory but unexpected glances at trees and gazing at the sky with puckered eyes denoting a near-smile. Even the unsusceptible man can have the event communicated to him by the behavior of his friends. "The delicate fingers of Spring," he will tell himself if he is of this particular disposition, "are busy again at their elegant traceries, and all of Nature is awakening at the gentle touch. For my old acquaintance, George Barnard, looks more than ever vacuous and the children in the streets are making an unseemly noise. This may be a good time to ask the boss for a raise."

But not so in Montreal, where the children of obdurate and intractable employers are unduly noisy even when blizzards sweep the streets in which they play and frozen passers-by wonder why the healthy, and mostly handsome, little faces are not dropping off with frostbite. For in Montreal the delicate fingers are kept from their rightful traceries until they can be withdrawn from thick gloves when the snow ceases to fall in April. Even then, none can look at the slot of sky imprisoned between the buildings, for all are too busy watching the treacherous, icebound pavement beneath their feet, or casting fearful, sidelong glances to avoid the deluge of slush from passing motorists. Moreover, the trees which line a few of the streets are too magnificently high for buds to be observed with any accuracy, while smaller trees have been isolated since the previous November in unvisited, snow-covered parks.

The only noticeable changes seem, to the distraught pedestrian, entirely unconnected with Nature.

The white coat of snow is shed from the pavements, and a vernal rippling is heard only in the gutters. Now do the inhabitants of Montreal tread yet more warily, for revealed to them, in its patchy splendor of brown and gray, is the hard, caked mass of ice accumulated upon the city since the first of the winter's snows. This is the time when the sand, strewn to prevent slipping, blows in clouds about the streets and into eyes and noses and mouths, when the Montrealer rubs his roughened skin reflectively and decides to change his heavy winter coat for a lighter one that would warm an Englishman or Frenchman through his severest winter. Now do old ladies, incredibly courageous, affix creepers to their shoes and venture into the streets as they have done the year round. Chains on car wheels rattle with a new vigor, and the backs of taxis describe furious arcs when brakes are applied. Non-Canadian visitors fall over repeatedly in the streets. A few people break their ankles. Montreal's erratic tramway system becomes more so.

After which, it rains. Sometimes the rainy spell lasts for weeks, permitting Canadians to deplore with clear conscience the vagaries of the English climate. The sand is laid, temporarily, local eyes clear, and St. Catherine Street becomes a mass of umbrellas, all of them carried by women, because for men it is considered better to be wet than be thought a little odd.

(For this same reason it is better also, in many circles, not to paint, sculpt, play an instrument, show an interest in music, read, write, admire scenery, like the theater, or converse in words of more than one syllable. In these same circles, however, it is permitted—nay, desired— that you attend the movies as often as possible, laugh at unfunny and improper cartoons, gawp at hypermammiferous illustrations in "girlie" magazines, pay one visit to Montreal's small museum to admire the Greek vase depicting returning satyrs and their steeds, recite *in toto* the monosyllabic broadcast made last night by your favorite comedian, sing any amount of songs so long as they are on the hit-parade, and publicly hawk-up in the streets. These are the circles that Dante did not deign to notice when he visited the Inferno.)

Then it rains, Stephen murmured to himself, adjusting his umbrella more directly overhead and resuming his main thought. And gradually the city's hard-packed coating begins to melt. Until one day you emerge from your door and see the most reassuring sight that Montreal has to offer, a beautiful, clear, uncovered patch of cement paving beneath your feet. You sigh deeply and consider changing your cumbersome overshoes for the more expeditious rubbers. Only a few days more and the efforts of conscientious citizens, combined with the industry of scrapers employed by the city, will have cleared the streets almost entirely and put an end to the hazardous slipping and sliding.

And now, perhaps, someone will look at the sky, for this is the very day when acquaintances are greeted with a recognition of the season. "Hello, seems like spring's here, doesn't it?" The delicate fingers have precipitated into indelicate action and given to each inhabitant of Montreal a resounding thump on the back, jarring at last the thoughts of men and, more especially, of women, to long-forgotten Nature—Who, it is well known, resides never less than thirty miles from the city.

Weather forecasts are heard anxiously, groceries ordered, children adjured, and finally the woman and her offspring depart to spend the following months in the summer cabin from whose precincts Nature has not budged since they departed the previous fall. The husband, able to visit only at week ends, remains behind for uneasy cooking and dilatory weekday adulteries. The partially abandoned city is taken over by American tourists, driving with the draped clothes hangers swinging merrily in the backs of their large and shiny cars, or sitting dejectedly on the front steps of overcharging rooming houses, lending to Montreal a fleeting resemblance to Keokuk, Ia. The heat descends.

But not yet; not until school is out and graduation over. The rain had ceased and Stephen stopped to furl his umbrella, smiling to himself at the pleasantness of life. He nodded as an unashamedly middle-aged woman passed by, and she returned his smile. He resumed walking and nodded again to the youth who closely followed the woman. The sun came out.

It was all simply a question of scale, he told himself. The circle to which one belonged was relatively unimportant so long as the maximum pleasure was derived from it and the maximum integrity contributed. By this yardstick he knew now that he had made a great many mistakes in the recent past, not the least of which, he reflected, concerned Duncan's book. What difference who paid the rent and supplied the food? The writing of the book, he should have realized, constituted an expression of integrity by Fabien and Duncan, to each other and to the circle they had elected to form. And as part of that circle, Stephen thought, I should have recognized the fact many months ago, for if a person like Bill can sense it, then it should have been transparent to someone like myself. I should have listened to Duncan more carefully that morning in the bedroom when I imagined that Bill had taken a dislike to me. I should have—

He detected the first formulation in his mind of self-excuse and dismissed the gambit as unworthy of his new self, dangerous to his new-found peace of mind. Excuses belonged to the era of his father, and there was no longer anyone to whom they need be made. There was no longer any God or any guilt, and the vague sense of uncleanliness that before was with him perpetually had now departed. Honesty and truthfulness; he mulled them over without shyness. The conception of integrity was embarrassing only at first usage. Afterward it became a veritable bulwark, a way of life.

He lifted his eyes to the clearing sky and thanked God for second chances. A joyous impulse caused him blithely to swing his umbrella, and he smiled at several more passers-by, some of whom smiled back. Every person pleased him and only the prospect was vile. How nice it would be to go for an ocean trip this summer with Fabien. There was plenty of money. Father had left it all to Mother, true, but Father had left a great deal more than expected.

Stephen hoisted his umbrella onto his shoulder as if it had been a rifle. Duncan killed my father, he thought, and I bear him no malice because I know it was an accident. Spring has come for me.

Up on the campus the brave buds would be opening and students passing through the Roddick Gate would be contributing something of beauty to the scene about them. Stephen quickened his steps and hurried toward McGill, whistling a little tune and pointing his toes meticulously.

II

"You are taking down too many, Stephen," protested Mrs. Hollis as he took down another of the paintings and leaned it against the wall. "Those pictures cost us a great deal of money. It seems a pity to put them down in the cellar."

"Don't worry," Stephen replied. "This place will really look like a sitting room when we've finished. What do you think of redoing it in fawn and French-gray?"

Mrs. Hollis sucked in her lower lip and flicked an imaginary speck of dust from the bookcase. "I don't know; it doesn't seem right, somehow, to be doing it so soon. Why not put the pictures away and let me get used to the room without them first. We could decide about the redecorating in a few weeks."

"I'd like to move all these Bibles, if you don't mind."

"Why—yes, I think that will be all right. You can keep your schoolbooks there. I have a Bible up in my room, and you can take one of those if you think you'll want one."

"No, thank you, Mother." It was an opportunity he had awaited. "I had enough of the Bible the night Father died."

In all the weeks that had passed this was the first direct mention between them of Mr. Hollis's death. Stephen's mother sat down on a chair and looked at him from placid eyes that were curiously at variance with the way her lips had suddenly tightened. "You've never told me who it was that called here that night. Was it the boy who came to dinner that time, the one with the red hair?"

Stephen shook his head, and the feeling of self-gratification amply repaid him for the lie even before it was told. This was something that Fabien would appreciate and admire. "No, Mother, it was a fellow I met at Chester's place one time. He must have heard us mention Esther, though why he should call her up I don't know except that he was a bit drunk."

Mrs. Hollis looked down at her hands. "That would explain it," she said. "I didn't like the boy with red hair. He was low-class."

"He is a little," Stephen admitted, and would have continued, but the approbation within him of his new-found loyalty was flowing too strongly and would permit no further condemnation. This was a glorious feeling—elevating and dignifying the whole of human kind. He added, "Duncan's had a pretty hard life, I believe, but he's okay when you get to know him. He certainly wouldn't want to help kill an old man he'd never met."

"Kill him? What did you say?" Mrs. Hollis got swiftly to her feet and began fussing at some ornaments on the mantelpiece, but Stephen had seen the startled fear that flickered across her face. "You musn't talk about it like that, Stephen. Your father was a very sick man, we expected him to go at any time. You've only got to ask Dr. Raddon and he'll tell you himself that he's surprised your father lasted as long as he did."

Stephen frowned impatiently. This was a line of conversation that must be halted before it proved to be a permanent and dreary bore. He crossed the room and leaned on the mantelpiece so that he was looking into his mother's face. "Why the protesting tone?" he asked. "You've nothing to reproach yourself with. You were a good wife, you brought up his children, looked after his home, listened to him when—"

He stopped as his mother began shaking her head. "There's something you don't know about," she said. "Just before he died that night, up in the study, he accused me of having stolen his children's affection from him."

"Pooh!" Stephen said, with an airy wave. "He wasn't himself that night."

But Mrs. Hollis was still shaking her head. "He said it to me often before. Ever since you were small children."

"What utter damn nonsense," Stephen snapped, bringing his fist down sharply upon the mantelpiece. "What did Father ever do to make any of us even like him?" He looked at his mother's stricken face and saw that this, for some reason, was the wrong method. Gently removing an ornament from her hand he returned it to its proper place and smiled softly. "Don't worry, Mother, the idea just made me angry for a moment. Father knew very well how fond I was of him."

"Were you? Were you really?"

"I was telling him so when I got home from the party that night. That's one reason why I went downstairs after you woke me up; I couldn't believe he wanted to throw me out of the house so soon after our conversation. I guess he just wasn't himself."

His mother's face cleared and he knew she believed him. "Dr. Raddon said it was liable to happen any time. Your father had been overworking himself for years. I pleaded with him to let Richard do more at the office, but he'd never listen to me."

"He had a mind of his own. I shall miss the discussions I used to have with him."

"I miss him, too," Mrs. Hollis said. "I miss him terribly."

Stephen looked at her sharply, seeking a sign that would tell him this was merely a performance of the anguished minuet formally demanded of the recently bereaved. With a shock of something like revulsion he saw that his mother was entirely sincere: a hint of tears glinted behind her glasses, her mouth was twitching at the corners. And now that he studied her closely it was obvious that what, during these past weeks, he had mistaken for placidity was in reality the stamp of bereftness, a resigned look of incompletion that probably she would wear until the end of her days. He became aware, all at once, of the strength of habit, the continual and peculiar form of sustenance that Mrs. Hollis had been drawing from her husband for so many years that its withdrawal had left her hungry, with an overwhelming sense of loss. Much the same sense of loss, thought Stephen, as one must experience on losing a gangrened leg. He said gently: "I know how much you loved Father."

It was a daring statement, ripping the very fabric of the Hollis tradition, but Mrs. Hollis showed no signs of surprise and Stephen was encouraged. "I can't help thinking," she said, "of the days when he was your age. He was a wonderful man."

"Yes," Stephen agreed warmly, and looked up to see Esther standing beside the doorway. "I'm glad," he continued, "that I was able to talk with him just before he died. When I think back, it was almost like saying good-by."

An odd mixture of emotions chased across Mrs. Hollis's face, then she glanced downward from the corners of her eyes and sighed. But when she looked again into Stephen's her expression was one of unmixed relief, and he knew that whatever had been troubling her was past. Only the loss remained behind her eyes. She said: "I'm glad you don't bear him any resentment for wanting to put you out that night."

Stephen gave her arm a reassuring pat. "He wasn't himself that night. The only person I'm angry with is Richard, for letting him work so hard."

Mrs. Hollis made no movement. "Richard has asked for a new car, but I can't let him have it until the estate is properly settled."

"And what does Esther want?" Stephen asked, grinning.

His sister came forward into the room, blushing to the roots of her hair and looking, Stephen thought, surprisingly less plain than usual. "Oh, shut up," she said. "I don't want anything. What are you all doing in here?"

"Stephen thought we might redecorate this room, but I'm not sure whether I'd like it or not. What do you think?"

"I don't care. I'm used to it this way."

"I think we should redo the whole house," Stephen said.

His mother opened her mouth to resist the idea, but before she could speak Esther blurted out: "Is that what you want, Stephen?"

For a moment he was unable to answer. The question, delivered with a directness quite foreign to Esther, had caught him off balance. He realized that he was vaguely frightened and looked at his sister for evidence that she was prosecuting some devious plan. But the plain face was blank, the eyes looking at him with only faint interest.

"Well, no," he said, "but I do have a selfish scheme up my sleeve. I'd like to take a trip to Europe this summer. My professor thinks it would help me in my studies, do me a lot of good. What do you think, Mother, could we afford it for a couple of months?"

She was watching him with eyes that had narrowed slightly. "I might manage it. Who would you be going with?"

"I don't know yet," he answered, unable to refrain from grinning. "But Duncan can't afford it and I wouldn't go with him if he could."

"I shouldn't want to think of you traveling all over Europe and boozing," his mother said, using the word so beloved of Canadian temperance members. "If you're sure you'll be in the right company I might be able to manage it. Father wanted you to get the best of everything from your education."

Stephen saw the expression of loss in her eyes become more

pronounced. He picked up an armful of paintings and said brightly: "Come on, Esther, give me a hand down the cellar with these things. We have to keep the place tidy." She trailed after him down the narrow stairs while he ran over in his mind the methods by which he could make an approach. His momentary fear of her had become more frightening in retrospect, and he must lay the ghost at once or be haunted by it forever.

"What do you think," he asked, ridding himself of his burden, "of repainting the hall and having black carpet on the stairs?"

She laid down the two pictures she was carrying. "I don't know," she said indifferently, and then she stared, probing his eyes, and Stephen knew they would be strangers to each other for the rest of their lives. How oddly awful, he thought, that we have grown up together and yet I have no idea of what she is thinking. Indirect approaches, filled with obscure family reference, were obviously going to be useless. He said to her:

"You were listening on the night Father died."

A long moment passed and she nodded, her face betraying nothing.

"You know, then, that I was lying to Mother up there in the sitting room."

"Yes, I knew." Her expression was slowly altering, her eyes began to shine. "I'm glad you did. There's no point in hurting her."

"The morality of an action," Stephen said, "depends on motive from which we act."

"You sound like Father."

"Hardly. It's a quotation from Dr. Johnson."

"Is he dead too?" she asked.

"Yes."

"So's Father." Esther moved closer to him and he thought she was going to cry. He was completely unprepared when she thrust her face forward, whispering fiercely, "And none too soon! I'm damned glad he is dead, the nasty old thing!" Imbued with a glorious sense of her own wickedness, she opened her mouth and called Mr. Hollis every bad name to which she could lay her tongue.

There were not many and few were strong, and soon she was reduced to a repetitive mickmack of improvisation that sent Stephen into gales of laughter as it terminated in "rotten old pig." Esther stood with her mouth open, gasping from her efforts, then she too began to laugh. "What a fool I am," she said. "I've wanted to say that to him ever since I was a kid."

"You can do anything you want, now," he told her.

She shook her head, her eyes clouding. "No, I can't. I can't even go to church with a clear conscience now he isn't here to force me. I want to go so much that it would be sinful to indulge myself."

"Now you begin to sound like Father."

"You know what I mean," she said, blushing deeply, and for the first time in his life Stephen became dispassionately considerate of a member of his own family. He bit back his derision of Chester Arden and patted Esther's shoulder.

"Cheer up. Do what you want, and I'll help whenever I can. Who knows, perhaps the Hollises will develop into a happy and desirable family once Mother has stopped missing Father quite so much."

"Yes," she said, and added absently: "I don't like Richard, though."

"Neither do I. He's a stinker. I bet he makes a mess of Father's business."

She moved away across the cellar so that her back was turned to him. Her head was bowed, and Stephen thought that from this view she looked very unhappy. "Are you and your friends having any more parties?" she asked over her shoulder.

No, he thought sharply, not that, and became acutely wary. One of the conclusions of his new existence was that Fabien and the family were two distinct spheres to be kept apart until each was translucently clear to him and easily manageable. For the time being one was infinitely more important than the other, and he knew instinctively that to bring them together, even briefly, would result in his being left with only the lesser. He said: "Everything has been quiet lately. Why do you ask?"

She turned and faced him squarely. "Do you know," she said, "that I'm thirty-five years old and I've never been to a proper party. I want to see what they're like."

If he voiced the thoughts presently in his mind it would mean saying good-by to all the ambitions he had for molding his family into the pleasant, poised group of which he could be proud. Esther would be immensely angry, and it was within her power to make others more so; a situation would arise, impossible to cope with, and there would never afterward be the gatherings in this house for which he so devoutly wished. And yet the mere thought of taking Esther anywhere near Fabien was impossible. Stephen had long since seen the folly of inviting Fabien to the house for dinner and was deeply grateful now that only Duncan had arrived. For Duncan was only a member of the circle, important as such, of course, and entitled to the loyalty and respect Stephen had learned to pay him during the past few weeks, but definitely not the central figure, the axis, as one might say. That position belonged alone to Fabien, and consequently anything that threatened

Fabien endangered the whole theoretical structure to which Stephen had become happily and obsessedly attached.

The thought of Fabien warmed him strangely. He looked at Esther and saw the bizarre improbability of bringing the two together. This was not jealousy, he knew, for a man was not jealous of his own sister. No—this was born rather of a regard for each of them. Neither was ready for the other and it was up to him to keep them apart until the time arrived when they were.

"What are you thinking about?" Esther demanded hopefully.

"It might be an idea to throw a party just after graduation. We could have it here in the house."

Esther shrugged and went listlessly to the stairs. "I suppose we could," she said, with a complete lack of enthusiasm. "Only the sitting room won't be ready by then, because Mother has to see whether she likes it without the pictures."

After she had disappeared from sight he began hunting around for the most dauntingly inaccessible place in which the paintings could be hidden. But he was still a little uneasy, and, all at once, he wanted to hurry to Fabien's house, that the feeling might be swamped and forgotten in the dedicated fierceness that seized him whenever he now crossed the threshold.

He thrust the pictures aside and hurried upstairs, sneaking out by the back door to avoid any questions. He felt better already.

III

There had been some excellent times of late, Stephen thought contentedly, contemplating where Fabien lay sprawled in an armchair, reading Saki. They had derived the ultimate possible enjoyments from the snow, driving religiously each week end to the Laurentians until the surfaces became too soft for skiing, sitting in the evening among the gaudily clad ski crowd, shouting songs and drinking between the glossy, roughwood walls of country taverns, driving home through the crisp air, still singing, skins tingling from snowburn and drink, spirits high. And there had been other small parties at the house, visits to movies at the University of Montreal, pub-crawls in the east end of the city where they wore their oldest clothes and walked in mock-danger, night strolls to the top of Mount Royal to see the city below them like a flung sackful of jewels, concerts at Plateau Hall, excursions to the dimmer recesses of the Redpath Library—nothing spectacular, but all astonishingly enjoyable. And there had been talk, and talk, and more illuminating talk, where one spoke freely of things that before had been but dim and timid thoughts, where ease and confidence flowed together.

How beautiful the human mind, the human frame; sweet the fruits of intercourse when one had realized at what times to bow to the wind or raise a gale oneself. In this joyous Wonderland one was a little like Alice, holding the piece of mushroom in either hand, nibbling first one side and then the other, growing taller or smaller as the occasion demanded. And, like Alice, one encountered delight where least expected: the hitherto flat and two-dimensional was growing roses; the almost extinct sang enchanting ballads; sheep were, after all, humorous; goats possessed melting beards; gnats made puns; eggs held a mastery over words though they were doomed to fall from a wall and shatter.

Stephen asked: "Is Duncan around?"

Fabien laid aside the book and reached for a cigarette. "What a gloriously lazy existence we lead, and what a good thing we can all afford it. Duncan's upstairs in the throes of final composition. The book, I understand, is almost finished."

"I guess he's excited," Stephen said. "That would explain why he hasn't been drinking so much of late. What will he do when it's finished?"

"I hope, permit me to read it," Fabien smiled.

"Patience rewarded," said Stephen, pleased at this genial manifestation of his new creed. He went over and sat on the arm of Fabien's chair, laying a light hand upon the shirted shoulder. "You're a very patient person, my friend, and I don't mean only with Duncan. Think of all the pains you took with me."

"My dear boy," cried Fabien, looking up with eyes that had grown round. "I've never bothered with you in the slightest. What on earth are you talking about?"

Stephen squeezed the shoulder and flung his arm along the back of the chair. "Forget it. I'm being unsophisticated. There are still a few things I haven't got the hang of. Do you think Duncan will let Bill and me read his book?"

"Bill has seen it as it comes off the typewriter."

"That's right, I remember the first time I came here," Stephen said. "Things were confused for me that night. I was upset because I was making a hash while all the time I wanted to make an impression on you. I'd taken a liking to you at first sight."

"How very embarrassing of you."

They smiled at each other, and Stephen impulsively gave Fabien's hair a little pull. How unbelievably pleasant to be sitting in this golden world where there were no antagonisms. Stephen got casually to his feet.

"My sister wants to meet you, thinks it would be nice if we had a party.

What do you think?"

"Delighted. She's quite nice, isn't she?"

"She's not bad."

In the pause that followed, Fabien stubbed out his cigarette, then he looked up again, his large eyes softened perceptibly. Stephen guessed what was coming and the self-ennoblement within him reached its flood.

"I know I've asked before, but what exactly happened the night Duncan phoned your sister?"

Stephen dropped back onto the settee. "Ask as often as you like: precisely nothing happened that could be connected with this house. My brother Richard thought it was a great joke, that's all."

"Your father never knew about it?"

"He was ill in bed. He died the following night, so no one had time to tell him anything."

"This is important to Duncan. He's almost convinced that he talked to your father and it's preying on his mind."

"He's being silly," Stephen exclaimed heartily. "My brother Richard is notorious for his warped sense of humor and his dislike of me. He was trying to make a fool of me that night."

"He succeeded for a while," Fabien said dryly.

"Yes." The assent was little more than an expulsion of breath. "He showed horrible taste to pull such a trick when Father was dying, and I'll do my best to see that you never meet him. He'd be out of place in our circle."

Fabien looked at him quizzically. "Sometimes you sound rather like a page from the Bumper Book for Boys. I expect you at any time to suggest a midnight feast in the dormitory because your Mum has sent you a hamper of tuck. Did you spend your childhood reading British school magazines?"

"This nation's slogan and standard excuse," replied Stephen, "is that Canada is a young country. My mother has given something far more substantial than tuck. This morning she promised that I could go abroad for the summer."

"Nice. Where?"

"Anywhere so long as I can convince her it has historical associations, and that shouldn't be hard." The words came out swiftly. "I shall be glad to get away, I need the change. Father's death still hovers about the house, and I figure that if I go away and come back the old life will prove to have been a former life. I am trying to start afresh, you know, I am trying to—"

He spread his fingers in a gesture of inarticulation, the urge to confide making him feel vaguely silly. And now a passage from a book of school-day reminiscences, written by an Englishman, did flash into his head. The author was walking with his very best friend through a lane near the cricket pitch. The tock of the ball sounded through the still summer air, the lazy applause of the spectators; and the boys were both twelve years old. "To whom, in all the school," asked the very best friend, "would you choose to tell your secrets? Would you tell them to Marsden?" The author had shaken his head and, "Fifth best," he said. "Then to Willis?" asked the friend, offhand, but again the author shook his head. "Fourth best," he said. And so they went to third and then to second best, but the first best was neither asked nor named.

Stephen knew of nothing like this happening in Canadian schools, and wondered whether he would be feeling differently if the existing Canadian educational system were different. He looked up in time to catch the sympathy on Fabien's face. "I don't want to sail under false colors," he said cheerfully. "I didn't like my father well enough to brood on his death."

Fabien's expression became inscrutable. "I'm really very sorry, Stephen."

"No need to be."

"Sorry for the childhood you must have led. I remember distinctly the suicidal horror with which I regarded my first pubic hair. How perfectly awful to reach the age of thirteen and not have a parent who would tell you the facts of life."

Underneath the flippancy the sympathy had returned. With fruitful communion so easily obtainable, harrowing confidences were needless, would impede rather than promote. Stephen locked his secrets deeper and presented to Fabien the smiling face of conviviality.

"You foreigners take these things far more seriously than we do. Father's position in Canada has been taken over by something called a teen-ager."

"More Canadiana?" Fabien asked with a shudder. "Poor families. I claim, with great pride, that my father used to beat me for eminently sound reasons."

"Are you fond of him?" asked Stephen, and was perplexed and pleased that his voice sounded mildly envious.

"Extremely. We shall spend days together, this summer, in public gambling places."

"You make me jealous," Stephen said, seizing the immediate opportunity for confessing so inopprobrious a fault. "God! I'd like to go with you." He looked at Fabien with inadvertent eagerness, and his spirits crashed.

Something was wrong. Fabien was trying to compose his features into an expression of polite regret. The room chilled and grew darker; the forgotten, familiar ache returned full force. Unable to bear hearing the rejection from Fabien's mouth, he rushed, gabbling, into the breach of silence.

"What a damned cheek I have, inviting myself like that. I mean, just because my mother says I can go abroad doesn't mean that I have to thrust myself on you, does it? I should think you've put up with me enough as it is without having to drag me around with you all summer. Don't you think so?"

His laugh rang through the room with a greater heartiness than he intended, and he stopped too suddenly, beset by an empty foolishness. "I'm gibbering," he said. "I told you that I needed a change."

Fabien shifted uncomfortably in his seat, more discomposed than Stephen had seen him before. The sight intensified his own uneasiness until he felt the sweat break out on the palms of his hands. And abruptly there came a clear conception of what the world would be like when Fabien had gone. The tiny, self-mocking voice failed to answer his summons, and he found himself fighting a desire to go down on his knees and implore Fabien to remain where he always could be seen.

A shudder of warmth ran through Stephen's body, and when he spoke his voice was unnaturally high and thin. "I seem to have projected an awkward situation," he said, and, to his horror, the attempt at a natural laugh resulted in a high-pitched snicker.

"Oh dear." Fabien's customary lightness was failing him. "Stephen, you do force me into the most awful gaffes. When my parents invited me for the summer they said there would be room for only one friend. I wish you had given me time to break the news more amiably than this."

"That's okay," Stephen said. "I guess you invited Bill."

"No; Bill claims to be spending the summer in harrying the British Columbia fish. I've asked Duncan to go along."

Fabien looked down at his knees, studying them with a little frown as if observing them for the first time. It would have been an insignificant gesture in anyone else, but Stephen perceived in it the appalling significance and knew, as the flush spread over Fabien's face, that he was being deceived.

"Whom did you think I was going with?" Fabien asked with a patently false pertness.

"It's natural you should take Duncan, you've known him longer. I hope you both have a good time."

"Thank you."

The silence became increasingly uncomfortable, and Stephen was aware of a typewriter clacking somewhere in the upper regions of the house. A bell rang faintly and the typing stopped, to continue again with increasing speed.

Fabien rose, yawning with an unsuccessfully attempted nonchalance. "We seem to have worked up a torridly uncomfortable atmosphere. What is it, Stephen? Have I done anything wrong?"

He hesitated in reply, weighing the treason he might commit against the suspected treason committed against him, wondering if he dare admit to himself that these last weeks had been a stupidly delusive adumbration. Then he looked into Fabien's face and the decision was made, the peace laved him. He said truthfully: "I'd been counting on coming with you this summer."

"Oh, damn!" Fabien balled a fist and punched it into the palm of the other hand. "What a wretchedly silly business. But my mother's theory that three's a crowd has amounted to an obsession since I invited two other friends home for the summer a few years back. They almost wrecked the house between them and seduced every maidservant in the district—not to mention some of the employers. Mother has become quite adamant about it. One, she claims, can be managed, two, never."

"I've thought of something," Stephen said, carefully watching Fabien's expression. "What's to prevent my coming along and putting up at a nearby hotel? I can convince Mother that anywhere in Europe has historical associations. Where do you expect to be?"

"This year," Fabien said slowly, his face a bland mask, "my parents have arranged to spend the summer in Rio de Janeiro."

Stephen was already rising, shaking his head with a dull certainty. Devoid though she was of learning, Mrs. Hollis would be convinced that no history of any consequence had ever been made in Latin America—a place, as even the most austere Canadian knew, of primitive, sexual dances, drink, and Roman Catholics. Moreover, the exhaustive enquiries bound to be aroused by so bizarre a journey would eventually reveal the presence in the party of Duncan. Though Fabien alone might conceivably be permissible—wealth calling to money and persuading Mrs. Hollis to loosen her purse strings through association—Duncan could only cause them to be tied in huger and more inextricable knots. Stephen moistened his lips.

"Do you think I could have a drink?"

Fabien nodded, taking his arm and leading the way across the hall. Stephen noticed that the typing had ceased upstairs, and he wondered if Duncan were leaning forward on his typewriter, gazing into space, thinking of the coming summer and Rio de Janeiro. Stephen, from somewhere, had heard of a street there with gay, multicolored paving; of the beauties of the harbor, the sugar-loaf mountain, the long, sun-swept beach, where Fabien would doubtless go swimming and Duncan, vainly exhibitionist, would loll beside him in the sand, talking of what they had done the night before and would do again tonight. The name of Stephen would not be mentioned, and they would laugh over incidents of which he would never know.

"A glass of wine," he said, as they entered the kitchen.

Fabien's face was clear again, almost insouciant, as he arranged the glasses on the table and drew the cork from a dark bottle. "Nearly the last of a very good sherry," he said. "I'd like you to have what is left of the cellar when I go away."

"My mother wouldn't allow it in the house."

"I forgot. Too bad. Your health."

The smooth, gratifying warmth slid down Stephen's throat. "But are you sure Duncan is going to like it?" he asked.

"The sherry?"

"Rio de Janeiro."

Fabien finished his glass and poured another. "Why not?"

"He's not a good mixer and possibly he won't get along with your parents. They might not like him."

Fabien looked thoughtfully at his wine. "I think it abominable that you don't; he's an extraordinarily nice fellow. Do you have something against him?"

"Nothing!"

Stephen felt the cry sing from his throat, so eager was he, in this time of doubt, to reaffirm his new faith. His open eyes had seen the rocky path of snare and pitfall into which, inadvertently, he was wandering, and his heart beat with a frantic anxiety to return to its pristine state of the early morning. He turned gratefully to the revivifying draught of truthful confession, glimpsing suddenly, before he spoke, how beautifully damned easy life was going to be in the future. This was the meaning of his father's insistence that Truth was a weapon; one spoke frankly and no weaknesses were left to be discovered; one's strongest defence was in the apparent defenselessness of transparent honesty. Tell all, and nothing remained to be forgiven; confess all, and be left pure, untainted, and without onus.

"To be frank, I used to hate Duncan's guts."

"Do you know why?" Fabien asked.

Stephen wrinkled his forehead. "I don't know, something to do with his book, perhaps; jealousy of the uncreative mind for the creative. Also I'm a guy who takes a long time to overcome first impressions, and when I first met Duncan I got the idea we had somehow clashed. I'd just bought a shirt from him, and he hadn't served me too well."

"You mentioned it before."

"But that's all over. I like him a great deal now I begin to understand him. I'm coming to see what you see in him."

"I'm glad," Fabien said, "but I don't think it was the book. Your book, my dear," he added, turning his head slightly, and Stephen wheeled to see Duncan entering the room by way of the back stairs. It occurred to Stephen that the entire social structure of Canada would be changed if Canadian houses were only built with more internal doors on the ground floors, and if the few doors included were not perpetually left open. He said: "Good morning, Duncan," and smiled.

"God's teeth," Fabien said, "you've taken another shower."

"Yes."

"Why?" Stephen asked.

Duncan blushed, the suffusion spreading from his forehead down to the towel that encircled his waist. "I like to be clean," he said.

He turned directly to Fabien, and Stephen saw tears shining in the corners of the reddish-fringed eyes.

"I've finished my book."

"My dear," Fabien said quietly. "How very nice for you."

"I've finished all of it." The red head nodded in a series of violent jerks, and Stephen could sense the shout of laughter that was welling up in Duncan's throat. "No more writing, no revision, no typing, nothing! I've finished it!"

The Scotsman walked across the room and dealt Fabien a light punch on the chest. "Thank you," he said, and punched again, a little harder. "Thank you for all your help." He laid his head helplessly on Fabien's shoulder and burst into a fit of uncontrollable laughter.

They were both laughing now, and Stephen felt the mutual import of the moment vibrating along his nerves. Already his lips were quirked in a smile and the first laughter came gustily from his throat as he crossed the room with open arms and impulsively pulled the locked pair to him. They stood together, all three, in the middle of the kitchen, heads close and bodies knit, the open mouths breathing the warm breath upon each other. The laughter grew louder and caught root, swelling into one of those inexplicable experiences of joyous hysteria.

This, then, was the reward for honesty and goodness and friendship, this sharing, touching, this loss of self in the proximity of the loved. There was not, and never could be, mirth enough to fill this moment, nor fuel in any place to engender this much warmth. He thought of his first Latin verbs, feeling at last the entirety of his body; and in the sped second his heart felt pity for the lost life of his father, who had not known, nor could ever now, that to touch was nearly the most beautiful verb of all. Duncan had sunk to the floor, clutching the falling towel about him, and Stephen bent down happily to assist him to his feet. "A drink," he cried. "An extra glass for the author!"

They sat around the table over the third glass of sherry. "When do I get to see the book? God knows I've waited long enough."

Duncan finished his drink and reached for the bottle. "Now I can get drunk purely for pleasure. No more hauntings, or searchings, or recordings, just a good, happy, unself-conscious process of becoming merrily stewed. I'm not showing you the book, Stephen, until after the publisher has seen it. They have female editors in Canadian publishing houses."

"What has that to do with it?"

"Do I see it?" Fabien asked.

"Not even you."

"And perfectly right, there is no earthly reason why I should. Duncan, when you are thoroughly drunk you are sometimes unbelievably charming. Let's get thoroughly drunk."

"A brilliant idea," Duncan said.

To sacrifice this moment of his greatest pleasure gave Stephen an additional pleasure, for he saw, with a clear eye, that he would be doing what was right. No one asked him to leave; on the contrary, they pressed him to stay; but he knew that for a while at least he was intruding. These two alone were responsible for the book, and the first sip from the cup belonged to them by right. Great as was his desire to share the immediate high moment, painful though its willful renunciation, he was beset with a deep contentment and a wider love at this opportunity for offering his selflessness to his friends.

And it is a plurality—they are both my friends, he thought, holding out his hand to Duncan. "I feel like a tart at a wedding," he said, "and I'm really going, whatever you say. But I want you to know how glad I am to have been present when you broke the news. It'll mean a lot when you're famous."

"Oh, but stay, Stephen," Fabien protested. "This deep and entirely unsuspected delicacy of feeling only makes you the more desirable as a companion. Come now! that's an excellent beginning. We shall sit at the table and tell each other how wonderful we are."

"You are, you both are." Stephen beamed mildly upon them, thinking how all at once they greatly resembled children. The sun was slanting through the window, the kitchen looked glittering and bright. He said: "You'll want to talk of the book and I know nothing about it. Also I'm in dire need of exercise, and it's my intention right now to walk to the top of Mount Royal."

"Good God!" Fabien said, aghast.

"Good-by, I'll probably see you later in the day." He waved his hand and walked out—through the dining room, across the hall, and out of the front door—feeling, as he met the open air, a positive aura of good will surround his body.

To his surprise the exercise, a spur of the moment inspiration, proved enjoyable. He stood on the Look-Out, atop of Montreal's mountain, gazing down at the smoking city and wondering idly how many others down there were aware of the simple solution to their problems. Tell the truth and shame the Devil; speak out and be unashamed yourself. It had been a relief to speak of his former dislike for Duncan—and see how Fabien had responded with a parting compliment! See, too, the pleasure experienced in so small an action as helping Duncan from the floor, the Forgiving and the Forgiven, no matter to which the individual descriptions were applied.

In point of fact, he thought, they are both participles, a present and a past, and he wondered if Duncan's attitude had changed, as had his own. An agitation rippled through him as he recalled the suspicions of plots and counterplots, the dinner, the phone call, Esther and Mr. Hollis; but he quelled easily the faint disquiet and grinned at his immediate recognition of danger, contemplating the city again and noticing how the river, no longer completely icebound, gleamed gray and silver in the sun.

For a few minutes he amused himself trying to pick out Fabien's house and, failing, fell to visualizing the bright kitchen where his two friends sat drinking. They would, of course, as they became steadily drunker, be talking about the book. And when Duncan was quite lit—soon now, for it was always soon with Duncan—he would be overcome with the magnitude of what had been done for him and would take Fabien upstairs to read the manuscript. Certainly if Bill had watched its construction, then Fabien would see the completion. And even should he privately consider it to be a jumble of trash, something Bill was not competent to judge, just as certain was the fact that the opinion would not be communicated to Duncan.

Perhaps, though, they were talking about Rio de Janeiro, mulling over their mutual delight at the forthcoming mutual pleasures, drinking, gambling, riding, swimming. Riding kit would suit Fabien even better than ski clothes, but how would he look in a pair of trunks?

Stephen leaned his elbows on the wall of the Look-Out and wondered once more whether Fabien's body was as brown as his face. Fabien, he thought, is almost prissy about revealing himself, which annoys my disgustingly healthy sense of curiosity. For the first time in months he thought of his father's hernia, and discovered that his face was glowing faintly red. He pondered further.

But too bad about Rio, if only for the reason that he especially wanted to meet Fabien's parents. They were seldom mentioned, but Stephen had long entertained a clear picture of the suave, slightly arrogant father and the beautiful, gracious mother, moving elegantly through the cool house containing the few, but fine, *objets d'art*. Probably they had leased a villa in Rio, white and stucco. Too bad about Rio, too really damned bad. He refused to think of it any longer.

But it was true that, whatever he thought, Fabien would not give his honest opinion of the manuscript—and there, balancing creativeness with friendship, lay a fine problem in ethics. First assume that Fabien was a competent judge of good writing, which undoubtedly he was, for literature, with Fabien, was second only to music, in which, for an amateur he was supreme. Right then: as a competent judge, which way did his duty lie? What would Stephen do in a similar position?

He walked down the shaded mountain path that led to the city, cogitating not too deeply, for the matter was comparatively unimportant, but playing a delightful game of morals which stopped only when he caught himself trying to inveigle Alfred North Whitehead into the triviality.

And that was exactly the word to describe it, for when viewed in perspective the book, like all modern writing apart from Mann and Gide, must surely prove to be trivial no matter how clever or artful its prosecution. Was Duncan also considering it unimportant? The matter was hard to judge. Right up until this morning Duncan had maintained a devious but deft display of torment over his writing, a line of conduct, thought Stephen, probably responsible for my suspecting him even to the length of thinking the book would never be finished. But Duncan proved with his dancing and his showers, his penchant for remaining unclothed, that emotionally he was unstable. His outward appearances, therefore, were not to be wholly trusted. There was more than something of the chameleon in the way he assumed what should be the prevailing mood, and more than likely the torment was only his conception of how a practicing writer should act.

If his book was rejected he would probably act for a while like a rejected author. It was only to be expected. But would he not, when the triviality of modern writing was pointed out to him, shrug his shoulders like the rest and realize the inconsequence of it? And if he was not at the moment comprehending the relative unimportance of his work, wouldn't it be kinder to prepare him in advance for the blow that was about to fall.

By the time he reached home, Stephen became aware with mild astonishment that he was worrying about Duncan. The position engrossed him to a degree where he was silent throughout the uninteresting lunch set before him. Only when he realized the dangers of self-flattery inherent in his mental attitude did he pause to do any definitive thinking, then excusing himself from the table he told his mother he was going out and headed again for Fabien's house.

He decided that, in a manner of speaking, he had deceived Duncan, and was doing so still, in hiding both the dislike and suspicions he had formerly entertained. He reflected upon the amount of clearance that must be done before commencing a new life, and resolved that the suspicions would be admitted immediately after the new affection had been declared. A clean sweep would be made, a truly fresh start; the straightforwardness exercised with Fabien would be extended to Duncan, and perhaps with the same rewarding results. Duncan would never, of course, assume the same stature as Fabien, but there was a draught to be drunk from even the smallest of vessels. He and Duncan would have a long talk.

Stephen let himself into the house and made his way quietly to the kitchen, intent upon an unassuming entrance lest anything boisterous break whatever alcoholic spell had been woven. The door swung open noiselessly, disclosing the glasses and the abandoned bottle. The room was empty, the house quiet. He continued on up the back stairs, treading softly until an odd, furtive feeling of guilt assailed him near the top. He stopped and shouted their names, one after the other, clearly. "Fabien! Duncan!" Perhaps they were drunk; he called again. Or perhaps only Duncan was drunk, and Fabien had gone to do whatever he did on those frequent visits to the consulate. Stephen made his way to Duncan's bedroom and pushed open the door.

Before an open wardrobe, where clothes hung carelessly, a towel lay upon the floor; another bottle and two glasses stood on a little table at the head of the bed. In the center of the counterpane, where someone obviously had been sitting, was an untidy pile of papers whose edges stirred faintly in a breeze from the open window. Stephen crossed the room, closed the window, and poured himself a drink in one of the dirty glasses. After that he sat down upon the bed, carefully straightened the manuscript that lay beside him, picked up the first page, and commenced to read.

He read with interest and detachment, sipping his drink sparingly, pouring another when the glass was empty. He noticed that the bottle was almost full and was pleased, for suddenly he was thirsty. He was certain someone would soon come in and discover him: they would all have a drink together and then they would talk. Fabien would have to bring up another bottle from the cellar.

Later, as he poured his fourth drink, he felt for a moment a little scared, but the smooth sensation of the liquor soothed him and he became once more interested and detached. Each finished page he turned on its face and added to the neat pile in the center of the bed. He guessed no one was coming after all.

He needed to turn on the bedside lamp before he was finished.

<h2 style="text-align:center">IV</h2>

"Me again!" the waiter snapped irritably, shrugging his thin shoulders. "Why the hell the city leaves a pile of dirty snow outside of this door every spring is beyond me. Don't the boss pay his taxes, or something?"

"He's pretty mad about it," the barman answered. "Asked if you still wanted it there in July. You'd better get it shifted tonight while there's no one here. What d'you say you wanted?"

"Two rye gimlets."

"That's what I thought you said. Recognize your customer?"

The waiter glanced surreptitiously to the table at the end of the room. "Never seen 'em before."

"The red-haired kid is one of old whatshername's boys, our regular-that-was. Don't you remember she brought him here one night and he got stewed?"

"Christ! she brought so many I lost count." The waiter's face showed signs of interest. "Y'know, I reckon one of her little friends finally knocked her off. She ain't been in here for weeks."

"She was too old for them to knock her *up*," said the barman, smiling complacently at his own humor, "so that ain't what's keeping her away. But don't worry, she'll be back here. They always are. Perhaps she'll come in tonight for Red there to introduce her to his pal. That other one sure looks like a guy who wouldn't care how he made a dollar."

"Yeah!" the waiter exclaimed bitterly. "I always had an idea she gave those guys money. And bitches like that never look at me."

"Too old," remarked the barman, laconically. "Not enough lead in your pencil. Here's your gimlets."

Stephen gave the polite waiter a large tip, sipped his drink, and settled more comfortably in the chair. Apart from an uncertainty how to begin, he was unperturbed. He said, nodding at his glass, "Good drinks."

"They all taste good to me," Duncan replied. He had been more or less drunk for the three days since his book was completed, and his eyes were like deep amethysts. "Fabien might join us later on, I left a note where we are. This is about the only place in town whose name I know."

"Those consulate affairs keep him fairly late," Stephen said. "I hope he gets here in time." And then he wondered if he spoke the truth for, since the other night, the truth related to Duncan had become harder to find. Why, for example, had he preferred to see Duncan alone, when last night he could have invited them both for a drink?

The question was only subsidiary to the main issue of friendship. He said: "A fairly decent place. Been here before?"

"I think I must have been, to remember the name."

They lapsed into silence, finishing their drinks, and Duncan called for a second round without saying anything to Stephen. "Hello," Duncan greeted the waiter.

"Hello, sir. Good to see you back again. How are the drinks?"

"Fine. Two more please."

The waiter returned speedily, and Duncan asked him to save the bill until the end of the evening. "Keep them coming," he said, and after they were alone he added to Stephen, "I must have been here before." The silence resumed.

"We don't appear to have picked a subject yet."

"I don't mind." Duncan smiled to himself, secretively. "Everyone talks too much, especially me. I keep Fabien up almost every night listening to me. I wonder he doesn't get fed up."

Stephen took a sip: the drinks *were* good. "There's something important I want you to know, Duncan," he said, "namely that I like you very well. It's silly to make a declaration, but I wanted to tell you because once I didn't like you and it's preying on my mind. I used to think some lousy things about you, and once or twice I may have voiced them. I'm sorry about it now, and anything you may have heard I hope you'll forget. I like you. There! That's all."

Duncan's smile expanded, became external, was projected across the table with such width that Stephen found himself examining the teeth. "Thank you for telling me. I always felt your dislike, but there was nothing I could do. It was a great relief when you shook my hand the other morning, and I'm sure Fabien was pleased. I've sensed now and then that the situation was bothering him."

"Possibly," Stephen said.

"We went out and got terribly drunk that day, you know. We both wished you were along."

"We can do it now," said Stephen, signaling for two more drinks. He pushed both across the table to Duncan, ignoring the protests. "I could never drink as much as you and I still have half this one left. Drink up! Your health! What shall we talk about now?"

"Why didn't you like me?"

"For one thing, until you produced the book I considered you a parasite."

"I see the point of view. Anyone who lives without production is a parasite."

"I guess you don't mean quite that," Stephen said, "but let's not pursue it until I get the rest of this off my mind." He paused. "For another thing, there was that business at my house. I thought you might have done it intentionally."

"That I did it at all was unforgivable."

"Exactly what my mother thinks. She doesn't like you."

"I quite understand."

"She thinks you're low-class," Stephen said, laughing, and he debated in his mind whether to continue. "Also there was the night you phoned my sister, but we'll not talk about that."

"If you don't mind, I would like to."

"There are painful associations," Stephen said truthfully.

"I quite understand." Duncan's smile had disappeared, his face was growing pale. "I'm sorry," he said, and it occurred to Stephen that throughout their acquaintanceship Duncan had been always apologizing for something. They sat looking at each other.

"My sister likes you, though."

"She's very kind." The pallor remained, but Duncan was attempting to smile again. "Shall we talk about Rio de Janeiro? I'm going there this summer with Fabien, to stay with his parents."

"Yes, I know," Stephen said. "There is something else I have to tell you. About your book."

"Oh, my book." Stephen inspected the teeth again as Duncan leaned forward. "What about my book?"

"I have read it."

Duncan went back abruptly in the chair and reached for his glass. "I don't understand you."

"I read your book."

"But that's impossible. I didn't show it to you."

This appearing and disappearing smile, thought Stephen, has something of the concertina about it. He said: "It was the afternoon you were out getting drunk with Fabien. I came back to the house for you and found the manuscript lying on the bed. I'm sorry. I couldn't resist the temptation. I know you didn't wish me to read it."

Duncan laid down his empty glass and picked up the second drink, draining it in one gulp. "Fabien didn't see it," he said. "Shall we have some more drinks?"

"I'm extremely sorry."

"It doesn't matter. Will you order me two? I have to go to the lavatory."

The drinks were on the table when he returned, and Stephen was lighting a cigarette. He extended the package and Duncan edged back into his seat, thrusting his face forward for a light from the match. "I was shocked," he said, mumbling because of the cigarette. "Silly!" Then he drank both drinks in rapid succession, shuddering slightly on the second, and added, "Some more," wigwagging to the waiter and turning his glassy eyes toward the bar.

The drinks must have been already prepared for the waiter brought them immediately. "The barman," he said, "said to say he's flattered."

Stephen nodded. "They're good. Sorry to keep you so busy."

"It's fine. So long as you're here I ain't shoveling snow. Did you see the pile of slush outside?"

"Yes, tough luck. Don't know what the city's coming to."

"You said it!" the waiter exclaimed. "Every year the same." He seemed inclined to further conversation, but Stephen turned his head away.

"These drinks are on me," he told Duncan.

"Thank you."

"I mean all of them. The money's a little more free since Father died. He didn't leave any to me, but I'm not complaining. When you're broke it's reasonably certain your friends are with you for your own sake. Once you get a little money—"

"What did you think of the book?" Duncan asked.

"You can never trust people about money. One of the reasons I disliked you at first was that Fabien is wealthy."

"What did you think of the book?"

Stephen drew on his cigarette and exhaled slowly, smiling. "Now how the hell am I supposed to answer that?"

"Truthfully," Duncan said.

"But listen man, I only skimmed through it, once."

"I value your opinion. Please. What did you think?"

With the tip of his middle finger, Stephen was gently edging his glass towards the center of the table. "To be perfectly truthful, then," he said, "I thought it stank."

There was a long pause while they looked at each other blankly, then Duncan put his elbows on the table and lowered his head into his hands, running his fingers over his scalp and disarranging his hair so that it sprang down over his hands and obscured the parting. "Yes," he said at last. "You are perfectly right. It stinks."

This was a greater calm than anticipated, and Stephen thought how much more shattering the blow would have been if received through a publisher's letter. All the same, there was pathos in the lowered head, and now the first duty had been fulfilled there remained the second, whereby the first was brought into perspective.

Stephen reached across and tugged gently at one of the red locks. "Hey, we have a lot more drinking to do."

The eyes that raised to his were, as expected, filled with tears.

"Can we get a bottle of wine?" Duncan asked. "Something cheap and strong and red. I have to do more drinking than you think."

It was Stephen himself who went to the bar, making the selection with a show of infinite care, grinning the while that Duncan should react with such close adherence to dramatic type. Emotionally the fellow was no more than a child; one had only to watch how his words were matched always by the naïve, unconscious gesture. Stephen returned down the length of the bar carrying the bottle of wine in his bare hands and placed it on the table with a flourish. "There!" he said.

To his surprise, Duncan looked animated, even angry. He looked, also, very drunk.

"What was the matter with my book?"

Stephen sat down, his mouth judiciously pursed, and put his elbows on the table, fingertips pressing together.

"Your situations are ludicrous, you haven't the faintest idea of construction, your characters talk too much and in a dialogue no one ever used, and every one of them is completely unreal."

"I knew them in the war," Duncan snapped. "You wouldn't know about that. I understand you spent the war behind a desk."

"I'm sorry you're being personal," Stephen said dryly, feeling the first throb of anger within him. "You asked my opinion and I can only repeat the things I've learned myself or picked up through talking to Fabien. So you may have known them in the war, or thought you did, but that doesn't mean you've got them on paper. The trouble is that you didn't know whether to analyze or sympathize and the characters varied from page to page. The result is a bloody mess."

"Your opinion only," Duncan said. "Wait until the publishers read it."

"Have you sent it to a publisher already? I'm sorry. I think you'll find his letter will confirm what I say."

He saw that Duncan was violently shaking his head and the anger burst into quick flame, scorching his tongue. "Don't be a dim-witted fool. The bloodiest idiot could see your manuscript is nothing but trash. It wouldn't have mattered if only the construction was wrong, you could have learned to remedy that. But the whole damn thing is wrong, word by word, and that's something no one in the world can teach you. You're just not a writer."

"Shut up!"

"The hell with you! You asked for truth and you're getting it."

"I have to write."

"You can't write. I suggest you go tomorrow and get back your old job, selling shirts. It's just about your speed."

Duncan sat up very straight, his eyes dry and expressionless staring at Stephen from a white face. "I know the book is a failure and I don't blame you for telling me. I asked for it. But I've just realized that you brought me out tonight with the sole purpose of enjoying yourself. You could have told me all this yesterday or the day before, but you wanted to get me alone, didn't you, so there would be no one to interfere with your idea of a good time? You're a stinking hypocrite, Hollis. You've sat there jabbering about friendship and the like, and all the time knowing that you loathe the sight of me."

"You're drunk," Stephen said.

Duncan's accent had become pronounced to a point where it was barely understandable. "I'm sorry for Fabien's sake, but with me it's a relief, for I've not liked you since first I saw you, with your posturing and your snobbishness and your silly prancing airs about nothing at all. You have the idea that life's a sausage machine where you feed in dollar bills at one end and get breeding from the other. And that's you exactly, Hollis—a dirty little sausage with all the nasty gray meat popping out whenever anyone sticks in a fork." Duncan drew a deep breath. "And if you think I'm being rude, I claim the precedent set me by you and your mother a long time since. I'll feel no need to apologize the morrow's morn."

"How peculiarly you say sausage," Stephen said. "You're drunk. You usually are. Why don't you go back to selling shirts?"

The fist caught him on the shoulder as Duncan lunged over the table, and in the next instant the waiter was between them, forcing them apart and down into their seats with a strength that was surprising in one who looked so frail.

"Don't get so playful, boys. We can all have a drink or two without any trouble." He looked closely at Duncan, and his mouth tightened. "You've had enough, chum. I think maybe I ought to throw you out. Why can't you behave yourself nice, like when you was here with your lady-friend?"

"It's okay," Stephen said, pulling a bill from his pocket. "Will that take care of it? We'll finish the bottle and leave."

"I'll bring the change," the waiter suggested, backing hopefully away down the bar.

"Keep it," Stephen said, with a wave of his hand. He turned back to Duncan. "You don't respond to the truth very well," he said levelly. "I should have been warned in advance. I don't like public scenes."

"How about private ones, Hollis?" A grin was spreading over Duncan's face, dispelling the anger from all but his eyes. "Bill tells me you had a very private scene with Miriam Sabel."

"What are you talking about, now?"

"Bill's word for it was very crude." The grin eased a little, and the anger in his eyes diminished noticeably. "I shouldn't be talking like this," he said soberly. "Fabien and I wanted her to have someone that night, and we were both glad. I hope you've seen her again."

Stephen was staring incredulously, the feeling of horror mounting in his throat until it threatened to choke him. They had known about it, devised it even. Oh God! how they must have laughed. He pressed his hands flat on the table and waited for his breath to come back, then: "She was a friend of yours. I wonder you didn't do it yourself."

For a moment Duncan faltered. "That sort of thing is messy," he said. "I—I like to be clean."

Stephen's voice was flat. "I suspected as much. You prefer messes like the one you made at my house that night."

"What?" Duncan went rigid. "What mess?"

"And I can assure you that Miriam Sabel likes you almost as little as my mother does."

"Why doesn't your mother like me?"

"She thinks you're low-class."

"Why doesn't she like me?"

The anger ebbed away and Stephen felt limp and chilled. He looked at the pitiably anxious face before him and saw the damage that had been wrought by his thoughtless straying into paths so recently forsaken. He had betrayed himself; had allowed to predominate the customs of condemnation and self-indulgence that had dulled his life for more than twenty years, leaving him alone and empty. Where, now, was the love and integrity that had lightened his burden these past weeks? Truth was still with him, but to what was it leading? Old habit must be destroyed and Duncan made a friend despite all opposition, for he was also the friend of a friend and, as such, must be doubly cherished. Stephen reached out and laid a hand on Duncan's sleeve.

"I regret losing my temper," he said. "I'm speaking sincerely when I say you're a friend of mine."

"What about the mess I caused?" Duncan asked.

"Drink your wine and pour me a glass."

"It is essential that I know. Please."

He had not yet decided whether he intended ever to tell Duncan the truth about it, but he perceived now that if the thing was kept suppressed in his mind an inflammation would be created that would nag and irritate into other ugly scenes like this one tonight. He looked across the table and saw the fear reflected in the blurred eyes that stared back at him. How could they be friends while the secret and the fear lay like twin films between them, obscuring their clear sight of each other? They would be unable even to speak freely until each word had been examined for the possibility of betrayal or revelation. He had sworn himself to truth, and so it should be. His touch slid down Duncan's sleeve and he took the hand, pressing it.

"Let's drink a corny toast," he suggested. "To truth and friendship."

"To truth," Duncan responded, drinking. "What mess did I make at your home?"

"I need your word not to repeat this to anyone."

"You have it."

"You feel all right?"

"I'm disgustingly drunk. Tell me anyway."

"I mean, you're not going to be upset?"

"Don't be so bloody arch," Duncan said. And suddenly he smiled as Stephen before had seen him smile only for Fabien.

No one else, not even Bill, had known this, and Stephen's heart swelled, spreading a glow throughout his breast.

"When you phoned the house, you were speaking to my father," he said gently. "He died later that same night, of a stroke."

Imperturbably, Duncan laced his fingers tightly together and laid his hands upon the table. "I see," he said quietly. "I read in the obituary column of the *Star* that he had died that night. They praised him highly; said he was a very religious man." He drew a shuddering breath and separated the hands to fold his arms. "So I killed your father."

"In a way," Stephen said. "No sensible person could hold it against you."

"I suppose not. That's kind." Duncan gave a short laugh, seemingly amused. "You've brought me nothing but stale news this evening, Hollis: haven't told me a thing I didn't already know. What else is there?"

He got to his feet, stumbling a little, and placed his hands on the table to maintain his balance. Then, without warning, he began to cry, long, grinding, noisy sobs that could be heard from one end of the bar to the other. The waiter was moving swiftly toward them and, remotely, Stephen realized he should do something, anything, to curtail the scene. But he was unable to move, rigid as iron, his eyes fixed in unwavering fascination upon Duncan. It was the most fantastically horrifying thing he could remember having seen, a man standing up like that to cry. Vaguely he felt that poems, whole symphonies could be written about it, terrible stories at which all men would tremble. Only when the waiter laid hands on Duncan was the spell broken.

"Okay, I'll take care of him."

"Get him out of here, quick!"

Stephen got to his feet and put an arm across the heaving shoulders, bearing heavily in an attempt to draw Duncan away. He was immovable, his feet rooted to the floor, his hands clenching hard at the edge of the table. Slowly he turned his head and stared at his tormenters without seeing them.

"I killed someone before," he said. "In the war. The blood came all over me and I couldn't get clean. There was nowhere to wash and they wouldn't allow me to change my clothes." Suddenly his voice rose to a shrieking crescendo. "I couldn't get clean! It came all over me and I couldn't get clean! I killed someone in the war and I couldn't get clean!"

"For Christ's sake get him out of here."

Before Stephen could intercede the waiter had twisted Duncan's arm behind his back and was hurrying the lurching form down the length of the bar. Stephen picked up the cigarette packet that lay on the table and placed it in his pocket, walking out slowly and steadily under the interested gaze of the barman. The returning waiter met him inside the door.

"He's lying out there in that heap of snow. Pick him up, take him home, and don't bring him back again."

Stephen surveyed the man from head to foot, curling his lip. "Wasn't the tip big enough?" He walked outside.

"Come on," he said, helping Duncan to his feet. "This time you really need a shower. Let's get home."

In the light from the street lamp Duncan looked greenish-pale and unutterably fatigued. His hair fell over his forehead, his eyes were almost closed. He made no attempt to brush off the slush that clogged the front of his clothing. Yet when he spoke his voice was flat, rational-sounding, without the slightest trace of his previous accent. His lips barely moved.

"We don't want Fabien to know about this," he said. "I'll start again at the store tomorrow if I can get my job back, so if you'll visit the house in the daytime we'll avoid seeing each other and Fabien won't feel the tension." He put a hand over his eyes and slowly pushed the hair from his forehead. "I don't want to see you again, Hollis. You make me sick— you and everything connected with you, including your bloody mother.

I did her a wrong and for that I'm sorry, but for nothing else. She helped make you what you are, Hollis, and you're bloody despicable."

"Twice you've said bloody," Stephen said. "You're doing well."

Duncan shook his head. "No I'm not, and neither are you. You're doing very badly. You want something so much that you don't care how you get it, even to the lengths you've gone tonight to get rid of me. You think it's a question of outside opposition, and that I'm in your way. You're wrong. What you want is beyond your reach. You'll never be able to bring it down to your level. You're going to find out your mistake."

"Is that all?" Stephen asked.

"Yes. I killed your father and I'm sorry. For the rest I hate your guts."

"Quite a long speech for a dark night. Go to hell!"

"After," Duncan said. "I have to go back to the store first. Good night."

He walked off down the road, head bent and shoulders rounded, with weariness marked in every line of his receding figure. The red head gleamed once as he passed a street lamp and then he was gone. Stephen saw him no more.

Four warm spring days later, after a busy day at the store selling shirts and talking to the customers, Duncan was equally dead with Mr. Hollis.

V

Three weeks had slipped by, and the sun was shining gloriously from a pale, pastel-blue sky. This was the most beautiful spring for years, Montrealers said, and, oh dear, they hoped it didn't mean a bad summer.

A few of the more venturesome children had already led the way by making their yearly visit to the park, where birds could be heard faintly singing above the inescapable din of Montreal's tramway system. Policemen were directing traffic with more than their customary balletic verve, lifting arms higher, pirouetting, gazing challengingly at the sidewalks where the ladies made bustling promenade in their new hats and the season's change of make-up. Heads long bent to winter's inclemency were at last raised, cautiously, a little higher. Down along St. Catherine Street the revolving doors were removed from entrances of the great, airless stores, and on Sherbrooke Street the trees whispered to each other in the stirring breeze.

The campus at McGill, inexplicably wider in the brightening light, palpitated with vernal hope.

"Think you're gonna pass?"

"Except organic chem."

"The goddam math paper is gonna fix me."

The sunshine flooded through the windows of the house in Westmount, revealing light patches on the wall, where previously pictures had hung. Mrs. Hollis sat in a chair, folding and unfolding her hands, the dark shadows under her eyes emphasizing the bereft look that had grown more profound during the past two weeks. She lifted her head listlessly as Stephen returned from the phone.

"Who was it?"

"Fabien. He wants me to go down. It sounded important."

His mother's interest rallied a little, a look of bitterness crept into her face and her voice grew harsh. "I should think you'd stay away from there after all the trouble that's been caused. Haven't we got enough of our own without you looking for more?"

Stephen assumed a patient expression. "Mother, I've told you a thousand times that neither Bill nor Fabien had the slightest inkling of Duncan's intentions. They were just as surprised and upset as I."

"It was only what you might have expected of such a person," Mrs. Hollis remarked with a sniff. "I wish you'd stay away. We've got plenty of trouble without everyone knowing you were a friend of his. The neighbors are talking."

"Not about that," Stephen said. "One of the benefits of living in a Catholic province is that the myth of the sanctity of life is maintained to the extent of keeping suicides out of the newspapers. Nobody around here knew Duncan, and they don't know he's dead."

"What about the people at McGill?"

"I wish you'd concentrate a little more on your own problem," Stephen said. "Have you talked to Esther again? I can't get a word out of her."

Mrs. Hollis's face assumed again the pitifully bedraggled look. "If only Father were here. He'd know what to do."

Stephen watched her without emotion, knowing that in a few days more his disappointment would have congealed into resignation. There was no remedy. His mother's spiritual incompletion was solidifying before his eyes. He said: "There doesn't seem to be anything *we* can do. Esther just sits looking out of the window with a smug expression on her face. She doesn't seem to care what people are saying."

"Chester Arden denies everything," Mrs. Hollis exclaimed with a hint of savagery. "But someone must have seen them; people don't talk for nothing. And now there's to be a special meeting at the church on Thursday. I shall never be able to hold up my head again."

"I don't see why not," Stephen said indifferently. "No one claims that *you* have been carrying on with Chester." He saw the expression on her face and laughed. "I'm sorry, but I can't see the situation as seriously as you do. Esther should consider herself lucky that people thought she had a reputation worth losing. As for Chester, he's so dumb he deserves anything that can possibly happen to him." Stephen laughed again. "I can't get over the thought of those two, and not a soul ever suspecting them. It must have been going on even while Father was alive."

Immediately he regretted the reference, for the look in his mother's eyes became more intense. How sad she looked, he thought, and how old. She said: "You never used to talk like that, Stephen. Those men you mix with are dragging you down. Your father would put you straight again if he were still here. He knew what was right and was never afraid to say so." She sighed. "He had great hopes of you, Stephen. I wish you were more like him."

"I'll try to be," Stephen said kindly. "But I can't do anything about Chester. He's avoiding me like the plague."

"We'll know better what's going to happen," Mrs. Hollis said, "after the special meeting on Thursday. Oh dear!" She screwed up her face and began most miserably to sob. "All the committee will be there—Mr. Trundell, Mr. Lamb, Mr. Pinger—all your father's old friends. What shall I do?"

He knew from the experience of two weeks that any attempt to comfort her would be useless. He could only stand by helplessly while the tears welled up behind her spectacles and trickled down her face. It occurred to him that, whereas Esther seemed to have become less plain of late, his mother appeared gradually to grow more unprepossessing. And suddenly he was oppressed by the drabness of his surroundings, the futility of the weeping to which he had listened since the first gust of rumor blew into the house. He said:

"Is there anything you want? I'm going out now."

"To that house?"

"I'll be back for dinner."

"Stephen, I don't want you to go."

"Don't be silly, Mother," he said.

"I won't have it."

"You don't have a choice, Mother. I'll see you at dinner."

Her tears had ceased. She stood up. She said: "I forbid it. I forbid you to go."

"Don't be silly, Mother. I'm grown up. You can't forbid me anything."

She came over to him and laid a hand hard upon his forearm. "Stephen," she said, "you're dependent upon me for everything, so I should have some say in the way you conduct your—"

"Good Lord!" he snapped, "Father!" and shook off her hand. The gesture was more forceful than he had intended. She receded two stumbling steps before regaining her balance. He said: "Don't ever think that you can direct me."

They were facing each other. She was quailing before him with a movement that was wholly, horribly familiar. The expression in her eyes was changing, the light flickering and dying and returning again—replenished, placated, weirdly triumphant. The incompletion of the past weeks had vanished and her spirit was whole again, her drawn face was excited, fearful.

She was looking at him in exactly the fashion she had always looked at his father. In an instant of clarity he began to fight the lurking future.

"I shouldn't have done that, Mother," he said. "I hope I didn't hurt you."

"It was my fault," she said listlessly. "Is there anything special that you'd like for dinner?"

"Anything you like." He rubbed his forehead. "Look, I have to go to Fabien's today because it's important, but in the future I'll not go so often." He knew he was lying.

"Oh, it doesn't really matter. I shouldn't have said what I did. The money is as much yours as mine."

Perhaps if he kissed her. He moved very slightly, and very slightly she retreated. So what the hell! Maybe it was all his imagination. He would think of it at greater length when he had more time. He said: "Well, I'll be seeing you."

"Yes," she said. "I'll try to get something nice."

He went out swiftly. What a peculiar business. The balmy spring air enfolded him as he emerged from the front door. He walked down the street conscious of Esther's serene, more than satisfied gaze following his progress from her post at the bedroom window.

Well, good for Esther! for having realized all along that sex was important. It explained the unexpected expression that she had worn for Duncan when he came to dinner. If Stephen had seen her in the company of more men he might, perhaps, have realized about her and Chester long ago. Good, again, for Esther!

And good for sex. He had not known before what the poets meant when they spoke of spring's besetting power, but now it was only in poetry that he could find a response for the languid, yet strangely urgent feelings that lay unresolved in his limbs and flittered in the hitherto undiscovered sections of his mind. He must discuss the matter with Fabien. Fabien would understand and advise. The relationship had been closer since Duncan went, putting them on a more intimate footing both with each other and the profundities. Even under such tragic circumstances the development had proved gratifying.

Stephen had not dwelt upon the thought of Duncan's death.

He bitterly regretted that their last time together had been unpleasant. Moreover, there was a tiny, nagging suspicion at the back of his mind that he might, unconsciously, have forced Duncan part way along the road by suggesting so vehemently that he return to his job at the store. Not until after his death had Stephen remembered the horror with which Duncan had described the work, that morning in the bedroom. But, poor little devil, he was at rest now. How shocked he had been to think that he might have contributed to the death of Mr. Hollis.

In the mild afternoon air, Stephen discovered that he had begun to perspire. What a wretched evening they spent in that bar and how abominable, in the light of after events, had been his own behavior. He should have realized how mentally unstable the kid was and treated him accordingly—gently, as Fabien had. Although, strictly speaking, he had not been such a kid after all. The inquest revealed that he was twenty-five, a little older than Stephen himself. Not much else had been revealed, for Stephen was not called upon to attend, while Fabien, quite naturally, showed no inclination to discuss the proceedings. Stephen— after preliminary questioning—had abandoned the subject as too painful for either of them.

Duncan had left no farewell communication of any sort, and Stephen wondered if this, in part, accounted for the surprising lack of grief manifested by Fabien. True, a certain air of melancholy had descended upon the house, an atmosphere that invited walking on tiptoe; but apart from an almost indiscernible restraint, a tendency to talk less frivolously, Fabien's demeanor remained remarkably unaltered. There was, Stephen thought, something callous in the complete dispassion of Duncan's departure, a trace of ingratitude in the abrupt, unfeeling way he had terminated this most intimate of friendships. Fabien, perhaps, at the back of his mind, regarded the absence of any message to himself as a slap in the face; or it might be, after all, that he was not so fond of Duncan as Stephen had suspected. The only time any emotion had been displayed was on that shocked day when first they learned the news, and that, in all probability, was mainly reflex action. It was an interesting problem, but Stephen did not puzzle over it.

By far the greatest portion of sorrow had been shown by Bill, who, even now during exam time, sat around the house on every opportunity with his features composed in gloom and a bewildered expression in his eyes. He talked more often, these days, of fishing, and frequently asked Fabien to play *Das Lied von der Erde*, listening to the whole recital in complete silence.

"I don't get it," Bill had said. "His book was finished, he was going on a holiday, he had everything he ever said he wanted. What did he do it for? Why didn't he come to me if he was in trouble? I'm sure I could have helped him."

No one made any comment, and Stephen thought how stupidly maudlin Bill looked.

It was becoming increasingly obvious that Duncan had been the cementing force in the relationship between Bill and Fabien, for of late they had less and less to say to each other. Fabien no longer used the affectionate, slightly derisive nicknames to Bill, and Stephen guessed that in the past they had been really meant for Duncan, a sort of cushion-shot of fondness. He also guessed that Bill would not be around much longer, and felt relieved. Of late Bill had taken to turning his bewildered stare upon Stephen. It made Stephen uncomfortable. He hoped, without really caring, that Bill would not be there this afternoon.

He opened the front door, and a murmur of voices came to him as he crossed the hall. He reached the threshold of the sitting room and halted, smiling already in the startled shock of pleasant precognition.

The man could be none other than Fabien's father. He sat in an armchair, holding a glass of wine, his legs casually, elegantly crossed, a look of polite, intelligent interest on his handsome and disciplined face. Although clad in an excellently tailored brown lounge suit, there was something about him that suggested a uniform, an effect heightened by immaculately groomed brown hair showing no trace of grey and a small, clipped, military-looking mustache. He carried an air of extreme good breeding. In the moment before the man got to his feet Stephen thought how different life would have been if he had grown up with such a father.

"You must be Stephen Hollis."

Stephen extended a hand and gave a slight bow. "How do you do, sir. I've been greatly looking forward to meeting you." He came forward into the room and saw that Bill and Fabien had risen from their chairs.

"Stephen," Fabien said, "this is Mr. Alexander McSurt, Duncan's father. May I offer you some more wine, sir?"

"Thank you, no, though I must commend you on its excellence. I hope Duncan was able to sample your cellar from time to time."

"Don't worry yourself," Bill said. "He got good and stiff whenever he felt like it."

"I'm so glad." Under the mustache the bright teeth gleamed briefly. They all resumed their seats. Stephen walked to the settee in a frightened daze.

"I wish you could stay longer, sir," Fabien said.

"Thank you, but I fear it's essential that I catch my plane in a little while. Time, tide, and business, you know, wait for no man—especially the steel business." He smiled amiably. "And, to be frank, I'd sooner get away as quickly as possible. I'm not much of a hand at pilgrimages to the grave, and all that sort of thing. I can never see where there's anything much to be gained by it."

Bill picked up his glass of beer and took a deep swig. "Anyway, Alec, we'll have our fishing this summer if you stay out on the West Coast. You'll get the best sport you ever had in your life."

"Ah!" Duncan's father exclaimed, nodding his head. "Now I am looking forward to that. Nothing like a spot of good fishing. Will either of you gentlemen be with us?"

Stephen came out his daze long enough to realize that he was being addressed. "I haven't been invited, sir," he said.

"Nor are you likely to be," Bill growled.

Duncan's father looked from one to the other, smiling. "You're all exactly as he described you in his letters. It's quite uncanny."

"What did he say about us?" Stephen blushed a deep crimson as all eyes turned upon him. "I beg your pardon," he said hastily, "they were private letters, of course."

"Of course," Bill snapped, and Duncan's father continued smiling.

"I begin to think that perhaps he was a writer after all," he said, and turning to Fabien he added, "I am pleased that he was able to spend his last days here."

"We all enjoyed it," Fabien said. "He spoke of you often."

"Did he? That surprises me rather. We saw very little of each other, you know, what with my being always away and Duncan and his brother going off to school when they were ten. It might have been different had their mother lived."

"I didn't know Duncan had a brother," Bill said.

"Oh yes, they were twins. Terribly attached to each other they were, had to do everything together, even to running away from school and joining the army when war broke out. Silly affair, actually, because at the beginning the British Army claimed that it wouldn't accept boys under twenty. Damned silly affair! Unfortunately, Hugh was killed at Dunkirk."

"I'm sorry," Fabien said, and Bill looked fixedly into his beer glass. Stephen edged a little nearer, wondering what Duncan had written that made his father appear to be speaking only to the other two.

"Oh, it wasn't too hard for me, really. Naturally I was upset, but I didn't know either of the boys very well. To tell the truth, I had some difficulty in telling them apart. They were very like, you know, red hair and blue eyes and quiet—very much like their mother, both of them. But Duncan took it very badly. He was in an army hospital for a long while afterward and then they sent him on sick leave for six months or so. I didn't see him because I happened to be in India at the time, but from what people tell me I gather that he was in rather rough shape. Not a scratch on him, you understand—he came through the war quite unscathed—but terribly upset mentally. He was devoted to Hugh."

"I wasn't in the war," Fabien said.

"Glad to hear that. Nasty business, totally unsuitable for boys like you and Duncan and Hugh." Duncan's father stroked at his mustache with a forefinger, looking thoughtful. "I think I *will* have a little more wine, if I may. I must be leaving soon for the airport."

Fabien came forward with the decanter. Bill refilled his own glass from a bottle of beer that stood on the floor beside his chair. No one offered Stephen a drink. He stared at the disciplined, faintly humorous face and tried to think of something that would give him entry to the conversation.

"I was in the air force," Bill said, "but we never had anything as bad as Dunkirk."

Duncan's father rolled the wine meditatively around his palate and swallowed slowly. "Pretty grim show," he said. "The boys spent two days on the beach before the boats arrived, being strafed all the time. After Duncan came to Canada I ran into a chappie who was with them, and he told me a little about it. It seems that Hugh was pretty badly messed up and there was nothing anyone could do, not even move him when the boats got there. It must have been rather hard on Duncan. This other fellow told me they had to drag him away before he would leave. Remarkable, isn't it, how British soldiers look out for each other at times like that. Of course, Duncan wasn't very old."

In the smothering atmosphere that suddenly filled the room Stephen wished that even Bill would look at him in order that he might convey to someone, if only by facial expression, the triviality of any misunderstandings he had had with Duncan. The very first opportunity and he would admit to having been wrong, pointing out at the same time how little it had meant either to himself or, more especially, to Duncan. Surely no one with Duncan's upbringing, no person who shared the same background as this tall, cool, immaculate gentlemen could have paid any heed to those gentle gibes about parasitism and store clerks. Stephen groped through his mind, seeking a total recall of everything that had passed between himself and Duncan on that last night. His memory became totally obscured.

The precise voice of Duncan's father was recounting something about the seriousness of the brother's wounds. Stephen forced himself to listen.

"One doesn't like to think of anyone suffering an agony like that, especially a member of one's own family. I don't at all blame Duncan for acting as he did. After all, you know, nobody expected any decency from Jerry, and he simply couldn't leave Hugh to die like that. This other chap, the chap I ran into, said they got as far as the water's edge and Duncan ran back. He was crying, the chap said. They went after him but it was too late. Hugh was already dead. After that, as probably you know, they all dumped their rifles in the sea so Jerry wouldn't get them. A shockingly grim business, but I can see Duncan's point of view. The only trouble was that afterward he couldn't see it himself. He was cool as a cucumber, I'm told, while they were crossing the Channel, but just as soon as he set foot in England he cracked up. They had to send him to a hospital immediately. I suppose he never really got over it. I'm sure it was the reason he avoided me afterward when we could have been together. I wouldn't have minded. There must be quite a few young men walking around today in similar positions."

"Oh Jesus," Bill said, in a voice that shook with horror. "How bloody, christly awful. Why didn't he tell us."

"He would have wanted you to know now, I'm sure. He said in his letters that, apart from Hugh, you were the only friends he had ever known."

"I loved him," Fabien said.

"Did you?" Duncan's father pulled a snowy-white handkerchief from his pocket and blew his nose, covering almost all of his face. "If only I'd known the boys better," he said, then he carefully replaced the handkerchief, looked at his wrist watch and got to his feet. "I really must be going or I shall miss my plane. Can I get a taxi easily? They're enormously difficult in England."

"I'll call one," Fabien offered, moving toward the hall.

"Don't do that! No!" They all turned sharply as Stephen almost shouted the command. He moved his lips and more words came out. He said: "I mean, it's almost quicker to just go to Sherbrooke Street and pick one up. I could walk down with you, sir."

"That's very kind, but I mustn't bother you."

"It's no bother," Stephen said desperately. "I'd like to do it."

"Well, in that case, thank you." They had all risen and were standing about the room in the awkward poses that precede farewell. Duncan's father held out his hand. "Awfully glad I had time enough between planes. Good-by, Bill. I'll be seeing you in a few weeks when my business is concluded."

Bill wrung the hand warmly. "You'll get the best goddam fishing you ever had. So long, Alec."

Duncan's father turned to Fabien, looking for a moment incongruously shy. "Well, lad," he said, "I'm not a religious man, but God bless you. God bless you. I know now what Duncan meant in his letters. We shall be seeing each other again. Good-by." He moved forward and gave Fabien a swift embrace, then he turned on his heel and walked quickly into the hall, saying, "Shall we go, Mr. Hollis?"

They went out of the house and down the street in an increasingly chilling silence that Stephen was prepared to break at any cost. From the corners of his eyes he looked at the striding figure beside him. It was the son of this man that Mrs. Hollis had dubbed low-class. No one could claim that it was entirely my fault, Stephen thought frantically. He said: "I don't live far from here, sir. I wish you could spare a few minutes to come home with me. I'd like my mother to meet you."

The eyes that turned upon him were Duncan's. He should have noticed it from the beginning. "Yes, it would be pleasant, but the time element is rather pressing, I'm afraid. Isn't this a handsome city. Duncan said it becomes beautiful when covered with snow."

"My mother would be pleased to put you up overnight, sir."

"Thank you. Some other time, perhaps."

The silence resumed. They were drawing nearer to Sherbrooke Street. "I wanted to see you alone," Stephen blurted out, "in order to express my sympathy. I liked Duncan an awful lot, but there were times when we didn't see eye to eye. Did he mention anything about it in his letters?"

"He didn't speak of you a great deal." The eyes turned away, ranging the street. The voice filled with a peculiarly flat politesse. "Excuse me, Mr. Hollis. I gave Duncan a liberal allowance, but I know he always spent rather freely. If he owed you any money, I trust you will speak up."

"No, sir," Stephen said, flushing scarlet.

"Forgive me. I understand he took a job in a local shop. It must have been for the experience."

"He was writing a book."

"Yes, I believe so. I've asked his friend Fabien to handle anything that may come of it. An extraordinarily decent fellow: I'm almost convinced I met his father in Budapest before the war. Good family, I believe. Not many left in that part of Europe these days."

"The world is in a bad state," Stephen said. It was fatuous.

They were standing at the curb. An occupied taxi sped past. Another was cruising towards them from a distance. "Are you," Mr. McSurt enquired politely, "one of the friends Duncan made while working at the shop? I'm sorry you didn't get on together."

Enmeshed in a web of dread and humiliation Stephen was incapable of explaining the tortuous intricacies of his exact relationship with Duncan. The words, formulated and waiting in his mind, refused to advance beyond his throat. The silence bore down. A hand flicked beside him. The cab pulled up with a faint squealing of brakes. He had accomplished nothing.

"How delightfully simple it is to get a cab in Canada." Duncan's father opened the rear door and climbed in. "Good-by, Mr. Hollis. I doubt that I shall be in Montreal again. If you are ever across the water, please feel free to call on me."

"Thank you," Stephen said numbly. "Thank you for letting me walk down with you."

"Don't mention it," Duncan's father answered with a polite smile. Good-by, Mr. Hollis." He leaned forward. "Dorval Airport, please."

The sunshine flashed brightly upon the back of the cab and the head in the rear window glowed red. Stephen watched until it disappeared around the corner, standing with his feet apart on the sidewalk, fists clenching and unclenching in frenetic spasms. He had to see Fabien. He had to go immediately to Fabien and discuss Duncan's father. Fabien would be kind and gentle. Fabien had been kind and gentle with Duncan, and now Stephen needed it.

But he did not turn back to the house. With lagging steps he started along Sherbrooke Street, his heart filling with a painful compassion for the memory of Duncan, whom he now sought to comprehend for the first time. Poor, pitiful Duncan, caught in the inescapable lime of circumstance. Poor, miserable search for cleanliness that had ended in conscious defeat when in Notre Dame de Grace the train had passed over the cumbered tracks and the unhappy soul was catapulted to its fearsome destination.

The compassion pressed outward with iron hands against the inside of his breast, and the breath came shuddering from his parted lips.

Fabien would know. Fabien would understand.

The fear passed over him like the licking tongues of an arctic wind.

VI

It was six hours before he let himself into the house. They would not have heard him yet, for he was treading softly and the piano was playing in the sitting room.

He was drunk. He had been drinking steadily since the departure of Duncan's father. From Westmount, where taverns were forbidden by pride and law, his feet had carried him to the first drink on St. Catherine Street and, after that, to place after less distinguishable place. He had been sick at one establishment and for a while had considered himself lost, but at the fifth or sixth place—he couldn't remember now—his thoughts had begun to resolve into a perspective upon which his mind at last could gaze with a modicum of detachment. It was an admittedly jagged vista, full of misunderstandings and snobbishness and unfortunately expressed truths, but it was one for which no one could justly be asked to accept the blame. Fabien would see that instantly when it was explained to him. Stephen stood still and listened.

Fabien would offer him a drink, and after a while, when Bill had gone, they would talk and talk until everything was threshed out, conclusions were reached. Toward the end, Stephen would describe the experience with his mother this afternoon, how it had upset him, and then Fabien would invite him to stay and they would sit up half the night talking about Duncan, perhaps in the same room where Duncan had once sat.

Fabien would understand.

The hall was dark except for a dim, yellow streak that shone from the sitting room. Stephen made his way to the door, treading a little heavier now to be heard above the sound of the piano. He was coming as a friend, and friends came not softly. And now that the pattern of Fabien's previous existence was broken, now that there was no one with whom he could sit talking late at night, Fabien needed a friend. Not Bill, for Bill was inarticulate and imperceptive, blind to the nuances of suffering to which the human spirit was subjected. Fabien needed someone who could talk, and understand when he talked.

In the sitting room a throat was cleared, the piano grew louder, plink-plinking a tune that was palpably absurd. Stephen leaned against the dark wall and smiled as Fabien began singing the song from *Alice in Wonderland*.

> "'My notion was that you had been
> Before she had this fit
> An obstacle that came between
> Him, and ourselves, and It.'"

He walked into the room and looked smilingly toward the piano, and his own intoxication mitigated a little to see that Fabien was ferociously drunk. The hands were lifting unnecessarily high in the air, the slender fingers coming down upon the keyboard with a verve, a burlesque flourish that was self-derisive. The broad back was rigid, the lolled-back head showing eyes stare-wide and foggy. Stephen watched while the treble hand lifted elegantly from the keys and took a glass from the long, filled row that stood in a perfectly straight line along the top of the piano. It was an achievement! Fabien drank the contents at one gulp without relinquishing for a second the ludicrous tune that continued in the bass.

Stephen dropped down on the settee. "Hi!" he said cheerfully. "I'm drunk."

"Everyone seems to be," said a voice.

Beyond the circle of the room's only lighted lamp, Bill sat huddled in a corner peering out from the shadows at Stephen.

"It's a mistake not to be," Stephen said. "Everyone should be drunk."

"Everyone should be quiet," Fabien said, without looking round from the piano. "I have a last verse and I especially wish to sing it to Stephen."

His right hand stroked a brilliant flurry from the top of the keyboard, and he began to sing again, his baritone voice louder, more musical.

> "'Don't let him know she liked them best,
> For this must ever be
> A secret, kept from all the rest,
> Between yourself and me.'"

He laid his hands in his lap and roared with laughter. "Do you like that, Stephen? In one significance it is unbelievably funny."

"In all significances," Stephen agreed, having trouble with the word. "You've done a wonderful job. How about the other tune?"

"Oh, that!" Fabien lifted his index finger and struck three times, hard, on middle C. "Stay on the settee, Stephen. Tonight I want company without having to look at it. This has been a most trying day. Did you get Duncan's father off all right?"

"Yes," Stephen answered, for it was too complicated to be explained right now. Later would do, when Bill had gone. He sprawled gratefully, happy at the candor of Fabien's dismissal and no longer perturbed by Bill's unwavering stare from the corner, nodding in recognition as Fabien commenced a Chopin nocturne.

"Let's talk, before we all go crazy," Bill said. "Leave the piano alone."

Fabien played on. "Bill has been like that since the mailman came. He managed to contain himself over Mr. McSurt, but the mail was too much. He wants to talk. And he liked Duncan's father."

"Didn't you?" Stephen asked quickly.

"I know what I'm giving you for Christmas, Stephen," Bill interrupted. "A nice, permanent little flame like on the tomb of the Unknown Warrior. You can spend the rest of your life fanning it into a great big blaze."

"Naughty," Fabian said. "Naughty Bill, in a temper because no one will talk with him."

"I will," Stephen said lightly, "if someone will give me a drink. I'm dying of thirst."

"Get a whole bottle from the cellar," Fabien suggested. "I think I once offered you the whole cellar." He laughed again, and Stephen was all at once afraid to leave the two of them alone. Bill was dangerous.

He said: "What's the matter, Bill?"

"The guy's a good head," Bill said to Fabien. "He'll have fishing like he never knew there was fishing. Him and my old man are going to get on fine."

"I see you're determined to talk." The hands scuffed out a brilliant arpeggio. "But don't expect me to stop playing. I won't."

Bill stretched his legs before him and allowed his arms to fall limply at the sides of the chair. His head came forward a little and, in the light, his face was fiercely sober. "We've been through this before," he said. "Why'd he do it?"

"Shut up, Bill. You're spoiling my music."

"I want to know."

"Is this private, or can I join in?" Stephen asked. His tongue was thick and halting; he was drunk after all. The room rocked and the fumes swirled round his brain.

Bill ignored the question. "There was no need. He had everything he ever wanted."

"He didn't have his brother," Stephen said. "We know now why he felt dirty and why he got on the railroad track. He was trying to wash off the blood and when it wouldn't work he chose to go in the way that was most like he remembered. You heard what his father said. Duncan killed his brother."

He drew back sharply, expecting a blow, as Bill hurtled across the room with clenched fists. "Shut your mouth about something you know nothing about! He would have told me, if that was the reason, when we used to talk about the war. I knew he'd killed somebody, but that wasn't it. Everybody killed somebody in the war, except you, Hollis."

"I know. I spent the war behind a desk."

"You're damned right. And did you ever kill anybody?"

"Yes."

Through the sudden roaring in his ears he heard Fabien whistling softly to his own accompaniment, and gradually the ground returned beneath his feet. When Bill was gone and they were in the bedroom, they would have a long talk. He looked up boldly into Bill's white face.

"Duncan had a morbid fixation about death. I even had to lie about the time my father died, to save his feelings."

"You needn't have bothered," Bill snapped. "We all read in the paper when it happened."

Stephen had not the least desire to weep, and yet his lower lip quivered. Again he had been deceived and his noblest intentions turned awry, brought to contempt. He said harshly: "Then why did you let me do it?"

Bill moistened his lips, unclenching his hands and dropping them to his sides. "It was an all right thing to do," he said, half-ashamed. "Did he really have anything to do with your father dying?"

To hell with Duncan, Stephen thought with savage impatience. He had been one of those insignificant people that friends try to endue with gigantic stature when death has intervened to prevent the illustration of discrepancies. History was full of them, and now a plot was afoot for Duncan and Mr. Hollis to walk side by side, casting their pseudoenormous shadows wherever Stephen chose to walk. Well, to hell with them both! He was sick of the sound of their names.

"My father's dead," he said, "and I don't know what Duncan thought. Are you trying to turn this into a murder mystery? Why don't you drop the subject and sit down?"

"Do, Bill," Fabien said from the piano. "If you had the least appreciation of music, you would be listening to me in rapt silence. Let's all have a drink and pick another topic."

"Don't stop playing." Stephen rose to his feet and stood face to face with the unmoving Bill. "You don't like me much, do you?" he said, and he was able genuinely to smile for suddenly everything had gone back to normal size, an Olympian calm had settled upon him.

Bill shrugged and turned away. "Let's have a drink. I'm a dab hand at getting people drinks."

When they had taken the first two from the line on the piano, Stephen counted the remainder and saw that there were eleven. Several empty glasses stood in a cluster around Fabien's feet, in imminent danger of being crushed every time he used the pedals. Stephen's smile grew wider. "We all need brightening up," he said. "Play something lively. What about the *Valses Nobles et Sentimentales?*"

The music when it came was more sad than he remembered. He had not noticed before the flat-champagne quality, the acrid disillusion of the chords upon which most of the melodies were pivoted. But it left him unmoved, detached, almost mocking, for the size of all things, apart from Fabien's hands on the keyboard, was diminishing, becoming less than normal, and Stephen felt himself expanding into a magnificent indifference. Another man's grief was his, and his only, incommunicable even though he invited you, as Ravel had done, to laugh with him at his own bitter suffering. Let them all grieve, for his father and for Duncan.

Stephen would remain dry-eyed—unsharing and uncaring. Both had been hoist on the petard of their own self-opinion, and only they were to blame for it. Both had assumed unnecessary proportions during their lives, but their lives were over now and they must be buried. He, Stephen, cared not one whit. They were no longer important. The feeling of power experienced on the night of his father's death returned with a rush, and he looked across at Bill's drawn face.

"I believe you thought more of Duncan than his father did," he said, and the waltzes drew to an end, the last mournful chord dying melancholy away like the sighing hush of a spent wave.

Fabien was continuing to play, improvising and modulating simple melodies, transposing them to a minor key. Bill dropped back in his chair, not looking to the piano where Stephen reached out his hand for another drink.

"He ought to have waited until the mail came," Bill said, looking at his untasted drink with repugnance and setting the glass on the floor beside him, tilting it so that some of the liquid spilled on his fingers. "Bloody fool, why didn't he wait?"

Slumped in his chair like that, Bill looked weak and ineffectual, his soft, western features slack, relaxing into stupidity.

"What difference would it have made?" Stephen asked.

"Oh, for God's sake," Fabien cried, beating a discord from the keyboard with his fists. "If you don't change the subject I'll start singing."

"That would be delightful," Stephen said.

And why did he suddenly feel like Miriam, when he hadn't even thought of her in weeks. Of course, it was exactly the sort of thing—that would be delightful!—that she had said at the party. Hag! But no matter what the ramifications, it had been all for Fabien's sake. All experience. With a swift, brushing movement he laid his hand briefly on the smooth head.

"Go on and sing something."

As the beautiful, disciplined fingers searched the keyboard the power within Stephen became tempered with a sense of intimacy so strong that he felt it must discover itself to anyone who watched. He glanced at Bill's lowered head, the cropped hair darkened by the dim light, and a wave of understanding came over him. Bill had been fond of Duncan to an extent where all associations were linked inextricably with his friend's red head. And now the head was fallen, the associations broken, and he was completely alone. Perhaps he had imagined they were leading a quadruple existence, that when one side of the figure was removed the others would close into a triangle, each measuring a corner bisected with grief. But if he has looked at me, Stephen thought, and at Fabien's rigid, indifferent back, he must realize by now his mistake. There is no grief here, no shared associations with which to bedeck and mitigate his sorrow. I can no longer look to the past and Fabien, obviously, does not wish to. We live in the present and anticipate the future, and to us the dead are irremediably dead. Poor Bill, with his solitary sorrow!

I am drunk, Stephen thought, beatifically drunk, and when Bill has gone tonight I shall tell Fabien I want to go to Rio. He walked over and picked up the glass that stood beside Bill's chair. "Have a drink," he said, with an exquisitely afforded kindness. "This will make you feel better."

Bill looked up, shaking his head, and behind them Fabien began to sing, amid the enmeshing counterpoint.

"'Little fly, thy summer's play my thoughtless hand has brushed away.'"

"There was a letter from the publisher," Bill said. "They liked his book."

"Good heavens!" Stephen exclaimed, beginning to laugh.

"'Am I not a fly like thee, and art thou not a man like me?'"

"They only wanted him to rewrite chapter three and part of chapter seven and they were going to publish. I'll show you the letter."

"I suppose they'll publish anything these days," Stephen said. "Neither Duncan nor I thought it amounted to anything."

There was a violent discord and Fabien leapt to his feet amid the sound of crunching glass, slamming down the keyboard lid with a violence that made the line of glasses ring loudly and brought a whining hum from the piano wires. The incriminatory words seemed to scamper almost visibly about the room, and Stephen could only stare with aching eyes at Fabien's back, waiting while the fear gathered in his gorge and slowly choked him. As in a slow-motion film he saw the arm come up and sweep the glasses with a tinkling crash from the top of the piano, then Fabien turned around slowly, his hands still raised, as if bestowing a benediction.

"I feel sick," he said.

The piano wires were quivering upon the air. There was a dripping sound and a tiny trickle of wine came creeping from beside the piano and circled slowly around the toe of Fabien's right shoe. Behind him, Stephen heard Bill rise to his feet amid the creaking of chair springs, then the wine glass was removed from his paralyzed hand.

"I didn't know you read Duncan's book," said the voice in Stephen's ear.

"For God's sake drop it," Fabien shouted. "I've had enough for one evening." He turned toward the hall, walking like an automaton, and stumbled to his knees on the threshold, the palms of his hands hitting the floor with a report that echoed through the house.

Bill was at his side, helping him to his feet. "Take it easy. You'll make yourself puke."

"Yes," said Fabien, straightening up and pulling down his jacket at the back. "Excuse me, I wanted to call someone. I'll use the upstairs phone and afterward I can take a shower. I feel filthy."

"Sure, that'll be fine," Bill answered, hooking an arm under the sagging shoulders.

They went together across the hall and up the black-carpeted stairs, their feet making no sound to break the silence that crushed with petrifying weight on every inch of Stephen's body.

He was one with the furnishings in the room, an object, an ornament, a piece of bric-a-brac. He had never before realized the hideous sentience of inanimate things, but now they began with foul subtlety to communicate with him, the winking shards of broken glass, the unspeaking notes of the piano, the beckoning soft convexities of the chairs. I've had too much to drink, he told himself feebly, but the process of thought was insufficient to break the concretion of his limbs and he could only wait while the danger mounted, the scream gathered strong. He had to get out, he told himself, into the fresh air, away from this room. All that remained in the world, now, was himself and this furniture. And Bill would be coming back in a very little while.

Upstairs, someone dialed the telephone. Stephen walked stiffly through the hall to the front door. As the cool night air blew upon him he began to run.

He refused to think about it. He refused to dwell upon this idiotic evening until it could be viewed dispassionately in proper perspective. He ran until the air burned torturingly in his lungs, then he slowed to a saunter, panting heavily, alone in the deserted residential street.

It was darker tonight, the lamps dimmer, one of those spring nights in Montreal when the sky is thickly overcast. He walked along fixing his attention on external things, the movement of a bush, a lighted window, the distant sound of car horns in the city below; deviating his thoughts to speculate hazily upon the lives of the strangers who moved through the streets down there, thinking of their relationship to each other and to himself. How constricted was life for the unwary: how much more constricted death. Tonight he would think of no one with whom he was familiar, thrusting from his mind even the persisting thought of Fabien.

The bitter taste of solitude came into his mouth, his faintly echoing progress through the street seemed but the footfalls of a ghost, pacing some forsaken desolation. He glanced over his shoulder for a reassurance from the city's reflected glare, and saw the other figure behind him, some fifty yards away, moving with unhurried tread, maintaining step, following.

Stephen ran again.

He ran until he thought his lungs must burst, then with painfully heaving chest he leaned against someone's gate and looked back along the street. It was deserted. He straightened up and resumed his way, laughing to think how really drunk he must be. It was the vague familiarity of the figure that had frightened him. Without the drink, he would not have fled. In the future he must cut it out; he was far from being in condition. No more drink.

Tomorrow he and Fabien would commiserate with each other over their respective hangovers. Tonight he would not dwell upon the matter.

He approached his home almost gaily, pleased that no lights shone from the windows, thinking it must be later than previously he had thought. This dislocation of time was another unpleasant aspect of drinking: it seemed years instead of hours since Duncan's father departed in that cab. Mr. Alexander McSurt. Too bad about him. He seemed, as Bill had said, a good head.

Stephen reached for the front door key in his pocket, whistling a tune under his breath, and the familiar figure stepped out from the shadow of the doorway.

"I came by another way," Bill said, "running all the way. Lucky for me I knew your address."

He was blocking the way, shifting his body so that Stephen was forced to take a step back against the wall.

"Hello," Stephen said. "What do you want?"

"What do you think? I want you."

"That's very flattering. What for?"

Bill hunched his shoulders. "I've been on to you, Hollis, since the night of that party. This is the end of the line."

"I was drunk tonight," Stephen said. "I am still."

"So much the better for me. I'm sober."

"What do you want?"

"I didn't want to do it at Fabien's place," Bill said. "Seems more like justice to do it here."

"If this is a joke, I don't get it and I'm tired of it. Let me through, I want to go to bed."

"After," Bill said. "First I'm going to fill you in."

"You're crazy."

This, he knew, was the reason for his panic flight. He said: "Does Fabien know you're here?"

"Why should he?"

"He wouldn't like this."

"Too bad."

The clenched fist caught Stephen squarely in the mouth, banging his head back against the wall with fearful force. He slid to the ground, reeling with pain, the rough surfaces of the bricks clutching at the fibers of his jacket.

"Get up, Hollis." Bill screwed the lapels of Stephen's jacket in one hand and dragged him to his feet. "Why don't you shout for the police? I'd like the neighbors to know you're fighting."

"You're crazy. I don't want to fight you." The words came out with difficulty. His lips were numbing, beginning to swell.

"That's fine," Bill said. "Makes it easier for me." The fist struck again.

His skull became a framework of pain. He tried to fall again, but the clutching hand at his coat prevented it. His brain whirled blackly and he sucked in his breath as Bill kicked him viciously in the shins.

"Don't do it," he gasped. "You read the book, too."

The hand jerked him forward until their faces were an inch apart and he could see the drawn line of Bill's mouth. "Now we've got something to fight about," Bill said. "I'm going to knock you until you can't see, or walk, or stand up. You're going to find out what war is like."

This time Stephen saw the blow coming and jerked his head aside, exultant as he heard Bill's fist hit the wall. "Okay," he said. "If you want it." He struck out fiercely and felt his arm go whistling harmlessly past Bill's ear.

An open hand struck him hard across the face, and the insult hurt more than the blow. He lunged forward, landing a punch on Bill's shoulder, and the other palm flicked smacking with a force that made his head ring. What a ridiculous way, he thought, what a bloody ridiculous way for two grown men to be behaving. And then he was caught by the throat and thrust back against the wall, while Bill's free hand beat a slapping tattoo, back and front, back and front, across both sides of his face.

"I've had enough," Stephen panted, his mind seeking frantically for distracting words. "Duncan and I were friends, Bill. Let me explain. Let's go and talk it over with Fabien."

"Leave Fabien out of this."

Now that Stephen refused to fight, the fists were clenching again, breaking skin and leaving blood with every blow that landed. The street grew darker and Stephen knew that soon the darkness would envelop him completely. He tried to concentrate on what Bill was saying in order to retain a hold, but all that came through was a jumbled mass of words with no connected meaning. And then he was lying on the ground, looking up, with Bill standing over him.

"Next time you want to pick on somebody," Bill said clearly, "pick on a guy without any friends."

The toe of a square-fronted shoe nudged into Stephen's temple and Bill drew back his foot, preparatory to a swing.

Stephen lost consciousness.

VII

He lay motionless, wondering where he was, while the frightening darkness mired about him broken only by the explosions of light that beat in agonizing rhythm to the throb of his pain-racked head. He was deathly ill, and he was lost. Cautiously he reached about for some object that might indicate his whereabouts, a long breath escaping him as the creeping hand encountered what was recognizably a chair leg. Then he was on a floor somewhere, still alive, alone.

Unless Bill was in this darkness, waiting.

He sat up quickly, too quickly, and fell full length again as the pain pierced a thousand places of his head. He remembered now and lifted a hand to his forehead, seeking the hub of the pain, the place where Bill kicked him. But there was no lump, no large bruise. The relief came from Stephen in a whistling sigh.

And suddenly he was convinced that Bill sat somewhere in the room, the arm of justice waiting to execute the primary law that demands the transgressor's eye. The hand flailed out, and Stephen sobbed as he clutched the chair leg a second time. Only for an instant he had imagined to hear the sound of a distant train whistle, to feel the sharp, cold metal of the tracks beneath his body. A cold sweat bedewed him as, with his free hand, he groped frantically in his pocket for a book of matches.

Cautiously this time, he sat up, edging his body gently until the chair pressed reassuringly against his spine. The matches fumbled in his shaking hands. The scratching sound was the most beautiful in the world, the tiny glimmer the most beautiful sight.

He was downstairs in his own home, sitting on the familiar carpet with his back to his father's chair. Easing himself painfully to his feet, he blew out the match and crossed the familiar territory to switch on the standard lamp. He glanced around the room and saw a few spots of blood on the carpet, two deep grooves that indicated Bill had dragged him part of the way. To his relief, there were no sounds from upstairs.

Well, they'll know tomorrow, he thought, prodding with gentle fingers at the rawness of his face. He would tell them quite frankly that it was none of their business, that the fight had occurred in the gym at McGill. An acute weariness overcame him and, as his body drooped, the fear surged back so strongly that he thought he must lose consciousness again. He slumped into his father's chair and waited for the dizziness to pass, seeking with closed eyes the first link in the chain of logical thought that would permit him to rationalize his position. The spell passed, and with it the fear, but in his head the pulsating pain remained. He opened his eyes and saw for the first time that the pictures had been brought back from the cellar and hung upon the walls. And then he remembered how his mother had looked at him.

Undoubtedly, Father had won. There would be no redecoration because Father would not approve, and today he had returned to the house to lead a coexistent life for as long as Stephen remained. Mrs. Hollis was no longer alone and incomplete, for in her mind the regime was re-established, the old tyranny had asserted itself; the need for oppression, lying across her puny spirit like a weal, was at last fulfilled. Without it, Stephen thought, she found her negativity akin to death. Only the bruises of mishandling can convince her that she lives. "I wish you were more like Father," she had said, and the threat was carried out, her existence was resumed, and hereinafter he could expect only the creeping attendance, the martyred resignation, the meek submission that had been Mr. Hollis's welcomed lot for all his married life. Talk, laughter, civilized intercourse, all hopes of these were gone. Fabien must never be admitted to this house in the future lest he turn away sickened, having seen Stephen through the dull and fearful light of Mrs. Hollis's eyes.

All the old hatred burst within him like an abscess. His father had established the kingdom and, against his wishes, the son was forced to inherit. Fabien would deride the specter as loudly as on the night of the party he had laughed at the living person. Mr. Hollis, dead, was as potently effective in holding them apart as he had been in life.

My father's death, Stephen thought, accomplished nothing.

He lit a cigarette with trembling fingers, drawing the smoke through his crushed lips and waiting for the sudden pounding of his heart to cease.

He died because he shamed me before Fabien, and it has accomplished nothing.

The tears sprang hot to his eyes. He dropped his splitting head into his hands, hoping for the relief of weeping, and loneliness surrounded him with a thousand whispering voices. The pain from his head seemed to seep down through his body, running along the bone structure with padded fingers, engendering in his flesh a flaming heat. And all at once he remembered the physical presence of Bill, the fierceness of his violence, and it was as though he sat in the center of a vacuum, devoid of motion, feeble and inept.

If Fabien knew what had been suffered, could see the evidence of the tears, then surely his gaze would rest upon Stephen as once it did on Duncan.

He peered at his watch through swollen eyes and saw that it was past two o'clock. Rising quickly from his father's chair, not bothering to walk quietly, he left the house, slamming the door violently behind him. Out in the street a taxi passed swiftly. He raised his voice in a shout and his spirits lifted aggressively as the obedient squeal of brakes shattered the stillness of the night. Let his mother hear, and believe this to be part of the despotic individuality he had been forced to assume. She had chosen the road, but he would walk it in his own manner, going his own gait and carrying the mantle she had given only on his arm. For he had a garment of his own to wear, a robe that was ripped by the ill-feeling and misunderstanding of others, but which he could wear proudly and with a flourish. Tonight he and Fabien were going to scrutinize every stitch and seam, and it would be proved beyond doubt that behind the tatterdemalion appearance lay the painstaking work and good intention of the honest craftsman. Fabien would understand. Fabien might even admire.

A positivity of purpose seized him so that he sauntered to the waiting cab almost arrogantly, giving his directions to the driver in a voice gratifyingly harsh and peremptory. There could not be two Mr. Hollises and if he, Stephen, pretended his father's role, then the father would be dead and the son could live his separate existence. It was a subtle point and he must speak of it to Fabien, making sure to draw the parallel with the Kantean edict.

"Drive on!" he ordered authoritatively.

The driver turned an essentially French-Canadian face and scrutinized Stephen intently. "You okay?" he asked.

"Sure! I picked the wrong two guys."

The driver puckered his forehead, shaking his head knowingly. "If people knew," he said, clucking his tongue. "These Westmount parties."

"Drive on," Stephen said again, more amiably, for it had amused him, as always it did, to hear how the French Canadian said West*mount* par*ties*. He leaned back in his seat, feeling the smile form behind his battered face, and began plotting the framework of what he would say to Fabien. When the taxi drew up silently after the short journey, a sketchy system had already been evolved, a progression of logical thought that reached from the first time he met Duncan up to the present moment. Not everything dovetailed, but the missing factors would emerge during conversation, or, failing that, it might prove amusing mentally to hunt for clues. Stephen inserted his key in the lock and hesitated a moment. It had occurred to him that Fabien might himself have missing information to supply, solutions to offer, motives to explain. This was the first time he had even entertained the thought. He turned the key and entered the house.

The previous silence lapped about him, different now, of a softer texture, the warm tranquillity that invites forgetfulness and rest at the end of a weary battle. Stephen crossed the hall, sensing from the atmosphere that Bill had not returned after his outburst. Probably he was too ashamed ever to return again. Stephen smiled.

It would be necessary to tell of what Bill had done, for there was no disguising the bruised face. He would explain that he felt no resentment and try to outline for Fabien the honest intent of Bill's motives, how he had been driven to error by an excess of grief. Fabien was going to be shocked, disgusted, but I shall tell him, thought Stephen, how in Canada we sometimes resort to fists because we have no solid ethnical background against which our perplexities can immediately crystallize to placating thought.

Stephen reached the top of the stairs. A beam of faint yellow light clove the darkness of the landing, issued from the room into which Stephen and Miriam had almost stumbled on the night of the party. The door swung back noiselessly on its hinges and Stephen entered, a strange, quickening excitement assailing him as his nostrils met the sweetish odors of sleep. Just over the threshold, he paused. The room was in darkness. The shaft of light was coming from the door, slightly ajar, of the adjoining bathroom. A vague disappointment possessed him that it would not, after all, be necessary to waken Fabien. It would have been, somehow, gratifyingly pleasant gently to shake him by the shoulder and feel the firm body stirring beneath his hand, see the wide eyes flutter open and assume soft recognition. He moved toward the bed to sit and wait.

Fabien lay full length, in silhouette, the covers folded neatly back below his feet, arms outstretched above his head, face buried in the pillow. Barely discernible in the darkness, his back moved with a steady rhythm, and in the way he reclined, not stirring, seemingly sunk into the bed, there was a sensuous, animal contentment—a sleep, untroubled by dreams, that was purely muscular.

A peculiar illusion of fiery warmth, not yet an actual feeling, crept over Stephen's limbs and into the region of his stomach, and the breath expelled suddenly, almost in a snort, from his nostrils. He lifted his hands and dropped them again, for they were trembling violently. The rest of his body had become suddenly rock-hard and sinewy, with every aching muscle thrusting out through the flesh.

"Fabien," he called hoarsely, for now the thought of touching the figure, shaking it to wakefulness, filled him with a violent revulsion. "Fabien, you've left the bathroom light on."

The long silhouette moved and changed its shape, the legs stretching farther, pointing the toes in a languid yawn, the arms opening lazily across the pillow.

"My dear, I'd fallen asleep," Fabien murmured drowsily, and he rolled over, the whites of his eyes gleaming bright in the gloom as he blinked in sleepy pleasure.

"Stephen!"

Fabien sat up abruptly, his voice rasping and loud. "What are you doing here at this time of night? What do you want?"

He could think of no immediate answer. Almost automatically he was going to say You, but he remembered that Bill had already made that reply once this evening, and it now became inadequate. He stood mute, waiting for some utterance that would help clarify the inexplicable feelings that were coursing through him, but there was no precedent upon which to fall back and the words that tumbled to his brain were soiled with inadequate familiarity. As the outline of Fabien's hand reached for the bedside lamp, Stephen began gently to sweat.

The room became filled with light.

"Pass me my robe," Fabien said, pointing across the room to where it lay draped across the back of a corner chair.

Stephen remained unmoving, staring at the naked figure before him, watching the chest rise, the packed muscles of the diaphragm flutter, with each breath that Fabien drew. The body was darker than the face, much darker, a deep olive brown that covered him smoothly from the neck right down to the arched insteps of his feet. Even the inner sides of his thighs were brown.

Stephen took one step nearer to the bed. Fabien is a foreigner, he thought.

"What happened to your face?"

It no longer mattered. Stephen shook his head. "I want to talk to you," he whispered. The words cut at his throat like gravel. In the plunging confusion of his brain, the clear-cut scheme devised in the cab became lost. He could no longer think of what he wanted to say.

Fabien waited, staring. "Did Bill do that?"

Stephen could only nod, watching, as Fabien raised himself to a sitting position, the multiple swelling and subsiding of the flesh, as if each individual portion of the moving body was endowed with independent life. Behind his bruised lips, Stephen's tongue became dry as a piece of leather.

"He certainly changed your appearance."

Fabien leaned his back against the head of the bed, his hands on either side pressing the mattress until the muscles stood out on his forearms. "Did he hurt you?"

A wave of fatigue swept over Stephen, so intense that he had forcibly to restrain himself from sinking to Fabien's side upon the bed. His face was burning and the tears pricked hotly at his eyes. He nodded his head slowly. "He hurt me pretty bad."

"Good!"

The word cracked in the air savage as a whiplash, but harmlessly, far above Stephen's head. He watched the stony expression melt from Fabien's face, the lips go back until he could see the teeth; but it meant nothing to him, for there was no contact: they were separated by an impalpable curtain of air that shimmered between them like the rising of a heat haze.

He is angry with me, Stephen thought, and the processes of his thinking seemed to belong to someone else. I must reach him across this gap, explain to him all those things I thought of in the cab, keep on talking until I am sure he understands. It is only grief that is incommunicable, not love, and only Bill has grieved.

He moved forward, raising his arms, and his outstretched hands penetrated the curtain that lay between. And now they were together, for they were close. The intangible current of understanding was flowing one to the other.

"I want to talk to you," Stephen whispered and he laid his hand upon the bare shoulder. He broke into a violent trembling as the hot flesh scorched his palm, searing through to his whole body.

He knew he was lost. There could be no turning back, even did he wish it. Dimly he wondered if this was the goal to which he had been blindly traveling since first they met, but the impression, inextricably tangled with images of his father and Duncan, refused to vitrify, and he could only stare down to see his own realization mirrored in Fabien's eyes, watch as the eyes widened and became blankly waiting.

And now his actions were no longer his own. Unable to prevent himself, he ran his gaze over Fabien's body, seeking some sign that would indicate what could not be read in the eyes. "I want to talk to you," he said again, and the words burst into the atmosphere unnaturally loud, meaningless, idiotic.

"There is nothing we can possibly say," Fabien said. "Please go."

"Why are you angry?" Without releasing his hold Stephen slowly reached forth his other hand and gripped Fabien's other arm, just below the opposite shoulder, kneading the hot, firm flesh with fingers that were all at once surprisingly, frantically strong. "Fabien," he said, almost sobbing. "Why are you angry with me?"

"Please remove your hands and get out!"

The fingers stopped their movement and gripped tighter. In a single passionate impulse Stephen jerked the unresisting body to him, almost lifting it from the bed, drawing the face close to him until he could feel on his cheeks the cool jets of air that expelled from Fabien's nostrils. "I want to talk to you. I have to make you understand."

"I understand perfectly," Fabien said coldly, and the blank look was gone, changed to an expression of revulsion that turned his face to coldest white marble. "I suggest you get out of here before you are sorry. And please don't bother to come back. I have no wish to see you again."

"Don't say that." There was no stopping now, for the tears in his eyes had overflowed and sobs were shaking his body. "I love you, Fabien. You've got to understand. Everything that I did was for you, you must believe me."

The strength had ebbed away, leaving him weak with a weariness that threatened to drag him to the ground. He felt his hands slide from Fabien's shoulders and down the smooth reaches of the body. He could do nothing to arrest their progress, for he was dying, cell by collapsing cell, under the withering repugnance that looked at him from the eyes into which he stared.

It must not end like this—he must not be driven away, not now when all the obstacles between them had at last been removed. Fabien must be forced to listen to him, feel what he was feeling, understand his torments, forgive.

With a sob of desperation Stephen flung himself upon the bed, reaching out with groping hands to draw to him the only thing in his life he had ever truly wanted. "Don't send me away, Fabien," he cried, and he was gasping, as at the end of a long race. "Let me stay with you. Put your arms around me and tell me that I can stay."

"You fool! You bloody fool! You misunderstand me. I am a foreigner." Stephen lay with his face partly buried in the pillow, his arm flung out across the naked chest. A passionate stream of unknown language hissed into his ear, then he felt the vibrations go humming through Fabien's unmoving body.

"You'd better come in now," Fabien called.

It was inexplicable only for an instant. Stephen heard the faint squeak of door hinges and knew that someone else was in the room, and then an insane fear gripped him, for all at once he expected to hear his father's voice thundering a denunciation. Slowly he raised his head, wrenching his unwilling hands from their last touching of Fabien, the fear retained, though already his mind had rejected Mr. Hollis and the succeeding image of Duncan. He turned to a sitting position, knowing that it would be Miriam.

The lips were smiling, the eyebrows raising in amused surprise over shining eyes. Framed in the doorway of the adjoining bathroom, a hand upon her hip and the other holding together the thin negligee that was her only garment, stood Crystal.

"Well, I *am* surprised, Stephen. I didn't know." She removed the hand from her hip and waved it once, sharply, in his direction. "Whoops! Stevie dear," she said. "Whoopsie!" And she began to shake with laughter.

In a purely reflex action he leapt across the intervening space and slapped her violently across the face.

"No, Fabien, don't bother." She stood looking toward the bed while the mark of impact grew more deeply crimson upon her cheek. "He's had enough beating already, and it's not really his fault. All he needs is a little medical treatment."

"What an abominable situation," Fabien remarked faintly.

"He's drunk. I expect he really meant to see Matt Lambert."

"Shut up," Stephen said, and it was like a whimper.

She turned cold eyes upon him and he saw her fist clench. "Why don't you go home, you lousy queer? You're not wanted here."

"He never has been," Fabien said in an indifferent voice. "I do wish he'd go away and not come back."

"You heard what the man said, Stephen." Crystal put her hand back on her hip and smiled again.

"Come to bed, my angel," Fabien said. "He knows his own way out."

She brushed past Stephen, the smile growing more tender, and he heard the bed springs creak a little under the added weight. He walked from the room without looking back. Crystal said softly, anxiously, "Are you all right?" and Fabien answered in a low, unfamiliar voice, "Thank you, my dear, I think so. I think so." He heard nothing else. He was feeling his way along the landing, down the black-carpeted stairs, the silence behind him forcing him from the house, forming an impenetrable barrier through which he could never return.

There was no pain now, only a numbness, and behind the bruises he could feel his face already assuming its unalterable cast. The front door closed behind him. He walked through the deserted streets, wishing that he could weep, wondering how his mother would sympathize tomorrow about the lacerations on his face.

VIII

The sunlit weeks were past, golden, glorious, arduous. The voices of teachers no longer rumbled in their ears, the classroom smells of chalk and ink were fast disappearing from olfactory memory. They had gathered on the campus under the eyes of proud parents and visiting pedagogues. They had applauded each other and themselves. They were emptying the city as the tourists poured in.

Beneath a pile of dirty laundry in the luggage of William Dexter Prescott, B.Sc., the rolled sheepskin lay forgotten as completely as the ceremony, two days ago. Rattling swiftly westward he looked with interest from the train window and reached into his pocket for the gold cigarette case that had been Fabien's parting gift, snapping it open with a flourish to read again the inscription, a facsimile of Fabien's own elegant handwriting.

What a good head, that Fabien! Pity he wasn't coming back to Canada, but that business with Duncan had affected him more than he had ever shown. A thing like that could put you off a place for a good long time—like not wanting ever to go back to England where you'd been stationed in the air force.

Duncan and Fabien. A sadness, a not altogether unpleasureable melancholy, filtered through Bill's mind. You often met good heads and knew them for a while, but then they went and you were alone again, just like the war. But you were better for having known them, most of them anyway, and it wasn't so bad really, for there was always fishing and a glass of beer and the chance you would meet a stranger with whom you could talk about what the war was really like.

Christ, he should have talked more to Duncan, different to what he had. He might have found out what was bothering the poor kid. He had thought for a while it was only that creeping bastard Hollis, getting up the kid's nose; it wasn't, but the idea had got somehow lodged in his head. That was the reason why, on the night he felt so goddam low, he had given Hollis that beating up. A bloody good beating up. But what was the difference, the guy had it coming to him anyway. He hadn't liked him from the first. A crawler, always intriguing. You never knew what he was up to, and he was always up to something, that was for sure.

Bill drew reflectively on his cigarette and thought of Duncan's father. Now that was a good head if ever there was one—sort of open-mannered, with no tricks. They were going to have some great times fishing together. He knew just the place. And didn't the guy say he had spent the war in India and Burma? That was something new. It would be interesting to compare experiences.

But they wouldn't talk about Duncan, although there were bound to be times when they caught each other's eye and knew they were both thinking about him. That sort of thing had happened a lot in the war. You met someone on leave who'd known a guy that you'd known and who'd been killed. You looked at each other and then you looked away. It gave you a strange sort of feeling. And come to that, you could almost say that Duncan had been killed in the war.

The magnificent scenery moved slowly past the window. Bill looked out and began seriously to think of fishing. Summer was a-coming in.

And would it be any better than last summer, Crystal wondered, sitting in the last coach of the same train. She grinned. Damn it to hell! and it had held so much promise—though to be fair she had to admit that he had not made any concrete proposition. For a while she thought he might be persuaded to stay until the end of medical exams, held later than any others, but no, it had all come in two days—the booking, the exquisite string of pearls, the last grave farewell at the dockside.

"Good-by, Fabien."

"Good-by, my darling. I have loved you."

"Will you write?"

"Perhaps."

She knew he would not. It no longer mattered. Certainly it had not been true love on her part, that much she had realized on that awful night when he lay for hours in her arms and sobbed like a child. Perhaps all men were really children, no matter what their age. So. Anyway, he had been perfectly lovely and she had not a single regret. Maybe next term—

Her absently wandering eye encountered that of a fellow traveler, a tall fellow with dark hair, handsome in a bony sort of way. She guessed he was about thirty. It pleased her. She decided he looked rather attractive, and they exchanged a smile.

Her fingers went to the pearls about her neck. But ah! she thought, you should have seen the one that got away.

Next term—well, next term she might even see a lot more of Stephen. He was a nice enough fellow and only a little bit odd and she liked him, and probably all he needed was a short, medical talking-to, something to put him on the right path. And there was, of course, the question of that enormous amount of money his father had left him.

Crystal fell to cogitating on the loss of her most precious gift. How wonderfully pleasant it had been, and actually she felt much better for it, more of a doctor, somehow.

She returned to her book.

"Can I help you, madam?"

"Just looking around," said one of the middle-aged women, and the other asked: "What happened to the red-haired clerk who used to serve at this counter?"

"I'm sorry, madam. I've only been here two days."

"Well, never mind." They moved farther up the counter.

"I expect he left," the second woman said. "I used to like talking to him. He knew every bit of gossip in the city."

"Oh?"

"He was the one who first told me about the Hollises."

"Oh, everybody knows that," said her friend. "Did you see that shameless cat in church last Sunday?"

There was a knowing nod. "They're getting married, you know."

"I should think so. I was surprised he was able to get another position. Somewhere way up North, isn't it? Good job it's a long way away."

"It can't be much of a congregation," her friend said. "Bit of a comedown for him. How awful for her family."

"Not so bad for that brother with all the money his father left him. He got the lot, you know."

"Yes, the red-haired fellow told me about that, too."

"Did he? Oh then maybe he was the one who told Mrs. Parkman."

"I told you. He knew everything."

"Can I help you, madam?" the two-day young man asked of the third middle-aged woman.

Miriam smiled at him, thinking how pathetically young and gawky he looked, her eye surreptitiously scanning the counter for some sign of Duncan. She had seen him a few weeks previously, back behind the counter, and on that day the uncertainty had caused her to flee. But now she was content, secure in her belief, and even the lack of positive proof occasioned by his absence caused her no disquiet.

He was to have been the acid test, for in retrospect he had emerged as the sweetest through asking the least and permitting her to keep the most. She even suspected that he had partly understood her. She had often, on thinking it over, tried to return the compliment of the suspicion by endeavoring to understand him, and sometimes it left her with a vague feeling that she had perhaps done him an injury. How did he feel about that? She would like to make amends, to apologize to him. Silly when she didn't know what to apologize *for*. But it didn't matter that he was no longer here. The simple fact of being able to come in, coolly to enter, proved beyond doubt that she no longer needed a testing. God! how restful it was.

"I want some really nice white shirts," she said. "For my husband. The very best you have."

She looked at her watch, a little anxious lest she be late for the meeting of the Hadassah Society. There was a prevailing rumor that she might be asked to join the group who paid visits to the young soldiers up in the Queen Mary Veteran's Hospitals. It should be interesting.

Fabien turned from the rail, the sleeves of his immaculate white shirt fluttering in the sea breeze. From farther along the deck a girl waved to him. He lifted his hand in response, and a young officer waved back from an upper deck, not seeing the girl on the level below. Both were smiling expectantly, waiting for him to join them. He turned back to the rail and contemplated the infinite blue of the ocean and the sky.

With each succeeding mile to the south, *la fatigue du nord* was peeling from him like the multiple skins of an onion. Perhaps in the future he would return to Canada for more skiing, but not for a few years yet, not until acquaintance had become old. A pleasant country, but strange. A little too much snow and for too long, and not enough singing birds. He had liked the people—the ones he passed in the street, Bill, Crystal, those who came to the party—such uncomplicated people. If one were more like them.

But what a ghastly, unendurable bore had been Stephen Hollis with his probing, his unending piddling about, his constant yearnings for heart-to-heart talks. How exactly like him to have discovered about Crystal in that gruesomely embarrassing manner—although it had been something of a relief to realize that one was not after all deceiving him with her. One had thought that they were close friends until the shocking way she had spoken to him on that unfortunate night.

Not that it didn't serve Stephen right, after his behavior, after his poisonously bad manners in reading Duncan's book. (That book. How badly written in spite of all Duncan's efforts. It was an achievement of sorts to have followed the publisher's instructions and rewritten sections of it without changing the style. One hoped Duncan was not displeased with it. Dear Duncan.) Yes, poisonous manners. Fouler than that. On thinking it over it was Stephen's manners that constituted the worst of his many bad faults. Hint after hint, and he had had neither sense enough, nor taste, to stay away.

How blue the sky and the sea. It reminded one of *Das Lied von der Erde*. Strange that Bill, of all people, should have liked *Das Lied*, and Duncan cared for it not at all.... Allüberall and ewig, blauen licht die Fernen.... Ewig.... Ewig.

No, he was still posing. It must stop. Tomorrow he was landing, he would be with his parents, no longer a foreigner. He tried to think in his own language. He had grown accustomed to English. The crests of the waves lifted whitely.

Ewig. No comfort for the wayfarer but in the blueness of the infinite distance he was obliged to travel. A voice. I suppose there is no way of helping anyone. Duncan had said that. And now the blueness of eternity had swallowed him forever. The red head and the eyes of him. Poor sweet Duncan. Sweet Duncan.

Fabien lowered his head and the salt tears fell down his smooth brown cheeks, dispersing on the breeze before they could reach the ocean.

The long weeks had passed.

"Hey, cheer up," Harrigan said brightly, carefully balancing his glass of beer as he plumped into the chair opposite Stephen. "You look like you're on a crying jag. Worried about marks or something?"

Stephen shook his head and looked across the table. The sight of the spotty, friendly little face brought him an almost painful sense of relief, rendered less acute the feeling of loss that lay about him. Involuntarily he held out a hand, causing Harrigan hurriedly to put down his glass. "Good to see you."

"Sure is," Harrigan said, beaming widely.

"Been quite a time."

"Yeah, I looked for you on the campus, but you weren't there."

"I was away awhile," Stephen said. "I had a slight accident, but it's okay now."

"Good."

Harrigan paused, obviously searching for ways to continue the conversation. "Going away for the summer?"

"No. That is, not for a while. I might make arrangements later."

Harrigan sipped at his beer, and they sat in silence. He seemed excited about something, and when, accidentally, his eyes met Stephen's he colored and looked away hastily.

"I was wondering," he said, gazing at the table with feigned unconcern, "whether you'd like to go to a party tonight? Some of the boys who're still in town are getting together for a few drinks, and they asked me to ask you along. I guess it'll be all right, though nowhere near as good as the one you asked me to. Gee, I enjoyed myself that time, didn't you?"

"Yes," Stephen said.

"Your pal sure knows how to put on a show. Think he'd like to come tonight?"

"He's gone away."

"Oh! Hope he has a good summer."

"He's gone for good."

The words had not been said before, nor even thought, and now they curved through the air in a tremendous arc of impossibility. Stephen got to his feet. "I have to make a phone call," he said, and went to the public booth in the corner of the tavern, willing to take any chance, no matter how desperate, to maintain the last contact, to relive at least a little of what he could not bear to allow to die.

Even could she give him no information, her mere bodily presence would assure him of his past good intentions, lift, perhaps, a little of this groaning weight that pressed so painfully upon his conscience. He dialed the phone.

"Hello," said a male voice.

"Could I speak to Mrs. Sabel, please."

"She's not in."

"When will she be back? It's very important."

"Could I take a message?"

"No, it's personal."

Marvin Sabel quickly made his decision. He was home more frequently these days, and this was the fourth young-sounding voice he had intercepted since the morning Miriam called him in Chicago. There was a great deal of pity in his heart, and he wished again that he could think of something that would put them straight, set them on the right road; but, pity or no, they must not be permitted any longer to batten on Miriam. How she first got into their clutches he neither knew nor cared, neither would he ever ask her, but the situation had to end right now. A finger of self-condemnation scratched at his mind, and he wondered how much his neglect had contributed to what she must have endured in the past. What unbearable peak of suffering she had aroused his suspicions?

He said: "How old are you?"

"That's none of your business."

"It's a great deal of my business. I happen to be Mrs. Sabel's husband."

He expected the phone to go dead, as it had three times before, but after a pause the young-sounding voice spoke again, edged with weariness.

"Your wife is a very fine woman, Mr. Sabel. I'm sorry to have bothered you."

"That's all right," Marvin said. "I hope you won't call again."

"I promise you that. Good-by."

"Good-by, and thank you," Marvin answered. "And good luck."

Stephen hung up and went back to the eagerly awaiting Harrigan. There were a great many wet marks on the table, adjoining rings where the glasses had been set down, and he wished the waiter would come and wipe them up.

"How about the party?" Harrigan asked cheerfully. "Matt Lambert said to bring you if I have to drag you there."

"Yes," Stephen said. "Thanks for the invitation. I'll be glad to come."

The flow of gratitude at Harrigan's persistent friendship was, he knew, disproportionate, but to nurture it was his only hope of emerging from this long, black tunnel. The light of being wanted would be his guide, even so small and dim a candle as the affection of Harrigan. Stephen smiled faintly over his glass, at his own hyperbole and because, momentarily, he was fond of his companion.

"That's better. I wondered when you would brighten up," Harrigan said affably. "In your position I'd be laughing all day."

"But you're not in my position," Stephen answered, and the smile faded.

"No. Wish to hell I was."

"Why?"

"No worry about marks or work: women, luxury, friends, everything you want. What I wouldn't give to be in your shoes."

"I haven't the faintest idea what you mean."

"Go on," Harrigan said, beaming merrily. "All the guys know. Mind you, I don't blame you for trying to keep it a secret. You'll have all sorts of people trying to mooch from you, thousands of them."

"What are you talking about?" Stephen asked.

Harrigan's expression became conspiratorially waggish. "Fear not, my boy, I shan't tell a soul."

"About what?"

"Quit kidding, Steve."

"About what?"

Harrigan was suddenly acutely uncomfortable. "I was talking about the three hundred thousand bucks your old man left you." He tried to cover the ensuing silence by sipping noisily at his beer.

"You're talking nonsense," Stephen said dully.

"Aw, come on, I'll buy you another beer, Steve."

Stephen slowly drained the remains of his drink, tilting back the glass until it lay across the bridge of his nose. "But there is no use your keeping it a secret," he said, "if everyone already knows."

"Did I make a boob?" Harrigan asked unhappily. "If it were me I'd go around telling everyone I met. Would you like that beer, Stephen?"

"No thanks, I have to be getting home." Stephen rose to his feet. "You say all the guys know? Matt Lambert and the rest? All of them?"

"They were all talking about it in the Union this morning. They're awful glad for you."

"Yes," Stephen said, "they would be. Yes. Well, so long. I'll see you later."

He turned, not listening to what Harrigan called after him, and walked away from the tavern out into the bright sunshine. He wondered if it were going to be a really hot summer this summer, and only when he stood waiting for the Sherbrooke Street bus did he realize that he knew neither the time nor the place of tonight's party.

And it was too late to go back and enquire. Infinitely too late. He sat staring out of the window, watching the people whiz by, and as the bus nosed into Westmount he began trying to guess what there would be to eat this evening, at the meal, at home, with his mother.

THE END

DOUGLAS SANDERSON BIBLIOGRAPHY
(1920-2002)

Dark Passions Subdue (US, 1952)

Final Run (UK, 1956) aka *Flee from Terror* (US, 1957) and *Un bouquet de chardons* (Fr, 1957) both as by Martin Brett

Night of the Horns (UK, 1958) aka *Murder Comes Calling* (US, 1958) as by Malcolm Douglas

Cry Wolfram (UK, 1959) aka *Mark it for Murder* (US, 1959) and *La semaine de bonté* (Fr, 1958) as by Martin Brett

Catch a Fallen Starlet (US, 1960) aka *The Stubborn Unlaid* and *Cinémaléfices* (Fr, 1960) as by Martin Brett

Lam to Slaughter (UK, 1964) aka *As-tu vu Carcassone?* (Fr, 1963) as by Martin Brett

Black Reprieve (UK, 1965) aka *White Man Dead* and *Couper cabèche* (Fr, 1964) as by Martin Brett

No Charge for Framing (UK, 1969)

A Dead Bullfighter (UK, 1975)

As Martin Brett

Exit in Green (US, 1953) re-written as *Murder Came Tumbling* (UK, 1959)

Hot Freeze (US, 1953) aka *Mon cadaver au Canada* (Fr, 1955) and *Heisser Schnee* (Germany, 1975) as by Malcolm Douglas

Darker Traffic (US, 1954) aka *Blondes are My Trouble* (US, 1955) and *Salmigonzesses* (Fr, 1956)

Flee from Terror (US, 1957) aka *Final Run* (UK, 1956) and *Un bouquet de chardons* (Fr, 1957).

The Shreds published as *Sables-d'or-les-pains!* (Fr, 1958)

The Dead Connection published as *La came á papa* (Fr, 1961)

A Dum-Dum for the President (UK, 1961) aka *Estocade au Canada* (Fr, 1961)

Shout for a Killer published as *Chabanais chez les pachas* (Fr, 1963)

Score for Two Dead published as *Le moîne connait la musique* (Fr, 1964)

As Malcolm Douglas

Prey by Night (US, 1955) aka *A boulets Rouges* (Fr, 1956) as by Martin Brett

Rain of Terror (US, 1955) aka *And All Flesh Died* and *Le Fête a la grenouille* (Fr, 1956) as by Martin Brett; and *Alptraum auf Italienisch* (Germany, 1975) as by Malcolm Douglas

The Deadly Dames (US, 1956) aka *Du Rebecca chez les femmes* (Fr, 1956) as by Martin Brett

Pure Sweet Hell (US, 1957) aka *Zum Sterben hat jeder mal Zeit* (Germany, 1975)

Murder Comes Calling (US, 1958) aka *Night of the Horns* (UK, 1958) as by Douglas Sanderson; and *Ruh in Frieden, lieber Schatz* (Germany, 1974) as by Malcolm Douglas

www.ingramcontent.com/pod-product-compliance
Lightning Source LLC
Chambersburg PA
CBHW070927190726
48292CB00004B/1140